GET "SOUL MATE" FOR FREE

To instantly receive the novella Soul Mate *for FREE, featuring characters from my Helheim Wolf Pack series, sign up to my newsletter at*
authorlaurendawes.com

To Phil; for all the usual reasons

USA TODAY BESTSELLING AUTHOR

LAUREN DAWES

HALF

A HELHEIM WOLF PACK TALE: BOOK FOUR

CAST

PROLOGUE

She tracked her prey with sharp eyes. She'd been in the club for a long time, looking for the most suitable male to bring into the fold. The corner booth she had commandeered afforded her the perfect viewing platform from which to visually stalk the many humans drinking, making out and fucking around her.

She crossed her long legs once, drawing the attention of every male within a twenty foot radius. They watched with their mouths open, the scent of their growing lust battering against her skin. Fluffing her hair, she ignored them all, glancing down at her manicured nails to inspect them for chips.

Damn, she had one already.

"Well, hi, baby," a male drawled. She took her time to look up, her eyes climbing his body slowly. When they finally landed on his face, there was a cocky grin in place. "Can I get you a drink?" he asked in that same slow way.

She narrowed her eyes and shook her head. "I've already got one, thanks."

Despite her answer, he placed his drink down onto the table and lowered himself into the other side of the booth, one arm casually hanging over the back of the seat. His hand lingered on his whiskey glass, his fingers running over the lip.

She studied him. The human had a square jaw covered in fine stubble, his blue eyes were heavy with lust, and his arrogant mouth was turned up slightly in the corner. He would do, but she had to be sure.

"What's your name?" she asked, propping an elbow up onto the table top and leaning her chin in her cupped palm. The guy's blue eyes dropped down to the spill of her breasts pressing perilously close to the edge of her Donna Mizani mini dress. He swallowed, and his eyes shot back to hers when she cleared her throat. She arched a brow at him, waiting for his answer.

"Kade," he replied.

"Kade," she replied in a voice dripping with sex. He nodded even though she hadn't asked him a question. "As much as I'd like to talk with you, my seriously deranged ex-boyfriend is in the club, too. I've tried breaking up with him, but the guy won't listen. He stalks me, follows me around." She leaned in a little closer. "He's probably watching us right now."

Kade's eyes drifted around to the dozen or so men who were actually watching them. "Which one is he? I'll make sure he leaves you alone."

She smiled. "The guy over there in the black t-shirt, dancing with the blonde girl. He's trying to make me jealous," she pouted. Kade's eyes fixed on the couple she'd just seen out of the corner of her eye. His top lip lifted off his teeth when the man in question glanced in their direction and frowned.

Reaching across the table, she took hold of his hand and squeezed his fingers carefully. Injecting a little fear into her voice, she said, "But you probably shouldn't say anything. He's a Marine. He'd probably just kick your ass."

Kade growled and stood up, his hands curling into fists. "I can take him," he spat.

She watched him stalk off toward the couple then sat back and watched the vicious fight that broke out between the two men. Kade was a dirty fighter—going for the low blows at every opportunity. When blood was finally spilled, she felt her wolf padding closer in her mind. Kade beat the other man so badly that he was left barely breathing on the club's floor. The woman he'd been with was screaming for help as Kade walked back toward her. His fists were covered in blood. There was a triumphant grin on his face along with a dark look of satisfaction in his eyes.

Fresh blood was spattered on his pale blue shirt. Standing, she reached up and thumbed away some blood that had made it onto his chin. Pressing herself against the front of his body, she felt the heat of his body, smelled his sweat and his growing arousal.

"Thank you," she whispered low into his ear. "Want to get out of here?"

Kade turned and pulled her close to his side. The crowd parted before them. She glanced over her shoulder at the poor bastard who had been on the receiving end of Kade's rage and felt...nothing. She laughed throatily.

It had been too damn easy.

ONE

Pain.

Agony.

Torture.

Torment.

All these words filled Alex's head. He thought he was dying. He wished he was, but deep down inside he knew differently. He wasn't dying. He was being fucking punished for pining after a woman he could never have.

Another roll of intense pain ripped through his body, forcing his breathing to become harsher and harsher with every passing second. The next wave crested, following closely behind the previous one, leaving Alex's body weak and convulsing.

His eyes cracked open, breaking the crust of sweat and tears that had sealed them shut. The sun was long gone, having probably set hours ago. Alex knew he should have been cold—it was the middle of winter, after all—but the snow around him had turned to slush where it was in direct contact with his body. Lifting a hand to his forehead, he ignored the shake and placed his palm against his damp skin.

He was burning up.

The bite on his right hand had finally stopped bleeding, but not before making the ground around him turn pink. In front of him was a trail of blood that would lead anyone who bothered to look for his sorry ass to the tree he was currently propped up against. He didn't expect anyone to come looking for him though. He didn't have any friends left.

Ever since losing Saskia, he had turned into even more of a bastard than before. His subordinates at work avoided his eyes whenever he stalked through the office looking to pick a fight just so he could feel again. There was only one man who would meet his eyes and Alex wasn't even sure he was human.

Vaile Wolfe seemed to watch his every step, looking at him like he was a stray dog that needed to be put down for being a nuisance. Hell, Alex even felt like he was a stray. Nobody wanted him.

Nobody would notice he was gone.

He winced when another wave of pain traveled up his arm and into his chest. Lifting his hand up close to his face, Alex inspected the wound that he had no doubt would kill him. If he had the strength, he would have gotten his ass up and out of there, but what was the point? He had nothing to live for anymore. What was he going to return home to, an empty apartment? A job he fucking hated? He was living in a world without a sun because he had lost Saskia.

"Yeah, good one, Alex. You're having a fucking pity party all on your own."

He heaved a sigh and kicked his legs out. Letting his head drop, he closed his eyes and waited for death to take him...

He woke up with a deep breath, the crisp morning air trickling in through his nostrils. Birds twittered in the trees around him, but instead of enjoying the noise, it was like nails down a chalkboard. He shifted his legs feeling the blood sloshing about in his limbs after being still for so long.

Alex looked down at his chest, surprised to see he was still breathing, still functioning as a human being even though he felt far from it. He squinted against the weak sun filtering past the bare branches above his head, feeling like his retinas were getting a once-over with high-grade sandpaper. Scrunching them up tight, he dropped his chin to his chest and took in a deep breath.

"Christ, even that hurts," he grumbled to himself since no one else gave a good damn about him. His lungs burned as he filled them with fresh air, settling into a steady simmer when he concentrated too much on the sensation. Lifting a hand to his forehead, he wondered whether the fever had broken overnight. It had.

He took another hit of the fresh morning air, wincing when the scent of death carried into his nostrils. His eyes swiveled around, searching for the source. His gaze eventually dropped down to his mangled hand. Bringing his hand closer to his face, Alex sniffed at the wound.

"Fuck," he muttered. The thing was infected now. Well, if exposure didn't kill him, the bite sure as shit would. "Fuck," he repeated, letting the back of his skull roll back into the tree trunk behind him. It was going to be a long, slow, painful death. His lids slid shut again, waiting for the end to come...

Alex jerked awake; something had woken him. He tried to sit forward only to feel all the muscles in his body seize up. He would have screamed, but even his tongue was useless. The best he could do was make some feeble mewling sounds at the back of his throat that sounded as weak and as pathetic as he felt. Breathing heavily through his nose, he waited for the pain and the paralysis to subside.

That was when he heard it: the sound of a soft-footed tread, and it was getting closer. Moving just his eyes, Alex glanced around the clearing and realized that neither the wound nor the cold was going to kill him; it was going to be a goddamn wolf or cougar. He was a sitting duck—crippled, surrounded by blood and dripping in fear. A branch snapped behind him, and he tried to move his hand, finding his fingers had finally unfrozen from their repose. He tried his other hand, able to bend it at the wrist and then the elbow. His body was slowly starting to function again.

Trying to remain calm, he looked around for something to use as a weapon. His gaze landed on his Ka-bar sitting half buried in the snow a few feet away from him. That would be his only choice if he were to defend himself against whatever wild animal had decided he would be an easy meal.

With a grunt of pain, he pushed himself off the tree. He landed on his side. Cold snow pressed against his cheek, sliding down the collar of his shirt. His major muscle groups obviously didn't want to play nice yet. Forcing his mind on his arms and legs, he coerced them to start moving, his heart rate ratcheting up to oh-fuck speed when he heard the predator getting closer, curious about his obviously impeded movement.

Spreading his fingers out, Alex tensed his muscles and pushed his upper body up off the snow. Dragging his feet underneath him, he attempted to lift himself up off the ground. But his legs had other ideas. With a bitten-back curse, he collapsed onto his hands and knees.

Breathing heavily, he looked up at his target. The handle of his hunting knife was sticking out of the snow like a taunt. His fingers curled into the snow under his palms and he growled in frustration before freezing as a giant off-white paw appeared in his line of sight, not more than an inch away from his knife. With a lump in his throat, Alex's eyes drifted up until the beast's giant head was in focus. Its bright orange, intelligent eyes stared back at him.

"You've got to be goddamn kidding," Alex said softly. It would figure that the animal that had given him the wound would come back to finish the job. Ignoring his more base instincts to stay still and lower his eyes, Alex pushed himself up into a stand, propping himself up against a nearby tree trunk when his legs threatened to give way. He stared the animal in the eye, not giving up his right to live just yet.

His legs shook violently, but he tried to hide the shake from this animal that seemed more intelligent than any regular wolf. Opening his arms up wide, he said, "Go on then. Finish me off!"

The wolf stayed where it was, cocking its head to the side in what looked like confusion.

Enraged, Alex lunged for the animal, but it only danced back a few steps and watched as he fell into a heap. He hauled himself upright and glared at the beast with contempt. "Get out of here and let me die," he spat, leaning back against another tree trunk, defeated. He groaned as a dull throb began in his frontal lobe, his lids sliding shut to stop some of the light still irritating his eyes from getting in. What he was really waiting for was the wolf to just finish him off. He couldn't understand how one little bite could incapacitate him so completely, other than thinking the infection was moving quickly through his body now.

When Alex opened up his eyes again, the wolf was gone. "Fucking figures," Alex mumbled, eyes sliding shut once more. "I'm not even worthy of being eaten." A moment later, though, he was woken by the rich metallic smell of blood. At his feet lay a dead rabbit; its pure white fur was spattered in scarlet blood, its black eyes like buttons buried in all that fur. Alex felt hunger bubble up within him. Falling to his knees, he took the carcass with both hands and brought the torn open belly to his mouth. Warm blood and fresh meat saturated his tongue. His jaws clamped down on the fresh kill, taking it into his body, letting it nourish him.

He groaned around his mouthful, chewing only twice before swallowing. He felt it hit his stomach, and he groaned again at how good that felt. He hadn't realized just how hungry he had been. When he was down to chewing the bones of the rabbit, he sat back on his heels and looked at his hands. They were red up to his elbows, small chunks of flesh and entrails hanging onto his skin and in the fine hairs on his arms. An indescribable urge overcame him to lick the small morsels from his body, and he didn't fight it.

He dropped the skin of the rabbit onto the ground beside him and leaned back against a fallen tree, simply staring out into the lonely forest. Fatigue began to weigh heavily on him, forcing his brain to turn off from any higher thinking. Heaving a heavy sigh, Alex let his eyes slide shut.

SAXON SHOOK OUT HIS SHAGGY CREAM-COLORED COAT AND BACKED AWAY from the clearing. The bastard was still alive—still fighting. He was well into the Change now. Saxon could smell that, could smell his scent all over him. Why had he even done that? Why had he risked his own life to bite the human his sister Saskia had found so charming? He barked a laugh, the noise coming out as a cough in his lupine form. He damn well knew the reason he'd done it.

He'd done it for Saskia.

Saxon looked around the forest. He was far from home. Alex had somehow dragged himself farther and farther away from where Saxon had originally bitten him, getting closer and closer to the territory of the newly extended Alfheim pack boundary to the north. After the final battle, Rhett had allotted the newly freed territories to the other packs, but chose not to take any more for the Helheim pack. They had the largest territory in the first place, so taking more would have just caused problems between the allies.

Saxon's steady lope ate up the snowy ground. He ran for at least three hours before finally arriving back at his car parked up on the hard shoulder of a fire road deep within the forest. Still panting, he began to change back into his human form.

The tingle started in his toes first, quickly spreading into his feet. When his arms and legs felt the full effect of his change, he grunted in pain, a small whimper breaking free of his throat. His back began to tingle then burn, his pale fur being sucked back into his body with frightening speed.

Frigid air kissed his oversensitized skin, the scream coming out of a human throat this time. Saxon blinked his wolf's vision from his denim-blue eyes and groaned as he straightened up. Sweat dampened his forehead, his body shaking with the effort of shifting back.

Bracing his arm against the top of his car door, he bowed his head and drew in a few deep breaths through his mouth to settle his pounding heart. The realization of his actions had suddenly swamped him.

Alex was still alive, and instead of letting him die from the Change, he had fed him a rabbit. Saxon shook his head, angry with himself for so many reasons. He had condemned his sister to a loveless mating, and he would punish himself until the end of his days for doing that to her.

Angrily, Saxon opened up the door and pulled out his boxers, jeans and shirt. Slipping them on, he shoved his feet into his work boots and laced them up tightly. He slid on a jacket and got into the car, glancing at the clock when he fired up the ignition.

"Damn it." He would be late for dinner with Saskia and Ezekiel if he wasn't careful. Putting the car in gear, he swung it carefully in an arc on the icy road and hit the accelerator, gravel and snow spitting out from his tires as he got traction.

Saskia had moved out of the apartment they had shared together for almost fifteen years, and moved into the little house Ezekiel had bought when they agreed to the mating. It was just what Saskia had always dreamed of living in: a cosy house with a wrap-around porch and window boxes filled with daisies and begonias—at least they would be once spring rolled around again.

Saxon pulled into the shovelled driveway, the grit and salt crunching under his feet as he got out. He breathed out deeply, watching his breath fog up in front of his mouth. When he turned around, Saskia was on the porch, a broad smile on her lips.

"I thought you'd forgotten," she said, stopping when Saxon motioned for her to stay where she was.

"Don't come down here, Sass." He walked up the steps and placed a soft kiss on her cheek. "I got held up running an errand. I wouldn't miss being able to spend time with you, sis."

Saskia wound her hand under his arm and settled it into the crook of his elbow, pulling him toward the door. "So, brother, how are you?"

He held open the screen door for her. "I'm good. We're busy at the shop, but I like it that way."

Saskia shook her head in the same way she used to when they were living together. "You work too hard."

"I don't have anything else to do now that you're gone," he replied, shrugging out of his coat and hanging it on the peg by the door. Saskia's smile faltered a little around the edges.

Before Saxon could ask what was wrong, Saskia's mate, Ezekiel, emerged from the kitchen. An apron was wrapped around his waist, a smudge of flour on his face. Wiping his hands on a dishtowel, Ezekiel offered Saxon his hand, his eyes slightly lowered in deference.

They clapped palms and Ezekiel reached for Saskia. She smiled weakly at her mate and made an excuse to get them all some drinks. Saxon watched the disappointment pass quickly over Ezekiel's features, but he'd hidden it from his eyes when he looked at Saxon once more.

"Is everything all right between you two?" he asked, sitting on one of the small loveseats in their living room. The other male let out a breath edged with frustration and sat down on the opposite couch.

They'd been mated a little more than six months, and although Saxon didn't know what being mated was like, he could only imagine what a sharp learning curve that could be.

Ezekiel glanced over his shoulder in the direction of the kitchen where the sound of cupboards being opened and closed could be heard. He opened his mouth, closed it and ran his hand along the back of his head. When he finally looked up again, he looked almost apologetic.

"I don't know," he finally admitted. "Before we were officially mated, I thought she was warming to me, but something's changed in the last few weeks."

Saxon leaned back into the cushions and nodded. He knew exactly what that "something" was. It was around the year anniversary since the Uprising, around a year ago that Saskia had made her mind up not to pursue Alex and do her duty by choosing a mate from the allied packs.

"Do you know what's wrong with her?" his brother-in-law asked. How could Saxon tell him his sister still loved a human male? "I just want her to be happy," Ezekiel murmured.

"I know," Saxon replied just as softly. "She's always been a little skittish, though, so just give her some time, all right?"

Ezekiel nodded and glanced up as Saskia came back into the room, her eyes darting between the two of them. She placed their drinks down onto the coffee table in the middle of the sofas and took a seat beside Saxon, snuggling into his side.

He was taken aback by her display of affection. They'd been close before, but their parents' death had ended that. He threw an arm over her and felt the tension ease from her body.

"So what's for dinner?" he asked, picking up his beer and taking a sip.

"Pot roast with an apple pie for dessert," Ezekiel said, looking confused. When he noticed Saxon staring, he grabbed his own beer and placed the bottle to his lips.

"How are things at work, Sass?" he asked, dropping his gaze from her mate.

"It's good. My first-graders are really cute and so well-behaved this year."

Saxon nodded and took another sip. He suddenly felt like he was sitting in the middle of a fight neither party knew they were involved in. He cleared his throat, excusing himself to go to the bathroom.

Splashing his face with water, he knew he'd made the right choice in biting Alex now. This life Saskia had found herself in wasn't what she wanted. The only consolation was that Ezekiel was a good wolf—a kind, loving male who would only want the best for Saskia. If Alex somehow made it back into her life, maybe Ezekiel would give her up just so she could finally be happy.

He was almost at the end of the hallway when he heard his sister and her mate talking in whispered voices.

"Saskia, please," Ezekiel pleaded.

"I'm fine, Zeke. Nothing's wrong," Saskia replied.

"You don't have to lie to me. These last few weeks have been different... you've been different."

She laughed lightly, trying to brush him off. "It's nothing you have to be concerned with."

"But I'm your mate. I want to be concerned if something is bothering you."

"It's nothing," she repeated more forcefully this time. "Besides, I don't want to talk about this while Saxon is here."

Ezekiel was quiet for a time before he sighed. "All right. But I want to talk about this after he's gone. I deserve that much."

Whatever reply his sister was going to give died on her lips as he reappeared from around the corner. He gave her an encouraging smile, which she returned.

"So, I'm starving. I don't know about anyone else," he announced.

Ezekiel gave him a tight smile. "I'll go check on the progress of the roast."

TWO

Saskia waved goodbye to Saxon from the front step of the porch, wringing the dish towel in her hands tightly. She was alone with her mate again, and her anxiety was threatening to take over. For six months she'd been living with a kind of terror. She thought she'd been covering it up well enough until Zeke had called her on it.

He'd said she'd been acting weird, and he wanted to know why. But how could she tell him? How could she tell her mate she was still in love with a human she had only kissed once? Yes, it was only one kiss, but her body remembered with crystal clarity just how it had felt.

Saskia's fingers found her mouth, her lips tingling from the memory. Her stomach clenched and she had to squeeze her thighs together to stop herself from moaning out loud. Her kiss with Alex had been the single most passionate experience she had ever had. And although Ezekiel was sweet and tender and patient with her, he was not Alex.

She turned around, coming face to face with her mate, who was standing in the open doorway, a look of consternation and concern on his handsome face. Approaching her, he brushed some of her pale hair from her face, his hand lingering on the side of her neck.

"Are you all right? You look flushed." Pressing the back of his fingers against her forehead, he frowned. "You don't feel warm," he murmured.

She smiled weakly. "I'm fine." She took a step backwards and let his hand fall away from her. Moving toward the door, she said, "I'm going to bed. Will you be okay with the dishes?" She waited for his answer, guilt gnawing at her.

"I was hoping we could talk." His voice sounded almost desperate.

"I'm really tired."

He let out a frustrated sigh. "All right then. I guess we can talk tomorrow. We can go out to dinner if you like."

"Sure. That'd be great," she replied in a soft voice before retreating to their bedroom.

Shutting the door behind her, she let out a breath and bowed her head. When her stomach stopped twisting, her eyes roamed around the darkened room. Zeke had let her decorate it in whatever way she'd wanted. She chose rich fabrics in burgundies and golds for the linens. The window coverings were the same, and votive candles and larger scented candles in hurricane vases were on every available free surface.

Closing the door behind her, she went about lighting a few of the candles and shutting off the lights. She rubbed her shoulders and groaned. She needed a soak. Padding into the bathroom, she started the bath, tipping in rich-smelling bath oils to help relax her muscles.

Kicking off her shoes, she undid the button on her jeans and shimmied out of them. Pulling her shirt up over her head, she stood in front of the mirror in her panties and bra, staring at the reflection of the woman whose heart hadn't just been broken, but had been blown to bits. There was no hope of repair now though. It had a permanent fissure in it, and although she wanted to love Ezekiel, she knew she never would.

There was only one man who would have her heart, and she hadn't heard from him in over a year.

Her chest rose and fell with a heavy sigh before she forced her mind away from the guy. It didn't do her any good pining away for him. He probably had another girlfriend by now. Why would he wait around for a woman who'd been engaged to another man? Deep down, though, she hoped that he hadn't moved on, that he'd refused to let the idea of the two of them being together ever leave his mind. God knew it had never left hers.

All through her mating ceremony, she had thought of Alex. When she repeated the words to bind her to Ezekiel, she was reciting them to Alex. When she looked at Ezekiel's happy, beaming face she was seeing Alex's face.

"Enough, Sass. That's enough now. It's been more than a year. He doesn't want you. He never sought you out after you told him you were engaged." Not that he ever would though. He was too honorable for that.

Stepping out of her panties and unhooking her bra, Saskia lowered herself into the tub and turned the hot tap on a little more with her foot. When she was comfortable, she turned off both taps and let her head fall back against the bath pillow.

She must have dozed off because the next thing she knew, Ezekiel was rapping gently on the bathroom door.

"Saskia?" he asked, trying the handle. It wiggled, but didn't open. He let out a sigh. "You know you don't have to lock the door."

"Sorry," she called out. "Silly habit. I'm just in the tub, but I'm getting out now."

Wrapping herself in a fluffy robe, she unplugged the bath and watched the water swirl away. She was suddenly envious of it. Why couldn't she just swirl away?

When she stepped out of the bathroom, Ezekiel was sitting at the end of the bed, his head bowed. He looked up and smiled slightly before slipping past her and standing in front of the basin to brush his teeth.

Saskia walked to the tallboy set in the corner of the room and pulled open the top drawer to retrieve her pyjamas. Her fingers ran over the soft fabric, holding it to her chest before finding some underwear to go under it.

Zeke had finished in the bathroom, stepping out wearing a pair of pyjama bottoms and nothing else. He was a handsome male with a body many females would have loved to have beside them, warming their beds. But when Saskia looked at him, all she saw was the life she had before, a life she could never have again. That life, where Alex had been the main part of it, was nothing more than a pipe dream now.

He threw back the covers, and Saskia watched the muscles in his chest, shoulders and arms work in sinuous harmony. She sighed and stole away into the bathroom to get changed. She still couldn't bring herself to undress in front of him, which was strange considering how nudity simply wasn't a big deal in werewolf society. She guessed her sense of propriety just got too ruffled at the thought of any male laying eyes on her naked body.

Saskia and Zeke had consummated their mating of course, but she didn't enjoy herself with him. There was no spark between them, which meant when he touched her, she shied away. Letting the robe fall from her shoulders, she drew the soft, warm fabric of her pyjama top over her head before stepping into her underwear and matching pyjama bottoms.

She brushed her teeth quickly, turned off the light and stepped back into the bedroom. Zeke hadn't extinguished the candles yet, leaving the room wrapped in a sort of fragrant, sensual glow. Clearing her throat nervously, she slid under the sheets and immediately rolled onto her side away from him.

No sooner had she settled than she felt Ezekiel's strong hands stroking her shoulders, her back. Squeezing her eyes shut, Saskia let him touch her even though she hated it. She could not deny him. She was his mate and certain things were expected of her.

She felt his shift in weight over to her side of the bed, pressing against her back. His thigh pushed between her legs in a possessive way. An arm was wrapped around her waist now, playing with the buttons on her pyjama top gently.

Saskia felt the length of his arousal lying semi-stiffly against the crease of her backside. She jumped when Zeke's warm lips found their way to the soft skin at the base of her skull.

"Saskia?" he asked hoarsely. "Is this all right?"

She nodded. She didn't trust that her voice wouldn't crack. The hand around her waist started undoing the buttons there, exposing her bare skin to him. She sucked in a hushed hiss when his warm fingers caressed her stomach, inching closer to her breasts.

His fingers cupped one of her breasts, kneading it, fondling it. Saskia bit her lip to stop herself from crying out at the small invasion.

His hand released her warm flesh and trailed down her side, pulling the waistband of her pyjamas over her hips. Ezekiel's hand stroked the back of her thighs, coming to rest on the rounded arch of her buttocks. He massaged the flesh there for a moment, his length hardening further and pressing against her with each caress.

She managed to hide her whimper as that same hand reached between her legs. His fingers ran over the fabric of her panties, pressing against her. She wasn't even close to being aroused, but Ezekiel was prepared.

Sliding a finger past the barrier of her panties, he dipped it into her body. It drew a moan from her throat which only spurred him on. He moved with a steady rhythm, gently plunging into the warm well of her body, his fingers mimicking what the lower half of his body wanted to do.

Saskia felt the moisture begin to pool. Zeke did too because he withdrew from her body and slid her panties and pyjama bottoms all the way down off her hips. There was more fabric removed from his body and suddenly the hot blunt head of his erection was there, pressing insistently at her opening.

With one hand on her hip, Ezekiel pushed himself into her core. Her inner muscles tightened at the invasion. Zeke stroked her skin, nuzzled her neck, murmuring for her to just relax. Saskia took in a tremulous breath, and let the tears that had been trembling in her eyes falls softly.

Ezekiel pushed and retreated, his speed gradually intensifying. She knew he wouldn't last very long. He never did. It had been nearly two months since he'd last attempted to make love to her.

Her tears smeared on the pillow beneath her head, soaking through, disappearing. Ezekiel never noticed, though. She was just an empty vessel for him to spill his seed in. God forbid she should fall pregnant to the male even though that was what all the pack was waiting for.

Zeke jerked to a sudden stop before his pace increased, a shuddering breath rustling her hair. "I'm...coming..." he panted, his hot breath blowing strands of her long blonde hair into her face with each word. She shut her eyes tightly and waited for the end.

It came with Zeke calling out her name, his hand curling around her hips and squeezing. She felt him jerking within her, his hot seed jetting inside. He pulled free almost immediately, letting her clean herself up.

If she was fertile, there would be no way to stop his seed from sprouting, but she had to try anyway. Stealing away into the bathroom, she pulled open the cupboard doors, moving a few bottles out of the way until she found her stash of the morning after pill. She popped the pills from their foil and swallowed them with a mouthful of water from the faucet.

Saskia looked in the mirror, stared at her reflection. Her hand curled around the discarded foil tray under her palm. Is this what her life had been reduced to, having sex with her mate then trying frantically to prevent a pregnancy?

With the shake of her head, she wrapped the tray with toilet paper and hid it in the trash. When she opened the door, Zeke handed her pyjamas to her, with a sad look on his face. She took them, mumbling her thanks and walking to the side of the bed. Sliding them back on, she got under the covers and closed her eyes.

ENZEKIEL SHUT THE ENSUITE DOOR BEHIND HIM FEELING AS IF HE HAD just violated his mate in some way. Well, he had, but damn it, he had needs, too. Jerking off in the shower every other day only got him so far, and since it had been two months since he'd last had sex with Saskia, he simply couldn't wait.

Seeing her come out of the bathroom wrapped in a fluffy robe, her cheeks pink from the heat and her skin smelling of the expensive French bath oils she liked to use, made his constantly simmering desire for her roar to life. Wanting to mark her as his as often as possible drove him more often than not. But Saskia always flinched when he reached for her.

Not really good for his ego.

Bracing his arms on the edge of the basin, he bowed his head and let out a deep breath. He was still naked, his cock hanging limply out in front of him, the scent of her covering him.

Hearing Saskia cry, smelling her tears, made him feel like an asshole for taking her as he had, but he had been unable to stop, driven by an internal, animalistic need. What he wouldn't have given to know what was really wrong with her. What he wouldn't have given to stop.

"Tomorrow," he muttered to his reflection. He would find out the reason tomorrow at dinner. Ezekiel cleaned himself off and switched off the lights. The warm glow of the candles had been extinguished, the scent of their ended lives drifting lazily through the air.

Saskia was already asleep on her side, her small body curled into a tight ball with her knees brought up to her chest. He got into the other side of the bed, lying on his back, thinking about how to make Saskia love him.

THREE

Alex woke up feeling stronger than he had in a few days. His body still ached and protested with each move he made, but it was no longer incapacitating. Using the tree behind him, Alex got himself up into a semi-standing position, his fingers clutching at the trunk to keep him steady.

Looking around, he tried to look for a familiar marker in the landscape, but couldn't see a damn thing. He wondered how far he'd actually gone into the forest on his hunting trip. Obviously it was far enough for people not to be able to find him easily.

But that had been the point.

He grunted as he pushed himself fully upright, swaying a little as the world in front of his eyes pitched. Looking down he saw the blood on his hands, creeping up his forearms until it ended at his elbows. He knew he should have felt something other than delight when he remembered feasting on the rabbit, but there was something about consuming the flesh of a weaker creature that just suddenly felt...right to him.

Forcing his mind off the memories of warm flesh parting between his teeth, Alex studied the bite on his hand. It was still open, but weeping a clear liquid now. Maybe he was supposed to survive this. Maybe this was just a test for him.

Alex squinted up into the early morning sun and started off in the direction he thought the highway was in. His body reminded him he wasn't running at one hundred percent capacity, which roughly translated to a slow zombie-like shuffle around the trees and underbrush. He was sweating before too long, but he pushed on, watching the sun slowly move across the sky. When it finally made its decent into the western sky, he was exhausted.

He stopped, his legs giving out from under him. As his ass hit the ground, it jolted his entire body and awoke the headache that had been simmering in the background all day as he'd walked. Now it roared like a dying beast inside his head. He sucked in a shallow breath as it relentlessly battered against his skull with hurricane force. Gritting his teeth, he held his head in his hands, begging a god he didn't believe in to stop the agony. Night was falling quickly on him, the temperature plummeting with the dying light.

Alex found a dead tree with a hollow big enough for him to fit inside and hunkered down for the evening. He must have walked at least fifty miles today. He shouldn't be too far away from a highway, or at least a home. Taking one last look at his surrounds, he shoved his hands under his armpits and closed his eyes.

ALL THE AIR RUSHED OUT OF CASEY'S LUNGS, STUNNING HER FOR JUST A minute. Rolling up onto her feet again, she shook out her russet-colored coat and bared her teeth at the wolf who had just tackled her to the ground.

Hunter only smiled at her, his big wolfy grin stretching out his lips and showing all his teeth. Not only was he her big brother, but he was her beta, too, but even that only got him so much leeway in Casey's book.

He was the tallest of all her brothers, his black as pitch coat highlighted by a streak of white starting at his left ear and covering half his face until it dipped below his chin. His yellow wolf eyes were dancing with enjoyment, laughing at her.

She snorted and kicked some snow up into his face, barking a laugh as she caught him by surprise. Before he could retaliate, she darted off into the trees once more.

She and her four brothers were doing a patrol for any lone wolves out on their boundary lines. It was only recently they began discovering more and more Bitten wolves roaming around on their turf, and their alpha, Acario, had stepped up the patrols.

They couldn't figure out who was biting them. Nobody in the pack had a good enough nose to pick up their maker's scent, so the best they could do was either rehabilitate them if they weren't too far gone, or kill them if they were.

Casey caught a glimpse of her youngest brother Riley up ahead. He was just a flash of strawberry blond fur darting between the trees. Flattening her ears against her skull, she ducked her head down, making her body more streamlined, and stalked after him.

Her pads sank into the three-inch-thick snow at her feet, blanketing the sound of her approach as Riley stopped at a stream for a drink. He lifted his head and sniffed the air, causing Casey to freeze in position. She was downwind of him, but prayed the wind didn't change direction.

Dropping his head once more, he lapped at the cold water twice more before finally noticing she was there. He glanced over his shoulder and took off, splashing through the stream and spraying water everywhere.

Casey was about to give chase when the wind shifted direction and a new scent burrowed into her nostrils. The scent wasn't a Bitten wolf...at least, he wasn't yet. She paused for a second, wondering whether she should go and get one of her brothers.

That was the only rule Hunter had placed on her if she was going to come out on patrol with her enforcer brothers—if she smelled a Bitten wolf, she had to go and get one of them straight away.

She huffed, unable to understand why they treated her so differently. She wasn't able to do anything without their permission. Casey wanted to become an enforcer, too. Her idol was Leona, a wolf from a pack that no longer existed. She had been an enforcer. She had been the Captain for the pack, and that's what Casey wanted to be.

Deciding she would go it alone, Casey turned her back on the line her brothers had been tracking and ventured out on her own. With her nose on the ground, she sniffed out the scent, weaving in between the trees until she came to a clearing. There was a groan. She circled around the ten foot wide space, eyes searching the underbrush, ears straining to pinpoint the source of the noise.

The acidic stink of vomit hit her nostrils, then another groan and retching. Scrunching up her nose, Casey warily approached the only area she hadn't checked yet—a hollowed-out tree trunk. The pungent scent of vomit got stronger, and she recoiled.

From just the other side of the felled timber she could see the male responsible for making all the noise. He was on his hands and knees, his forehead damp with sweat. He was dressed in black hunting boots, black cargo pants and a hooded parka. He didn't even know she was there.

His whole body shook, straining to purge his body. Casey recognized it for what it was. She was no stranger to the symptoms she had seen a dozen times before. The male was about two days into the Change. He would also have an almost unbearable headache that would only get worse the more he puked.

He groaned and sat back on his heels, his hand shaking as he brought it up to wipe his mouth. The male had dark hair, but was going grey around his temples. His face was pale and gaunt, his expression fierce despite his body fighting off the infection. She looked over his body for the bite. It could have been under his clothing for all she knew, but she caught sight of it when he ran his hands through his hair.

It was a bad one, but it was weeping clear liquid. He would probably survive the Change if he was taken care of properly—given shelter, food and a place to rest his bones, because his whole body was going to be coming apart really, really soon.

Raising one paw, she was about to step into the clearing and show herself when a low growl trickled into her ears from behind her. Peering over her shoulder quickly, she saw a pair of angry yellow eyes glaring back at her.

Quickly doing the submissive thing, Casey spun around, lowering her head and tail. She trotted over and began licking at her big brother's chin. He snorted sharply and she looked up into his questioning eyes. Wagging her tail slightly, she tossed her head in the direction of the clearing.

Oliver and Dylan, her two other older brothers, marched forward, corralling her so she was behind Hunter. But now she couldn't see anymore. She tried to jostle for her position once more, but Hunter took her by the scruff of her neck and growled just once. That was all it took.

Casey stayed put.

Oliver and Dylan disappeared past the brambles before Hunter and Riley joined them. Casey couldn't hear anything and it was driving her crazy. She whined, pacing from side to side, unable to disobey the order from her beta.

There was a growl then the human swore. "Oh, just fucking great! What is it with me? Do I smell like a delicious wolf snack? Fuck!"

Casey cocked her head to the side. The human wasn't scared of being surrounded by four giant wolves. Perhaps he didn't realize what it meant. She whined again, dying to go past the last of the brambles and see for herself what was happening.

She needed to talk to the human, needed to explain what was going on, what was going to happen to him. Even though this was technically against her orders, she relaxed herself and called on the Change, feeling her body twitching with the start of her shift.

Her skin shivered and writhed beneath her thick red coat. Casey began to pant, her toes cracking and reforming into the shape of her human fingers and toes. Leg muscles shaking, she forced herself to stay upright as all of her joints suddenly came apart at the same time.

A whine vibrated through her vocal cords, her lids squeezing down on eyes the color of an overcast sky. Her top lip lifted in a small grimace, her brain trying to fight back the pain.

A low sweeping sting crawled up her skin. She fell into the snow, her breathing labored. Her muscles twitched, her thick red pelt being sucked back into her body. She likened the feeling to getting road rash—being scraped down with coarse sandpaper followed by a treatment of Brillo pads and a good dose of direct flame to the skin.

Casey's head dropped onto the snow, the pain finally receding. She looked down at her scarlet painted fingernails and smiled. Pushing herself up to standing, she stepped buck-naked into the clearing with her brothers.

They had the human backed up against a tree. Their teeth were bared, saliva dripping hot and fast from their gums. Casey was dwarfed by her brothers, but her size had never stopped her before. Shoving her five foot four body in between them, she eventually pushed through to the front of the group.

The human's eyes widened when he got an eyeful of Casey. Not bothering to cover herself, she cleared her throat and dragged his attention away from her small chest.

"Who the fuck are you?" he asked with a noticeable tremor in his voice.

Casey's stare intensified. Hunter growled at the guy's tone. The human's hazel gaze darted to her brother then back to her.

"What's going on? Who are you, and why aren't those wolves attacking you? Why are you naked?" His eyes were wild. "What's going on?"

Casey took a step toward him, which was closely shadowed by Hunter. She glanced at him quickly, asking him to trust her just this once. He shook his head, his yellow eyes narrowing on the human.

With an exasperated sigh, Casey ignored him and approached the guy anyway. Hunter was standing between them a second later, his hackles raised, a threatening growl in his throat.

The human, to Casey's surprise, stood his ground, glaring defiantly at her brother. This male either had a death wish, or had dealt with wolves before.

"What's your name?" she asked, trying to shove Hunter out of her way. He was nearly three hundred pounds as a wolf, so that was no easy feat. Her beta held his ground even as she swore at him to stop being such an asshole.

Hunter apparently didn't appreciate that because he turned and nipped her on the arm. Blood oozed immediately, and Casey decided not to push it. When she glanced back at the human, his eyes were wide.

"He bit you."

She shrugged. "Just a scrape. He could have snapped my arm in half if he wanted to."

Hunter's yellow eyes slid her way and she smiled. "Well, you could have and if our mother hadn't torn you a new one the last time you did it, you would have again."

"You know it?" the human asked.

Casey looked at her big brother and knocked her shoulder against his front leg. "*He's* my big brother. He's just protecting me."

"From who?"

"You."

The stranger's eyes widened in response before they slid shut like he was in pain.

"It's a headache, right?" she asked. Oliver stepped up to stand beside her, blocking the cold wind that had started blowing. She reached out to touch his side. "You've been bitten, haven't you?"

The human nodded, his gaze darting between the black and brown wolves at her side.

"Alex," he eventually replied.

"I'm sorry?"

"My name. It's Alex."

"I'm Casey," she replied. "This is Hunter and Oliver." She glanced over her shoulder. "Riley and Dylan are back there." On cue, they stepped forward and flanked Hunter and Oliver so there was a line of wolves in front of him.

"You have four brothers?"

She shrugged, drawing the man's eyes to her arm.

"The bite...it's already healed." He seemed to trip and stumble over the words.

Casey nodded. "It began healing almost as soon as I was bitten," she replied steadily, watching the man unravel.

"H-how?"

"It's in my blood."

"What are you?" he asked, his gaze bouncing between them all.

"The same thing you are. I'm a werewolf."

FOUR

Alex truly believed he was hallucinating. Hell, it wouldn't have been the first time.

"A werewolf?" he repeated.

The girl—Casey—nodded once, her fire-red hair bobbing up and down with the movement. As he looked at her face, her eyes shifted from green to grey then back again. The headache he'd been suffering from for the past day at least roared to life again, throbbing like it wanted to beat its way out of his head.

He groaned and massaged his temples. "A werewolf?" he said again just to make sure.

She shrugged her slender shoulders—her naked shoulders—and grinned at him. "At least you will be shortly."

Throb.

Throb.

Throb.

"I don't understand," he said, not raising his voice for fear of aggravating his already pounding head.

"You've been bitten. You're halfway through the Change already. But if you thought what you've experienced so far was painful, wait until your wolf literally claws its way from your body in the next twenty-four to forty-eight hours."

She was still smiling as she spoke.

Fucking unnerving.

Alex blinked. The words she was saying grammatically made sense, were in the usual subject, verb and object order, but to him it all sounded like bullshit—a huge pile of what-the-fuck that he was having trouble swallowing. "Huh?"

She took a step toward Alex and the huge black wolf let her, his striated fur contrasting with the sulphur yellow eyes. She crouched down in front of him, and Alex did his best to ignore her nakedness. She reached for him, her unbelievably warm fingers touching his temple where the headache throbbed the strongest. Her tentative touch turned into a full-handed check of his temperature, her hand sliding against his forehead.

She turned and spoke to her brothers. "He's passed the fever stage. We don't have much time."

"Don't have much time for what?" he asked.

Casey glanced back and gave him a lopsided smile. "Before you're going to pass out. Come on. Get up." She stood up and motioned for him to do the same. Alex let out a breath and stood on unsteady legs.

"Where are we going?" he asked, fingers digging into the bark of the tree he was using as his crutch.

The biggest of the wolves growled and swung around, the other three following. Casey took his hand and tugged him after them. "Back to our place. You'll see our alpha if you're still conscious in the morning."

Still conscious? Fuck, no. He wasn't going anywhere with this strange woman and the four steroid-hopped wolves she was claiming were her brothers. He planted his feet, surprised when Casey had no trouble dragging his weight even though his feet had stopped moving. "What'll happen then?" he asked, his mind churning through the options he had in that moment.

He came up with nothing.

Zip.

Zilch.

Nada.

Fuck.

"We'll help you through your first shift and then you'll officially join the pack."

"We?" he asked.

Casey smiled cheerfully. "My alpha and my brothers...and me, of course." She turned to face him. "That is, if you make it that far."

Well, that was pretty ominous. Alex shook his head, but let the small woman lead him out of the forest. It turned out he wasn't too far from a road. There was a big truck parked up on the shoulder that all the wolves were standing around.

Casey opened one of the rear doors, leaning in to get something before ushering him inside. "You don't want to see what's going to happen next." She pulled on a pair of jeans and a jacket, zipping it up and shivering a little. Motioning for Alex to move over, she slid in beside him and shut the door.

He looked out the windshield and peered into the darkness. "What's going on out there?" he asked. He could see the giant wolves prowling around, their bodies seeming to vibrate violently. They looked agitated, snarling and snapping at each other.

Suddenly, the largest wolf—Hunter—seemed to simply buckle, his body contorting painfully.

What the *fuck* was going on?

Casey pulled on his shoulder, dragging him back into his chair. He hadn't realized he'd scooted that far off his seat. "Nothing you want to see," she replied. "Close your eyes."

"I don't think so," he snapped back. If his years on the Force taught him anything, it was to never take your eye off the threat.

Casey rolled her eyes. "Just do it already."

Eying her for a long minute, Alex let out a frustrated breath, then did as she asked and waited. With his eyesight gone, his other senses came alive. He could hear animalistic howls that turned into masculine screams. He heard wet sucking sounds followed by pops and grunts. Trying not to let his imagination go too crazy, he focused on the smells contained within the car.

Blood—tangy and sharp—was the first discernible thing, then the smell of himself from not having washed for a few days. Forest and earth tangled in with all three, and then there was Casey. She smelled just like she looked—sweet—although Alex couldn't quite put his finger on the exact scent.

The sound of the car doors popping open and the rush of winter air opened his eyes. Alex looked at the hulking men pulling clothes off the other seats and putting them on.

The man on the driver's side had dark hair with a white streak through it. His eyes were blue—the same blue as a cold winter's day. He looked at Alex, his jaw working, yellow chasing the blue from his eyes for a moment.

"That's Hunter," Casey told him, giving her brother what looked like a disapproving look. "Oliver," she said pointing to the male in the front passenger seat. Oliver was not as wide as Hunter, his hair brown and shaggy, his eyes brown.

"Dylan." Casey inclined her head toward a male version of her—at least where his hair was concerned. It was the same red, and Alex could see the family resemblance. Dylan had eyes a few shades darker than Casey's, which changed to dirty red before he pulled a shirt over his head.

"And that's my baby brother, Riley," Casey announced happily. Her youngest brother had strawberry blond hair and hazel eyes with a violet twist.

"Case, I want you up here with me," Hunter ordered from the front seat. Casey gave Alex an apologetic smile, shrugged and climbed up into the front to sit between her two brothers. Now he was sandwiched between Dylan and Riley on the back seat. The two males were big. So was Alex. It wasn't a happy seating arrangement for anyone concerned.

He was squirming in his seat, trying to get comfortable, when a low growl sounded. Pausing, Alex felt his pulse beginning to pound harder, the instinct to run from a predator too damn obvious. He remained rigid in his seat, sucking in air quietly through his mouth to calm his racing heart. Alex fixed his eyes ahead of him, concentrating on taking stock of his surroundings. The fact that they hadn't blindfolded him must have meant something.

They drove for some time, the headlights of the truck skimming off the slick blacktop. Not knowing where they were going was driving him crazy.

"Where are we?" he asked, bursting the bubble of silence that had fallen over the truck. Casey glanced over her shoulder, the glow from the dashboard illuminating half of her face, bathing it in pale light while the other half remained in shadow.

"You're in Alfheim pack territory."

"Alfheim?"

She shrugged. "That's the name of our pack," she replied before turning back around to look through the windshield. Casey looked so small wedged between the bulk of her brothers.

Deciding he probably wasn't going to be getting any other information from her or her brothers, Alex zipped his lips and tried to gather as much information as he could about his location. Of course, the pitch-blackness swirling past the windows did nothing to help with that, but he did it all the same, trying to focus his eyes despite the pounding in his head.

His eyes were beginning to feel incredibly heavy, the gentle vibrations of the car relaxing his brain, setting up the alpha waves of sleep until he was suddenly jerked awake. Blinking, he looked around to see that they had stopped in front of a house that looked like it was straight out of a kid's cubbyhouse brochure.

The air was crisp as he got out, making him shiver. Waves of violet light were just touching the horizon. Around the sprawling wooden house, all the trees had been cleared, leaving it bare. Smoke wisped from the stone chimney on one side of the steeply-pitched roof and snow dusted the wooden shingles.

As Alex looked over the house, Oliver came and took him by the elbow and led him up the stairs behind the others. Casey was first through the door, kicking off her boots and shucking the jacket directly onto the floor.

A sharp pain sliced behind Alex's eyes, dropping him to his knees with the severity of it. Clutching his head, he looked up to see lights zigzagging across his vision. He shifted back onto his heels, but that only made the pain worse.

His stomach clenched hard, his throat already working itself up to vomit again. Alex must have groaned Casey's name because the next thing he knew, she was there, her warm hand gliding across his forehead.

"Help me get him into the basement room. We're losing him."

Another hand snaked under his armpit and began lifting him. Alex groaned again, the throbbing intensifying with each and every movement.

"Get him on the bed." Alex's hearing began to get spotty, fading in and out. He'd kept his eyes shut the entire time, afraid that if he saw the room spinning, or ridiculously bright lights in front of him, he'd lose what little he had left in his stomach.

There was a softness beneath his head that he willingly sank into, sighing gently. His head was still pounding, but the room was dark and as the other people retreated, it fell into blissful silence. This was what he needed.

Darkness.

Silence.

A little time-out from the what-the-fuck situation he'd found himself in.

His eyelids cracked open to the most beautiful sight he could ever hope to see. Saskia sat beside him, her denim-blue eyes soft and concerned. She smiled at him, and the ice wall he'd built around his heart cracked and began melting.

"Saskia? Are you really here?" Alex asked.

Saskia reached over and lightly ran her fingers over one eyebrow, stroking his skin until his eyes felt heavy. Lifting one heavy limb, he tried to reach for her, too.

"Saskia, I thought I'd never see you again."

"Shh," she whispered, a tear rolling down her cheek.

"Baby, don't cry. I'm all right."

Her gaze fell to the tear that had dropped to the sheets between them. When they rose to his face again, her eyes were bright aqua. A sudden surge of awareness filled him. He knew what it meant. He knew who was staring out at him. It was one word and it was a word that had been thrown around before: wolf.

FIVE

Brax slumped back into his desk chair and let out a deep breath. Thank fuck that was over. Hitting a few more buttons on the keyboard, the screen he'd been looking at blinked out into nothingness, the light on the camera latched onto the top of the monitor going out.

His body was slick with sweat, the vinyl G-string he had been sporting leaving indentations on his hips. Brax stood up and stretched out his spine, feeling everything pop, his whole body relaxing from the lack of tension. It had been a marathon session that he'd set up in the hopes that he would become distracted enough with performing that he wouldn't think of his old home and his best friend.

He groaned when he realized what he'd just done.

"Fucking idiot," he muttered, taking the bottle of Lag sitting on his coffee table by the neck and putting it to his lips. As he all but fell onto the leather sofa, his mind drifted. It had been over a year since he'd left the Helheim pack, but it felt as if he'd walked out on them just yesterday.

The look on Rhett's face as he realized he had no pull over him anymore almost made Brax change his mind completely. It was only his oath to his new alpha, Mathias, that had made him walk, but it had been the hardest damn thing he had ever had to do in his life.

Sucking back another mouthful, Brax felt the liquor funnel down his throat, hitting his chest with a cruel burn. It had been over a year since he'd last spoken to Rhett. It had been over a year since he'd lied to his best friend.

I'll call. Promise.

He hadn't called. He'd even gone as far as to ditch his cell and get another. He'd also come close to just changing his whole damn name, but the thought of all the paperwork involved with that particular endeavor made Brax's brain hurt.

His phone beeped, dragging him back to the present kicking and screaming. Taking another hit from the bottle, Brax jerked forward to get the thing off the table, hissing when his naked skin peeled from the leather with a ripping sound.

"Goddamnsonofabitch!"

Mental note: naked body + sweat x leather sofa = fuckload of unnecessary pain.

Brax palmed the phone and unlocked it, looking down at the text message that had popped up onto the screen. Well, wasn't that a surprise.

It was from Ulf, the beta of the Asgard pack. Brax read the text a few times before locking his phone and gingerly standing up again. His beta wanted to see him in twenty. Abandoning his beloved Lag on the coffee table, Brax wandered naked toward his bathroom.

After hitting the shower and coming up smelling of roses, he dressed in a pair of black slacks and a black silk button-down. He felt like an asshole being dressed as he was, but when the beta wanted to speak to you, you damned well better be looking good when you did it.

Shoving his feet into a pair of loafers that felt equally as uncomfortable as the rest of his ensemble, Brax slid a Beretta into the waistband of his pants and then slipped on a jacket to conceal it. Palming his keys and phone, Brax left his studio apartment in town and took the elevator down to the garage level of his building.

Business had been good in the last year—so good in fact that he'd upgraded his car. Sitting in his parking spot was a brand new Audi R8 coupe, all shiny and new-car smelling. Hitting the button on his key fob, the lights flared and died. He slid his body into the cavity of his new baby and started her up.

"Oh man," he murmured, enjoying the feel of the engine rumbling through the entirety of his body. "So the right decision."

Brax reversed from his spot and left the apartment complex garage. The pack house was only a ten minute drive away. Situated just outside the city limits, it was smack bang in the middle of a rich, white-collar neighborhood. After passing through the multitude of new security measures in place to protect the alpha, Brax crept up the long drive and pulled up behind a hulking Hummer parked in front of the house.

Ulf was already at the door. The guy was built like a wrestler—stocky and small. His blond hair had grown in a little, taking away some of the scary-factor from his wolf's rust-red eyes. They clapped palms and the other male stepped back to let Brax inside.

"What's up?" he asked once they were inside.

"Not much."

All right. So Brax was obviously not going to get a whole lot of information out of the guy.

"What was with the urgent meeting?"

"Mathias wants to see you."

Oh, fuck.

Shaking off the worry, Brax stepped toward the alpha's office door and knocked. Waited. Then waited some more. Eventually he heard Mathias's voice through the wood.

"Enter."

Brax did just that, finding himself in yet another place that reminded him of Rhett and his former life. After the death of Antain and the burning down of their old pack house, the Helheim wolves had come here for sanctuary, but also to plan the battle that ended the war with the Dragos pack.

"Take a seat," Mathias murmured, not looking at him. His eyes were fixed on one of the dual screens on his sleek, glass desk. Brax sat down on the aesthetically pleasing, yet highly-uncomfortable, low-lying sofa opposite the all-that-modern of Mathias's desk.

When Brax closed his eyes, he could still see Rhett sitting behind the thing, giving orders, kicking ass.

"You've been with us nearly a year now, Brax," Mathias said, breaking his train of thought.

"Yes, Alpha."

Mathias sat back in his chair, his eyes fixed on Brax's. When those watchful eyes slipped to green, Brax dropped his gaze to the alpha's chin.

"You seem to keep your nose clean."

Brax realized it was an observation rather than a question. "Yes, Alpha."

"What do you do for work?"

"I'm self-employed."

From his periphery, he could see Antain's brows had popped. "Is that so? A young businessman, are you?"

Brax shrugged, keeping his eyes low. "Of sorts."

"What sort of business are you in?"

Ah, fuck. He did *not* want to talk about this with his alpha. Antain hadn't known what he'd done for cash, and Rhett certainly hadn't known. So Brax coughed up the lie that had served him so well in the past. "IT."

Mathias nodded. "And business is good?"

The last few months had been crazy-insane. He'd wanted to stay busy, to keep his mind occupied as the anniversary of his departure rolled on round like it didn't give a fuck that it still hurt. Brax cleared his throat. "The last few months have been very profitable."

"Profitable enough for you to be able to take a little break from it?"

"Alpha?" Brax asked, finally lifting his eyes for a lingering second.

"I've been in touch with some of the other alphas from the west coast. It seems that there's someone biting humans and leaving them for dead or the Change. As a result, there are more Bitten wolves crossing territorial borders. A lot are too far gone to be assimilated into a pack, but some have made it through unscathed."

"I don't understand."

Mathias sat back in his office chair, steepling his fingers in front of his mouth. "I'm sending Ulf out to talk with the other packs, to figure out what we're looking for, because no doubt, sooner or later, we'll also be getting our fair share of trespassers."

"And you want me to go with him?" Brax surmised.

Mathias nodded. "Yes. I want to see how you handle yourself out in the field. We need more enforcers. I know you worked under Antain as an enforcer when it was necessary, but I'm thinking of a more full-time kind of position. Would that be something you'd be interested in?"

Brax closed his eyes. This is what he'd been waiting for. This was his way out of his other job. It was becoming so damn tedious now. It was as if his whole life had lost its color completely.

"Excuse the language, but fuck, yeah."

SIX

Saskia slid her old apartment key from her pocket and twisted it in the lock. Saxon wouldn't be home yet, but she needed a bit of quiet time first, to think through what she was about to do.

The door opened softly, allowing Saskia to slip inside quickly and quietly. She turned on the lamp by the door and looked around the apartment she used to live in. Life had seemed so much simpler then. She heaved a heavy sigh and kicked off her favorite pair of ballet flats.

Dropping down onto the overstuffed sofa, she curled her legs beneath her and just sat there absorbing her former life. Looking around, she noticed not much had changed. The furniture was all the same except for the coffee table that had been smashed up in the fight between Saxon and...

Alex.

"Damn it," she muttered. It always came back to him. She glanced at her watch, keeping an eye on not only how much longer her brother would be, but also how long until she'd be required to go to dinner with Ezekiel.

Her mate was trying to understand what was bothering her, but bringing up another male, another *human* male, was not going to be well received. She shut her eyes and wondered how she was going to tell him. He could, of course, demand she tell him and she would have no choice, but he would never do that to her.

"Saskia?" Saxon asked. Her head whirled to face him, her heart starting to pound wildly in her chest. She hadn't heard him come through the door. Taking a few deep breaths to slow her racing pulse, she smiled at her big brother.

"What are you doing here?" he asked, dropping a sports bag at his feet. He wasn't wearing his usual mechanics overalls for the first time in...well...ever.

"Since when do you go to the gym?" she asked, eying his sports shorts and running singlet sceptically.

He grinned. "Nice to see you, too, Sass."

Her cheeks colored and she dropped her gaze. "Sorry. How are you, Saxon?"

He sat down beside her, removing his shoes while he spoke. "I'm good. And I started going to the gym after you left home since I had no reason to come home straight away."

"You must be so relieved not to have me as a burden anymore," she replied, trying not to let his words wound her.

"It's not that, Saskia, and you know it," Saxon said softly, putting a tentative arm around her shoulder. She wiggled closer to him, snuggling up to his side and breathing him in. His arm tightened around her, his chest rising and falling.

"Is everything okay?" he asked, his deep, resonant voice rumbling through his chest. She nodded, dislodging the fresh tears that welled as the question was asked. She sniffled and sat up, wiping the errant tears away with her fingertips.

"I don't even know why I'm crying," she said.

"Tell me what's wrong."

She fixed him with an exasperated look. "You know the reason, Saxon."

He glanced away then back at her, his wolf's bright orange eyes blazing for a few moments. She felt her own wolf answer his beast's call. "Alex, right?"

"Yeah." Her voice was barely audible.

He blew out a breath. "Zeke's getting suspicious. You know that, don't you?"

She nodded. "I do. In fact, he organized a special dinner for tonight so we could talk about whatever's been bothering me."

When she looked back at Saxon, he was staring at her, setting the hairs at the back of her neck on end. She fidgeted in her seat. "Want to talk to me about it? Maybe I can give you some advice."

Saskia glanced at the galley kitchen and stood up. "How about I put on some tea while you shower and then I'll tell you about it?" She held her breath while she waited for his answer. She needed a little time to wrap her head around what she was going to say.

Saskia breathed a sigh of relief when Saxon nodded and left her with the tea-making duties. She worked with an almost robotic efficiency as she boiled the water and warmed the pot. Pulling two mugs from the cupboard, she set them onto a small tray along with a jug of milk and the sugar bowl.

She had just finished rifling through the cupboards for some cookies when Saxon reappeared, his dirty-blond hair wet from the shower. Placing the teapot onto the tray along with a small plate of cookies, Saskia turned to take them into the living room when Saxon relieved her of the tray.

Giving him a smile of thanks, she followed her brother back to the sofa.

Saskia picked up the pot to pour, but her hands were shaking so badly, her brother took over that, too.

When the hot mug of tea was finally cradled in her hands, she let out a deep breath and began telling Saxon all of her concerns.

"I don't know why I'm thinking about Alex now, but he consumes my every thought, every second of my day. I can't shake him from my memories, and honestly, I hope I never do," Saskia said, talking down into her tea.

"You think you've made a mistake mating Ezekiel, don't you?" Saxon asked.

"Yes and no. Zeke is a good wolf. He treats me well. He doesn't push me into doing anything I don't want to do, but always at the back of my mind, I'm worried that he could change his mind about me, about deciding to stay here in Buxton. He could make us pack up and leave tomorrow, and I would have absolutely no choice in the matter."

"And you're worried he'd do that?"

"If he finds out about Alex, he might. I mean, I haven't seen or heard from Alex in over a year now. I assume he's still living in town, but maybe he's moved somewhere else. In any case, I can't image Zeke wanting to stay in the same city as the man I..." she paused, unsure what to say next.

Saxon took another sip from his mug after blowing gently over the surface. "What was it about Alex that attracted you so much?" he asked, seeming genuinely curious.

"I don't know how to explain it really. His soul...spoke to mine, I guess."

Saxon nodded, frowning a little. "I've never experienced that so it's a little hard for me to understand."

Saskia took his hand in hers and squeezed gently. "You will someday."

He laughed gently. "I wouldn't count on it. Our name has been tarnished permanently by our parents' actions. I'm not expecting any female to want me."

Saskia's heart ached for her brother, and she was once again reminded of what a great guy he was. "So what do you think I should do?"

"Well, you could tell him and wait and see what the consequences are."

Saskia shook her head resolutely. "I can't. If I tell him I love Alex, he'll move us away from Buxton for sure."

"Or you can pull yourself together, forget about Alex and focus on the male in your life now. Zeke is honorable. He has a good bloodline and your mating has helped to repair the rift between us and our old pack."

Saskia swallowed roughly over the lump that had formed in her throat. "What if I can't?" she whispered, placing her mug down onto the new coffee table in front of her. "What if Alex haunts me until the day I die?"

Saxon put his mug down and took her hands into his. "Then I suggest you get very good at pretending Zeke is the only wolf for you. Let's face facts here: Alex hasn't contacted you in over a year. He hasn't tried to come around and see you. He hasn't turned up at your work. Maybe he's respecting your decision to move on."

She nodded, whispering, "He is an honorable male."

Saxon squeezed her hands. "Honorable, yes, but not in your life. Don't throw away what you have with Zeke on a hope. For all you know, he's found another woman to share his life with."

Saskia knew he was trying to soften the blows, but that thought had entered her head before; however, she had banished it before insidious roots of doubt could form. She let out a deep breath. "I know you're right, Saxon, but somehow my heart and my head are telling me completely different things."

Saxon was quiet for a moment. "Let me ask you this: who has been there for you the last year? Who has cared for you, fed you, clothed you?"

"Ezekiel, of course."

"Then be logical about this. Alex is gone, but Ezekiel is here. Don't throw everything away for a human."

Saxon was right, of course. Her eyes alighted on her watch and she stood up suddenly. "Oh! I have to go," she announced. "I'm going to be late."

"Where are you meeting Zeke for dinner?"

"He got a reservation at *Valentino's*."

Saxon whistled through his teeth. "He's putting in the effort."

Saskia nodded, but she knew once she got to the restaurant, all she would be able to think about was Alex. That was where their first date had been... where their only date had been. Plastering a false smile onto her lips, Saskia collected her handbag and slipped it onto one shoulder.

"Thanks for the talk, Saxon."

"Anytime, sis."

She turned to leave when Saxon called her name. She faced him once more and waited.

"I just want to tell you how awful I feel for pushing you into mating Ezekiel. It was for the good of the pack, but I still feel like a bastard for doing that to you."

She shrugged. "It wasn't anything I wasn't prepared to do. My sense of honor would have gotten to me in the end anyway. You just shoved us along a little faster."

Standing up onto her tiptoes, she kissed her brother on the cheek and left the apartment feeling slightly lighter than she had before. She had finally reached a conclusion. She wouldn't tell Ezekiel everything. Why rock the boat when Alex wasn't even in her life anymore?

Saskia arrived at *Valentino's* at the same time as Zeke. She resisted the urge to pull away as he gently guided her through the restaurant, past all the other diners with eyes appreciatively appraising Zeke at her back.

"Here's your table for the evening," the maître d' said, pulling Saskia's chair out for her. Her heart beat erratically against her ribs for a second as she realized they'd been seated at the exact same table she and Alex had shared before.

"Is something wrong?" Ezekiel asked softly into her ear. She shook herself a little, shrugging off the haunting memories.

"I'm fine." Taking the proffered seat, she turned to look at the menu that had been handed to her. Zeke took the seat opposite her so he was facing the door.

"You look nice," he commented congenially.

Saskia glanced up from her menu. She didn't. She was still in the dove-grey pencil skirt and scarlet blouse she'd worn to work that day. "Thank you. You do, too."

Ezekiel smiled at her, reaching across the table to touch her fingers. Letting out a breath, she smiled back at him then resumed looking at the menu.

Their server came and took their orders and while they waited for their drinks to arrive, Saskia physically felt the uncomfortable silence settling between them. Her mate cleared his throat suddenly, drawing her eyes up to his face.

"How was your day?"

"Fine. Yours?"

He gave her a sad smile. "Busy."

Saskia nodded and began playing with her fork, straightening it then moving it around again. Their drinks finally arrived and she gulped down her wine until Zeke's raised brow stopped her. With a small embarrassed smile, she put her nearly empty glass down and waited.

"The reason I brought you out to dinner tonight was so we could talk, Saskia," Zeke said, his fingers idly playing with the label on his boutique beer bottle. "I know something's wrong, and I want to help you with it. Now before you tell me it's nothing, let me just say that whatever you have to say to me could never make me love you any less."

Saskia's eyes darted to his face, seeing his sincerity mirrored in his eyes. He truly did love her, and she realized with unshakeable clarity that she did not share the same feelings for him.

Steeling herself, she looked her mate in the eye and smiled. "It's nothing, really. It's just that the last year has been a rollercoaster ride for me. First, it was the suitors then the fight then..." she hesitated. What she was going to say was, "Alex giving up on me completely." Instead she said, "Getting mated to you."

Ezekiel gave her a genuinely warm smile in return for her admission. "Getting mated to you was the best day of my life, but I can see how strange and overwhelming it must have been. You'd been living with your brother all that time, and then you had to live with me and keep a house and everything else." He frowned, pinched the bridge of his nose with his thumb and forefinger and let out a breath. "Anyway, it's been a rough year for you. I get that you're still adjusting, but all I ask is that you let me share the burden. I'm your mate. I'm here for you through thick and thin."

He gave her hand an encouraging squeeze and Saskia returned the gesture. "Thanks, Zeke."

His smile reached his eyes. "Anytime."

CASEY GOT UP TO STRETCH HER SORE MUSCLES AGAIN. ALEX WAS STILL on the bed, still unmoving from when her brothers had thrown him on there.

After much debate, her alpha—who also happened to be her father—agreed to let Alex stay until he finished the Change. Judging by his almost comatose sleep, she knew he wasn't far from it.

Walking the perimeter of the room, she shrugged her shoulders and did some lunges to stretch out her stiffening muscles. Dropping down to the floor, she did fifty push-ups before flipping over onto her back to do the same number of crunches.

She'd always believed physical strength was a necessity. She never wanted to be underestimated by anyone—especially an enemy.

"Saskia, wait," Alex mumbled suddenly. Casey jumped to her feet and approached the bed. Alex was shaking his head frantically, sweat beading on his forehead and neck. His eyelids were still firmly shut, but his lips were moving.

Dragging the chair she'd just vacated a little closer to his bedside, Casey sank down onto it and watched him with fascination. Who was Saskia?

"Saskia, please. Give me...chance." Alex groaned and finally lay still, his tightly fisted hands relaxing once more. Casey watched as his breathing eased. Alex's eyes opened slowly, his hazel irises focusing on her. He frowned and brought his hand up to his temple.

"Headache?" she asked brightly.

Alex groaned. "Not so loud."

"I've got aspirin for you." She helped him sit up and gave him the two pills and a bottle of water. Alex took them from her, dropped them into his open mouth and cracked the seal on the water bottle.

He drank thirstily, not stopping until the bottle was empty. She took it from his hand and placed it back onto the rickety bedside table. Alex lowered himself back down onto the bed, his eyes warily watching her.

"Who's Saskia?" she asked.

"How do you know about her?" he demanded angrily.

Casey put her hands up in the universal sign for calm-the-fuck-down. "You were just moaning her name in your sleep."

Alex's cheeks immediately flamed with color, causing Casey to giggle.

"I wasn't *moaning* her name," he spat when she wouldn't stop laughing.

"How would you know? You were asleep."

He glowered at her. "You're really irritating. Has anyone ever told you that?"

"All the time," she grinned. "So, who's Saskia? Your girlfriend? Your wife? No? Your lover?"

Alex snapped his teeth at her—a very wolfish gesture—and turned over onto his side so his back was to her. "What are they going to do to me?" he asked.

"Keep you here until you go through the Change."

He barked a harsh laugh. "My change into a wolf, you mean?" Sarcasm dripped from every word, but Casey ignored it just like she always did.

"That's the one," she replied happily, sitting back in her chair and propping her legs up against him. "You'll get the pleasures of having fur and fangs and all those good things."

He snorted. "I don't believe you."

"What? That you'll be changing soon or about werewolves in general?"

"Both," he spat back petulantly.

"Well, I hate to break it to you, but both things are very, very true. You saw my brothers shift. There's your *werewolves-aren't-real* theory shot out of the water."

He was quiet for a moment. "I don't know what I saw."

Now it was Casey's turn to snort. "Bull. Shit. You know what you saw. Your brain is just making you believe it was something else."

"Werewolves aren't real. Neither are vampires and fairies. They're figments of a deranged mind."

"Whatever," she replied. He'd see soon enough. "So, who's Saskia?"

"I don't want to talk about her," he growled back.

After a long silence, she asked, "Alex, where do you live?"

"Buxton."

Buxton was like the center of Helheim Wolf Pack territory. "Whoa," she breathed.

"What?"

"Nothing," she said quickly. "It's nothing. It's just where we found you... you're a long way from home. Your family must be missing you."

"I don't have any family to miss me."

"Friends?" she ventured.

He shook his head slowly.

"Well, what about work colleagues? Surely your boss must be missing you by now."

"I am the boss."

"Own boss, huh? What do you do? Run your own business or something?"

Alex didn't reply, so Casey pushed his legs where her feet were resting. Eventually he sighed and answered her.

"I'm a cop."

"Oooo, what kind of cop?"

"A cop who doesn't like answering the questions of a deranged little girl with brothers the size of small cars, that's what kind of cop." He sucked in a breath. "Just leave me alone, Casey."

"Umm, ouch. Okay." She dropped her feet to the floor and moved to the door. "I'll be back to check on you again soon." Alex rolled over and stared at her with hollow eyes. She pointed her finger at him and made a little circle with it. "Yeah, all this anger and hostility are classic symptoms of an impending shift."

Without another word, Alex rolled over again. Casey tapped on the door three times and was let out. Hunter was on guard duty this time around.

"How much longer?" he asked, his eyes raking her body to see if she'd sustained any injuries while being in the same room as Alex.

"An hour. Maybe less. He's *really* irritable."

Hunter smiled, revealing one dimple in his cheek. "Maybe he's irritable because he's been talking to you."

Casey slugged her big brother in the chest. "I have no idea what you're talking about." With a wink, she turned around and made her way up the stairs.

SEVEN

Saxon had walked Saskia down to her car, making sure she was safely driving away before going back upstairs. He'd been surprised to see her there, and even more surprised she'd told him as much about her feelings as she had.

Climbing the stairs up to the apartment, he realized that although he had made the right decision by Saskia in biting Alex, it was a gamble. There was still no guarantee that he would come back for her. There was a chance he might already be dead from the Change.

He knew Saskia was having second thoughts about her mate, and that he, Saxon, was the reason she was having them. If he hadn't been so damn bullheaded about the whole getting mated thing, she wouldn't have settled. But the reality was that Alex wouldn't have been an appropriate choice for her. He was human. She was not.

Unlocking the apartment door, he pushed inside and looked around. Why the hell was he bothering to hang around? Getting changed into a pair of dark jeans and a white button-down shirt, he slipped his feet into a pair of boots and grabbed his keys.

Out on the street, he shoved his hands into his pockets to blend in with the other humans huddling against the cold. The bar he was heading toward was as seedy as shit, but it was a place where he could keep his head down and not be bothered. All he wanted to do was try to get good and wasted.

A warm wall of stale air and spilled beer hit his nostrils when he opened the door. Stepping over the threshold, his eyes scanned for threats before he slumped down onto one of the stools at the bar.

"What'll it be?" the bartender asked in a bored voice. Saxon looked up into his face. He was thin with a beaked nose that only made his face look longer than it really was. His flannelette shirt hung off his shoulders, his cheap jeans equally as baggy.

Brushing his mousy-blond hair from his eyes, the bartender snapped, "I haven't got all night."

"Jack. Straight up."

The guy grunted and pulled a dirty glass from under the bar top. The bottle of Jack was next. He emptied the rest of the bottle into the glass and pushed it in Saxon's direction.

Picking up his drink, Saxon drained it in one swallow, the bartender's bug eyes watching him the whole time.

"Another?" he grunted.

Saxon placed the glass down onto the bar a little more forcefully than needed and winced. "Keep them coming."

The human grunted again and shuffled to the other end of the bar to get another bottle of whiskey. Saxon kept his head down while he waited, but it wasn't too long before he smelled the overwhelmingly strong perfume of a female approaching him.

"Fuck," he said in a hushed breath, lifting his eyes to check on the progress of his drink. Damn, the guy was still trying to fit the pourer into the top of the bottle.

An arm slid over his shoulder. Saxon couldn't stop the growl from coming out, feeling it vibrate past his tightly-pressed lips. The woman hesitated for a moment.

"Did you hear that?" she asked in a low voice, her lips brushing against the shell of his ear as she spoke. He ground his teeth together and shrugged out from under her.

"Hear what?" he snarled.

"It sounded as if a dog just growled."

Great. Just fucking great. "You're hearing things."

Saxon still hadn't turned to look at her, and by the way her fingers flexed into his shoulders again in an attempt to draw his attention, it was bothering her.

He was just about to tell her to fuck off when the bartender came back over to stand in front of him, the bottle of Jack in his hand. Saxon watched him pour another drink for him, the guy's eyes fixed on the female draped over Saxon's shoulder. She must have been showing a bit of skin.

"Thanks," Saxon mumbled, taking a long drink from the glass. The bartender moved to walk away, but Saxon called him back. "Leave the bottle."

The male's brow arched over one beady eye, but he nodded and left the bottle on the scarred bar top less than an inch from Saxon's bunched up fist.

"What's your name?" the woman asked.

Saxon finished the rest of his whiskey. "Are you still here?" He poured himself another drink. He threw that one back, too, wincing at the burn.

With an angry huff she moved away, the scent of her cloying perfume leaving with her. "Thank fucking Christ," he muttered.

"I'd be careful of that one," the bartender said. Saxon looked up wearily.

"Why's that?"

"She's a pro—a real piece of work."

"Thanks for the warning," Saxon grunted back, pouring another couple of inches into his glass.

"You seem pretty intent on destroying yourself tonight."

"That a problem?" he snarled back, feeling his wolf beginning to get agitated by the alcohol.

The guy put both his hands up in front of him. "Nope. Just saying, is all."

Saxon sighed and closed his eyes. "I'll pay you double my tab tonight if you keep the whiskey coming and the conversation to zero. We got a deal?" He met the human's watery brown eyes and watched him flinch.

The bartender nodded. "Yeah, we got a deal."

———

CASEY STEPPED OUT OF THE SHOWER, WRAPPING A TOWEL AROUND herself. The shower had felt good. This was the first opportunity she'd had to change out of the clothes she'd been in for almost a whole day. She'd been too concerned about Alex to leave him before he woke up again. He was so close to the Change, and the next few hours were critical.

After dressing in a long-sleeved tee and jeans, Casey wandered down the hallway in search of her father. She needed to talk to him to find out what he planned to do with Alex once he completed his first shift. Her pack hadn't taken in too many Bitten wolves without a lot of suspicion first.

She'd just reached his office door to find it cracked open a little. Pressing herself against the wall, she listened for a moment.

"Casey wants to let him stay," Hunter said, his voice getting louder and softer as he paced across the length of the office.

"There's no guarantee he'll make it through the Change though." Oliver's voice had the same low tone as Hunter's—something they got from their father.

"Maybe not," her father said, "but he's made it this far. The odds are in his favor."

The clinking of glass echoed through the otherwise quiet room. It didn't matter what time it was; as far as her father was concern, any time was time for a drink.

"Hunter, how's his temperament?"

A long pause filled the space, and Casey found herself holding her breath. Being her father's beta, Hunter's opinion and recommendations were listened to more often than not.

"He seems okay. He doesn't appear to be violent. In fact, he appears to be quite sceptical of the whole thing."

Riley snorted. "That'll change."

"Would he fit in here?"

"There's no way to tell."

Not being able to see the men talking was driving Casey crazy. She stepped forward to peer past the crack in the door and...

"Tell me again where you found him," her father asked. He was sitting on the edge of his desk, the glass of scotch resting near his hip. His greying hair gave him a distinguished look, but behind his green eyes, his wolf was still powerful enough to control any other.

"About a mile out from our farthest border," Hunter replied. He dropped onto the sofa next to Oliver.

"Where'd he come from?" her father directed the question to the entire group assembled in front of him.

Oliver shrugged. "Don't know. He's been in and out of consciousness."

"Has anyone spoken to him?" her alpha demanded. Casey shivered, feeling his power wash against her skin. She took a cautious step away from the door, the floorboard beneath her foot creaking loudly.

Her father's head whipped around to the door, his wolf's black eyes shining through the green. His gaze darted away and a second later the door opened. Hunter stood on the other side, the irritation clear on his face.

Despite her wolf cowering away, Casey straightened her spine and began to push past her brother. Taking her by the shoulders, he stopped her without really even trying.

"No, Casey."

She glared up at him. "What do you mean, no? I have every right to be in here too."

"No, you don't. This is for enforcers only."

She huffed and propped her hands on her hips. "Exactly. Enforcers only. I'm going to be an enforcer, so you might as well let me in now."

Hunter looked over his shoulder at their father. Acario's lips were thinned and his eyes were hard. He shook his head once, and Casey let all her pain show through.

"Father, please!" she begged. "It's not fair. I can help!"

"No, Casey," he replied, his voice hardly raised above a whisper, but the power that carried it to her ears made her knees buckle.

"Please," she whimpered, tears forming in her eyes. Angrily, she wiped them away before her brothers and father could see, but the distressed look in Oliver's eyes told her she'd failed.

Shaking her brother's hands off her shoulders, she straightened her spine and tilted her chin. She would get her way. She had to. "He's spoken to me. I know where he comes from. If you let me in, I'll tell you."

Her father stood up and walked toward her. Although Casey's heart was pounding hard against her ribs, she gritted her teeth and stayed strong. Acario's hands cradled her head, his thumbs wiping away the fresh tears.

"You're in no position to make demands of me, child. You will never be an enforcer. Get your head out of the clouds, Casey. Now leave us. Your mother said she needed help getting dinner prepared."

"But—"

"No!" he boomed. "No, you will go and help your mother now and that's an order."

"But—" she tried again.

"I'm also prohibiting you from seeing the Bitten male. He could be dangerous, but the effects of the Change might be holding him back."

"But that's not what Hunter said." Her green eyes fell on her brother. "*Tell him.*"

Hunter shook his head and turned his back. Casey bit the side of her cheek. He was being a coward by not standing up for her. He *knew* Alex wasn't dangerous.

"Casey, leave us now," her father said. The compulsion to follow his order took hold. Her wolf supplicated herself to his and she turned around, dejected, and stomped through to the kitchen.

EIGHT

Saxon tipped his head and sucked back the last of his whiskey before placing the glass back onto the bar. The bartender—Earl—as Saxon had found out gave him a reproachful look from his corner of the bar before his eyes swiveled away.

The place was nearly empty and Saxon was far from being drunk enough. With less than an inch left in the bottle of Jack, Saxon emptied it into his glass and took a deep sip. He squeezed his eyes shut and rode the burn.

"Can I get a vodka, please?" a woman snarled from beside him. Saxon's nostrils flared as he took in the scent of her irritation and stress.

"What a fucking day I had," she said, turning to him. Saxon blinked, his eyes automatically dropping to her mouth. When her lips flexed into a smile, he forced his brain to look at the whole package. Christ knew, his cock wasn't interested in seeing anything more, but Saxon wasn't in the habit of listening to his dick.

The woman had brown hair that couldn't be called dark or light. It was somewhere in between, falling in soft waves over her shoulders. Her eyes were grey and hard. She had a small scar on the side of her nose where a piercing would have once been.

She smiled again, showing him her perfectly straight, perfectly white teeth. "Bad day for you, too?" she asked, her eyes darting to the now empty glass and bottle loitering in front of him.

"Something like that." His voice sounded like gravel. Saxon cleared his throat.

"What happened to you?" she asked, picking up the glass of vodka Earl had just parked in front of her hand. She gave the other man a grateful smile and threw back the liquor in one go. Saxon licked his lips hungrily as the slope of her throat was exposed to him. His wolf liked how submissive she was being even if she didn't realize it.

"What's your name?" he asked, cursing himself for even engaging her in conversation. He should just pay his tab and leave, but his cock had other ideas. Saxon couldn't even remember the last time he'd gotten laid.

She smiled at him—a genuine smile, he thought. "Buy me another and I'll tell you," she replied, humor dancing in those hard grey eyes.

He nodded and without breaking eye contact with her, he called, "Earl, get the lady another vodka and another Jack for me."

Earl grunted in the way Saxon was becoming to recognize was his acquiescence. A moment later, he reappeared with their drinks.

The woman raised her glass to Saxon. "To new friends," she said, her mouth curling up at the corner.

"To new friends," Saxon murmured in reply, his cock jumping at the implication of his words. He swallowed a mouthful of whiskey and placed his glass down deliberately. "So, what's your name?"

"What's yours?" she countered.

"Saxon." He stuck his hand out to her.

Her grey eyes dropped to his hand, her tongue creeping out to moisten her lips. A wave of lust radiated off her body. "Sandy."

"Short for Sandra?"

"Short for Sandy," she replied, placing the lip of the glass to her mouth.

"All right, Sandy-short-for-Sandy, what made your day so horrendous?"

"My lecherous excuse for a boss," she huffed.

"Made you work late?" he asked. It was well after ten o'clock.

"Nope," she replied, popping the "p". Saxon's eyes latched onto her lips again, his hard-on straining against the zipper of his jeans.

He scooped up his glass and took another sip. "What then?"

Sandy swiveled on her stool, her knees in between his legs. He gulped, hoping she didn't look between his thighs. "He propositioned me. He said that if I fucked him, he'd give me a raise and a better office."

Saxon let out a breath. "Fuck."

"Yeah. I said I'd only do it if it was for a corner office," she added seriously.

Saxon schooled his expression carefully. "I hear people would do anything for one of those corner offices."

Sandy's serious expression finally cracked and she smiled at him. "You don't really think I'd fuck my boss for a corner office, do you?"

Saxon shrugged. Now that the word "fuck" had been thrown around a little that was all he could think of. "I don't know how attractive your boss is."

Sandy laughed, throwing her head back. The few people left in the building glanced their way, shaking their heads. When she finally gained control of herself, she said, "I told him I'd rather fuck the entire office for nothing at all rather than spread my legs for him. He's, like, fifty years old with halitosis and a comb-over."

Inside, Saxon laughed. If she thought her boss was old, she'd find his ninety years fucking hysterical. Not that that would ever happen. A sobering thought.

"Look, Saxon," Sandy said, her hand landing on the top of his thigh. He sucked in a hiss and reached for his drink, draining the last of it from the bottom of the glass. "You wanna get out of here? My place is a few blocks away."

Letting out a breath, Saxon said, "My place is closer."

Taking her hand, he stood up. Shoving his free hand into his pocket, he pulled out some cash and threw it on the bar. Earl's brown eyes lit up, and Saxon knew he'd overpaid, but with Sandy sucking on his earlobes, he just couldn't seem to concentrate.

By the time they'd made it to the door of the bar, Sandy's lips were on his throat, nipping and sucking his skin into her mouth. Saxon groaned, his erection tenting the fuck out of his pants. As soon as his apartment door was shut behind them, Sandy's eager fingers were tearing at the buttons of his shirt. He let her go, his own hands dropping to cup her ass. Her mouth found his, her tongue twisting and writhing with his.

"Bedroom?" she whispered, her hands fumbling with the button on his jeans.

"That way." He nodded toward his bedroom door and let her take the lead. Kicking the door shut behind them, he worked the small zipper at the back of her skirt down and pushed the thin material away.

"Pants. Off. Now," she said, playing with the top button of her shirt with a seductive smile on her lips. Saxon pushed his already opened pants off his hips, letting them pool at his ankles. Sandy's eyes dropped to his groin and she bit her bottom lip.

Fuck, yeah.

"Your turn," he replied. "Strip."

Sandy smiled wickedly, turning her back to him. He couldn't hide the groan as he saw the pale blue French knickers she was wearing were the ones where half her fine ass was hanging out. Turning around, she started undoing the buttons on her blouse and slowly stripped out of it. She made a show of losing one half then the other before reaching behind her to unclasp her bra. Standing naked before him, she playfully slid her fingers over his chest, down his waist, before gripping him firmly at the base of his cock and applying a little pressure.

He groaned and jerked his hips back, forcing her to release him. He dropped to his knees and stripped her of her panties. She was smooth between her legs—something he noticed human women did. But he was a little old-fashioned. He still liked his women to have a little hair there. Sliding his finger through her folds, her grip tightened on his shoulders as she let out a shuddering breath.

Dropping his head, Saxon replaced his finger with his tongue. Long, languid strokes played at her flesh, drawing fresh whimpers from her throat.

Before too long, her whole body was flushed with heat, her skin carrying a fine sheen as he worked her to her first orgasm.

After she rode the high, Saxon picked her up and took her to the bed, laying her down. She was boneless and smiling up at him as he climbed her body and positioned himself between her thighs.

"Protection?" she whispered.

Saxon groaned mentally, but pulled open his bedside drawer and fumbled around for the box of condoms. Christ, he hoped they were still good to go.

Ripping the foil packet with his teeth, Saxon rolled the condom onto his erection and found his place again. Sandy arched her back, thrusting her breasts into his face. Taking the invitation for what it was, he latched onto one of her nipples and rolled the tight bud of flesh around with his tongue.

Her hips pressed insistently against his cock. He felt the head of him find her opening and with one strong thrust, he was deep inside her. Giving her a few moments to get used to his size, he started rocking against her, finding a rhythm that would bring them both to orgasm.

It didn't take long for Saxon. He felt his balls begin to tighten, the deep feeling of impending release rushing up on him. Sandy's fingers were around his biceps, holding on and demanding he give her more.

But he didn't have any more to give. Beads of sweat moistened his brow. His mouth was in a firm grimace. He tried to hold on, but when Sandy's inner muscles began to tighten around his cock, he knew it was all over.

He barked a curse at the ceiling, pumping himself into her until she came too, her body clamping down on his cock, milking him that little bit more.

After they had both come down from their highs, Sandy pushed some of the long waves from her face and breathed, "I should have come to the bar earlier."

"Why's that?" he asked, sliding out of her body and sitting on the edge of the mattress. Snapping a few tissues from the box beside his bed, he unrolled the condom and cleaned himself up.

"You could have lasted three times as long if you didn't have all the liquor in you," Sandy replied, her finger drawing figure-eights on his back.

Saxon stood up to dump the used condom in the bathroom. After washing his hands, he looked at himself in the mirror and sighed. This was the part he hated. He couldn't have a strange female sleeping in his apartment. His wolf wouldn't let him rest. Shrugging into the bathrobe hanging on the back of the door, he flipped off the light and walked back into the bedroom to send Sandy home in a cab.

He found her curled over onto her side, already snoring lightly. Fuck. The sheets were down near her feet, so he pulled them over her naked body and he went out into the living room to wait until she woke up.

IN HIS TIME AS A COP, ALEX HAD BEEN SHOT, BUT THAT PAIN WAS nothing when compared with the excruciating pain he was experiencing in this moment. It seemed like every time he dragged in a breath, his lungs were filling with acid while his skin was being scrubbed raw with razor wire. Even his finger and toe nails were hurting.

Behind his eyelids, his head throbbed in time to his racing heart, pounding out a rhythm that shouldn't have even been possible to sustain life. He moaned, sucking in a sharp breath as even his jaw and teeth hurt. Christ, even his tongue hurt.

"Shh." A soft voice washed over his senses. He rolled his head in the direction of the sound. "Don't fight it, Alex."

Casey.

It was Casey.

Alex forced his eyelids to open, his retinas burning as they also had the acid and razor wire treatment. Something cool touched his forehead, making a relieved moan escape his throat.

"What's...happening?" he slurred.

The coolness went away for a moment. "You're going through the Change."

"What...mean?"

"Your wolf is emerging from your body for the first time. Don't fight him."

"Going...to...die," Alex managed to spit out.

Casey laughed easily. "You're not going to die. You'll see."

Even though he couldn't see it, Alex could hear the smug satisfaction in her voice. He still didn't believe her. How could he? There was no such thing as werewolves.

The pounding in his head got worse. He groaned and tried to place his hands over his ears, but yelled out in pain at the sudden movement. It seemed as if all the muscles in his body had shut down in tandem, holding him hostage inside his head, barred in by the pain.

"Make...it...stop," he gritted out.

"I will," Casey said. She got up from the chair she'd been straddling and went to the door. Opening it just a crack, Alex smelled one of Casey's brothers on the other side.

"Casey, what's going on?"

"It's fine, Hunter. He's fine."

There was a soft growl before Hunter said, "He's not fine. He's going through the Change. Get out of there, Casey. Now!"

"All right. Give me a second." Casey closed the door. There was a metallic click, then she let out a shaky breath and came back over to the bed.

"They won't be able to get in here. I have the only key."

Alex watched her mouth form the words she said to him, but he didn't hear them. All Alex could focus on was the dirty scent of fear slowing seeping from her body.

Prey, an insidious voice whispered.

Weak, it said again.

A huge *thump* sounded, dragging his thoughts back to the room. The door was shaking on its hinges and Casey was up on her feet, her back to him.

Now, the voice whispered again so seductively.

Attack. Now.

Alex shook his head, looking down at the floor beneath his feet. When had he sat up? When he looked up again at Casey, the voice was more insistent.

Attack.

Weak.

Prey.

He groaned, cradling his head in his hands. It suddenly felt very full in there.

"Alex? Are you all right?" Casey asked. He glanced up to find her across the other side of the room. Her fear was a stench that filled his nostrils, further aggravating the voice in his head.

Wolf, the voice said.

Wolf? Alex thought. *What in the hell does that mean?*

"Alex? Is your wolf talking to you?" Casey asked in a stuttering breath. She was pressed to the wall now, the look of panic plain on her face.

"Is that who's talking to me?" he asked, standing up and stretching out his aching muscles. The pain was gone now, a new feeling of anticipation burning through his blood. The sharp tang of anger came from behind the door.

"Casey! You get out here right now. He's not stable!" Hunter yelled.

Alex heard the buzz of a growl only to realize it was coming from his own throat.

"W-what is your wolf saying to you, Alex?" Casey asked.

"Prey. Weak. Attack."

Yes. Prey. Weak. Attack, his wolf rumbled in agreement.

Prey.

Weak.

Attack.

Alex shook his head to clear the voice away, although he still felt its presence within him.

"Is he talking to you?"

Alex nodded. He closed his eyes and the silhouette of a giant snarling beast shuddered to life. A wolf. His wolf. Its fur was black with grey flecks around its muzzle and ears. Its eyes were intelligent, the color of a blazing sunset. With its lips pulled back from its gums, he could see the razor sharp teeth it would use to rend flesh from bone.

Attack, his wolf urged again. Alex couldn't not listen to his wolf. It was protecting him. He understood that. Casey was afraid of him, and things that were afraid of him were unpredictable—dangerous.

Attack.

Alex crouched down lower to the ground, his eyes fixed on Casey now cowering in the corner. Her eyes were wide, darting around the room—landing on the door behind him. He smiled. There was no way for her to escape now.

"Casey! Goddamnit! Open this door *now!*" Hunter boomed.

Her green eyes bounced back to the door, her bottom lip trembling. "I-I can't. He's cornered me."

The roar that sounded from beyond the door made Alex cringe, but his wolf would not be swayed.

Attack.

Alex's eyes fixed on Casey's jugular. So exposed. So delicate. All he had to do was bite. All he had to do was cut off her air supply and she would be dead. And his wolf could feed. He took a step toward her, licking his lips.

"Alex?" Casey squeaked, trying to hide her trembling body.

Attack!

NINE

Casey's wolf was whining to get out, scratching at the sides of her ribs, pawing against the inside of her head. *She* understood the danger presented in the room, and she wanted out to take care of it.

Casey on the other hand knew she could take care of it herself. "Alex?" she said, hoping he hadn't heard the squeak of fear in her voice. By the way he took another step toward her, he had heard it and decided she was prey.

Showing weakness in front of another wolf was never good. Casey gulped and looked over at the door. Hunter was still pounding against it, demanding she open it for him. But it was too late. Alex's wolf was getting stronger, speaking to him. His self-preservation had probably kicked in, and although she wasn't seen as a threat, she was being seen as weak.

Which could end in only one way.

Casey licked her lips nervously, wondering how she was supposed to get out of this one. A warning growl broke free of Alex's lips, and her head turned quickly to look at him. He was so incredibly close to shifting for the first time, and if she was still in the room with him, he would tear her to shreds.

"Casey! Open this goddamn door!"

"I'm fine," she replied, not raising her voice. "Really. I'll be fine with him."

The sound of furniture crashing outside the door made a nice change from a hammering fist.

"Hunter?" she called. The ensuing silence filled her with dread. He'd left her. He'd left her there. "Hunter?" she called again, desperation leaking into her voice.

Alex was yet to take his eyes off her. Mere feet away now, he lowered his body even closer to the ground as he prepared to leap at her.

Dropping her gaze to the ground, she raised her chin and exposed her throat. It was a gamble. Alex saw her as weak, and being submissive to him could go one of two ways. He could see her submission as giving up, or he could see it as an opportunity to attack her while she wasn't looking.

Letting out a deep breath, Casey waited. Her heart was pounding so hard in her chest she thought it would crawl out of her throat. She let out another deep breath and watched as Alex's feet appeared in front of her.

"Casey?" he croaked. She raised her head, but kept her eyes on his chest rather than look in his eyes. "Casey, look at me."

She lifted her eyes the final few inches and looked into his black eyes. He began to smile, but his expression contorted into a grimace as a shout broke free from his lips. Stumbling back, Alex fell to his knees and clutched at his head. Casey took a few steps toward him causing his head to swing up. Pain-filled eyes met her face. They swam from black to orange. His wolf was trying to push out.

"Casey? What's happening to me?" he gasped, his voice much lower than normal.

"You're going through the Change, Alex," she replied softly. "You're going to be fine. Just don't fight your wolf. Let him guide you."

"It's fucking agony," he breathed in reply, his fingernails digging into his hair. "I'm dying."

Casey shook her head. "You're being reborn."

ALEX KNEW ONLY ONE THING: PAIN. IT WAS PLAYING HIS BODY, PLUCKING at the strings of his subconscious, threatening to drag him under and beat him. Death would have been a blessing, except that Casey was adamant he wasn't dying.

Clutching harder at his skull was the only way to stop the feeling that something was going to come bursting out of it. He felt too full. He was sharing his body with something else—something feral and wild writhing under his skin. It was sending images of biting through still twitching flesh and warm blood spurting out onto his tongue.

But the thing that bothered him the most was that those images didn't bother him. He liked how the images made him feel.

Wolf.

It was only one word, but goddamn, it felt right. His muscles, which had been so loose and liquid before, suddenly seized. His elbows dropped to the floor, his body rigid; a cold sweat broke out under his arms, on his back and on his brow.

Casey's scent was suddenly filling his nostrils, jacking up the pain. His skin prickled with a sudden fire, his bones aching, his head pounding like a thousand tiny fists had gone to work on the inside of his skull.

The growl in his head frightened him. He managed to look up and see Casey crouched beside him, her eyes changing from green to steel grey.

"I can see your wolf, Alex," she murmured. "He's looking out through your eyes."

He let a growl out and Casey stood up, backing away. "Casey," he managed to squeeze out between breaths. "Stay...away...from...me." He sucked in a lungful of air. "Hurt...you," he added when she started shaking her head at him.

A surge of power ripped through him, throwing him onto his back. His legs scissored back and forth, his hands bunched into tight fists. Every inch of his skin was on fire, every hair follicle being plucked free of his skin and being replaced by a white-hot needle.

He yelled out hoarsely, wishing Casey was not in the room. Whatever was going to happen to him couldn't be very pretty. Breathing through the excruciating pain, he looked at her.

"Leave. Now."

"No," she whispered.

"Leave!"

"No!" she screamed back, crossing her arms over her chest.

"Casey! Get the fuck out of there!" another male's voice yelled and Casey's head jerked up to look at the door.

"That's a fucking order!" the voice added. Casey stood up on shaking legs, her body willing, but the expression on her face telling Alex that her mind wasn't. She approached the door apprehensively. She slid the locks free and opened the door.

An older looking male stuck his head in the room, his green eyes swimming with black shadows as he evaluated Alex. With flared nostrils, he spat a nasty curse and pulled Casey from the room. Through the door, Alex listened to their conversation.

"Casey! What in the hell were you thinking? He could have killed you. Don't you realize how close he is?"

"Father, I know. I was just trying to help him through it."

"He would have killed you. You're my only daughter, and I will not have you risking your life for a Bitten wolf!"

A Bitten wolf. That was exactly what Alex was. He felt the beast beneath his skin, invading his blood and his muscles. He felt it press against his subconscious, presenting itself in flashes of fur and fang.

Wolf.

"Please, Alpha. Let me go back in there," Casey begged.

"No. You're to stay out here with me. We will wait for this to be over."

More could have been said, but Alex's mind had turned to other things.

Out, his wolf demanded.

"How?" he asked, gritting his teeth and beating back the pain assaulting his body in waves.

Out.

"How?" he repeated, screaming out wordlessly as its claws raked up against his ribs. He looked down the line of his body, half expecting to see his sides punctured. His skin felt too hot, stretched too damn tight. He had to get out of his clothes.

Struggling into a sitting position, he stripped the tee and pants from his body. His skin felt as if it was melting against his muscles and bones. He looked down at his ribs when he felt his wolf beginning to struggle against him, watching as his skin moved from pressure beneath it.

He would have been scared of what he'd just seen if he'd had the strength to react, but he didn't. He was immobile, watching and feeling his wolf starting to dig its way out of his body.

Alex tried to keep his breathing even, his thoughts lucid. He was about to fucking die, and there wasn't a damn thing he could do about it.

OUT!

Alex screamed as his head felt like it was about to explode. He was sure Casey would be seeing bits of his brain matter strewn all over the carpet when she walked back into the room. The pain that had started at the top of his head slowly drifted down to his forehead, his eyes, his ears, his cheeks and jaw.

It kept moving, picking up pace, snowballing the pain. The bones in his shoulders seemed to shift and dislocate, his elbows following suit. Soon it was his hips and knees. He screamed when his bad knee popped free of its socket.

Alex was vaguely aware his whole body was changing shape. Rolling over onto his side, the movement released a whimper from his throat. Every single point on his body ached, throbbing with his erratically pounding pulse.

When he looked down, he saw his fingers twitching—moving independently of his thoughts. His neural pathways must have been firing randomly. He was fucking dying and he wouldn't be leaving a pretty corpse behind. He howled in pain when his fingers began changing shape—becoming shorter, his nails turning into claws. The pain was the same in his feet, and a quick glance down confirmed it.

Where his fingers and hands, toes and feet once were, there were now lupine pads and claws. He squeezed his eyes shut and bit down on the inside of his cheek. With labored breaths, he wished himself to finally wake up from the nightmare.

It couldn't be real.

It just couldn't be.

A raw scream exploded from his throat. His jaw hurt, and when he ran his tongue over his teeth he could feel the blunt shapes were gone, and sharp fangs replaced them.

The pain subsided slowly and Alex let out a shaky breath. Unsure whether he could stand up yet, he lay there panting, listening to how his chest sounded different from before. He had just closed his eyes to sleep when the sensation like that of having hot oil thrown on his entire body brought him back to consciousness with a howl.

The fire traveled over his entire body. It felt as if he was writhing in agony for hours, but only seconds had passed. When it was finally over, and the pain receded, Alex let his thoughts blank out to nothing. He was checking-out of whatever fucked-up situation he had just been through.

When his lids slipped closed, there was only one thing he was thinking of. Saskia.

Mine, his wolf agreed.

TEN

Ulf picked up Brax the following morning for their road trip west into Jotenheim territory. After throwing his gym bag into the back of the Hummer, Brax got himself settled in the front passenger seat. He cleared his throat, and he could have sworn he heard an echo.

"Your ride is pretty nice. It's got nothing on mine though," Brax said to his beta, sliding his eyes to the side to watch his reaction.

Ulf's top lip curled. "That little tin can you drive? This baby could roll right over it," he said, running his hands over the top of the steering wheel in a loving caress.

Brax grinned. "Only if you can catch me."

Ulf barked a laugh. "Whatever, asshole."

As a beta, Ulf was good. Even as a friend, he was all right, but he wasn't Rhett...annnnnnnd Brax was right back where he didn't want to be: thinking about Rhett and Indi and leaving them both when they were at their lowest.

Brax huffed and cranked up the radio to drown out his thoughts. He knew he'd done the right thing by leaving. He couldn't be around Indi while he was addicted to her bite. It had been a year, though, and he was pretty sure he wasn't hooked anymore.

"Brax, you there?" Ulf said, turning down the music.

"Umm, yeah. Sorry."

"Something on your mind?"

He turned to look at the other male. "*My* mind? Nope, there's nothing going on in my mind."

Ulf glanced between him and the road, but didn't say anything more. Brax fixed his gaze out the passenger window, watching the world slip by. The Jotenheim pack house was still a few hours' drive away, and with Brax unwilling to discuss his deepest and darkest secrets with Ulf, he let his mind drift off as the Hummer ate up the distance.

Brax was jolted awake by a sharp shake on his shoulder. He blinked, the fuzzy image of Ulf's face coming into focus.

"We're here," the guy said, slipping out of his already open door. Brax looked through the windshield at an apartment building probably no larger than four stories high. The stucco façade was painted a natural stone color, the windows arched around the top.

"This is where the alpha lives?"

Ulf glanced back at him over his shoulder. "He owns every apartment in the building. He and the majority of his highest ranking enforcers all live under the same roof."

Brax tipped his head back, squinting at the building. "How big is his army?"

"Bigger since the battle last year."

Brax grunted.

"Are you coming or what?" Ulf called over his shoulder. Brax got his feet moving, marching after Ulf like a good little enforcer.

When they reached the large foyer doors, Ulf hit the buzzer for the penthouse, static filling the space.

"Yes?" a female replied on the other end.

Ulf hit the button again, getting up nice and close to the intercom. "It's Ulf from the Asgard pack."

"Come on up. Avon is expecting you," the female replied. A buzzer sounded, and the door clicked open. Brax looked up as he passed through the doorway, noticing the security cameras and sensors dotted throughout the lobby.

Ulf punched the "up" button on the elevator, falling into a relaxed stance as he waited—his arms behind his back, his feet shoulder-width apart. Brax stood at his shoulder, mimicking him. When the doors opened, Ulf stepped into the car and hit the button at the top of the panel.

When the doors opened up once more, Brax got an eyeful of an intensely modern apartment—completely unexpected after seeing the outside of the building. The sweet smell of caramel wafted through the air. Brax drew the scent into his nose. He'd always loved the smell of caramel.

"You must be Ulf," a woman said, the heavy scent of caramel getting thicker. Brax's eyes flipped open. He didn't know why, but he simply had to see this female's face. The petite brunette in front of him ducked her eyes when she met Brax's intense stare.

"Yes, I'm Ulf. It's nice to meet you," Brax's beta said, offering the woman his hand. He watched, fascinated, as the female looked at Ulf's outstretched palm then away nervously, biting her plump bottom lip in a way that made blood rush south of Brax's belt.

"Avon told me to show you through to his study. If you'd like to follow me?" The woman turned, and Brax would have followed her to the ends of the earth if she'd asked. He wondered who she was. She'd said "Avon" instead of "my mate", so she could be an unmated pack member. All he knew was that he had to know her.

"Shit," he cursed softly, jogging to catch up to Ulf, who was already out of the foyer. Down the long hall, Brax passed by large, bold oil paintings and sleek glass furniture. He followed behind his beta as they entered another room—a room where the scent of caramel grew stronger and Brax's growing erection was making a nuisance of itself.

Avon was reclining in an armchair positioned toward a fireplace. Brax took a surreptitious look around the room, taking in the almost rustic decorating style and cozy rather than crisp lines. He also kept an eye on the woman. She was tucked away in the corner, as far away from him as possible.

Brax smiled at her, and she dropped her eyes, turning her body away from him. He frowned. Women usually fell at his feet when they saw his dimples.

"Andrea, you can leave us now," Avon said gently.

So, her name was Andrea. Brax was captivated by her, by her dark hair and pale eyes. She was petite and delicate with a fragility to her that made him want to care for her.

"She's not for you, wolf." Avon's harsh voice cut through Brax's thoughts. His head swung around, his wolf trying to push forward. All year, he'd been working hard on controlling the other half of himself better, but he continued to be front and center, pushing back when Brax tried to pull him away.

Avon's eyes were barely holding his beast back, the pale blue color like ice chips glinting back at Brax. Dropping his eyes, Brax tilted his head a little to the side, showing the more dominant wolf his throat in submission.

"Forgive him, Avon," Ulf said softly. Brax hated that the guy was speaking for him. He'd obviously fucked up here, but he could stand up for himself. But sometimes being a wolf was more about following orders and falling in line rather than being who you were born to be. Brax wasn't a fuck-up, but right now he felt like one.

"I apologize if I've caused offence," he said, eyes downcast.

Brax could still feel Avon's wolf in the room, suffocating, stifling. Brax's wolf finally backed away, but was still buzzing with anger.

Avon grunted, his attention returning to Ulf. "I'm glad you're here. Kade will be here soon."

"Thank you for allowing us to come and speak with him. Any information he can provide us with will help us to pinpoint exactly who we're looking for."

"Of course, of course." Avon waved Ulf's words away. At the other end of the house, the doorbell rang. Brax watched the open doorway, hanging out for one more look at Andrea. She walked past a moment later, pausing to look into the room as she did. A smile broke out on Brax's lips when she looked his way. She hurried off, a startled deer escaping the hunter.

"That'll be Kade," Avon replied, finally standing up. Both Brax and Ulf followed the alpha from his office, heading in the direction of the elevator. The saccharine scent of caramel preceded them, making Brax's body go into meltdown. Andrea was standing beside the elevator, waiting for their guest to arrive. Brax took a second to look the female over. Yeah, he liked what he saw. She was carefully avoiding his stare, choosing to keep her eyes fixed on her feet.

The elevator door sprung open with a soft chime, drawing everybody's attention. Brax took a step backwards as the new wolf took a tentative step into the room. His eyes were lowered in deference as he addressed Avon.

"Alpha, you wished to see me?"

"Yes, Kade. Thank you for coming so soon," Avon replied, walking toward a white leather sofa in the far corner of the room. Brax took his lead from Ulf, following Avon to where he was currently sitting. Once everyone had sat down, Avon asked Andrea to bring them all some coffee.

Brax watched her leave, noticing when she put a hand on the wall to steady herself for a moment. He only paid attention to the conversation going on in front of him once she was out of sight. He dropped his eyes when Avon caught him staring.

"I won't warn you again," the elderly alpha said, his words a snarl.

"I'm sorry," Brax replied. He had to keep his eyes to himself otherwise he was going to piss the guy off. When Andrea returned with a tray of mugs, Brax kept his gaze on the floor, staring hard at a loop in the pile that had come loose. When she was gone, Brax picked up his coffee and took a shallow sip. Damn, he could still smell her.

"Kade, this is Ulf. He is the beta of the Asgard pack. His alpha sent him here to ask you a few questions."

"Ask *me* questions?" Kade asked, surprised. He looked between Avon and Ulf, completely ignoring Brax. That was fine by him. It would give him time to catch another glimpse of Andrea.

"They want to know about who bit you."

Kade's body stiffened suddenly, his eye movements become more frantic. His nostril flared. He licked his lips. The male was nervous as all fuck. But why?

"It's all right, son," Avon murmured, placing a hand on the other man's forearm. "You're all right." Turning to Ulf, Avon added, "He had a pretty horrific experience when he went through the Change."

"What happened?" Brax asked, his eyes narrowing on Kade.

Avon cleared his throat. "The wolf who bit him strung him up between two trees afterwards. He had no way of getting himself free. One of my enforcers stumbled across him in the backwoods. If we hadn't found him, he might not have survived the Change on his own."

"Who bit you?" Ulf asked, his voice like gravel.

Kade shook his head. "I'd been working late, looking after a dog we had in for surgery—I'm a vet," he added, his face twisting into a strange grimace. "At least, I used to be a vet. Animals don't seem to like being around me much now. Anyway, I'd been in the clinic late when a man brought in his dog. It was big— bigger than any dog I'd ever seen. At the time, I thought it was part wolf and, as it turned out, I wasn't too far off. The dog bit me and I treated the wound.

"A few hours later, there was a knock on my front door. The same guy had come around to see if my injury was okay. He'd said he felt really bad about his dog biting me. I invited him in and the next thing I knew, I was being hit in the head and shoved into the tray of a truck. When I came to, I was strung up between two trees." Kade shivered. "I blacked out a lot during that time," he said in a soft voice. "When I finally came to again, Avon was there. He told me what was happening to me. He took me in, and the rest is history, I guess."

"So it was a male wolf, too?"

Kade nodded. "Yeah. A big black wolf with yellow eyes." The guy shook his head, his eyes glazed. "I'll remember those eyes for the rest of my life."

"Did the guy say why?"

Kade jerked away, a stuttered, unsteady motion. "Why, what?"

"Why you were bitten? Why they chose you?"

"I didn't know it was premeditated," he replied. "I just thought it was a case of wrong place, wrong time."

Ulf sat back in his seat. "Maybe it was. Who knows?" He glanced over at Brax and raised an eyebrow. Brax shook his head in reply. There was nothing else they needed to know. They had the color of the wolf. That was a good enough start.

Ulf and Brax stood in unison, Avon and Kade watching them. "That's all we need for now," Ulf said, moving toward the door.

"Are you sure?"

"Yeah. We'd better keep moving. Mathias wanted us back in a few days." Ulf offered the alpha his palm. "Thanks for allowing us to speak with Kade."

Avon nodded. "I just hope it helped."

ELEVEN

Ezekiel pressed the button on the garage door remote control before he hit the end of the driveway. The thing trundled open slowly, groaning and protesting with each revolution. Saskia's car was already parked on the left, the engine ticking away softly as he brought his car to a stop beside it.

It had been a day or so since the dinner at *Valentino's*, and he still felt horribly frustrated by the whole situation. He knew Saskia wasn't telling him the whole truth, although what she did tell him had been a surprise. He hadn't thought about what choosing a mate would have been like for her, or to witness a violent fight between two males over her.

He had been in the kitchen at the time of the fight, but he'd found out later that it had been between a young wolf from the Asgard pack and a human male. He didn't know many details other than the man she'd been with had tried to get physical with her, and when that happened, the human had stepped in.

Although he couldn't understand why the human was there, he was grateful that he was able to pull the other wolf from her. She had been badly shaken, but refused to end the party. He believed it was then that he started to fall in love with her.

She had such strength and will to do the honorable thing. It was a fine trait to have in a mate. Besides, he had been wondering about the brother and sister whose parents had disgraced his pack so spectacularly.

"Zeke?" Saskia asked.

Ezekiel looked at his mate through the windshield and smiled. How long had he just been sitting in the front seat reminiscing? Long enough for Saskia to come looking for him.

"Is everything okay?" she asked, pulling open the passenger door and sliding inside the car. Her scent engulfed him, settling his wolf down in an instant. He didn't like being away from her for too long; it was the same instinct all mated males had.

He smiled when she touched his hand where it clutched at the steering wheel. "I'm fine, darling."

She looked away, a slight blush crawling up her neck and cheeks. She was the perfect specimen of femininity and the perfect mate. She was obedient, gentle and devoted. She cared for her appearance, and he had never seen her once without makeup on.

"What were you doing out here?" she asked him curiously. Her hands were held together in her lap, her fingers twisting together. He could smell her anxiety, and he had hoped after all the time they'd spent together that she would learn to trust him, and maybe even love him one day.

He sighed. He couldn't rush it. "I was just thinking about how lucky I am."

The blush made a comeback and she looked away. "I have dinner waiting for us on the table. Come on in before it gets cold."

Saskia slipped from the car and shut the door. Ezekiel followed behind her, taking one of her hands and twisting their fingers together. Saskia gave him a little smile and led the way into the dining room.

As he was becoming accustomed to, the dining table had been set with their best linens complete with fabric place settings, and napkins held together in ceramic rings. The cutlery was lined up perfectly, and in front of both settings were a red and white wine glass. A pot roast was in the center of the table, a bowl of vegetables and mashed potato on either side of the platter.

"I hope you're hungry," she murmured, walking behind him to take his suit jacket from his shoulders. Ezekiel shrugged the jacket from his arms and watched her stow it on the back of one of the spare chairs.

He pulled out the chair directly to his right where he usually sat at the head of the table. Two bottles of wine sat at his elbow and he offered them to Saskia.

"Red, please."

With a nod, he began to pour some into her glass. "Maybe you won't be able to have this for a little while if we're lucky," he mused as he twisted the bottle to a stop. Saskia whipped her head around to stare at him, a look of shock on her delicate features.

"Zeke—" she started.

He waved his hand toward her. "Forget I said anything, Saskia. It's too soon, I know." But he did want to have children with her, and he wanted them soon. He thought maybe that if they had a child, everything else would smooth out. She would be so devoted to their baby that she wouldn't have time to feel sad or confused as she did now.

But that was wishful thinking.

She hadn't been a virgin when they'd mated, but they hardly spent enough time together for there to ever be a possibility of her falling pregnant anytime soon. In fact, every time they did have sex, she stole away into the bathroom immediately to wash away any sign of him. Was she ashamed to bear his child?

He watched her delicately eat the thin slices of meat from her plate. He could see the conflict written all over her face, and although she had told him everything was fine, that she was simply overwhelmed by everything that had happened in the past year, he couldn't shake the feeling that she wasn't telling him the whole story.

What she needed was a break away from life, from its trivialities and the grind of going to work. Even he could benefit from a break.

"Saskia," he started, making her pause. "How easy would it be to get a Friday and Monday off work?"

"If I asked far enough in advance, it shouldn't be too difficult. Why?"

He slid his fingers over her free hand resting on the table top. "I thought it would be nice to get away for a long weekend. We could go anywhere you want."

Her fingers curled into her palm, forming a fist beneath his hand. "Why?" she breathed, her eyes firmly fixed on her plate in front of her.

Had her breathing kicked up?

He sighed and released his hold. "I just thought it would be nice to get away. Maybe it'll be a chance for us to get to know each other in private, without your brother breathing down our necks."

She finally lifted her eyes to his face and there was a fire burning in them. "Saxon doesn't breathe down our necks."

He laughed gently. "Maybe not yours. But I feel that he does mine. There's a lot of pressure knowing your brother is watching my every move." He sat back in his chair and crossed his arms over his chest. "I know you love him, and he means a lot to you, but—"

"He's the only family I've got left," she said, a sting in her words.

"Well, that's not exactly true, darling. You have me now."

Saskia dropped her fork. It clattered against the China plate. "I don't want to go away for a long weekend, Zeke. I want to stay here."

He shook his head slowly, somehow knowing this was going to happen. "Darling, I just want to get away for a bit. I know you didn't tell me everything the other night. I was hoping we could relax together and you would open up to me. You can trust me, Saskia."

"I know that," she mumbled, picking up her wine glass and taking a sip.

He blew out a frustrated breath. "Well, if you don't want to go away for a long weekend, why don't you tell me the reason you've been so cool toward me these last few months? And don't tell me 'nothing', because I know that's a lie."

Saskia closed her mouth and looked forlornly at her plate. "There's nothing wrong," she said quietly.

"Sass, we both know that's a lie. I just can't understand why you won't tell me the real reason you've been so detached."

A tear leaked from the corner of her eye, smudging her perfectly applied eyeliner. "I can't tell you because I'll hurt you." She turned, surprising the hell out of him when she took his hand. "And I don't want to hurt you, Ezekiel. You're a good man. What I'm dealing with is just something I have to do on my own."

He wanted to tell her she was being ridiculous, that he was there for her no matter what, but instead he simply said, "Okay."

Her gaze shifted around his face, searching for something. "Okay?"

"Okay. I'll let you handle whatever it is you're dealing with unless I can see that it's starting to hurt you."

She nodded.

Ezekiel thumbed the tears from her cheek, adding, "Promise me you'll tell me if it gets too much?"

She looked stunned for a moment before nodding slowly.

They finished their meals in silence, both contemplating what they'd just said and agreed to. Ezekiel was just hoping he was doing the right thing.

SASKIA BEGAN CLEARING AWAY THEIR PLATES, GLASSES AND CUTLERY, shooing Ezekiel away when he tried to help.

"Thank you for the offer, but I've got this."

Taking the platter of meat from her hands, he said, "I insist. You cooked. I'll clean up. Why don't you go take a bath or something? Go unwind after a long day at work."

Saskia stared at him for a moment before nodding and making her way toward the bedroom. Why couldn't she just find a way to love Zeke? How many other men would be doing what he was now? The answer? None. He was a once in a lifetime kind of find.

Slumping down onto the end of the bed, Saskia levered her flat shoes off with her toes and stood up to run the bath Zeke had suggested she take. Opening up the taps, Saskia looked through the cupboard until she found her favorite bath oils and tipped a generous amount into the slowly filling bath.

Wandering back into the bedroom, she grabbed the cordless phone and took it into the bathroom with her. With the water level slowly rising, Saskia stripped out of her remaining clothes and let her hair out of the loose bun she'd secured that morning. Her blonde hair cascaded over her shoulders, tickling her bare skin.

Eventually she ventured into the water, letting the heat work away at her stresses and worries. Not for the first time, she wondered whether she would ever get over Alex. There was no doubt he'd made a huge impact on her life, but she was being a fool if she let the memory of someone she barely knew interfere with the life she had now.

A good life with Ezekiel.

She stared at the phone perched on the edge of the tub, unable to bring herself to pick it up and call Saxon. He had enough to deal with without her whining in his ear. But it had felt good to talk to him before. It almost felt like their relationship had reverted back to how it had been before their parents' disgrace.

Almost.

She could hear Ezekiel moving around in the bedroom, probably getting changed out of his suit and putting on some sweats and a tee that would highlight the strong definition of his stomach muscles. There was no doubt her mate was very attractive. If only she could purge her body of Alex then maybe she could let herself fall in love with her mate.

Perhaps his suggestion of a long weekend away hadn't been a bad one. She's just overreacted. She realized that now. It was just that the idea of being away from her home set the panic button off in her head. Her worst fear would be that Zeke would take her back to his old pack, which was as far as you could get from the Helheim pack.

And the thought was terrifying.

But the more he explained, the more she could see he was just trying to look out for her. She sighed and ran a wet cloth over her shoulders, squeezing out the excess water so it trickled down between her shoulder blades and between her breasts. Saxon was right. She had to get over her infatuation and focus on the great man in front of her now.

"Zeke?" she called.

There was silence on the other side of the door for a moment before her mate replied. "Is everything all right?"

"It's fine...I was just wondering whether you could come in here and..." She sucked in a breath. It was now or never. "Wash my back for me?" she finished, already feeling a hot flush creeping up her neck.

The door opened a little, and Zeke's head appeared around the door jamb. "Did you just ask me to wash your back for you?" he asked, seemingly dumbfounded.

She nodded. From where he was standing, he wouldn't be able to see her bare body yet, and by the look of naked lust in his eyes, he couldn't wait to, either. He slid the rest of the way inside, closing the door behind him. He seemed to be gathering his thoughts as he made his way closer, his eyes running the length of her body.

The front of his sweats tented with his erection, and Saskia was both fascinated and embarrassed by his reaction to her. How could he find her desirable when she pushed him away so much? How could he still want her?

Noticing where her eyes were transfixed, Zeke gave her a hasty smile and turned around, reaching down into the front of his pants. When he turned around again, the erection was gone. As he lowered himself to the ground, he whispered reverently, "You're beautiful, Saskia. Have I told you that?"

She blushed again, but nodded. He did tell her she was beautiful. She just didn't have the nerve to accept his compliments before.

"Thank you," she whispered, clutching the wet cloth in between her fingers a little tighter.

Zeke cleared his throat, motioning with his hand for what Saskia was so tightly holding onto. She handed it over and leaned forward a little to give him the access he needed.

Wrapping her arms around her knees, Saskia rested her head on her thighs. His first touch was tentative, lingering on her skin when she didn't flinch away from him like she always did. Saskia remembered to breathe in deeply through her nose to keep her body from trembling. Zeke's strokes started at her shoulders, sweeping along the breadth of them slowly.

Eventually he became bolder. Standing up to perch on the side of the tub, his free hand began rubbing her shoulder, massaging the muscles she didn't know were tight until a little pressure was put on them. She groaned in pleasure, feeling the tight knots in her shoulders beginning to melt away under his skilled fingers.

His other hand—the one with the cloth—swept down her spine. Saskia threw her head back, her eyes closing. It was like heaven—the equally soft and hard touches from Zeke.

Dropping the cloth into the water, he swept the hair away from her neck, his thumbs pressing into the muscles there. She felt her embarrassment creep up her neck as she moaned again.

"I love that sound," Zeke said in a husky voice. "I wish you did it more when I touched you."

His candor caught her by surprise. His hands were soon replaced by his mouth, his tongue darting out and swiping away droplets of water from her skin. She gasped, startled by the sudden soft touch.

"Is this okay?" Ezekiel asked softly, his voice hoarse. "I can stop if you want me to."

"No," she breathed. "Don't stop."

His fingers slid across her shoulder and down to the dip of her collarbones. She held her breath, waiting for him to touch her breasts.

"I want to take you to bed." His voice was in her ear, his breath tickling her. She nodded, not trusting her voice yet. She was about to stand up to get out of the bath when Ezekiel's strong arms wound around her body. One arm was under her knees, the other behind her shoulders, lifting her effortlessly from the warm bath water. Her skin felt both hot and cold at the same time, her nakedness breaking out in goosebumps where it was directly exposed to the cool air.

Cradled to her mate's chest, Saskia felt incredibly small. His bicep cushioned the back of her head, his chest radiating warmth she wanted to snuggle up against. She felt his strong, hard stomach against her side, the scent of him and his wolf drifting into her nostrils.

Somehow he had worked the knob on the bathroom door and opened it, striding through the bedroom with purpose. Saskia could feel his eyes on her, and when she looked up, she found his wolf was staring out.

With her heat pounding out a tattoo, Ezekiel lowered her to the mattress, snagging the soft, velvety throw from the bottom of the bed and draping it gently over her bare shoulders. Saskia pulled the ends together, huddling under the supple blanket.

Zeke stood before her, his chest heaving. His erection had sprung free from his waistband, and was now standing proud and true out from under the fabric of his pants. Saskia's eyes quickly darted down then back up again, her cheeks suffusing with heat.

She had never been comfortable with men's reactions to her.

"You can look at me, Saskia," Zeke said. "In fact, I like it when you look at me."

Forcing her eyes back down, she watched as her mate gently removed the sweats from his hips, revealing his hard length. She gasped when he took himself into his hand, his palm rubbing up and down the shaft. Her eyes darted to his mouth when he moaned.

He suddenly licked his lips. "I wish this was your hand, Saskia."

"I—" She was not ready for that. Saskia had lost her virginity in college, if bare penetration could be called losing her virginity. Her hymen had been long gone since she rode horses when she was younger, so her first and only sexual experience had been disappointing at best.

The closest she had ever come since was with Alex…and the kiss that could have gone much further if she had had the spine to just let her feelings for him be.

Stop thinking about Alex right now, she chastised herself. She was with her mate—the only male she had in her life.

Zeke shook her out of her stupor by taking her hand and placing it where his had been a few seconds before. His skin scorched her, but instead of pulling away like she wanted to, she maintained her grip. His sex felt hard and soft at the same time, a steel rod wrapped in velvet.

She released her hand when Ezekiel's hips began to undulate slowly.

"No, baby, don't stop. Please," Zeke begged.

What was she doing? She couldn't do this. She didn't want to do this. "I'm sorry, Zeke. I can't," Saskia said, burrowing her hand under the blanket, pulling the edges closer together to hide her nakedness from him despite all he had seen before. The sound of clothes being dragged back on brought her head back up. Zeke had pulled his sweats back into place, his erection not as prominent as before.

Saskia felt the first of her tears spill over her lashes and dribble down her cheeks. She couldn't even bring herself to make love to her mate. Oh, how she hated this feeling of loss, this feeling of longing for something she never really had in the first place.

"I'm sorry," she cried. "I'm sorry."

Her chin was being tilted up and, through her tears, she could see Zeke.

Remorse shone from his eyes. With the pads of his thumbs, he brushed away the tears now streaming down her face.

"I'm the one who should be sorry. I shouldn't have pushed you so far. I know this is still hard for you."

Saskia tried to drag her eyes away, but Zeke wouldn't let her.

"Sass, look at me. I'm sorry. Please, forgive me?"

"Of course," she murmured.

"Do you want to go to bed?" he asked gently, releasing her face from his hands.

"Yes." Saskia's voice was barely a whisper. Why did she suddenly feel so dirty? "I think I'm going to take a shower first though," she tacked on, getting up and wrapping the blanket more firmly around her shoulders. As she walked back toward their bathroom, she heard Zeke let out a frustrated breath, but he remained where he was.

With the bathroom door firmly shut behind her, Saskia let all the emotions pour from her. Wracked with guilt, she dropped to the ground and began to weep. She wept for Alex. She wept for herself. She even wept for Ezekiel and the loveless mating he had found himself in. But most of all she wept for the love she had so stupidly given up on. Duty and honor had driven her to do as Saxon had bid, but she should have listened to her heart. It was broken now; it was cracked and smashed into a thousand tiny pieces she had no hope of reassembling again.

Her heart had died when she walked away from Alex.

And she knew she would never love again.

TWELVE

Casey had worn runnels in the floorboards outside the containment room. Constructed from steel-enforced concrete, it was werewolf-proof, vampire-proof and probably atomic-bomb proof, too. The metal door had even more reinforced steel running through it. There was only one way in or out, and that could only be achieved if you had the key.

"Would you stop pacing?" her youngest brother asked from his corner of the room. Casey glanced up, first looking at Riley then Dylan, Oliver and finally Hunter. Their father had left a while ago, demanding to have a report as soon as the Change was complete.

She shook her head and continued pacing back and forth, back and forth. She couldn't keep still. She had been listening to the screams and groans coming from the other side of the door for near-on two hours now. Casey could only imagine the pain Alex must have been suffering though. Stopping in front of the door, she ran her fingers through her hair and let out a frustrated groan.

"Was that you or was that him?" Hunter asked, jerking his chin in the direction of the room at his back. Casey realized then that she hadn't heard anything from Alex in a little while. Could it all be over? Could he have survived the final hurdle and completed the Change? There was only one way to tell. Without giving her brothers any warning, she wrenched open the door, slid inside and jammed the spare key they didn't know she had into the lock. She heard the bolt slide into place.

"Casey! Goddamnit!" Hunter bellowed, pounding on the door. She let her back rest against the thing while she surveyed the room. Alex was lying on the ground, his huge barrel chest heaving up and down with labored breaths. She let out a shaky breath of her own, unaware that she had been holding it in the first place. She took a step away from the door, only to stop dead. A low growl of warning filtered through the air, setting the hairs on her arms and neck on end. Closing her eyes, she could see her wolf slowly retreating into her body. She was scared of Alex and his wolf.

Steeling herself, Casey took another step only to receive an even louder growl this time. Her heart kicked up into her throat and the alarm bells sounded. She didn't believe Alex would hurt her, but his wolf was another story. This was a bad idea.

Retreating back, Casey fumbled for the key in her pocket. Unwilling to take her eyes off Alex, she reached out blindly, her fingers inching along the smooth steel until she found the lock. The pins chattered along the cylinder as she slid the key in, the sound too loud in the otherwise quiet room. Just as she turned the key, Casey was thrown off-balance as the door was opened from the other side.

Unable to catch her footing in time, she stumbled forward, her muscles stiffened and braced for the impact.

"Fuck!" one of her brothers said. She couldn't have been sure which one though, because as soon as she managed to get her eyes to focus, she was staring into the eyes of one very pissed off newly Bitten wolf.

Alex's eyes were veiled in pain—two bright orange orbs nestled in black fur flecked with pale grey. Casey's gaze immediately dropped, getting stuck on his mouth. With his top lip curled back, gleaming white fangs were all she could see.

Annnnd then there was that growl again. This one said the time for warnings was over. His mouth opened, ready to snap, when two hands were suddenly on her, pulling her back. Shoved roughly behind the backs of Hunter and Dylan, she peered between their arms.

Alex was up on his feet now, backing away from the two dominant wolves, his eyes darting between them and looking for an exit at the same time. A sharp rap on the door indicated the arrival of their father, who stalked into the room riding his power as alpha. A whimper leaked from Casey's lips, her knees going weak as all that authority washed against her. Her wolf wasn't strong enough to stand up to the onslaught, and she cowered away from it, submissively lowering her body and bringing her tail between her legs.

"Get her out of here," Acario growled, his voice a few octaves lower than normal. Casey's arm was suddenly gripped by Oliver. His brown hair fell over his eyes as he looked down at her, and she could see his wolf's piercing emerald green eyes looking through her.

"Don't hurt him!" she yelled as she was dragged from the room.

"You don't get a say in this, Casey," her father roared, his eyes solid black. "How dare you put yourself in danger like that."

"I wasn't—"

"Thinking," he spat out. "I know. You never do." His hard, black gaze flipped to Oliver. "Get her out of here now, and don't take your eyes off her for a second. You hear me?"

"Yes, Alpha," Oliver replied. To Casey he said softly, "Come on, Case."

"No!" she screamed as the last image she saw was of Hunter, Dylan and her father closing in on Alex. "You're scaring him!"

Oliver gripped her arm tighter, placing his mouth beside her ear. "Shut. Up. Casey. You're only making things worse for yourself."

Casey immediately shut her mouth, having not really been spoken to like that by Oliver before. He was usually the one who was the calmness to Hunter's anger, the humor to Dylan's snide remarks. He was the one to patch her up after a nasty fall, the one who slid the rest of his dessert over to her when she'd practically inhaled hers and was still starving for more.

Outside the room, Oliver took her by both arms and stared hard into her face. She couldn't tell whether he was going to tear both of her arms from her sockets and beat her with the bloody stumps for her stupidity, or wait until her father and other brothers came out so he could do it with an audience.

"What were you thinking?" he breathed, pulling her close and crushing her against his giant chest. Confused, Casey stood there and let him hold her. "What were you *thinking*?" he repeated. "Going into a room with a newly Changed wolf? Putting yourself at risk like that?"

Casey felt the first tear slide down her cheek. Angrily, she wiped it away. She knew what she was doing. She was trying to help Alex through his Change. And she could have if they'd let her.

"Why do you want to help him so much? All the other Bitten wolves we've given sanctuary to for the transition, and you've never batted an eyelid. Why him? Why now?"

Casey shrugged, because she simply didn't have an answer to that question. And now that Oliver had said it, she began to wonder. *Why Alex?* All the others had been given the same treatment, left to their own devices for the Change whether they survived it or not. What was it about Alex that made her care?

"I don't have an answer for you, Oliver. I just...have to help him." For some reason, he was important. She just had no idea why that might be.

The door to the secured room opened then, Dylan's athletic frame filling the space between the jambs. Casey's eyes drifted down to his shredded and bloodied shirt and her heart bounded into her throat.

"What happened?" she asked.

"He won't talk to us until he knows you're all right."

"Father?" she asked, pulling away from Oliver.

Dylan shook his head. "Alex."

THIRTEEN

Alex didn't understand the reasons why, or how he was suddenly on two legs again, but he was glad he was. Sitting on the bed, his naked body was covered in sweat like he'd run a marathon or ten, back-to-back. But that couldn't have been the case because he was still in the same godforsaken room as before.

"Where's Casey?" he asked, not for the first time. While he'd been completely out of control of his actions, he remembered his wolf lunging for her when she'd fallen. It had meant to hurt her, but thankfully her brothers had managed to pull her out of the way just in time.

"She doesn't concern you," a man said. He was about a foot taller than the eldest brother—older too, although by how much he couldn't say. He looked as if he was in his mid-thirties, with red hair about five shades darker than Casey's.

"You're her father," Alex said.

The man's black eyes seemed to bore down into him, searching his soul, finding his wolf. Alex flinched as his wolf shied away, his tail sinking between his legs. Out of some unknown instinct, Alex dropped his gaze, choosing to look at the man's chin instead.

"I am, but more important, I am her alpha—Acario. This is my territory you are in. And it is with my permission and beneficence that you stay...for now."

"What happened to me?"

The alpha pulled a steel chair toward him and sank into it. "You shifted for the first time."

"Shifted?"

"Into your wolf."

Alex squeezed his eyes shut and remembered the whole thing like a film playing behind his eyes. His body had broken and then rebuilt itself in the form of his wolf. He remembered the claws and the teeth. He remembered the fur and the base thoughts to attack the threat and try to escape.

"What happened after you came into the room?"

"You don't remember?"

Alex shook his head.

The male sighed, his huge chest heaving up and down. "I forced you to shift back."

"Why? How?"

"Because it is in my power. This is why Bitten wolves need to have a pack to take them in. They're volatile and dangerous. I subdued your wolf and forced him back so we could talk."

Alex licked his lips. Damn, he was thirsty. Hungry, too. His eyes darted to the door. "Where's Casey?"

"She's outside."

"I don't believe you. I want to see her."

"Answer some of my questions first and then I will fetch her."

"No. Get her now. I need to see her now. I need to know she's okay."

The alpha's lips pursed for a moment before he glanced over his shoulder and nodded. The red-headed brother peeled away off the military-style rank and opened up the door. Flashes of flesh shone through his partially shredded shirt and Alex wondered whether he had been responsible for the damage.

Although he couldn't see Casey, he could smell her; his nostrils flared as he took in the faint scent of fear and the more acrid one of anger.

"What happened?" she demanded.

"He won't talk to us until he knows you're all right."

"Father?" she asked.

"Alex."

Half a second later, Casey was in the room, her eyes finding him on the bed, naked and on display. She went to him, despite her brother reaching out to grab her, despite the warning in her father's voice.

She glanced quickly over her shoulder at them all then looked back over at Alex. "Are you all right? Were you hurt?"

"I'm fine." Now that she was closer, he could see that she had been crying. Damn. He felt like an even bigger piece of shit. He must have scared the pants off of her. He took her hand in his, stopping her from clucking over him like a mother hen.

Pulling her down to his eye level, he asked, "Did I hurt you?"

"No."

"My wolf—" he began to say, unable to think up a suitable excuse.

"It's fine. He felt threatened. I fell directly into his line of sight. It wasn't your fault."

"I could have hurt you," he replied, his voice rough. Fuck. Why did he care so much that he almost hurt her?

Pulling the blanket from the bed, she settled it over his shoulders and got cozy beside him.

"Casey," her father warned.

"You wanted to ask him questions. Ask him," she replied, sitting back and pulling her knees to her chest. Alex wondered why her father simply didn't order her to leave his side instead of letting her dictate how things were going to get done.

Whatever.

She was there.

She was safe.

And she was still his only ally.

With his anger still clouding his face, Acario said, "Fine. Where are you from?"

Alex pulled the blanket closer to his skin. "Originally Chicago."

"Is Alex your real name?"

"Yes."

"What were you doing when you were bitten?"

"Hunting."

"What were you hunting?" This question came from Hunter, his hand resting on the back of his father's chair.

"Wolves," Alex replied with a smug smile. He watched with perverse pleasure as Hunter's hand dug into the steel.

"Where?"

"What?"

Acario said, "Where were you hunting? Where did you park your car?"

Alex scrubbed a hand over his face. It seemed like a million years ago that he'd left his apartment and just driven until he was deep in the woods. "What day is it?" he asked.

"Monday," Acario said.

"I left on Friday morning to go hunting. I took a day off work to get away from life for a while."

"Why?"

Saskia.

Alex ground his teeth together. "None of your business," he growled. The two men flanking the alpha took a step toward him, but were stopped with the smallest gesture from Acario.

"*Where* did you go hunting?"

Alex shrugged. "Maybe fifty miles from Buxton."

A collective hiss engulfed the room. Alex looked around, confused. "What's with the hissing?"

"Buxton—" Big Red began to say, but zipped his flapping gums with a glare from Acario.

"What job do you do in Buxton?"

"I'm a cop. What's with the twenty questions? I don't see how any of this is your goddamn business."

"Watch your tone, wolf," Hunter growled, his eyes flashing from blue to yellow. Alex now knew that was his wolf peering out, because he could feel his own wolf creeping closer in his mind.

Alex shook his head, closing his eyes for a minute. Saskia's eyes had changed colors, too. They'd been dark blue one minute then aqua the next. Could it be possible?

"I said, were you particularly attached to your job in Buxton? Because you cannot go back there." Acario's voice drifted into his ear, breaking Alex's thoughts.

"Huh?"

"Your job. You can't go back."

"The hell I can't."

"He's right," Casey said softly beside him.

Turning his head, he gave her a look. "Why not?"

"The Helheim Pack is the only pack in the country that won't tolerate Bitten wolves on their turf. They don't rehabilitate them like we and many other packs do."

"What do they do with them?"

"Kill them," Acario said, drawing Alex's attention. "The alpha sends his beta and captain to kill them. The captain of the enforcers is also nicknamed the Butcher. I'll give you three guesses as to why that might be."

Alex shrugged off the last piece of information. If there was a chance he could get to see Saskia one last time, he'd take it. And if there was a chance that Saskia was also a werewolf, he had to know that, too.

"So what does this mean for me?" Alex asked.

"It means for now, we will keep a close eye on you, see if you can assimilate into our pack. If you so much as raise your voice to one of our wolves, I'll know about it and you'll be reprimanded. Three strikes, you're out."

"And if I don't conform?"

"I'll confine you to this cell until we can gather the pack for a public execution."

"There's no ground in between?" he asked, looking for the loophole.

"I'm afraid not, Alex. You didn't ask for this life, but it is the life you are now living. There are rules that must be followed. Our pack is large enough for you to find a place of your own, get a job, find a mate. Do whatever you want, but don't leave our boundaries. If you do, we'll find out and bring you back."

And with that Acario stood up and led the way from the room. Casey's brothers started to trail after their alpha except for one.

"You coming, Case?"

Alex glanced over in time to see her shake her head. "Not yet, Oliver. I'm going to hang with Alex for a little while."

Oliver sighed and nodded his head as if he was expecting that answer. "I'm going to be outside for the next half an hour. If you're not out by then, I'm going to come in and get you." He glared at Alex before shutting the door behind him.

"They seem fun," Alex drawled, standing up to retrieve his clothes. Casey watched him wince, his muscles having gone cold from disuse after his shift. She stood up, wrapping her arms around her midsection.

"How was it?" she asked.

Alex pulled the shirt over his head. "Hell just about sums it up."

"Hungry?" she asked, smiling, already knowing the answer.

"Starving."

"All right, we'll get you something to eat, *if* you tell me why you were out hunting in the middle of winter with a pissed-off attitude and no supplies."

"That's none of your business," Alex grunted back, pulling on his pants and doing up the fly carefully. "It doesn't matter now anyway, does it?"

"How so?"

"Well, according to your father I can't go back to my former life."

Casey flopped down on his bed, rolling her head in his direction. "It's true."

"So just drop it already."

"Why do you want to go back there so bad?"

"I don't," he replied, his jaw tight. "There's nothing there for me anymore."

"But there was before?"

Alex glared at her, but she wasn't cowed by the show of aggression. Grinning, she sat up. "You can't scowl me into submission. You've seen who I grew up with and I've learned a thing or two about getting what I want in a houseful of men."

Casey kicked her legs off the side of the bed, swinging them.

"Has anyone ever told you how annoying you are?"

"Yep," she said, still grinning. "Just ask my brothers...and my father...and my cousins...ah, hell, ask the whole pack. They'll all tell you the same thing."

Alex sat down beside her. "Why did you come in here while I was...out of control?" The serious tone of his voice made her pause for a moment.

She stopped swinging her legs and brought them up under her body. "I knew you wouldn't hurt me."

"I almost used your face as a chew toy," was his reply. The sound of devastation in his voice tugged at her heart. She shrugged and looked down at her tightly clasped hands.

"I just want to be something."

"You are something."

Casey looked up at him, cocking a brow.

"You're a pain in my ass," he drawled slowly, a grin transforming his constantly scowling face so much that Casey had to blink to make sure she was still looking at the same person. "What do you want to be?" he asked gently.

Nobody had asked her that before. "An enforcer."

"Enforcer?"

"Yeah, like Hunter and Oliver and Dylan and Riley. A soldier. I want to do stuff to ensure the pack survives."

"So why can't you?"

Casey snorted, rolling her eyes when Alex frowned. "I'm female, which means my place is in the home raising pups."

It was Alex's turn to laugh this time. "You're a little young for all that, aren't you? What are you, like, fifteen?"

Casey slugged him in the shoulder. "Whatever, asshole. But...promise you won't flip out on me?" she asked, her serious tone wiping the smile from Alex's face. He nodded. "I'm actually sixty-nine."

"Bull. Shit."

"It's true. Werewolves age slowly. I was born the year after the Second World War ended."

"How—"

"Does that work?" Casey shrugged. "Our blood has some pretty powerful healing abilities, which also happens to translate over to keeping our cells youthful—strong."

"Will it be the same for me?" Alex asked, his eyes fixed on the ground beneath his feet.

"Sure will. The only thing that'll hurt you now is a slug to the head or being cut by silver." She leaned into him like she was sharing a secret. "And FYI, silver poisoning can and will kill you if you don't take care of it straight away."

"Got it."

Alex's stomach chose that moment to growl loudly.

"Food?" Casey asked, sliding off the side of the bed.

"God, yes." Alex stood up, stretching out his back and groaning a little.

Casey led the way through the door and into the hallway of their basement, which doubled as a gym-slash-man cave. At one end there were separate weight and cardio rooms. On the opposite side, a foosball and pool table took up the floor space where large, cheap sofas lined the walls, facing the plasma TV.

Oliver was leaning over the pool table, one hand curled under the end of the cue. His wolf slipped for a moment, checking she was still in one piece before he refocused on his shot.

"We're going to get something to eat. You wanna come?"

He put down the cue quickly. "Sure," Oliver said. Walking over to her, he draped his arm over her shoulders and dragged her closer to his body. She knew he was only trying to protect her from the other male, but there was nothing to worry about. Despite the fact that Alex had just had his first shift and was likely to go through many more spontaneous shifts in the next twenty-four hours, she knew his control over his wolf was strong. She could see it in his eyes when they were talking. Not once did his wolf peer out, and that was a feat many Bitten wolves couldn't control for at least fifty years.

FOURTEEN

Saskia slipped from the warmth of her bed and glanced over her shoulder. Ezekiel was still sleeping peacefully. She was sure he'd fallen asleep at least an hour ago, but wanted to make sure he was well and truly out of it before attempting anything.

With her legs overhanging the side, she dug her toes into the carpet and dropped her head into her hands. Well, that had been an epic fail. She felt so foolish for even trying to let down the walls she'd built around her heart. With a soft sigh, she bent at the waist, scooped up the dressing gown she had discarded on the floor and slipped both arms in; the delicate scent of her bath oils was still clinging to the soft fabric.

Dropping to her knees, she pulled a small carry-on sized suitcase out from under the bed and quietly opened it. After filling it with a few clothes and essential toiletries, she got dressed in jeans, a bulky cable-knit jumper and leather boots. Piling her blonde hair on top of her head, she tied a hair elastic around it and checked on Zeke once more.

He hadn't even moved.

Backing from the room slowly, Saskia shut the door and let out a deep breath. Leaving her mate wasn't something she had ever planned. It wasn't even something she had ever contemplated before, but she was unable to see any other way. She wasn't being fair on him by staying, and she wasn't being fair on herself by living a lie. And although she had tried to banish Alex completely from her thoughts, she simply hadn't been able to. He had branded himself on her soul.

Walking through to the front hall, she paused briefly at the small table where all the keys were kept. Taking her own car would have been preferable, but she couldn't risk Zeke waking up with the sound of the engine. Saskia gripped the handle on the front door. This was it. There was no turning back now. Flipping the lock and depressing the handle, she sucked in a deep breath of the icy air that gusted into the house. She carefully shut the door behind her and began walking down the front path.

The garden beds—usually filled with daffodils and dahlias in the spring and summer months—were blanketed by snow. The birdbath in the middle of their cottage garden had an inch of water frozen solid in the center of the shallow depression.

She looked at the garage longingly as the winter wind whipped snow up into her face. It wasn't that she was particularly cold. It was just that she wanted to get out of there as soon as she could.

Ducking her chin into the top of her sweater, Saskia focused on putting one foot in front of the other, making her way to the one place she knew she wouldn't be turned away from.

The closer she got to the city, the more traffic buzzed around the streets. Luck was on her side when she hailed a cab that actually stopped. The man popped the trunk and got out to help with her case. Once inside the warm car, she gave him her brother's address and sank back into the seat.

The clock on the dashboard said it was nearly one in the morning, and by the burning in her eyes, Saskia knew that had to be true. She pinched the bridge of her nose and let out a breath, glancing up to see the cabbie watching her through the rearview mirror.

"You running somewhere, miss?" he asked with an accent that sounded too cultured to be coming from his mouth.

"No," she replied steadily, fixing her gaze on the window beside her. Her reflection looked back at her, tears glistening on her cheeks. Rubbing her fingers under her eyes, she tried not to think about how Zeke would feel when he woke up to a cold, empty bed in the morning.

Lost in thought, she hadn't realized they'd arrived at their destination until the cabbie popped open the trunk and got out. Fumbling with the door handle, Saskia slid out into the cold night air, trembling with the guilt of what she'd just done.

"How much do I owe you?" she asked the man as he placed her small suitcase at her feet. Pulling out her purse, she took out a twenty and offered it to him.

He waved away the proffered money. "No charge, miss."

Before she could ask why, he gave her a sad smile and climbed back into the car. She didn't even get to say thank you. With a small sniffle, Saskia picked up her case and pressed against the glass door into her old apartment building.

Exhausted, she took the elevator up to the third floor, shuffling out of the thing when the doors opened slowly. In her pocket sat her old apartment key, which Saxon had insisted she keep. She was glad for it now. Sliding it into the lock, she twisted her wrist. The familiar smells of home welcomed her inside. Without turning on any lights, Saskia shut and locked the door behind her.

"Sass?" Saxon asked. Saskia spun around, squinting at the sudden flood of light. His finger still lingered on the light switch closest to his bedroom door, his rumpled hair and boxers telling her she'd woken him anyway despite her best efforts to slip in unnoticed. "What's going on?"

The look of concern on his face undid her. Saskia's eyes were suddenly blurry. "I—"

The next thing she knew, her face was buried in her brother's chest, her nose in the space between his neck and shoulder. His hands rubbed gently down her back, and she was only vaguely aware he was murmuring softly to her.

"Come and sit down."

Saskia willed her legs to move, and they obeyed. Shuffling her feet over the carpet, she sank down onto the sofa beside her brother. Her shoulders had rolled forward and her breath was hiccupping out of her throat.

"Tell me what happened." It was more of a demand than a suggestion, but she was too exhausted to fight him on it.

"I just couldn't handle it anymore."

"Handle what, hmm?" Saxon had lifted her face up with his finger under her chin, his fingers wiping away her tears.

"The lie," she replied, chin trembling. "I tried. God, I did try to love him, but I just..."

Alex.

That single thought sent her over the edge again, a fresh wave of tears crashing down her cheeks. She broke down, her face in her hands, her whole body shaking.

"You couldn't," Saxon surmised, rubbing her back once more.

Through bleary eyes, Saskia looked at her brother. The breaths she was dragging in were ragged, but she had to tell him why.

"Zeke came home this evening with a plan to go away for the weekend."

"To work things out?" he asked, snapping a tissue from the box on the coffee table.

Saskia nodded, her throat suddenly tight. Fighting back the tears, she swallowed and tried to speak again. "When I heard he wanted to go away, I automatically thought he was trying to move me away from Buxton and from you and from..."

"Alex?"

"Yes," she replied on a whisper. "I know it's stupid. He doesn't want me. If he did, he would have contacted me."

Saxon let out a frustrated breath she was well versed with. "Saskia, you know there could never be anything between you. He's a human. You know how it goes with female wolves; they have to mate a male wolf."

"I know that. My head knows that, but my heart is screaming at me to ignore the rules, to follow it instead. I guess when Zeke said 'go away', my first thought was 'I'm never going to get a chance to accidently run into Alex at the grocery store' or 'I'm never going to catch a glimpse of him on the street somewhere.'"

"But you recognize the fact that even if you did, nothing could ever come of it unless by some miracle he's been bitten by a werewolf."

Saskia laughed at the absurdity of it. "I know. No Helheim wolf would risk it, and he probably wouldn't even survive the Change if he did."

Saxon's hand suddenly stopped rubbing those circles on her back, and Saskia peered at him. He looked almost...remorseful.

"What is it, Saxon? You look like you've just realized you've forgotten to do something important."

He blinked at her then gave her a thin smile. "It's nothing. Besides, your problems are more important right now. Tell me what else happened between you and Zeke. I can't imagine one little argument would send you running."

"It didn't. After dinner, he suggested I go and take a bath. I did and while I was soaking, I was thinking about what you said about loving the male I had rather than one who wasn't there." Saxon nodded in encouragement when she faltered. Taking a deep breath, Saskia continued. "I..." This was hard to talk about with her brother. She swallowed. "I don't initiate...intimacy with Zeke. He's the one who always starts it."

Saskia watched as poor Saxon's mouth thinned out and he looked a little green.

"Anyway, I initiated it this time, but I couldn't go through with it. It felt like I was lying to him even more, and I couldn't do it to him, or to myself."

"So you left?"

She nodded. "I waited until he was asleep, but yeah, I left. I couldn't sleep in the same bed with him. I can't live in the same house as him."

Saxon stood up suddenly, pacing in a tight line in front of her. "You have to go back, Sass."

"But I don't want to. Haven't you been listening to anything I've been saying? I don't love him. I can't stay with a male I don't love."

Saxon dropped to his knees in front of her and took her hands in his. They felt warm and familiar as they wrapped lightly around her fingers. "You have to, Saskia. You're not just ruining your life here, you're ruining Zeke's, too. He'll forever have a reputation for not being able to keep his female."

"Saxon, please don't send me away."

He shook his head, his denim-blue eyes never leaving her face. "I'm sorry, Sass. I'll let you stay the night, but in the morning you'll have to go home. You're a mated female now. That means you have responsibilities."

Before she could argue her point any further, Saxon abruptly stood up and strode toward his bedroom door. With his hand on the handle, he stopped, but didn't turn around.

"Your bedroom is the same as it was before. Try and get some sleep, and maybe in the morning you'll be thinking a little more clearly..." He paused and Saskia was sure that was the end of the conversation.

"I love you, Saskia. You know that, don't you?"

She whimpered. "Yes."

His head dropped, his shoulders slumping forward. "Good. That's good. Good night, Sass."

HANDS DOWN, THAT WAS THE HARDEST THING SAXON HAD EVER DONE. Turning his sister away, forcing her back to a mate she didn't love—he felt like a piece of shit—but it was the right thing to do. It was his duty to make sure she went back to Ezekiel.

Leaning back against his closed bedroom door, he wondered if he had done the right thing by forcing her to choose, by forcing her to forget about Alex. He laughed. What a fucking hypocrite. If he was so focused on getting her mated for the good of the pack, why in the hell did he bite Alex?

He'd done it for Saskia.

He'd done it for her happiness.

It was a gamble, and only God knew whether Alex had actually made it through. But Saxon had had to try. Running a hand through his hair, his wolf whined and brushed up against his side.

Well, there was no use trying to get back to sleep now. He was well and truly up. On the other side of the door, he could hear Saskia wandering around before her bedroom door finally clicked shut.

Saxon, please don't send me away.

Those words had wounded him like none others had before. If they were blades, he would have been haemorrhaging out from the damage they'd done. But even as much as they had hurt, they had been necessary. Saskia couldn't throw her life and reputation away on a *what if*. What if Alex had survived? What then? Was he just going to waltz back into her life? Was it all going to be peachy? Somehow Saxon didn't think so.

I'm sorry, Sass. I'll let you stay the night, but in the morning you'll have to go home.

She would have to go home to her mate in the morning, and she would never know just how much it would tear him up to see her go again.

Unable to handle the silence and his incessant thoughts, Saxon pulled open his bedroom door and listened. Saskia's light snores could be heard coming from down the hall. He stepped out into the kitchen, pausing by the drying rack to pull out a squat glass then filling it with ice. Next was a nice strong hit of Jack.

Taking the glass to the sofa, he slumped down onto it and took a long drink. Despite the fugitive hiding from her own mating in her bedroom, Saxon felt strangely light at having his sister home again. He'd taken for granted having her in his life, so when she was gone, he felt it like he was missing a limb.

He sat there until his whiskey was gone. Contemplating another, he actually made the trip into the kitchen to pour a second drink, but stopped himself. Instead, he inched his way down the hall and cracked open Saskia's bedroom door.

Her room looked just as it did when she was living there. He couldn't bring himself to rearrange anything, almost hoping that she would eventually come back to him. His sister was curled up in a ball in the middle of her bed, her knees pulled up to her chest, her mouth slightly open as she slept. She looked relaxed—a lot more relaxed than she did when she'd first arrived, in any case.

With a soft sigh, she stretched her body out and lay flat out on her back, her hands resting gently on her lower belly. Saxon had a crazy thought then that maybe she was pregnant, but after inhaling deeply, he couldn't smell any differences to her body.

Retreating from her room, he shut the light off in the hall as he went past and returned to his room. He had to at least try to get some sleep. In the morning, he'd be dealing with a whole lot more drama.

FIFTEEN

Alex closed his eyes and drew in another breath. Night had finally fallen. He could smell it in the crispness of the atmosphere, the stillness of the air. Falling back from the small open window set into the basement bathroom, he looked at himself in the vanity mirror.

He couldn't believe he was still breathing. All the pain that had rampaged through his body made him think he would simply just pass the fuck out and never wake up again. Touching his cheek, his fingertips rasped over his rapidly growing whiskers. He'd kept himself clean-shaved for work, but he liked this look.

His eyes were the same black as he was used to seeing in the mirror, except that now flashes of orange passed through the inkiness.

Brother. The word whispered through his mind. His wolf, who seemed capable of only single words, spoke to him once more. Brother. Yes, he supposed his wolf was like a brother now.

Alex ran a hand through his dark hair finding it felt the same as before. That was the funny thing, though; he looked and felt the same yet he was irrevocably different. He was a werewolf now—an idea that he still wasn't one hundred perfect comfortable with, but how could he argue with the evidence?

He flexed his fingers, remembering when claws and paws had replaced them so violently.

Up above him, floorboards creaked and groaned as the family walked around. Alex would wait until the house was quiet and then he would make his escape. He was planning on going straight through the basement door since nobody seemed to be locking the damn thing, but maybe they did it when he was asleep—locking him in his room until morning.

After taking a shower and changing into some fresh clothes, he returned to find a tray of food waiting for him. His stomach growled at the anticipation of filling it. He had eaten only a few hours ago with Casey, sitting at the kitchen bench, surrounded by stainless steel appliances and a top of the range double-door fridge.

The thing had been stacked to bursting with food.

"Feeding an army?" Alex had asked Casey as she'd made them four sandwiches each. Casey had just started pulling cold meats and salads from the different compartments when she'd looked over her shoulder at him.

"Feeding my brothers," she'd replied, smiling. "All that won't last for another two days," she'd added, waving her hand in the direction of the open doors.

Alex had whistled through his teeth, and was going to ask more questions about her brothers, but the sight of the food Casey had been placing on the granite bench in front of his face made his mouth water.

He'd been so damn hungry that Casey had given him two of her sandwiches. He'd finished them all before she could get to her last one. Apparently shifting made you hungry.

Alex sat down on his bed, pulling the tray into his lap. In the bowl there was a thick beef stew with about half a French breadstick beside it. To finish it all off, there was a decent portion of peach cobbler with vanilla ice cream. Alex had just finished his last mouthful of cobbler when there was a knock on the door.

"Come in," he called. When the wood inched open, he inhaled, dragging in the sweet scent of Casey. Her fire-red head popped around from the side of the jamb, a mischievous smile on her face. Alex lowered his spoon, dropping it into the empty bowl.

"If you've come in here to drill me for more information about why I want to go back home, you're wasting your time."

She snorted. "I never waste my time." Alex could tell she wanted to say more, and she sure as shit didn't disappoint. "I think I need a bedtime story. Feel like telling me who Saskia is?"

He put a lid on his anger before he answered. "Nope."

"Is she why you want to go back home so badly?"

"I don't want to go home so badly. If I have to stay here, I'll stay here. Like I said, there's nothing left for me at home."

She smirked at him, but kept her lips pressed together as if holding in a laugh. Frustrated, Alex shoved his tray at her and said, "Take this with you when you leave, will you?"

Those bright, intelligent eyes of hers clouded over with rage. "I'm not your maid," she replied, spitting the words at him. "Take it up yourself." Angry, she stood and stalked from the room.

Alex stared at the offending tray and an idea struck. Giving Casey a ten minute head start, he picked up the tray and left his room. Up at the top of the stairs was a door totally pimped out with locks. Bringing up his free hand, he tried the handle, expecting it to be locked. It turned against his palm and squeaked open. Alex stepped through, and shut the door behind him. The kitchen was empty, all the lights on the bottom floor turned off. Carefully placing the tray next to the sink, Alex pivoted and moved toward the basement door.

This was his chance, and he didn't have much time.

Downstairs again, Alex went through the small chest of drawers looking for a coat. On the third try, he found his hunting jacket and put it on. He took one last look at the room and left, moving quietly up the stairs once more. When the basement door snicked closed behind him, he headed in the direction of the back door. Flipping the locks, he opened it up, catching a whole lot of fuck-that's-cold right in the face.

A creak of floorboards sounded overhead and Alex got moving. Sliding outside, he shut the door behind him and started walking into the winter-covered forest behind the house. Looking up, he found the North Star then began to walk in the opposite direction. He had to be north of Buxton. The air was chillier here, but the vegetation was near enough the same. He figured he couldn't be more than a couple of hundred miles away from home.

A couple of hundred miles of slogging through the snow in the middle of the night.

Christ, he should have thought this through.

He was well within the cover of the forest now, the silence around him pressing against his skin. With his heavy breathing fogging up around him, he kept his eyes on the sky, watching the stars to keep his course.

He'd just jumped up from a ditch when the sound of frozen branches cracking and splintering against the fresh powder split the quiet, cold night air. Alex stopped, dropping to the ground and making himself as small as possible. His wolf, who had been quiet for a while, was suddenly marching forward in his mind.

Stalk.

Hunt.

Alex ignored its commands, swiveling his eyes in their sockets as whoever was following came toward him. They weren't crashing through the brush, which told him they knew how to hunt. His nostrils flared, pulling the gentle breeze into his nose.

He let out a small growl when the sugary sweetness of Casey's scent filtered through. Getting to his feet, he brushed off the snow from his body and whirled around in time to see Casey pushing past one last snow-laden bough.

Removing the hood of her jacket from her head, she smiled at him and cocked a hand on her hip. "Leaving me, Alex?" she asked, her voice saccharine enough to give him a toothache.

Alex couldn't stop the groan. "Go home, Casey." He turned around to start walking again when she pulled up alongside him. He snuck a glance at her from the corner of his eye. "You're not going to run home to tell Daddy I've escaped?"

"Nope," she replied, pushing a low-lying branch out of their way.

He didn't bother with the sly look this time; he straight-up stared at her. "Why not?"

She stopped and pushed some hair from her face. "Because I'm coming with you."

Alex's eyes narrowed, realizing the little sneak had left the door unlocked on purpose, and had given him the idea to leave after dropping off his dirty dishes. He could have wrapped her up in a hug if he hadn't still been furious that she'd followed him. He continued walking.

"No, you're not," he said. "Go home, Casey. There's no reason for you to get into trouble."

"What if that's exactly what I want?" she shot back, irritated.

"Why would you want to do that?"

It was her turn to groan. "Why wouldn't I? Come on, Alex. You've known me for a couple of days now, and what have you learned about me?"

"You're annoying?" he said, helping her over a fallen log.

She waved off his hand and legged it over herself. "Besides that, smartass."

"I give up," he muttered, glancing up at the sky once more.

"I don't exactly like being told what to do."

Oh yeah, that was Casey.

"And I don't like following orders that are sexist and stupid."

He stopped and turned to her. "Sexist *and* stupid? Helluva combination there."

She looked at her brightly painted fingernails. "Whatever. Like it or not, I'm coming with you, so just suck it up."

"Give me one reason why I should let you come with me?"

"Because you're going the wrong way. Buxton is that way," she replied with a know-it-all grin, pointing to her left.

Alex cursed and checked the sky once more. "I'm following the North Star."

Casey followed his finger up to the bright star he was following. "That's not the North Star."

"Sure it is," he replied acidly. "I think I know how to follow the stars."

She laughed. "Well, if you knew how to follow the stars, you'd know that was actually the Big Dipper you're pointing to."

Alex scanned the sky above them, finding the brighter North Star much farther away.

"Fuck."

"Just face it," Casey said. "You need me."

He huffed. "I don't *need* you, Casey."

"Fine. You want me here," she shot back, raising an eyebrow, daring him to disagree.

"You're delusional. You do know that, right?"

She waved his insult away. "Some say delusional. Others say awesome."

Checking he was going the right way this time, Alex started off in the direction Casey had pointed. Behind him, he heard her follow.

"I'm not going to be able to get rid of you, am I?"

"Afraid not."

Alex had a long walk ahead of him, and it wouldn't be a good one with a pounding headache, which he had no doubt he would get if he kept trying to argue with Casey. So he let her follow him.

CASEY SMILED TO HERSELF. HAVING FINALLY WON THE ARGUMENT, ALEX had resigned himself to having her as a travel companion, which was great because Casey needed a change of scenery. The only downside to all this Boy Scout stuff was that there was no less than four hundred and fifty miles of forest to traverse before they even got close to Buxton.

That meant her father and brothers had ample time to come and find them, to bring them back in. The only chance they had was to make it into Helheim territory before they were found. Her father wouldn't risk crossing the boundary without first asking permission from Rhett.

The temperature was dropping thanks to the cloudless night. Luckily for them, their bodies were like Space heaters, keeping them warm without the usual need for layers.

"So, since we're officially traveling buddies, tell me about Saskia."

"How about I don't?" Alex shot back with a dark glare over his shoulder.

Interesting. A touchy subject. It only made her want to poke some more. "Come on, Alex. At least give me a hint? Just a little hint?"

"No," he snarled.

"Okay, how about this: I ask you a yes or no question and all you have to do is say yes or no in reply and I'll take over the detective work from there."

"Will you drop the whole topic if I do this?"

"Probably," she replied sweetly. Like hell she would, though. If she found out a little bit of information, she was so not going to let that go.

"Fine," he grumbled, holding a branch out of the way for her to pass.

Casey clapped her hands together excitedly. "Okay. Okay, is Saskia your wife?"

"No."

"Girlfriend?"

"No."

"Mother?" she asked, confused.

Alex snorted. "No."

"Well, who is she then?" she snapped, her hand hitching up onto her hip.

"That's not a yes or no question," he replied smugly.

Casey huffed and folded her arms over her chest. "Come on, Alex. You're killing me here."

He was silent, but she was sure he had muttered "I wish" under his breath.

She decided to try a different tack. "What if I tell you something personal about me first? Would you tell me who Saskia is then?"

Alex stopped, his shoulders slumping forward. "How personal are we talking here?" he asked without turning around.

Casey stepped up to his side and turned to face him. "Crawl-under-a-rock-and-die personal?"

He seemed to think about that for a moment. "Only if you go first. If I think it's personal enough, I'll tell you about Saskia."

Casey chewed her fingernails before sticking that same hand out to Alex. "Deal."

"Deal," he replied, shaking her hand in agreement.

"Okay, here it goes...until recently, I still wet the bed."

Alex arched an eyebrow at her, clearly not believing a word. Ah well, it was worth a shot.

"All right, fine, that's a lie." She let out a deep breath. "If I tell you this, you absolutely can*not* tell anyone."

He nodded, but looked uninterested. "Deal."

"I mean it. If you breathe a word of this to anyone, I will hunt you down and kill you."

Alex's expression didn't change. All she got was a stiff nod. Slowly, Casey turned and began walking again. Alex stomped along beside her, letting the silence settle before she was finally ready to tell him.

"Last year, while my mother was out shopping and my brothers were all out, I came home early to find my father fucking another female pack member in his office."

Alex's footsteps hesitated for just a second before resuming their rhythm.

"He's still fucking her, and I heard that she's now pregnant. She herself has a mate, so they're probably passing the kid off as his, but I know it's my father's."

Casey wrapped her arms more firmly around her middle and ducked her chin into the top of her jacket. Discovering her father's infidelity had been tough on her. All her life, she'd looked at her parents' relationship and aspired to have the same thing.

But after seeing that, she didn't want to take a mate. Males couldn't be trusted when it came to that sort of thing. That was why she was pushing so hard to do the opposite to what her father wanted for her. He wanted her mated and spewing out pups, but she'd be damned if she let that happen to her.

A heavy arm was suddenly wrapped around her shoulders.

"I'm sorry you had to see that, Casey," Alex said. "Girls always model their idea of their future husbands on what they see their fathers do."

Her vision was suddenly blurry and she rubbed the tears away before Alex could see them.

"My father did the same thing. I guess that explains why I never settled down with just one woman."

She wiped her nose and sniffled. "So you had a girlfriend?"

"The last girlfriend I had was well over a year ago. If you can believe it, I had about a dozen relationships in a year once—not all of them healthy."

"So many," she breathed. Casey was used to male wolves being so incredibly loyal to their mates, but her father had wiped that notion from her head. She supposed humans really weren't much different. She swallowed and broached the subject she was dying to find out about. "So, who's Saskia if not your girlfriend?"

Alex sighed and removed his arm to shove his hands into his jacket pockets. "Saskia...is...the love of my life."

"Is? You still love her?"

He nodded.

"How'd you meet her?"

He smiled, and she could practically see the love radiating out of him. "She saved my life."

"How?"

"I got beaten up pretty bad by a couple of guys. I must have passed out because when I woke up, I was at her place. She brought me into her house without knowing a damn thing about me, patched me up, gave me somewhere to rest."

Casey pushed her hands deeper into her own coat pockets. "How romantic."

"After I saw her smile, I couldn't get the image out of my head. I found out where she worked. I showed up with flowers and asked her out. Eventually she said yes and we had one date, and then..."

"And then?" she asked, glancing over at him.

He let out a breath, the frustration clear. "And that's it. We had one date, and she ran out of there like I was carrying the Ebola virus. I found out later she was engaged to someone else."

"Engaged? But she went on a date with you?"

"Yeah, well...that's it. That's who Saskia is."

Casey knew he wasn't giving her the whole story, but there was still time. She would get it eventually.

THEY WALKED UNTIL THE SKY BEGAN TO LIGHTEN WITH RIBBONS OF PINK and purple. The sun was rising and they were incredibly close to the Helheim territorial border. Casey was exhausted, but wouldn't allow them to rest until they crossed that invisible line that would prevent her father and brothers from seeking her out.

"How much farther?" Alex asked. He looked haggard. He needed to rest just as much as she did. Looking up, she saw the small river that divided the territories.

"We just have to cross that river and we'll be in Helheim territory."

Alex gave her a stiff nod and picked up his pace even though he looked close to dropping. Casey kept up with him too until they reached the white banks of the river. It was frozen over, but she was reluctant to cross that way. Looking up and down the banks, she found a tree that had fallen, its long trunk spanning the distance over the water.

"This way," Casey said, leading Alex over to the log.

"Let me go first," he murmured. "To make sure it's safe," he added when Casey rolled her eyes. Well, what do you know—Alex was a gentleman.

Alex climbed up the side of the trunk and walked across the top without even a wobble in his step. Casey followed, taking his hand to help her down on the other side. She shivered at being in the territory of another wolf pack. It was dangerous, but danger was her middle name, and this was an adventure she wouldn't miss for the world.

SIXTEEN

For a split second before Saskia's eyes opened, her whole body stiffened. She knew when she opened them, Ezekiel would be beside her, leaning in to kiss her on the mouth and murmuring his good-mornings to her. She would get up and look out their bedroom window, wishing for a different life. But when Saskia finally forced her lids to open, the sounds of the city drifted into her ears, and the window that looked out into the yard wasn't there. In one huge rush of relief, she remembered where she was.

She was home.

Throwing the quilt from her body, she sat up and rubbed the sleep from her eyes. The sun hadn't even risen yet, but Saskia felt amazing. Drawing the scent of her old bedroom into her nose, she smiled.

Which made her frown.

She hadn't been happy in so long. It almost felt as if she were a completely different person now...until she went back to her mate.

The lightness Saskia had felt dissolved in an instant. Glancing at the clock, she saw that she still had an hour before daybreak. Dressing quickly, she stepped out into the living room, making sure to keep her steps light. She found the keys to her brother's car in the dish by the door and left the apartment behind her. She began driving out of town, her wolf now whining at her to find a stretch of quiet forest to hunt in for a little while. She tried to remember the last time she'd let her out, to let her feel the wind whipping through her fur. By the insistent shove against her brain, it had obviously been a while.

"All right, all right," she muttered. "I'm almost there."

Saskia must have driven to the farthest border of the territory when she finally pulled up onto the hard shoulder and put the car in park. Popping the lock on the door and pushing it open with her foot, she slid from the front seat and began stripping off her shoes and clothes.

Flurries drifted around her, making lazy little circles through the air around her head; they landed in her hair, sticking there. Letting out a breath, Saskia called forth the Change to take over her body.

It was her extremities that tingled first—her fingers, her toes. The tingling extended into her arms and legs eventually engulfing her entire torso. Forcing her muscles to relax, she let her wolf take over.

She started panting when pain surged through her body like a giant wave. Bones popped, and her skin stretched and split—giving way to her wolf's form. Falling to her knees, the gravel beneath the snow bit into her knees, but that pain was a drop in the ocean compared with the agony she felt as her glossy blonde fur covered her body.

As the sting receded, Saskia just lay there for a moment, collecting her thoughts, doing a mental check of her body. Slowly, she climbed to her feet, shook out her coat and padded off into the dense underbrush of the forest.

Burs snagged in her fur as she brushed past them, her pads making a soft *pff, pff, pff* sound as she moved. Her ears were constantly swiveling, listening. Her stomach growled, reminding her that she hadn't stopped to eat breakfast, or even grab a banana from the fruit bowl.

The small furry creatures of the morning were just beginning to stir, her wolf becoming fixated on the sound of them moving around. Before Saskia knew it, her feet were moving, her paws sinking down into the snow. After tracking for a few minutes, the scent of a rabbit infiltrated her sinuses, sending her on a new course. Brushing past the low branches, her nose stayed stuck to the ground, a constant stream of scents entering her nose, registering with her brain.

When the trail she was following began to become more concentrated at the base of a tree, Saskia began digging, her paws dragging the snow away, getting her closer to her breakfast.

As her jaws closed around the rabbit's neck, it let out a squeal. Warm blood and flesh filled her mouth, her sharp teeth tearing at the fur and skin. Saskia dropped the rabbit and began to strip the meat from the bones. The snow around her turned pink, and steam rose from the exposed body cavity.

***

ALEX WAS SO GODDAMN TIRED THAT HE DIDN'T EVEN KNOW WHICH direction he was going anymore. Hadn't he already walked past this same cluster of ferns before?

He groaned.

Whatever.

According to Casey, they were still moving toward the city, and right now, that was enough for him. The petite female was still at his back, still yammering away like he gave a fuck what she was saying.

Damn that girl. She had made him talk about Saskia even though he'd promised himself that he wouldn't. Hearing her secret brought a whole lot of I'll-never-talk-about-this-to-anyone right back to the forefront of his mind. What she'd said about her dad was just how it had been with his father.

And it sure as shit explained a lot about Alex's attitude toward long-term relationships.

Perhaps Alex needed to redefine his. As it was, he was firmly in the a-month-is-long-enough department. If he wanted any chance with Saskia, though, he was more than willing to throw that idea out on its ass.

Stepping over yet another small cluster of lady ferns, Alex's eyes swept over the tiny clearing he found himself in. The breeze had kicked up, sending an achingly familiar scent through his nose and into his brain.

Lust tore through his body, his body reacting, hardening.

Mate, his wolf whispered.

"Whoa, what's with the growling?" Casey asked, sidling up beside him. "And the erection?" she added, giggling. Alex looked down. Yep. Sure enough, he had a massive hard-on, and why wouldn't he? Saskia was nearby.

Mate.

Yep, heard you the first time, buddy, Alex said to his wolf. With his eyes scanning the forest, Alex tried to get a visual on the woman he had to make his.

Mine, his wolf shot back, somehow sounding irritated. Alex stepped forward, brushing past the snow-covered limbs, stepping over the fallen trees. Casey followed behind him, and by some miracle her mouth stayed shut.

After a few minutes of walking, the sound of bones crunching under teeth broke through the dawn calm of the forest. Zeroing in on the sound, Alex stepped past the trunk of a white oak and stopped—his breath hovering in front of his mouth.

Saskia stood a few feet away from him, tearing apart the rabbit she had caught. Her aqua eyes were closed, her ears relaxed, and Alex realized that she didn't know they were there yet.

Casey appeared at his side, breathing steadily. Her eyes widened. Glancing back at Alex, she pointed and mouthed the words, "Is that her?" to him.

He nodded. There was a low growl and when he looked back, Saskia's piercing eyes were fixed on them both. With her lips peeling away from her teeth, blood highlighted the sharpness of her fangs.

Alex took a step closer. Casey grabbed him by the arm. "Stop," she hissed. "She'll attack."

Alex shook his head. "No, she won't. Give her a minute to catch my scent."

Casey reluctantly let him go. "It's your funeral."

"Case? I'll be fine," Alex stated calmly before turning back to Saskia. She had squared up to him now, her eyes darting between him and Casey. Waving Casey away, Alex heard her curse him before stepping back.

Alex dropped to his knees. He wouldn't have done this in a million years to any other wolf, some unknown instinct telling him that it would be a death sentence, but with Saskia—*his mate*—he knew he was safe.

Licking his lips, he closed his eyes and tilted his head back, exposing his throat to her. His wolf was brushing up against his ribs, rolling over onto his back and giving her his throat, too.

The wait to see if Saskia recognized him was agonizing. With his pulse roaring in his ears, he could feel a small trickle of sweat coasting down the length of his temple, his cheek, his chin.

The first sign that she had come closer was a small chuffing sound as air was dragged in through her nose and expelled through her mouth. Alex's hair moved with the action, his face getting blasts of heated, blood-tinged air.

She whined and Alex opened his eyes, coming face to face with his aqua-eyed wolf. Saskia pawed at the ground, pushing her head up under his chin and rubbing along the length of his shoulder. Alex let out a breath he didn't know he was holding and let his body relax. Keeping his arms down at his sides, he felt his wolf pushing forward in his mind. When his wolf's and Saskia's eyes met, Alex could feel the possessiveness beginning to flow through him.

She was his.

Mine.

"Alex?" Casey asked from behind him. Saskia's hackles immediately rose, and she put her body between Alex and Casey. He rose to his feet, resting a hand into the ruff of Saskia's neck.

"It's okay," he said. "She's a friend."

Saskia backed away, but kept growling softly.

Casey approached warily. "Is she going to attack me?" she murmured.

"I don't think so," he replied, looking down at Saskia.

With a whine, Saskia turned and trotted off in the opposite direction.

"I think she wants us to follow her."

"Gee, you think?" Casey replied with a smirk.

Alex was so damn happy to have found Saskia that he let that snide comment slide. Giving Casey a little shove, he said, "Come on."

SEVENTEEN

Zeke woke up the next morning grateful it was the weekend. And he had so much to look forward to. Although Saskia hadn't said they would go away, he was going to start looking for little B&Bs to go to. He wanted somewhere that Saskia would automatically fall in love with, and then hopefully she would fall in love with him, too.

Rolling over onto his other side, he began patting his hand around on the other side of the bed only to find it empty. His eyes flew open and panic gripped him immediately, but he forced his heart to slow, for his brain to process. She wasn't there, so maybe she was in the bathroom.

Tilting his head, his tired eyes focused on the bathroom door, but it was open and the room was empty. The kitchen, maybe? Straining his ears, he listened for the tell-tale signs of breakfast being made, but all he got in return was silence.

All right, he'd let himself panic now. Throwing the blankets from the bed, he slid his feet into his slippers and drew on his dressing gown. Where could she be? The thought that she'd run out on him crossed his mind for a half a second, but he wouldn't let the idea take root. She wouldn't disgrace him like that. She was probably out at the store getting something nice for breakfast, or out for a run or something.

In the kitchen, Zeke opened the fridge first then the pantry. Both were fully stocked with their usual breakfast foods. Returning to the bedroom, he found Saskia's running shoes still under her side of the bed. He did notice something else as he peered under the bedframe though. The small carry-on she kept under her side of the bed was gone.

"Oh no," he murmured, popping up onto his feet once more. Jerking open the drawers of her dresser, he was horrified to discover some clothes were missing. Legging it out of the bedroom, he paused with his hand on the internal door that led into the garage. Gathering his courage, he opened the door only to discover her car still there. Slamming the door shut, he stalked through to the kitchen and grabbed the phone from its cradle.

Punching in her cell number, he paced, his anger fighting for domination over his concern. Her phone rang out, and he talked himself into believing she was out somewhere and couldn't hear it.

He glanced at the time on the microwave. It was only just after seven. Nothing but cafes would be open, and even then they couldn't be that loud.

Slumping down onto a stool by the phone, he forced himself to think. Where could she be?

"Saxon," he all but growled, standing up and going to collect his car keys. He should give Saxon a courtesy call first considering the hour, but Zeke's anxiety to make sure Saskia was okay was too much, demanding he go now and find her himself. His wolf was on board with that idea, too.

In the garage, he buckled himself into his car and hit the door opener on the visor. The garage door opened agonizingly slowly, the whited-out landscape filling the rearview mirror. He reversed out of the drive, shutting the garage door as he went, and started heading downtown to Saxon's apartment.

There was little traffic on the roads, which was great because Zeke wasn't sure how well his stress levels would do with the added pressure. Finding a park in front of the building, he got out and jabbed at the intercom button on the wall.

It took a while, but eventually Saxon's sleep-heavy voice answered.

"Yeah?" he barked.

"Saxon? It's me."

"Zeke?" He sighed, then said in an almost resigned tone, "Come on up."

There was a buzz and Zeke pulled open the door. He rode the elevator up to the third floor, walking purposefully toward the apartment he hoped was harboring his mate.

The door opened before he could knock, and the expression on Saxon's face told him everything he needed to know.

"She's here?" he asked, stepping inside and shucking his coat.

Saxon took it from his hands, opening up a closet door and putting it on a hanger. "She came around about one o'clock this morning."

Ezekiel closed his eyes up tight, a combination of relief and fear clamping down on his body. He was glad she was safe, but afraid of what her running in the middle of the night meant.

Zeke sat down heavily onto the sofa, turning to Saxon. "Did she tell you why?"

He nodded, looking grim.

Zeke swallowed past the lump in his throat. "Well?"

"I think you should hear it from her."

He nodded woodenly. "Where is she? Still asleep?"

For some reason, that irritated Zeke. She was still sleeping soundly after running out on him in the middle of the night. Wasn't she upset? Wasn't she feeling guilty for what she'd put him through that morning?

"No. She was gone before I got up, but her bag is still here, so she'll be returning soon."

"Do you know where she's gone?"

Saxon shook his head and stood up. "Can I get you some coffee while you wait?"

"Sure."

Ezekiel watched his brother-in-law start the machine and grind the beans himself. The rich, heavy aroma of coffee soon permeated the apartment, easing some of the tension in Zeke's shoulders. If Saskia had spoken to her brother about why she ran, she might even tell him.

Hopefully.

"You know I like you, right?" Saxon asked, holding a cup of coffee in front of his face. Ezekiel shook himself. How long had he just been staring out into space?

Accepting the cup, he replied, "Yes."

"You should know that I told her she could stay the night, but she had to go home to you in the morning. I won't allow her to ruin your reputation."

"So she's thinking of leaving me?" he asked, his voice hollow.

"She's... You need to speak to her. She's the only one who can tell you how she's feeling."

Zeke nodded. Saskia was going to leave him, but Saxon had talked her into staying. Had he been so unbearable to live with? Had he pushed her too far? He thought back to the night before—how his desperate need to be with her had made him touch himself in the most inappropriate way in front of her. He was such an idiot. Saskia was a proper female, with sensibilities, with good manners. Of course his behavior had offended her.

"She shouldn't be too much longer," Saxon said, offering him a look of sympathy.

Zeke didn't need it from him, but he took it, sitting there, waiting for his mate to return.

***

Casey was following Alex, who was following Saskia. She didn't really have a good feeling about it, but what other choice did she have? She was an Alfheim wolf in Helheim territory without permission. She'd be killed if found, but maybe if she stuck with Alex, she would be able to explain the situation to the Helheim alpha.

"Umm, you didn't tell me Saskia was a werewolf," Casey said, talking to Alex's back.

"I didn't put the pieces together until I became one."

Casey thought that was weird, but whatever. "Where do you think we're going?" she asked, taking up a position at Alex's side. Saskia was ahead of them, her pale fur being dusted with snow each time she swept past a shrub.

"Don't know. How far from the city are we?"

Casey shrugged. "I'm not sure. Maybe fifty miles?"

He looked up at Saskia then back to her. His wolf had been front and center for a lot of the time since they'd discovered the female. "She wouldn't have run all this way from her place to here. She must have a car somewhere."

Alex suddenly stopped, pushing a branch out of her way and waving her through. Casey jumped over a small ditch and found herself on a small road. Alex stood beside her, his gaze on Saskia, who was approaching a car parked up on the shoulder. He started after her, but Casey pulled him back.

"Give her a few minutes."

"Why?" he asked, his eyes fixed on the spot where Saskia had ducked out of sight behind the car.

"She's shifting back. Remember what I said about that? It's not pretty."

He nodded and relaxed his muscles. She could practically see the cogs working in his head.

"She's safe."

"I know," he replied, eyes still unmoving.

"Man, oh man, you got it bad," she muttered. Casey could practically smell the pheromones in the air. Had he known what she was before he was bitten, or was that some kind of silver lining in the whole Bitten wolf situation?

"Alex?" a voice asked from behind the car. He was moving before the end of his name was spoken. Casey followed, peering over the edge of the trunk when she got there. For her nosiness, she got a growl from Alex that she promptly ignored.

He glared at her. "I don't want you to see her naked."

She snorted. "Please. I've been a wolf since I was born. Being naked in front of each other is like breathing in front of each other: normal."

Saskia was shaking, a combination of a quick Change and the cold hitting her hard.

"Alex, check her car for clothes."

He looked reluctant to leave until Casey smacked him in the arm. "Now," she ordered.

She smiled as he growled again, but did as he was told. Crouching down, Casey hooked an arm under Saskia's and pulled her up to her feet. The female looked at her warily, her nostrils flaring.

"You're not one of us," she whispered.

Casey shook her head. "Nope. I'm an Alfheim wolf."

"What are you doing here in our territory?"

"Saskia, get dressed. Please," Alex said, announcing his arrival spectacularly—Casey was shoved out of the way as Alex muscled his way past her, helping the other female to dress. The whole time, Saskia was looking up into Alex's face, a look of wonder in her eyes.

Yeah, it was a real Hallmark moment.

Alex led the woman around to the passenger side of the car, relegating Casey to the back seat. As soon as all the doors were shut, her wolf sat up, suddenly alert. Puzzled, Casey drew in a breath and held it. This couldn't be Saskia's car. It was definitely a male's, and his scent made her heart trip in her chest.

Suddenly her skin felt too damn tight for her body. "Umm, whose car is this?" she asked as Alex started up the car.

Saskia turned around to look at her. "My brother's. Why?"

"No reason," she replied quickly, trying to breathe through her mouth. She was so not going to drag any more of that masculine spice into her nose if she could help it.

Casey sat back and tried to focus on something else—anything else. Oh look, she found a quarter in between the seats. She pocketed the coin and glanced up when Saskia sucked in a breath, on the verge of speaking.

***

"ALEX, WHAT HAPPENED TO YOU?" SASKIA ASKED. THE WORDS WERE barely whispered, but Alex's head snapped around like she'd used a loud speaker.

"Look, I know I was MIA from your life, but—"

She shook her head. "No. Not that. What *happened* to you?" She leaned forward and inhaled once more. "I did read the scent right. You've gone through the Change, haven't you?"

"Yes," Alex replied, his voice like gravel.

"When? How did this happen?"

Alex cleared his throat, glancing back at the road. "I went hunting on Friday. I just...had to get out of town for the day."

"On Friday?" she murmured, lost in her own thoughts as she looked out the windshield. She knew the significance of that date. Had he realized it too?

"Yeah," Alex replied softly. "Friday made it a year since our first...and only...date."

"Oh, Alex, I'm so sorry I ran out on you. I've thought of nothing else for an entire year."

"Even on your wedding day?" he asked, his tone icy. "You *are* married now, aren't you?"

She cringed at the malice that had laced his words. "Mated," she replied softly. "We call it being mated, and yes—even then."

"Why did you agree to go on a date with me if you were already promised to someone else?"

She turned to him, wanting so desperately to reach out and take his hand. "I wasn't at the time. I had to lie to you."

"Why?"

"Because you were human and I'm...not. You have to understand that there are rules I have to abide by. I can only get mated to a male from my species."

"Even if you don't love them?" he asked. When he turned to her, the look in his eyes nearly made her heart break. "You don't love him, do you? Because if you did, you would have forgotten all about me."

Saskia closed her eyes, feeling the tears roll down her cheeks. He was right. If he had meant absolutely nothing to her, she would have forgotten about him by now. But she hadn't because she still wanted to hang onto the feelings he invoked in her.

Dashing away the tears, she looked at his handsome face again. "If you were bitten on Friday, where did you go? Surviving the Change is difficult."

He grunted, flipping on a directional signal to get onto the first sealed road they'd seen in a while. "Casey and her brothers found me. Took me in. Fed me."

Saskia looked over her shoulder at the petite female strapped into the backseat of her brother's car. Her red hair was hanging loose around her shoulders, her green eyes watchful. "And where did you find him?" she asked Casey.

"On the edge of our territory," Casey said. "Closest we can figure is that he walked for almost two hundred miles after he was bitten. He was about two days in when we found him—severe headaches, vomiting."

"And your alpha let you look after him?"

She shrugged. "We've been finding a lot of Bitten wolves on our land and *we* like to rehabilitate them. We leave killing them only as a last resort."

Saskia turned her body back around. Her words were a dig at how Antain had run the pack for so many years, but the rules were the rules. It meant keeping the pack's bloodlines pure.

"Alex, why did you come back here?"

He glanced between the road and her, his eyes guileless. "I came back here for you."

Saskia's chest tightened and she looked out the passenger window, pensive for a moment. "Why now?"

"I'm sorry?"

She faced him again while her heart still hammered frantically in her chest. "Why now? It's been a year."

He cleared his throat uncomfortably. "You were engaged to someone else. I respected your decision."

"And now I'm mated to him. So I'll ask you again, why come back now?"

Alex was staring hard through the windshield, watching the road for non-existent dangerous drivers. "Remember when I saved you from that asshole who tried to get into your pants at the party?"

She nodded. How could she have forgotten? He had been so fierce in protecting her. He'd had the reaction most mated males would have had toward their females if they had been in the same situation.

He continued, "Well, I didn't realize what it meant at the time, but I saw your eyes change color. It wasn't the first time either. And then when I met Casey and her brothers, I noticed the same thing happened to them. I now know that it was your wolf pushing through your eyes. When I realized you were also a werewolf, I thought maybe that would change things between you and me."

"Alex—" she interrupted.

"But," he said, stopping her from saying anymore, "*if* you're mated, I'm going to respect that."

She sat back into her seat and let his words wash over her. He had come back for her, and he was going to respect her mating to Ezekiel. He was even more honorable than she'd first thought. If only she had met him after he'd been bitten. Things could have been so very different for her.

Alex had just taken the exit that would take them downtown, back to Saxon's apartment.

"I know you don't live here anymore," he murmured as he pulled up to the front of the building, "but I don't think I could handle seeing where you live with your mate."

She wanted to tell him how bad things were between her and Zeke, but she kept quiet. There was nothing that could happen between them now. Their fates were sealed; hers in a loveless mating, his as a Bitten wolf. The repercussions of being on Helheim land would have to be addressed soon, and he would either be killed or sent packing back to the Alfheim pack, if they'd take him.

Without warning, a fresh wash of tears fell from her eyes.

"Hey, Saskia," Alex said, touching her shoulder gently. Her wolf was suddenly front and center, whining at her to let him touch her more. "Don't cry, baby. I'm sorry I said those things to you, but I want to be honest with you. I couldn't handle seeing where you live so happily with your mate. It would cut me up inside."

She shook her head, waving his explanation away. "It's fine. I'm fine. Let's just get upstairs."

Saskia led the way up to Saxon's apartment knowing that this would be the last time she would ever lay eyes on him. After she went home, he would be sent away and the life they could have had together would once again be a dream.

Taking her apartment key from her pocket, she slid it into the lock and twisted it.

"I'm going to hang out here for a bit," Casey said softly.

"Are you okay?" Alex asked.

"Don't tell me you're worried about me, Alex," she replied, forcing a smile onto her lips. "I'll just give you guys some time alone together first, okay?"

Alex nodded and Saskia opened the door wide, ushering her guest in before her.

While still pulling her key free, she called out to her brother. "Saxon, I'm home."

"Saskia."

The key fell from her fingers, landing with a dull thump on the carpeted floor. She spun around to find Ezekiel standing there, his wolf's eyes fixed on Alex.

EIGHTEEN

Saskia's gaze fell onto Ezekiel, taking in the firm set of his jaw, the crease between his eyes. She couldn't tell from sight alone whether he was angry or worried.

"Ezekiel, what are you doing here?" she asked quietly. She wasn't prepared to see him yet. And she definitely wasn't prepared for Alex to meet him.

"I could ask you the same thing," he replied equally as softly. His eyes were fixed on Alex, who was standing beside her. Taking a step forward toward Zeke, Alex mirrored her, earning him a glare from her mate.

She looked at Alex, shaking her head at him, hoping that he saw the warning in her eyes. To his credit, Alex backed away.

"Who's this?" her mate asked, his wolf pushing forward in his eyes. Saskia had never seen Zeke's wolf surge so quickly before. He was usually so in control.

"This is Alex."

Zeke's eyes darted to hers. "And you know him?"

"I... He's a friend," she replied.

"Where do you know him from?" Zeke commanded. Saskia flinched at the harsh tone of his voice, but let him make his demands. He was just a male trying to protect what was his.

"She saved my life," Alex said, speaking before Saskia could. She threw him a *let me handle this* look over her shoulder before turning back to Zeke.

"About a year ago, we found him in an alleyway. He'd been beaten up pretty badly. Saxon and I decided to bring him back here to make sure he was okay."

Zeke glanced at her brother to verify the story. Saxon nodded—a short, sharp movement, but the way his jaw muscles tightened said he didn't like being dragged into the conversation.

"Why haven't I met him before this?"

"He's been out of town."

"He's part of the pack?"

"Yes," Saskia replied at the same time as Saxon said, "No."

"Well, which one is it?" Ezekiel asked.

"He's not part of our pack yet."

Zeke seemed to be scrutinizing Alex. He took a step forward so that only a few feet separated them. Saskia felt the air thicken, her wolf responding to the two males going toe to toe. Her mate's nostrils flared.

"Rhett won't let him in the pack. He's a Bitten wolf."

"That's why he came back," she blurted. "We're petitioning to see if he'll make an exception."

Zeke eyed Alex like he was a piece of dirt. "He won't," he spat, giving Alex his back, insulting him and his wolf. She was shocked. She'd never known Zeke to be so disrespectful.

A growl vibrated throughout the room, although she couldn't be sure who was responsible for the sound. She simply moved without thinking. She stepped in between Zeke and Alex just as her mate tried to lunge for the other male.

Pressed between the two testosterone-fueled men, she had to fight for her dominance. Alex's body was pressed to her back, Zeke's chest to her front. Both men were taller than she was, both glaring at each other over her head.

"You should just leave now," Zeke spat, pointing a finger in Alex's face.

"I'm not going anywhere," he retorted, his voice dangerous, his body lethal.

"Bitten wolves aren't worth the air they breathe. Whoever bit you should be killed right alongside you."

"Watch your mouth," Alex replied, barely able to contain his growl.

Things were spiraling out of control quickly. Saxon waded into the fight, trying to pull Ezekiel away from Alex. The more the males jostled with each other, the more trapped Saskia felt.

She was suddenly light-headed, all the air she needed to drag into her lungs suddenly gone. She could see the men still arguing, but her hearing had gone fuzzy.

"Please," she whimpered, her body being tugged and struck with each movement of the men. Black spots popped up in her vision, and her gasping became frantic. She was going to pass out if she didn't get the air she so desperately needed.

She was going to...

Casey had been standing out in the hallway listening to the

men argue with each other. She hadn't even seen Zeke, but she already didn't like him. He was being way too much of an asshole even if he was Saskia's mate.

"Why haven't I met him before this?" Ezekiel demanded in a harsh tone.

"He's been out of town," was Saskia's reply.

"He's part of the pack?"

"Yes," Saskia replied at the same time as another voice said, "No."

Casey froze, her hand shooting out to catch the wall, to keep her balance. Her knees were already weak from being so close to the male—the same one whose scent had been all over the car. Saskia had said he was her brother. Casey swallowed past the lump in her throat, her wolf frantically trying to get out and have a look at the man just on the other side of the wall.

That was the real reason she hadn't gone in. She didn't care whether she was a witness to the sweet reunion or not. She didn't want to go in there because Saskia's brother was inside that room, and she needed just a minute or ten to catch her breath.

Casey felt the air begin to vibrate with a familiar ripple of testosterone. She'd witnessed enough of her brothers fighting over a female to recognize the signs that the shit had just hit the fan.

"Zeke, step off," Saskia's brother said, drawing her attention more than it should have. She wanted so badly to just glance around the corner and have a look at him. Her mind was throwing up all different kinds of scenarios though: blond hair like his sister, or dark hair, blue eyes, or brown eyes, green eyes. She had no idea, but she was dying to find out.

Saskia had fallen silent, her plaintive pleas having done nothing to stop the two males going at each other. What they needed was a firm hand. Gathering all her courage, Casey let out a breath and stomped into the apartment. Her brain took just a second to register the two wolves fighting. Saskia was squeezed between them like she'd thought her body in the middle could have stopped them.

The rest of her attention was on the sandy-blond haired man trying to pull another man off Alex. This must have been Saskia's brother. His nostrils flared at her arrival, his head spinning in her direction.

She let out a long, slow breath. Oh yeah, this was it. The world seemed to stop and melt away completely as their eyes met. She felt her wolf pressing against her skin, and there was no doubt she would be hovering in her eyes, too. His denim-blue eyes flashed orange, a wave of his unique scent hitting her nostrils and getting stuck in her sinuses.

He smelled like wood smoke in the middle of winter, a combination of comfort and heat that made her whole body suddenly feel very weak. A shout brought her attention back to the fight. Shaking off the effects of seeing Saskia's brother, Casey got right down to work.

She pushed herself between Alex and Zeke, finding Saskia's eyes fluttering, her breathing labored. She was going to pass out. Wrapping an arm around the other woman's waist, she drew her close to her body and, with her free hand, she swung out a fist and caught Alex in the jaw.

Alex stumbled back from her, a look of shock on his face. That made Casey smile, but she didn't have time to enjoy it. Making sure Saskia was still firmly in the line of her body, she spun around and wound up for another punch.

Zeke's momentum had pulled him toward her, making her punch doubly strong. Casey caught him in the nose, blood spurting out from where her knuckles connected with cartilage.

"Enough!" she yelled, her eyes swinging in between the two men on opposite sides of her body. Saskia's whole body went slack at that point, dragging her attention away. When none of the men offered to help, she carried the woman over to the sofa and laid her down gently, muttering about the chivalry of men under her breath as she went.

When she stood up again, she found three men staring at her. Avoiding the denim-blue gaze of Saskia's brother, Casey focused on Alex and Zeke.

"Got that out of your systems, boys?" she asked. "Good."

Alex was rubbing at the side of his face with a pissed-off expression while Zeke had his head tilted back to prevent any more blood from raining down on his shirt. His eyes were silver slits watching her carefully.

"Who are you?" Saskia's brother croaked. Casey's eyes closed of their own volition, her whole body both relaxing and becoming keyed-up at the same time.

Damn it!

"I'm Casey. And you are?" she snapped back, pretending to be pissed off.

"Saxon," he replied. "Saskia's brother."

"Oh, so *you're* the brother?" she asked, glancing down at her red fingernails, looking bored. "I'm surprised you couldn't take care of these two." She motioned between Alex and Zeke.

"I was just about to break them up," he replied.

Looking over her shoulder at Saskia, she said, "You should have done it faster then."

Saxon's eyes widened as they landed on his sister. It was almost as if he hadn't seen her pass out. He was crouched beside the couch within a heartbeat, running his hands over her forehead.

"Saskia? Can you hear me?"

The female mumbled something unintelligible, her eyes fluttering open slowly. "Saxon?" She jerked upright, looking around. "What happened?"

"You passed out," he replied, holding her up gently.

"Oh," she murmured. Her denim-blue eyes rose first to Alex then Zeke, taking in the bloody nose and the red marks on Alex's skin. "What happened to them?"

"I did," Casey announced, grinning. "You're welcome," she added when Saskia had nothing else to add.

Well, Casey figured the party was over. Glancing over at Alex, she cocked an eyebrow and asked, "You ready to go?"

"Go?" Saskia asked, standing up with Saxon's help. Casey tried to keep her eyes off Saxon, but failed when they glided up his muscular arms. Damn, the male was as sexy as hell.

Saxon smiled at her. "Thank you," he replied, his eyes smoldering. Had she said that out loud? With a blush burning her cheeks, she stomped over to Alex who was grinning like a fool. Giving him a sharp elbow to the stomach, she announced, "Let's give Saskia and Ezekiel some time to talk."

"That's the first intelligent thing I've heard all morning," Zeke said, his hand finally falling away from his nose. "Come on, Saskia. Let's go home."

Saskia hesitated, and Casey frowned. She was missing something, she was sure.

"Saskia," her mate urged, his extended fingers flexing in a *come-on* motion.

Still clutching her brother close, Saskia cleared her throat. "I'll be home soon, Zeke."

"Why won't you come with me now?" he asked, his angry, silver-eyed wolf fixing its gaze on Alex.

"Please, Zeke. I won't be long. I just need to speak to Alex for a moment."

Casey could see how much he was biting his tongue. He wanted his mate to go with him. Eventually, he gave her a stiff nod and moved toward the door. He brushed past Alex, causing him to stiffen. What an ass.

"I expect you home in an hour," Ezekiel announced as he clutched the edge of the door. "And don't leave this apartment."

Saskia nodded meekly, dropping her eyes to the ground.

"I love you," Zeke announced, waiting.

Saskia eventually met his eyes. "I'll see you at home." She offered the words up with a small smile, but Casey could see how much her refusal to reciprocate had hurt him.

Without another word, Zeke left, slamming the door shut behind him.

NINETEEN

Saxon breathed a sigh of relief as soon as the apartment door was shut. The fact was that Ezekiel could have dragged Saskia out of there; he had every right to, in fact, but somehow the guy had ignored his wolf's demands and simply left.

Saxon's eyes darted between his sister and the human male she'd once been infatuated with.

Except he wasn't human anymore.

He'd made it.

He'd gone through the Change.

The bastard had actually done it.

"So, that was your mate?" Alex asked, running a hand through his grey-flecked hair.

"Yes," Saskia replied, wrapping her arms around her waist.

"He seems like a real peach," Casey said, walking toward Saxon. Her words were meant for Saskia, but her eyes were on him. She blushed, dropping her gaze. She was clearly still embarrassed at saying he was as sexy as hell out loud. Casey was only a few feet from him. He could smell her scent so much more clearly now. To him, she smelled like his childhood, of going to the carnival with Saskia and their parents. She smelled of cotton candy and candy apples fused together—deliciously sweet and highly addictive.

Who was this female and where had she come from?

"Saxon?" Saskia asked.

Saxon refocused on the room. Casey was looking at him expectantly. Shaking his head, he turned to his sister and said, "I'm sorry. What did you say?"

Saskia folded her legs under her as she sat on the floor. "I said what's going to happen now?"

He blew out a breath and walked to the other side of the room so he could think clearly. Having Casey so close to him was driving his wolf crazy.

Mine, he said.

Saxon ignored the demand and switched on the coffee machine instead. "You're going to have to go home, Sass. I told you last night that you couldn't stay here."

Saskia looked at Alex quickly then back at him. "What do you think Ezekiel's going to do to me?" His sister's voice was small, vulnerable.

"He loves you too much to keep you confined to the house like a pet."

"He can't do that," Alex snarled, his hands curling into fists at his sides.

"Actually, he can. They're mated." Saxon pulled four mugs from the cupboard and set them on the kitchen bench. "That means he can tell Saskia exactly what she can and cannot do."

Casey snorted. "That's so sexist."

Saxon glanced at her. "Not all males are so strict," he muttered. He knew he certainly wouldn't be when he finally found his mate.

Casey flushed and looked away.

"So, you're just going to let her go back to him?" Alex demanded from his side of the room.

"She's not my responsibility anymore, Alex. She's Ezekiel's. And if you're really planning on trying to join this pack, you'd be best to remember that."

If you're really planning on trying to join this pack, you'd be best to remember that.

Saxon's words rang in Alex's ears. Was that what he wanted to do? Was it even an option? What he really wanted was to have Saskia back in his life, and if that meant joining her pack, then he guessed that's what he would have to do.

"I'm going to go and lie down for a little while," Saskia announced, rubbing her temples. Alex's body tensed. Was she hurt? Had Ezekiel hurt her? Had *he* hurt her? Just thinking that made his stomach seize up tighter than a stone.

"Are you feeling all right, Sass?" Saxon asked, pouring coffee into the third mug. "Maybe some coffee will help? Or tea?"

"Nothing can help me now, Saxon. I have to go back to my angry and hurt mate. I just need to rest up before that happens."

As she passed by Alex, she paused and glanced at him. Her beautiful eyes flashed aqua, and he could feel her wolf reaching out to his. His wolf whined and began scratching, desperate to get to her, to comfort her.

"Will you still be here when I wake up?"

"I guarantee it," he replied in a gravel voice. She nodded and he watched her walk through her bedroom door, giving him one last small smile before she closed it behind her.

Saxon had placed three mugs of coffee onto the table and took a seat in the armchair beside the TV. Casey was still sitting on the sofa, making herself at home. With a heavy sigh, Alex joined her, finding a space between Casey and the chair's arm.

"So what now?" Casey asked.

"Zeke is probably already on his way to Rhett to report the appearance of a Bitten wolf and an Alfheim wolf on pack lands."

"Fucker," Alex hissed under his breath.

Saxon pinned him in place with his dark denim eyes. "You may not like it, Alex, but you have to recognize and respect that Saskia has made her choice in a mate."

"Why him, though?" he spat back.

The male's chest rose and fell. "She had to choose a mate. She's well within breeding age."

That last statement made Alex clench his hands into fists. His blood pressure inched up too. The thought that Zeke got to touch his female intimately made him want to rip off each of Ezekiel's limbs and beat him with them.

He recognized the absurdity of his thoughts, of course, but somehow he couldn't stop himself. Perhaps it was his wolf sending the images of doing exactly that. Shutting his eyes, Alex sucked in a deep breath and released it slowly.

When his lids finally popped open, Saxon was staring at him. "I'm ashamed to admit it, but I was the one who was pushing her to get mated so quickly. After you showed up here—"

"And kicked my ass," Alex muttered, his body quickly remembering the kind of pain he'd been in. Saxon had used him like a crash test dummy against his household furniture. Alex looked at the sturdier, less pointy wooden coffee table where their drinks were sitting.

Yeah, it hadn't been wooden when he'd gone through it. Saskia had saved him from the beating though, and that was when they'd had their first and only kiss.

He never saw her again after that, and he thought he'd be okay with that. Except the minute she was out of his apartment, his heart had torn in two. The next year was a blur of booze and anger. He pushed everyone away from him, and instead of finding comfort in between a random woman's legs every other night, Alex couldn't stomach the thought of touching anyone who wasn't Saskia.

"I should apologize for that," Saxon said, dragging him kicking and screaming from his sad fucking thoughts. "You were a human sniffing around my sister, making demands."

"I loved her," he said, surprised he'd said it to her brother when Saskia should have been the one to hear those words first. He cleared his throat roughly. "I loved her then. And I love her now. There isn't anything I wouldn't do."

Saxon's eyes hardened. "That may be, but she's now off limits."

Alex didn't like how final that sounded. "I know that, but even seeing her for a little while has been worth it. Every second I spend in her presence will be treasured for the rest of my life."

Saxon grunted and looked away. Before he'd hidden his face though, Alex could have sworn he looked regretful. That would figure, though, if he had been the one to push her to get mated to someone she obviously wasn't in love with.

"Well, this has been great, but what are we supposed to do now?" Casey asked. She had her mug balanced on top of her thigh, one finger tracing the rim of the cup.

"You can't leave our territory without explaining yourself to our alpha," Saxon answered. His eyes were orange as he looked at Casey, and Alex noticed that he watched her quite often and quite closely.

"I'll call him and let him know you're here. Maybe if he hears if from me rather than Zeke, he'll be more lenient."

Casey yawned loudly, covering her mouth with the back of her hand. "Is there somewhere I can crash for a while? We've been traveling since late last night."

"Sure. You can take my bed. It's just through there." He pointed to the door beside the kitchen. Casey looked at it then back at Alex.

"You going to be all right for a while without me?" she asked with a smirk.

"Why wouldn't I be?"

"Cos you need me to fight your battles for you, clearly."

Alex flipped her off, making her laugh. "I'll catch you in a few."

With the door finally closed behind her, Saxon turned to Alex.

"She seems like a handful."

"You have no idea." Alex shook his head and took another sip from his mug, draining the last of his coffee.

"Do you know much about her?" Saxon's question caught him off guard.

"A bit. Why?"

"No reason," he replied quickly. "Only, Rhett will want to know."

"Then Rhett can ask her himself." Alex heard himself saying the words with a little too much force. He scrubbed his face with the heel of his hand. "Sorry. It's been a long night."

"Do you need to rest, too?"

"Yeah, I could crash out for a few."

"Okay. I've got some errands to run." Saxon stood up and placed his coffee cup on the table. "Take the spare bedroom down the hall. I'll be back in a couple of hours."

TWENTY

Ezekiel slammed the door of his car shut and just sat there for a moment. His wolf was banging around in his skull, demanding he go back to get Saskia and take her home with them. There was still blood on his chin from where that female had punched him in the nose. For half a second, he was sure that she'd broken the thing. Shutting his eyes, he let his head fall back heavily against the headrest.

Who was Alex to Saskia *really*?

And why did she take him back to Saxon's place?

Shouldn't she have taken them straight to Rhett? They were two foreign wolves in their territory. It wasn't as if it was a time for a cup of coffee and a catch-up. Well, if his mate wasn't going to do the right thing, then he would.

Glancing at the time, he decided to go home first and give it an hour before calling Rhett. As he drove back home, Zeke replayed every word spoken during the conversation.

Damn, he'd never been so angry, so territorial. He hated seeing Saskia in the presence of another male who wasn't a blood relation. It made his wolf's hackles rise. He guessed that's what it meant to be a mated male. Saskia was the most important thing in his life. He would fight for her. He would die for her. Clearly he'd get punched in the face by a petite red-head for her, also.

So distracted by his thoughts, he missed his turn-off. With a curse, he turned back around and corrected his mistake. When he pulled into the drive, the house looked the same as it always did, but somehow he felt as if there had been a momentous shift in the past eight hours.

Saskia's leaving in the dead of night certain shook him more than he wanted to admit. He hit the button for the garage door, stopping the car to watch the thing strain and work to get all the way up. Once inside, he killed the engine and closed the door.

Inside, the house was quiet, the lingering scents of him and Saskia in every corner of the four walls they'd been calling home for the past six months as a mated pair. He remembered showing it to Saskia for the first time. Her eyes had lit up, and he knew why he loved her so much. There was a light within her that left a warm, golden glow in him.

For him, she was like the very air he dragged into his lungs. The fact that she hadn't loved him as much as he'd loved her in the beginning had stung, but he had hoped with time that she would learn.

Being away from her now, knowing that things were strained, left him anxious for her well-being. Pulling the phone from his pocket, he dialed her number and put the thing to his ear. It rang three times before his mate's sleepy voice answered.

"Hello?"

"Saskia," he said softly. "Sorry, did I wake you?"

"It's fine," she replied. The sound of sheets rustling filled the empty space between them. "I just had to lie down for a little while after what happened."

"I'm sorry. I wasn't thinking straight."

"You were protecting your property. I get it."

Property? He shook his head angrily. "No, Saskia. I don't think of you as a piece of my property. You're my mate, my equal. I was protecting you from that other male."

"Why? He's just a friend."

Yeah, right. "My wolf went a little crazy when he saw you walk in with him. Blame it on him if you must, but know that I don't see you as a piece of property that I can stamp ownership on."

She sighed heavily. "I'm sorry."

"What for?"

"For leaving last night. I was overwhelmed with everything that had happened, and I'm sorry I didn't tell you."

He laughed softly. "A little warning would have been nice." He sobered as he remembered waking up that morning to a cold, empty bed. "I was so worried," he whispered.

"I know," she said back just as softly.

"If you need some more time with your brother, I understand."

"Thanks, Zeke. I'd like to spend the day with him, but I promise I'll be home tonight."

"All right. I'm just going to call Rhett."

"About what?" she asked, her voice sounding panicky. She probably thought he was going to break their mate bond. "Shh, Saskia. Don't worry," he cooed back softly. "I'm just going to report Alex and Casey to Rhett. He needs to know there are two foreign wolves within the territory."

"Do you have to report them so soon?" she asked.

"It's better that I do it sooner rather than later. You know the rules."

"I do," she admitted. "When?"

"I'll give him a call when I get off the phone with you."

"Okay."

"Okay." Zeke looked around the kitchen, thinking. "I'm going to make something to eat, but you rest up and I'll see you tonight, okay? What would you like for dinner?"

"You're going to cook?" she asked.

"Of course I am. Now tell me what you'd like and I'll have it ready when you get home."

Saskia's heart was pounding too hard in her chest.

"Italian would be great. Lasagne, maybe?" she said into her phone. Zeke was an exceptional cook, but never offered very often.

"Consider it done. I love you."

Why did he have to say those words? "I'll see you tonight," she whispered in reply and hung up the phone. She knew he was going to report Alex and Casey to Rhett, but that wasn't what scared her—it was what was going to happen to them then. She had just got Alex back. She didn't think she could handle losing him again so soon.

Although she had only slept for maybe twenty minutes, she couldn't have gone back to bed again. She was too wide awake—too wired for her brain to relax. Besides, if she let herself sleep again, she would dream again and her heart wouldn't have been able to take it. She'd seen her life with Alex unfurl. They were mated, they had children, they were happy together—truly happy. Even Saxon had found himself a mate who looked peculiarly a lot like Casey.

A gentle knocking on the door pulled her from the memories. Shaking her head, she said, "Come in."

Alex's scent swirled into the room. His human scent lingered, but the scent of the wolf was the one that called to her; he smelled of freshly cut wood and fresh powdered snow.

"Saskia? Can I come in?" he asked in a soft voice. When she didn't answer immediately, he added, "I heard your phone ring. That's how I knew you were awake."

The dream flashed in her mind's eye, playing through each scene. She could have been with Alex if she wasn't already mated to Zeke. The thought made her sad. "Come in," she answered, hiding the shake in her voice.

Alex nudged the door shut behind him and approached the bed. "May I sit down?"

She looked at him, surprised. She didn't think he would be so careful around her.

Unless it was because she belonged to someone else now? Yes, that had to be it. "Of course."

Alex perched on the very edge of the mattress, his weight making her body lean toward him. She sighed, closing her eyes, imagining how being flush beside him would feel.

"Are you all right? You look as if you're in pain."

Saskia opened her eyes. "No, not in pain." She gave him a small smile which he returned, but there was sadness in his eyes. She let out a shaky breath. "I can't believe you're here. I can't believe you're one of us now."

He shrugged.

"Did it hurt? Going through the Change?"

He rubbed at his chest. "I've been through worse pain."

She nodded, remembering the scars that covered his upper torso. "Being shot?"

"Losing you," he replied, looking irritated with himself. "Damn it. I'm sorry. I shouldn't have said that," he added, looking remorseful.

Her heart was beating a harsh staccato in her chest. That same spark they shared before was still there, and if it was even possible, stronger than before. She bit her bottom lip. "Why shouldn't you have said that?"

Alex's dark gaze smoldered on her face for a moment, increasing the loud *thump, thump, thump* of her pulse in her ear. There was such longing in his eyes, longing that would have been reflected in hers, too.

"Because I promised myself that I wouldn't say inappropriate things to you since you're mated to Zeke."

Saskia didn't know what to say to that. Clearing her throat, whatever she was about to say froze on her tongue.

Alex had just taken both of her hands in his, brushing his lips against the back of her knuckles. "I know I said I wouldn't say things like that, but damn it, I have to tell you this."

"What?" she asked, her whole body trembling.

"Just that I never stopped thinking about you. The day you walked out of my apartment broke me."

"But you moved on, didn't you? Started dating again?"

He shook his head, his expression serious. "I couldn't. How could I when every woman I saw couldn't match up to you?"

"Oh, Alex." She was melting inside. She'd longed to hear the words, but they were spoken too late.

"You've been haunting my dreams, Saskia. When I heard you were engaged, I knew I should have been angry that you hadn't told me, but I could never be angry with you. The only thing that's been keeping me going is the memory of our first kiss. Do you remember it?"

She nodded, afraid all the feelings she had for Alex would come tumbling off her tongue if she opened her mouth. She remembered everything about their first kiss—the hesitation, the longing, the taste of his lips.

"I think about it all the time. I think about what our future could have been like."

She couldn't stop the tears now. He was saying everything she'd ever wanted him to say.

"Don't cry, baby," he whispered, catching her tears with the tips of his fingers. "I didn't mean to make you cry. I just had to tell you before you went back to your mate. I had to make sure you knew."

"I knew," she replied softly, dashing the tears from her eyes. "I know."

"I've loved you from the very first moment I saw you. Do you know that, Saskia?"

She shook her head, unable to believe his sweet, sweet words.

"It's true. I loved you then and I love you now."

His words made her gasp. "Alex, you can't."

"I don't care if you have a mate now. You can't stop me from loving you."

"But we could never be together."

"It doesn't matter. If I get to see you every other day, I'll be happy."

She shook her head slowly. "Someday that won't be enough for you. You should find someone who will love you as much as I—" Saskia cleared her throat, banishing the words she was about to speak. She did love Alex, but what good would it do to tell him? It would only make this rejection and hopelessness all the more painful.

"You should find someone who you can share your life with. You should find a woman who will have your children, who will grow old with you."

He sobered. "I already have. I don't want anybody else."

"Alex, please," she begged. "You can't."

"I can. And I will," he replied, his tone brooking no argument. She realized then that he was a dominant wolf. She guessed he always had been, though. He kissed her palms this time, laying her open hand against his face. "You have to go back to him, don't you?"

She nodded, tears decorating her lashes.

"Then know that I love you and will always be there if you need me. For anything, Saskia. I'm serious," he said when she huffed gently.

"Even if I want ice cream in the middle of the night?"

He smiled. "I'll bring two spoons."

<h1 style="text-align:center">TWENTY-ONE</h1>

Casey flopped around onto her back, groaning in frustration. She was tired, but there was no way she could go to sleep—not while the scent of Saxon and his wolf surrounded her so completely. She'd been hoping he'd offer up his bedroom to her so she could do a little snooping to find out what kind of male he was.

After going through his drawers, she'd found out he was a boxers over briefs man, he liked the middle-of-the-range cologne selection and he had an unhealthy obsession with mechanics overalls, although she had found some nice dress shirts in his closet, which suggested he did dress up on occasion. As she'd touched his clothes, she so badly wanted to see him dressed in them so she could take them off him again.

Slowly.

"Damn, what are you? A female in heat?" she asked herself. "Just stop it and try to get some rest like you wanted to."

Casey tried to relax back into the pillows, even closed her eyes in the hopes that sleep would take her, but all that meant was all her other senses were on high alert. Like her sense of smell...and her hearing. From behind the adjacent wall, she heard the rumble of Alex's voice and the softness of Saskia's.

Casey liked the female. She was completely opposite to her in many ways, yet their fate tied them together: find a mate and breed. If only the way the alphas thought would change then she could be whatever she wanted to be. All she got now was a brush-off every time she suggested—gasp! Heaven forbid—something other than keeping a house and hunting for a mate.

Unable to stop hearing the conversation between Alex and Saskia, Casey laid back and listened.

"I've been through worse pain."

"Being shot?" she asked.

"Losing you," he replied. "Damn it. I'm sorry. I shouldn't have said that."

Casey so didn't want to be privy to this conversation or what followed. Lifting her weary body from the bed, she left Saxon's scent behind and opened up the door.

The male that had been haunting her was just coming through the front door. He first glanced at an opened door just down the hall then at Saskia's door, frowning. She guessed Alex was not supposed to be in there alone with his sister. Casey cleared her throat, and his deep blue eyes ratcheted to her face like he hadn't realized she was there.

"Casey," he said, his voice vibrating through her body, calling her wolf forward. She didn't want him to see how badly he was affecting her, so she straightened her spine and tried to make her expression say *Who else?"*

"Got it in one, handsome."

Damn it! Why'd I have to call him handsome, too?

The nickname earned her a smile that melted the marrow in her bones. "Couldn't sleep?" he asked.

She shrugged and moved toward the sofa. "Something like that." Casey put her feet up on the coffee table and crossed her arms over her chest.

"Make yourself comfortable," Saxon said, joining her on the sofa.

She was sure he was going for sarcasm, but lucky for him, she didn't always acknowledge it. "Thanks." She grinned at him, snuggling down deeper into the cushions, deeper into his scent. "So, you want to know about me, huh?"

Saxon's expression went from shock to suspicion.

"All you have to do is ask, you know," she added.

"Do you make a habit of eavesdropping?" he ground out.

She grinned again. "Of course I do. People say some pretty interesting things when they think I'm out of earshot."

"I bet they do," he grumbled, relaxing back into the sofa's cushions.

"So, what's the story with Alex and Saskia?"

"I don't know what you're talking about."

She gave him an exasperated look. "Were they lovers?"

"No. He pursued her, but...she didn't show any interest."

She snorted softly to herself. "You wouldn't have allowed any more than that though, would you?"

"Of course not," he relied crisply. "She was under my care at the time. If she was going to get involved with someone, I would have known about it, and he certainly wouldn't have been human."

This rhetoric was nothing new for Casey, so she let it roll off her back like she always did. "Now that Alex is one of us, what does it mean for her?"

Saxon glanced at his sister's closed bedroom door, and frowned once more. Alex being inside with his sister was driving him mad. "It doesn't change anything."

"But she's unhappy. Surely, you can see that. Hell, I've only just met the other guy and even I can see she's unhappy."

Saxon's spine stiffened. "She's mated now. Nothing is going to change that."

"Well, there is one way," Casey said slowly. "Zeke could break the mate bond with her."

"He wouldn't do that to her."

Death was a better option than breaking the mate bond, but Casey knew of one couple that had done it in her pack. They'd just stopped loving each other, and mutually decided to end it. The only downside was that the female was often shunned after the bond was broken. Casey thought it was better to be free and shunned than stuck in a mating that was loveless.

Saxon's chest expanded and contracted under his tee, and Casey had to look away. Why did he have to look so good?

Saxon gave her an amused smile. "Do you even have a filter, or do you just say whatever you're thinking?"

Casey's cheeks colored when she realized she'd put her foot in it again. Damn that male. He made her mouth and her brain stop cooperating. It took her a moment to recover and she forced her expression back to haughty indifference—an expression she didn't think was fooling anyone. "I don't believe in hiding the truth."

Saxon's gaze pinned her in place, his eyes smoldering, lighting a fire within her, too. Casey's skin felt too tight for her bones, and she shifted uneasily on the sofa. If he could get that kind of reaction from her just by looking, she desperately wanted to know what he could do with his hands and mouth. She licked her lips, tasting his arousal in the air.

Saxon shifted forward in his seat, and Casey's heart raced. Had he read her thoughts? Was he going to touch her? His feral eyes still watched her, but instead of reaching forward, he lifted himself off the sofa and excused himself. Casey watched him walk into his room, shutting the door firmly behind him.

Saxon let out a deep breath and slumped onto the edge of his mattress. Casey's scent was all over his bed, his sheets. He groaned and stood up, rearranging the sudden erection pushing against the inside of his pants. He had never wanted a female this badly before, and it was only her scent that was encouraging him. He could only imagine what would happen when they touched.

Stripping off his clothes, he walked into the small ensuite attached to his bedroom and turned on the shower. A little time with the shampoo and rinse routine would help him focus again.

Saxon stepped under the spray and tilted his head back, his eyes sliding shut. Behind his lids, the image of Casey materialized. She was wearing that cocky grin she had when she turned toward him on the couch.

I don't believe in hiding the truth.

Saxon groaned again, throwing an arm out on to the tile. He would have loved to have taken her right there on the couch, but social decorum dictated that was not the right thing to do while his sister was just in the other room.

Pushing the red-head from his thoughts, he focused on rinsing the suds from his body and stepped out of the cubicle. Wrapping a large towel around his waist, he quickly got dressed then found his phone in his discarded jeans pocket. Dialing the pack house, he put the device to his ear and waited for someone to answer.

"Hello?"

"Rhett?" he asked.

"Yeah. Who's this?"

"Saxon," he replied, running a hand through his hair.

"Saxon," Rhett drawled, "I was wondering when I'd be hearing from you."

He was? "We have a situation." Saxon didn't see the point in beating around the bush with this thing. Even though it would kill Saskia, he had to keep the pack's safety in mind.

"Sounds serious," Rhett replied.

"It is. Alex D'Angelo, you know that human male who broke Skylar's arm at the party, well, he's been bitten." Saxon winced a little over those last words—*he's been bitten*. Yeah, he knew all about *that* little secret. If Alex remembered anything from that time, he hadn't mentioned it yet, which was a good thing.

"I'm glad you called to tell me yourself. I just got off the phone with Ezekiel about it. He seems to think that you were harboring a fugitive."

"I was waiting until a more respectable hour to call."

"I appreciate that," he replied, the sound of leather creaking in the background.

"Did Zeke tell you anything more?"

"There's more?" Rhett asked.

"Alex came back with a female from the Alfheim pack."

"He already found himself a mate?" Rhett asked, not bothering to hide the surprise from his voice.

Saxon bit back a growl, then pretended to clear his voice. "No. She brought him here. I don't know anything more than that. I thought it'd be best to ask her all those questions in front of you."

"You're right. I'd prefer to question her myself. Bring them around to the pack house in an hour, and we'll decide what to do with them from there."

"No problems."

"Oh, and Saxon? Send Saskia back to her mate."

"You got it."

After hanging up, Saxon got dressed in a long-sleeved tee and fresh jeans.

Casey was just where he'd left her, except she was now asleep, curled up against the arm of the chair. Ignoring his wolf's insistent calls to take her to his bed, Saxon set his jaw and knocked on Saskia's door.

Opening it without getting the okay was stupid, but he didn't have time for this. Much to his surprise, she and Alex were sitting about a foot away from each other on the mattress, their curious glances fixed on his face.

"Alex, I just got off the phone with Rhett. He wants to see you and Casey at the pack house in an hour."

"All right."

"I'm coming with you," Saskia insisted, standing up and wringing her hands together nervously.

Saxon shook his head. "That's not my call to make, Sass. You have to go back to Zeke." He held her eyes. "Rhett knows the whole story now thanks to your mate."

"He *told* Rhett? What was he thinking?"

"He was worried about Alex being around."

"But—"

Saxon put his hands up in front of him. "It doesn't matter. I'll drop you home to Zeke on the way to Rhett."

TWENTY-TWO

Saskia's gaze dropped to Alex. He stared back, his wolf surging in his eyes for a split second before Alex was once again in control.

"Okay," she replied, looking back at her brother. Although he was the one doing the ordering around, she could tell he didn't like doing it.

But he was right.

She had to go back to Zeke and face him.

Sliding from the edge of the bed, Alex followed her brother from the room. He stopped as he left, giving her an encouraging smile before disappearing from sight. With a heavy feeling in her chest, Saskia pulled on her shoes and collected her purse.

With only a cursory glance at herself in the mirror, she stopped and went back for a closer inspection. There were bags under her eyes, evidence that the late night and early rise had done nothing for her complexion. The rough ponytail she'd done that morning was coming apart, wisps of hair surrounding her face.

And Alex had seen her like that?

Dropping her handbag back onto the bed, she undid the knot keeping her hair up and ran a brush through her blonde locks. When it had been somewhat tamed, she pushed it behind her ears and placed the brush back.

Taking a deep breath, she pulled open her door and closed it quietly behind her. Alex glanced over, his nostrils flaring ever so slightly, his eyes beginning to burn as they drifted down her face and neck, taking a leisurely circuitous route of the rest of her body.

She responded to his inspection, liquid heat pooling between her thighs. In her mind's eyes, she saw her wolf becoming submissive to the mate she knew she had in Alex.

"Saskia?" Saxon asked.

Dragging her eyes from Alex, she turned to her brother. Breathlessly, she said, "Sorry. What?" Saskia hoped her brother couldn't see the blush flushing her cheeks. Even if he didn't see it, he would have been able to smell how attracted she was to Alex.

He frowned, his eyes narrowing at Alex like he'd physically touched her to bring out that reaction. "I said are you ready to go?"

"Sure."

"Where's your suitcase?"

"In my bedroom."

"I'll get it," Alex rumbled, brushing past her.

"Where's Casey?" Saskia asked, hoping to draw the attention away from them.

"Bathroom. Once she's out, we'll be ready to go."

They all left together, but down at the car, Saxon insisted that Alex sit up front with him. Sliding into the backseat with Casey, Saskia played nervously with her fingers, her eyes fixed on the scenery that passed by her window. More than once she felt Alex's eyes on her, but she didn't dare look at him. It would have only made it harder to walk away.

Saxon pulled up at her house much too soon, and as she stared up at it, she forced herself to remember that Zeke had stayed in Buxton at her request, and that he was a decent male.

"I'll call you later," Saxon said to her through the rearview mirror. She nodded, turning her head to the petite female beside her when she touched her hand.

"It was nice to meet you," Casey murmured, "even if it was for only a short time."

Saskia nodded, tears filling her eyes as she knew this would more than likely be the last time she would see Alex. She couldn't see how Rhett would let him stay on pack lands now that he was bitten. She opened her mouth to say something, but before a word could be spoken, her car door popped open and a swirl of freezing air invaded the small space.

She blinked up at Ezekiel. Resting one hand on the top of the car roof, he had the door propped open with the other, bending his body forward so he was eye-level with the other occupants of the car.

"Saxon, thanks from driving her back."

"No problem," her brother replied.

"Going somewhere?" he asked, his gaze lingering on Alex for a few seconds.

"Yeah. Rhett wants to see them both," Saxon said. "I called him this morning about them being here."

Saskia noticed how Zeke tried to hide his smugness. "It's probably for the best. We shouldn't have foreign wolves wandering around unchecked. It endangers the rest of us."

From behind her, Saskia could have sworn Casey had uttered the word "douchebag" very quietly. She smiled because she had to agree. Zeke was trying to play it off as if his concern was for the pack, but it was clear he was just trying to assert his ownership of her.

With a sigh, Saskia touched Zeke's arm, drawing his attention. "I have my suitcase in the trunk."

He'd been giving Alex a hard stare, but he nodded and disappeared from the doorway. Without looking at anyone in particular, Saskia slid from the back seat, murmuring goodbye as she went.

Just as she shut the door, Zeke wound his arm around her waist, pulling her body into the line of his. She tried not to squirm as the car reversed from the drive and drove off. Once their audience was out of sight, Zeke removed his arm and clasped her hand instead, pulling her up onto the porch with him.

Reluctantly, she followed, closing the front door behind her. Zeke placed her case down in the living room, his expression unreadable for a moment before every emotion played across his handsome face.

His arms were suddenly around her, holding her carefully. "I'm so glad to have you home," he said over and over again, chanting it like a prayer.

Saskia felt tears prick her eyes. She hated hurting him. "I'm sorry. I know I've already said it, but I'm so very sorry, Zeke. I didn't think."

"Feel like telling me why you ran?"

She took in a deep breath. She had to start being honest with Zeke—really honest, not just saying she would then changing her mind like she'd been doing.

Pulling away from him so she could see his face, she cleared the tears from her eyes. "Put on some tea and I'll tell you everything."

Ezekiel didn't waste any time. As soon as he was in the kitchen, Saskia slipped away from the living room, dragging her suitcase behind her. By the time she reappeared, Ezekiel had two mugs of tea on the coffee table and a full pot sitting on the table.

"Thanks," she murmured, dragging the sleeves of her sweater over her hands before she accepted the cup. Her mate sat beside her, leaving them touching from hip to thigh. Saskia took a sip to settle the nervous fluttering in her stomach and began to tell him what she'd been keeping from him.

"Zeke, can I ask you to keep any questions you might have until the end? It's going to take a while for me to get all of this out."

He nodded. "Sure. Take your time." He placed a gentle hand on the top of her thigh, squeezing her knee ever so slightly.

"Before we were mated—before that party even—I found myself attracted to a human man."

Ezekiel's hand tightened where it lay, but a sideways glance from her made him relax once more.

She couldn't believe she was going to tell him all this. "He began asking me out, and I denied him until I finally gave in. We went out for dinner just once, and something he said to me then made me realize what I was doing. I had no right to be leading him on like that. There could be no future between us. He was human, and I...I was trying to run away from my responsibilities. When I got home, I told Saxon I was ready to see what males from other packs were interested in mating with me."

She took a sip from her tea, her throat already dry.

"You looked so beautiful that night," Ezekiel said softly. "Have I ever told you that?"

"All the time," she replied with a smile. "At that party, there was a fight where one of the younger males had his arm broken. The human I had been seeing had broken it. For some reason he had followed me to the pack house, and he saw the other male trying to..." Saskia flushed, and Zeke growled.

"He touched you?" It was a demand from his wolf. When Saskia didn't deny it, the growling got louder. "I'll kill him."

"Zeke, he had his arm broken by a human. I think he was humiliated enough by that."

"But he touched you without your permission."

"It's in the past." She patted him gently on the arm. "I told the man then that I couldn't see him anymore. Somehow he heard that I was engaged to someone, which I guess I kind of was. I was promised to someone else—I just didn't know who that someone was at the time. He came around to the apartment to confront me. Saxon almost killed him, too, for searching me out. I only just managed to stop him. I took the guy home, stitched up his injuries and left."

Saskia could see Zeke was chewing his own tongue to stop himself from asking a question. "Go on. Ask me."

"Did *he* ever touch you inappropriately?" he demanded again.

"No. He was always a perfect gentleman."

"Did you kiss him?"

Saskia's cheeks heated. She couldn't believe she was about to tell her mate the details of her and Alex's bare romance. "Just once, and I left his apartment straight after because I knew it couldn't go anywhere."

Zeke nodded. "Good."

"I didn't see him for almost a year. I thought he'd moved or something, although I was sure his work would have kept him in Buxton. I didn't know if he was even still alive until—" This was it. This was the bombshell. "This morning."

Zeke's fingers tightened, making her wince. He removed his hand and gave her an apologetic smile. "Sorry," he muttered. "You're talking about that guy, Alex, aren't you?"

She nodded.

"He's not human anymore though," he added softly.

Saskia's answer escaped on a sigh. "No, he's not."

Her mate frowned and placed his cup back onto the coffee table. Turning his body toward her, he asked, "So the reason you've been acting a little strangely these last few months is because..."

"Is because it was coming up on a year since everything happened from meeting Alex to the date to the kiss to the..." she paused. "It was a pretty crazy year for me. A lot of things happened. I thought I was over them all, but obviously I wasn't." She placed her cup next to Zeke's.

When she sat back again, he took her hands in his. They were warm and tender. "So, how does Alex's appearance affect me?"

She looked into his eyes quickly, the shock wearing off a moment later. "It doesn't affect you, Zeke." Biting her lip, she looked away. "I mated with you. I'm committed to *you*."

"What if he asked you to leave with him? Would you go?"

The vulnerability in his voice made Saskia look at him differently. He'd always seemed so collected and in control. Alex's appearance had shaken him—even before he'd known who he really was.

"I wouldn't go. I made my choice, Zeke, and I'm going to stand by it." He didn't seem to believe her. "I haven't been fair to you at all. I should have seen what a great guy I had a long time ago, but my head was filled with silly scenarios involving another man—a *human* no less."

"He's not human anymore though. He's a wolf now, and that changes things."

"Not for me it doesn't."

The hurt in Zeke's eyes burned. "How can I know that for sure?"

"You're just going to have to trust me."

"I do trust you. It's the male I don't trust."

"Zeke, tell me what I can do to make this up to you. I'll do anything you want. If you want to move from Buxton, we'll move."

His brows shot up. "Anything?"

"Name it. It's yours," she replied, touching her hand softly to his slightly stubbly cheek.

His dark eyes held fast to hers, a sense of longing in their depths. "A child." He swallowed. "I want us to try and get pregnant."

TWENTY-THREE

Casey watched the sprawl of forest take over from suburban houses, the trees streaking past in flashes of white and green.

"How much farther?" she asked Saxon, not really caring what the answer might be. She just liked the way his blue eyes darted to the rearview mirror to look at her.

"About a mile."

His answer didn't matter. She was going to ask again in three...two...one...

"How much farther?"

His eyes were narrowed when he looked at her this time, which only made him look sexier if that was even possible. "Were you even listening to the answer I gave you less than five seconds ago?"

"No," she replied, grinning when he growled. "Soooo—how much farther?"

"Ignore her," Alex drawled, turning to look at her over his shoulder. "I know I do."

Casey flipped him off and looked back to find Saxon watching her once more. "Eyes on the road, handsome. I don't want to ruin my pretty face by going through the windshield."

His wolf surged forward before he looked back at the slick blacktop they were driving on. Smiling smugly, Casey glanced out the window as they slowed to turn into a long gravel driveway. The forest followed them all the way down to a large circular driveway at the end of the road.

Saxon stopped the car behind some big environmentally irresponsible SUV and cut the engine. The sound of car doors slamming shut seemed to echo. Saxon led the way up the few porch steps to the front door, his fist rising to knock. Casey took a second to enjoy the view, liking the way Saxon's jeans were snug against that fine ass of his. His shirt was tucked into the waistband of his pants; her fingers twitched to pull the fabric free, to run rampant under his shirt all over his hot skin.

His head swung around then, his eyes flashing, the scent of his arousal hitting her nostrils. Damn, he could read her so well. Giving him a devil-may-care smile, she said, "I can't enjoy the view with you glaring at me like that, handsome."

He let out a frustrated huff just as the door to the pack house opened up. A huge wolf with military-style short hair and grey eyes filled up the doorway. In an instant, she could tell he was the more dominant wolf and dropped her gaze to his chin. She felt his eyes rake over her.

"Daddy!" a little voice called, drawing Casey's attention. She risked glancing up, seeing the Helheim wolf smile as a human woman approached him with a child in each of her arms.

"She wanted her daddy," the woman said, reaching up onto her toes to kiss his cheek. She handed over one of the squirming children. He took the little girl into his huge arms, cradling her gently against his huge chest.

"Saxon, Rhett's expecting you. Go on through."

"Thanks, Vaile," Saxon replied, stepping past the guy and walking farther into the house. Alex waved Casey through before him. She gave Vaile a wide berth and slipped around him into the hallway, but Alex stopped to talk to him.

"Wolfe," Alex said, offering Vaile his palm. By some miracle, Vaile took it. "When did you become a daddy?"

"About the same time you became an asshole," Vaile replied, his expression serious.

Alex actually looked chagrinned. "Yeah, well..."

"What the fuck happened to you?"

Alex shrugged. "I still haven't gotten my head around that."

Vaile grunted. "The alpha is waiting for you."

Alex nodded stiffly and turned to see Casey watching him. "You waiting for me?"

"Just keeping you out of trouble," she shot back, turning on her heel and marching down the hall. Alex already knew who Vaile was, but how was that possible?

Using her nose, Casey followed Saxon's scent to a door left open to the hall-way. Inside the room, she found an office that was quite modern. A large glass desk took up a third of the room, a sleek and expensive-looking computer monitor sitting in the corner of it.

Behind the desk was a leather chair that still smelled new. On the opposite wall to the desk were two large sofas, with a small fridge in between them acting as a table of sorts. On top of the fridge were some glasses and a few mugs.

Saxon was standing in front of a large bookshelf, looking at something he was holding. Sauntering over to him, she peered around his arm to see what held his attention so completely.

It was a photograph in an expensive gold frame. Saxon's smiling face stared back out at him, Saskia held close to his body. Saxon seemed to notice her then, his head jerking around, his nostrils flaring.

Casey cleared her throat. "When was this taken?" she asked, her eyes lingering on the easy, relaxed expression on Saxon's face. She liked seeing him like that.

"Last year," another voice replied from behind her. She spun around, her wolf already cowering at the power of the alpha who now stood before her. His mismatched eyes were relaxed, despite having a foreign wolf standing in his office. This must be Rhett.

Rhett took the photo from Saxon and looked down at it. "After the pack house burned down, and we had it rebuilt, I asked all the wolves of my pack to leave a photo of themselves to help build some new memories."

Rhett handed the photo back to Saxon, then moved behind the desk; he practically fell into the leather chair. "But you didn't drive all the way out here to hear about that, did you?" he asked, steepling his fingers under his chin. "Take a seat. We have some business to attend to."

Casey noticed that Alex was already sitting down. Saxon sat on the other side of the couch leaving Casey to occupy the middle. Vaile strolled in then, followed by another male whose dark hair and blue eyes made a shiver crawl down Casey's spine.

Vaile took up the space behind Rhett's right shoulder, and the other man took the left.

"What's your name?" Rhett asked. Casey's eyes were in her lap when the question was asked. Glancing sideways at the other men, it quickly became obvious the alpha was talking to her.

"Casey," she replied.

"And what pack are you from, Casey?"

"The Alfhcim pack."

Rhett leaned forward in his chair. "I don't remember getting a call from Acario asking permission to have one of his wolves in my territory."

Casey lifted her eyes to his chin. "He doesn't know—"

A phone began to ring, cutting off her words. Rhett glanced down at his desk and frowned. Picking up the phone, he held it to his ear.

"Hello?" he said. "Acario, we were just talking about you."

Casey's fingernails were suddenly digging into the tops of her thighs. Saxon shifted beside her, leaning in to whisper into her ear.

"Something wrong?"

She shook her head, trying to relax her body. Rhett was still talking to her father, throwing a lot of "uh huhs" and "yeses" at him. On more than one occasion, she could feel his gaze on her, but she dare not look up.

After what felt like a lifetime of holding her breath, Rhett finally hung up. "It seems like your father is a little upset you're gone," Rhett said.

From the corner of her eye, Casey saw Saxon's head swing around like it had just come unhinged; the question he wanted to ask was burning in his eyes. She ignored him, focusing all her attention on Rhett.

"I plan on leaving as soon as we're done here."

"That's good. But I still want to know what you're doing here."

Casey licked her lips and looked over at Alex. Her chest rose and fell as she drew in a breath through her nose. "It's a long story."

Rhett opened his hands. "I've not got anything else to do."

She nodded and slipped to the edge of the sofa. "I found Alex within our borders. From what I could tell, he was about two days into the Change. I had two options: either leave him there, or take him back to the pack house. I convinced my brothers to take him back with us. My father instructed us to keep an eye on him. If he pulled through the Change okay, we were going to absorb him into the pack, but..."

"But I didn't want to stay there," Alex interrupted. "It was my choice to leave, but Casey followed and I didn't stop her."

"You told him of the risks?" Rhett asked Casey.

"Yes. I told him he'd be killed on sight if one of the enforcers found him, but they didn't; Saskia did."

Rhett's eyes narrowed on Saxon. "Is that true?"

Saxon nodded. "Saskia went for an early morning run and came across them. She brought them back to my apartment."

"Why didn't she bring them here?" Rhett asked.

Saxon's denim-blue eyes rose for a moment before falling to his tightly clasped hands. "She wasn't thinking clearly," he replied.

"He isn't the first one we've found," Casey interjected, drawing the alpha's attention away from Saxon. "We've been getting more and more Bitten wolves on our lands. We've admitted more than a dozen in the past year."

"And the others?" the brown-haired wolf on Rhett's left asked.

"Terminated," Casey replied in a small voice. "They were too far gone; their wolf had completely taken over their humanity."

The male snarled, the sound only stopping when Rhett barked, "Sabel!"

Pressing on, she said, "I think whoever has been creating all these Bitten wolves is also responsible for Alex."

It was Vaile's turn to react to her statement. His grey eyes fixed on Saxon before ratcheting to Alex.

"You can't tell?" he asked.

She shook her head. "We don't have anyone in the pack with a nose good enough. We don't even know if it's just one person doing the biting, or if there are multiple people acting under the orders of someone else."

"And what more has your father done?" Rhett asked.

"The only thing he can do is accept the wolves that have made it through the Change, and to kill those who haven't. We don't know where to start looking for the culprit."

Rhett sat back in his chair, his hands folded in his lap. "Casey, I want you to go and wait outside. I need to speak to Alex for a moment. Saxon, you can join her."

Casey did as she was asked, standing up on suddenly unsteady feet and walking to the door. She gave Alex an encouraging smile and slipped from the room with Saxon on her heels. With the door shut behind them, Casey let out a deep breath and slumped against the wall.

"You're the alpha's daughter?" Saxon asked quietly. He was propped up against the wall opposite her.

"Yeah. So?"

He looked away. "Never mind."

When it was clear there was nothing else to be said, Casey settled down onto her haunches and leaned against the wall. Her mind had just started to drift when the sound of laughter coming from somewhere farther in the house snagged her attention. She stood up and followed the voices.

"Casey!" Saxon hissed behind her. Ignoring him, she wandered through a doorway and stepped into a large, modern kitchen. There were four females there; two werewolves, a human and one she couldn't place.

The unidentified female was standing at the bench, her head bent over some dough she was kneading. The human from before—Vaile's mate—was just lifting a young child from a highchair while another blonde female had another child with the same striking blonde hair and blue eyes. She realized they were twins. An older wolf sat in a comfortable-looking chair in the corner.

As soon as Casey's scent registered, the wolves and the female kneading the bread looked in her direction. Casey smiled and waved at the others, but jerked back in surprise at the woman behind the bench. Her eyes were a vibrant violet that seemed to glow.

"You're...you're..." Casey couldn't get her mouth and brain to work at the same time. "You're..."

"My name's Indi. And you are?"

"Casey," she replied. Indi was the felvair who had been the cause of the uprising a year ago. She was the reason the packs had gone to war. Without her blood, the chances of a female werewolf having a baby girl were about one in ten. *With* her blood, though, every pregnancy would result in a girl. And with the current male to female ratio in packs, more girls being born was a very good thing—especially for Casey.

"Why are you here?" another female asked, clutching the child carefully to her chest.

"I was bored," she replied without thinking. When she got some frowns, she cleared her throat and added, "I brought Alex home."

Nobody in the room seemed to react to that except for the human.

"Alex D'Angelo?" she asked.

Casey nodded.

"Where's he been?"

"He was bitten. I found him in my father's territory."

"Is he okay?" The child in her arms squirmed free and walked unsteadily over to the older woman in the chair.

"Seems to be," Casey replied, watching the little girl waddle. More questions were poised on the tip of her tongue when Saxon stepped up behind her.

"Come back to the office, Casey."

It wasn't a command she wanted to listen to, but she went with him, giving the women a wave goodbye.

"You can't just walk off and introduce yourself to the females of this house," Saxon hissed under his breath, taking hold of her arm and pulling her to a stop within an inch of his body.

She would have been really turned on if he hadn't been so damn authoritative. Pulling free from his grip, she crossed her arms tightly across her chest and gave him a cold look. "I don't remember giving you permission to touch me, or tell me what to do, handsome."

Saxon paled and took a step away from her. He looked down, his voice holding an edge she couldn't pick. "You can't just waltz off and do whatever you want to do, Casey. You're in the alpha's house now."

She snorted. "Sorry, but that's never stopped me from doing anything before," she replied. "Besides, if I want to do something, I'll just go and do it."

"Like following Alex?"

She smiled. "Yeah, like following Alex. And this, too." Without giving him any more warning about her intentions, Casey stretched up on her toes and pressed her mouth to his.

A surge of electricity pounded through her body at the connection, making her skin tighten and her brain short circuit. She had never experienced something like that before. It was as if she'd just been plugged straight into an electrical main, and her body was still sparking. Saxon wrapped his arms around her waist, dragged her closer to him and slanted his mouth over hers to deepen the kiss. A shudder rode her spine, goosebumps filling the skin on her arms. There was such passion in his kiss, almost as if he'd been wanting—*needing*— her for so long. She knew then that he felt it too—this connection between them.

The office door opened then, and just like that, the moment was over. Saxon jumped back from her, breathing heavily. Casey watched the way his eyes darted away from her to Sabel, who was standing in the doorway.

"Your turn, Saxon," he said.

"Okay. Thanks," Saxon muttered. He disappeared into the room without glancing back at her. Sabel followed. When the door was once again firmly shut, Casey felt her body become boneless. She touched her fingers to her mouth, still feeling Saxon, still tasting him.

"God. Damn. That man can kiss."

TWENTY-FOUR

Alex slouched back into the couch cushions as he watched Saxon and Casey leave the room. He felt balanced when they were there, and their departure left his wolf shifting uneasily. It was such a strange sensation, having another entity sharing the same skin as him, but in a way he also couldn't remember what life had been like before he'd been bitten.

"How much have you been told?" Rhett asked, not messing around. Alex liked that.

"About what?"

"Being a werewolf, but more specifically being a Bitten wolf."

He shrugged. "Not much. Figured I'd learn on the job."

Rhett's mismatched eyes narrowed on his face, and Alex fought not to squirm. Alex's wolf was cowering from the guy, his tail between his legs.

"He's showing his submissiveness to the more dominant wolf," Vaile said from his position on Rhett's right shoulder. "Instincts will save your ass more times than you'll know. Listen to your wolf."

Yeah, okay. Submissive. Alex could sense the power coming off Rhett. He could feel it coming off of Vaile, too. He thought back to all the times he got a strange vibe off of his best detective. It was like a tangible volatility. He was a living, breathing threat, but he hadn't realized at the time that it was his wolf doing all the talking.

Alex's eyes swung to the other male in the room. His dark hair was long in the front, shielding his blue eyes from view. He could taste the dominance of this one, but in his mind, Alex could see his own wolf snarling in challenge.

The guy took a step forward, causing Alex to jack-knife up from his chair.

"Sabel," Rhett said in a normal, almost bored tone. "Leave him. He doesn't know how it works yet."

"How what works?" Alex asked, still holding Sabel's eyes. A trickled growl filtered through the room, the smell of anger and irritation washing over him.

"I said enough!" Rhett said again. Inexplicably, Alex could feel his knees give out, forcing him back down onto his ass.

Breathlessly, Alex looked up again, not meeting Rhett's eyes. "What the fuck was that?"

The alpha's mouth quirked up. "Me. Pull that shit again and I won't stop Sabel from attacking you, and believe me you haven't got what it takes to meet him head-on just yet."

"He never will," Sabel spat back, his whole body vibrating.

"So," Rhett started, "you're now a Bitten wolf. There's just one little problem."

Alex shifted his gaze to Rhett's chest. "What's that?"

"We don't admit Bitten wolves into our pack. So, what does this mean for you? It means that tomorrow morning, you'll be returning to the Alfheim pack. I'll call Acario back to confirm, but it shouldn't be an issue."

"But I don't want to go back there. My life is here. My job is here."

"Get a transfer. It can't be that difficult."

Alex felt a tingle of anger surging forward. "I'm not going anywhere."

"I can't let you stay. Our pack is one of the last with a clean bloodline. We will not have it tainted if you mate with one of our females."

"There's only one female I want."

Rhett leaned forward in his chair. "Yes, from what I remember there was only ever one female for you. Saskia is mated. Werewolves do not take too kindly to other males stealing their mates away from them."

"It wouldn't be stealing her away. I can tell she doesn't love him."

"Be that as it may, Saskia would not leave Ezekiel for you. She is too honorable."

Alex knew that was the truth. Saskia wouldn't leave her mate for him. She'd made her decision. He should just leave. He should go back with Casey and try to start again. He sighed, defeated. "I know you're right, but I can't help the way I feel."

"Try to. Now, onto something that interests me more than your pining for a mated female," Rhett said. "What do you remember about who bit you?"

"He was a big motherfucker," Alex said, remembering sneaking up on the giant white wolf.

"Color?" Vaile asked. Alex glanced up at his detective and smiled a little. He had his professional face on.

"Pale. Not white, but not yellow. Like a cream color, I guess."

"Eye color?"

Yeah, he remembered exactly what color eyes it had. "Orange. Bright orange."

Vaile and Rhett exchanged a little glance Alex had no idea about. "Weight?"

"Fuck, I don't know. At least two-fifty. Maybe more."

Vaile leaned down to whisper something in Rhett's ear. The male nodded and focused on Alex again. "Vaile is going to take your scent to see if he can place who bit you."

"He can do that?" Alex asked, standing up quickly.

"Yeah, I can. Ever wonder why I'm so good on a crime scene?" Vaile replied, stalking toward him. "Just stand still."

Alex found himself obeying the order without a second thought. He stood rooted to the spot as Vaile hovered closer and closer. His nostrils flared a few times, a small growl slipping free of his throat. He'd only been there a matter of seconds when he pulled away, a sneer on his lips.

"It's who I thought it was," he said to Rhett.

"And who's that?" Alex asked, the detective in him needing to know.

"That doesn't concern you," Rhett replied. He sighed. "I want you to stay here tonight, Alex. Tomorrow you can return with Casey to her pack. Am I understood?"

Alex could feel the power in his words, could feel his will pressing against his wolf. "Yes, I understand."

Damn, he'd never done well with supplication. He was always the one giving the order, not taking any shit. He had to get used to a lot more than just turning into a wolf every now and again.

***

Saxon had never been so mortified in all his life. Casey didn't seem to have any moral standards whatsoever, but when her mouth had touched his, all thoughts of propriety left him. All he'd wanted was to touch more of her, to taste more of her.

Before his mind decided to leave on a Casey-completely-naked holiday, Rhett cleared his throat, drawing Saxon's attention to the more important things at hand.

Alex was escorted from the room by Sabel, the guy's hand wrapped securely around Alex's upper arm. Rhett sat behind the desk where he'd been before, and Vaile was standing at ease behind him.

"Saxon, I have a favor to ask. Casey will be leaving tomorrow to return home. Alex will be joining her. We're keeping Alex here overnight to keep an eye on his control over his wolf, but I need you to let Casey stay with you."

The situation wasn't ideal, but it was Rhett's order and he couldn't ignore it. "Okay."

"Swing by the house tomorrow morning with Casey and we'll see that they get on their way. That's all."

Saxon left the office, letting the door softly snick closed behind him. As soon as he was out in the hallway, Casey's sweet, sugary scent invaded his senses.

"What's going on?" she asked, standing up quickly from her place on the floor. "I saw Alex being dragged out of here by that scary wolf."

"Alex is being kept here overnight before he leaves for your pack lands tomorrow morning."

"Well, that's great, I guess." She looked up and down the hallway. "What about me?" Her small voice was amplified by how tightly she wrapped her arms around her torso; it was as if she was trying to protect herself from more than just a physical blow.

Saxon tried not to sound so excited about the next words to come out of his mouth. "You're staying with me tonight."

Casey's expression turned teasing, her body relaxing visibly. "Only if you buy me dinner first and treat me right, handsome."

Rolling his eyes, he led the way from the house. He felt her at his back, felt the way her eyes were lingering on the lower half of his body. His wolf enjoyed the way she stared, but the man was having a harder time accepting it.

Hard-packed snow crunched under his heavy work boots. Tilting his head back, he wondered how long the winter was going to be. It had seemed like forever already. The only bonus with weather like that was that there were more accidents from cars sliding on black ice. More accidents meant more cars coming in for repair at the shop, which also meant it kept Saxon busy.

And busy was good.

He popped open the driver's side door and slid inside. Breathing in deeply, he braced himself for being locked in with Casey. Cold air shot into the car when she pulled open the door, the draught carrying her sweetness in before she actually sat down. Saxon ground his teeth and glared out the windshield.

When she'd been in the back of the car on the drive over, he couldn't seem to keep his eyes off her. Whenever he could, he sought out her face in the backseat, hoping she would look at him, hoping she would smile.

Granted, she'd been the most annoying person in the whole entire world to have in the backseat of his car, he somehow he couldn't get enough of her. The slamming passenger door brought him out of his thoughts.

Shaking his head, Saxon started the car and shifted it into drive. Carefully maneuvering around the other parked cars, Saxon crept forward down the gravel drive.

"Is Alex going to be all right?" Casey asked softly. Saxon glanced over to find her staring out the passenger window. He watched her reflection for a few moments before the responsibilities of driving a car became too pressing.

"I don't see why not. Why?"

Casey turned her whole body to face him, her knees pulled up under her body. "Your pack kills Bitten wolves for no good reason."

There were tears in her eyes, and Saxon wanted to reach out to wipe them away. Stopping himself before he could do exactly that, his chest rose and fell gently as he thought. "They won't kill him. They'll let him return."

"Why? What makes him so different?"

"He has a history with the pack. Vaile and his mate are actually two of Alex's detectives."

Casey turned her head away, but kept her body toward Saxon. With a few shaky, jerky movements, she wiped the tears from her face. "Do you promise he'll be okay?"

"Of course." Saxon was irrationally irritated by her concern for Alex. "Can I ask you something?" he blurted out before he could stop himself. There was a serious malfunction between his brain and his mouth where Casey was concerned.

She turned to face him once more. She smiled slyly. "Only if I can kiss you again."

He jerked away from her words, his brain screaming "No!" but his body and his wolf screaming "Yes!" He was panicking. He knew it. Casey knew it. Goddamn! Why had she had to bring up kissing again?

Casey's satisfied laugh cleared his head for just a moment. "What's so funny?" he snarled without meaning to.

"You should have seen your face just now." She laughed out loud again, clutching her side. "It looked as if I'd asked you to inject yourself with radioactive material or something. Is the idea of kissing me so repulsive?" she asked.

Repulsive? Hardly. Saxon could still remember how her lips felt on his. He could still remember how his body had reacted to her heat. "Of course not," he finally replied stiffly. "But you just kind of threw yourself at me before."

She snorted. "I was totally yanking your chain. You're so damn uptight, Saxon. Has anyone ever told you that before?"

He grunted. *Uptight* was his middle name, apparently. He couldn't help it though. His parents' indiscretion had forced him to step up and take care of Saskia. "I did it just to get a reaction out of you," Casey added, still grinning although some of the shine had been taken out of it.

He ground his teeth. "Why are you so concerned with Alex's well-being?"

"Because he's my friend, of course."

"But you've just met him," he replied, keeping his eyes on the road.

"Maybe, but you just know when you meet someone whether you're going to be friends or not."

"It sounded to me like you annoy him."

He saw her shrug from the corner of his eye. "You might see it as being annoying, but Alex likes it. He's taken me under his wing. He likes me."

She sounded so damn sure of herself. He grunted, but said nothing more.

"You don't believe me, do you? Look, he could have left me behind when we left the pack house. I even told him which direction to go, but he let me follow."

"He could have just been using you," Saxon retorted, simply to get a rise out of her.

"Whatever," she replied. "Alex likes me for me."

"Unlike liking you for someone else?" he asked.

She snorted. "That's the story of my life." When he didn't say anything, she added, "I'm female for starters. That means I'm somehow more fragile than a male."

Saxon wanted to argue it was a fact, but he kept his mouth shut.

They were well within the city now. Keeping an eye on the rearview mirror, Saxon carefully weaved through the morning traffic. When Casey didn't elaborate, he glanced over at her. She had one brow arched in challenge.

"Got nothing to say about that one?" she snapped.

"What do you want me to say? That it's true?"

She huffed and crossed her arms over her chest. "Secondly," she pressed on, "I'm my father's daughter. Nobody wanted to piss off the alpha's daughter so I was treated differently when I was growing up and when I went to school."

"All right, so what is it that you want to do?" Saxon parallel parked up against the curb and cut the engine.

He opened up his door and stepped out into the cool morning air. He looked at Casey over the top of the car.

"Can we go upstairs?" she asked.

"Sure."

He unlocked the apartment building's glass front door, holding it open for Casey. Unwilling to stand in another tightly confined space with the woman, Saxon took the stairs up to his apartment.

Once they were inside, Casey sat down on the sofa, curling her legs beneath her once more. Saxon took the armchair opposite, not wanting to put himself any closer than he had to be.

She cleared her throat and looked at him. "Nobody has ever asked me that before." When Saxon didn't say anything, she added, "Promise you won't laugh if I tell you what I really want to do?"

"Sure," he replied. He knew he would do just about anything for her. Clearing his throat, he said, "You can tell me whatever you like and it'll die with me."

She looked down at her brightly polished nails and sighed. "What I really want to be is an enforcer."

"An enforcer?" he repeated, frowning. What kind of female wanted to volunteer for that job? He knew from his previous pack what kind of things he had to do in order to keep the pack safe. Had she thought all of that through?

Casey was looking at him cautiously. "You think it's a stupid idea."

"No, not stupid. Just...you do realize what's involved with being an enforcer, don't you?"

She nodded. "I follow my brothers around when they let me. I know that sometimes I'd have to kill other wolves. I know that sometimes I'd have to torture others and hunt vampires. I'm ready for that."

Saxon doubted that very much. In the Midgard pack, before his parents' fall from grace, he had been a rising enforcer. He could have been Captain if he'd been there a few more years. His wolf was dominant, but under Antain's rule he had to promise to remain a lower-ranked member of the pack. Back then that had been fine. Saskia had been his top priority.

But Saskia wasn't his responsibility anymore.

He looked at Casey and shook his head. Somehow this female had not only stirred his wolf to life, but also his ambition, with nothing more than her presence in his life.

"You don't think it's stupid?" she asked in a hushed voice.

"No. I don't think it's stupid. I think you know exactly what you want and that's a good thing. I had to give up a lot in order to join this pack, but talking to you has helped me to remember some of those things again."

"What did you want to be?"

Saxon brought one leg under his body, his elbow resting on the arm of the chair. "The same as you: an enforcer—a captain, actually."

"What happened?"

"My parents," he muttered, suddenly ashamed.

"I don't understand," Casey replied, standing up to perch on the free arm of his chair. Her cotton candy and candy apple scent fragranced the air, surrounding him and making his head slightly fuzzy.

Saxon sucked in a breath, leaned back and explained. "My father lost his job at the garage. He was a mechanic, too. We were in danger of losing the house. My parents couldn't see another way out. They began selling their blood on the black market to support Saskia and me."

Casey nodded, her expression solemn. "You obviously didn't know what was going on."

"Not at the time, no. That was the only reason we were allowed to leave and find another pack. Antain took us in and we've been here ever since."

"Why can't you become an enforcer now?"

He let out a frustrated breath. He couldn't believe he was discussing this with her. "That was the one stipulation we had to abide by in order to stay. I have to remain a low-ranking wolf, which means no enforcer job. I have to keep my nose clean and maintain submissiveness." He shrugged. "It's not so bad. The taint from our parents didn't seem to follow us here."

"And you're happy?" she asked, picking at the fabric of the armchair.

"As happy as I can be," he lied.

TWENTY-FIVE

Saskia felt sick to her stomach. She didn't think words could have that much power—to make you feel physically ill—but Zeke's had done just that. Her stomach clenched again, the words bubbling over in her mind.

A child.

"I'm going to be sick." Lurching from the sofa, Saskia ran to the bathroom off the hallway and threw herself down in front of the toilet. She'd only just managed to get the lid up before she heaved. Nothing came out, but black spots appeared when she blinked, pulsing with an impossible strength with each pound of her head. Sitting back on her heels, she pushed the hair from her face and stared into the empty bowl.

"I didn't think you'd physically get sick from the idea of carrying my child," Ezekiel said from the doorway. In an effort to stop any more black spots bounding up into her vision, Saskia turned her head just a little to look at him. His arms were crossed lightly over his chest, his expression lost somewhere between disappointment and regret.

"I'm sorry," she whispered. "I'm sorry. I'm sorry." She figured the more she said it, the more she would mean it, but if this is what happened when he merely suggested having children...

Zeke walked into the bathroom, dropping to his knees beside her. She whimpered when he laid his hand on her shoulder. "I know it's a lot for you to take in, but if you're serious about making a go of this with me, I'd like us to start trying for children as soon as we can."

She nodded, because that was what was expected of her, but she wanted to scream that she didn't want to have his children. Unfortunately, she really didn't get a say in it. She was mated to him, and the situation was hopeless.

"Saskia, I love you, but—" Zeke stopped midsentence as his phone started to ring. Standing up, he pulled the device from his pocket and answered it with what Saskia now knew as his professional voice.

"Kennedy," he said. "Yes, Ted. What can I do for you...yep...yep...damn it, all right; I'll be in the office ASAP." When he hung up, he gave her apologetic smile.

"You have to go into the office?" she asked.

"Yeah, sorry. I know it's a Saturday and I swore I wouldn't work any more weekends, but one of my high-profile clients was just arrested and I need to go and do some damage control with the media. Will you be all right on your own for a while? I shouldn't be any longer than two or three hours."

She sat back against the tub adjacent to the toilet and brought her knees to her chest. "I'll be fine."

Leaning down, he kissed her on the forehead. "I'm sorry. I'll make it up to you."

Saskia nodded, looking into his eyes. He turned to leave, but stopped at the door. "Thank you for telling me about Alex."

She counted his echoing footsteps as he walked through the house and left through the garage. When the door shut behind him, Saskia managed to get herself upright and standing in front of the vanity. She hardly recognized the woman staring back at her. The past twelve or so hours had been an emotional roller coaster she hadn't been able to get off of no matter how hard she'd tried.

Moving into the living room once more, she picked up the two dirty mugs and took them into the kitchen. She had just finished washing them and putting them in the drying rack beside the sink when there was a soft knocking on the front door.

Saskia wasn't expecting anyone. Looking through the curtains in the front window, she gasped. She stepped back from the window, letting the fabric slide through her fingers.

Fumbling with the locks, Saskia opened up the door. "Alex? What are you doing here? I thought you were at the pack house."

He ducked his head and rubbed a hand over the back of his head. "I was, but I couldn't stay there."

"Why not?"

He finally looked at her, his eyes molten. "I can't stay away from you." Saskia's whole body responded to the heat matched in his voice, her heart stuttering in her chest.

She shook her head, slowly removing all those illicit images from her mind. "Alex, you can't—"

"I know I can't, but I just...I can't not see you again. They're sending me back with Casey tomorrow morning. I spent a year staying away from you in the same city and it damn near killed me. I can't imagine living four hundred and fifty miles from you is going to be any easier, so I need this."

Suddenly aware that he was still standing on her porch, she opened the screen door and took a step back. "You want some coffee?" she asked with a smile.

"Coffee would be great," he replied, his voice suddenly graveled. He stepped inside and shut the door behind him. "Is Zeke around?"

"No. He's had to go into work for a few hours."

"So I get at least a few hours with you then," he muttered.

Although Saskia wanted to spend every second with Alex, she shook her head. "I can't let you stay for any longer than a half an hour."

"Why?" he demanded, his wolf pushing forward in his eyes. He'd taken a step toward her, too—just a hair's breadth away from touching her. But he didn't touch her, and Saskia wanted to cry out, to demand that he did.

Instead, she sucked in a steadying breath. "Because you shouldn't be here."

He grinned at her. It was cocky and she liked the way it looked on his lips. "Come with me then."

Laughing gently, she turned and walked toward the kitchen. "I can't do that, either."

"Why not?"

She stopped and, without turning around, she said, "Because I've made my choice, Alex."

Before he could protest, she rounded the corner into the kitchen. Her pulse was pounding in her ears, but she forced her body to work, to put one foot in front of the other. Filling up the water container on the coffee maker, she turned it on then began boiling water in the kettle for some tea for herself.

Alex was there when she turned around. Despite the long island bench separating them, she could feel him surrounding her.

"You made the wrong choice," he said softly. "You made the wrong choice and you know it."

"I made the right choice for me at the time," she replied, surprised her voice came out as steadily as it had. Inside, her emotions were churning violently.

"So you admit you made the wrong choice?" he challenged, walking around the bench that had been providing her with the only protection she had from him.

"It wasn't at the time," she mumbled back, looking at her feet to avoid the desire in his eyes—afraid that he would see it mirrored in hers.

Alex drew her face up with his finger under her chin. "But it is now." He pushed some hair away from her face. "Now, you realize that being mated to Zeke is wrong for you."

She shook her head, refusing the burning in the back of her throat to result in tears. "You were human. Saxon would have killed you. I didn't have a choice."

He reached for her, his fingers skimming down her arms and taking her hands into his. "You wanted me then like I wanted you. The only thing that stopped you was me being human. Is that right?"

She nodded, swallowing back the tears. She knew what he was doing. She knew what he was trying to make her see. "What's stopping you now then?"

The first tear escaped, sliding down her cheek. "I love him." It was the worst lie she had ever told in her entire life.

Alex jerked away from her like she'd just slapped him. His fingers slid free from her hands and she mourned the loss. "Bullshit."

Saskia met his glare, but couldn't hold it. Alex had seen straight through her.

"If you loved him—truly loved him—you'd be fighting a hell of a lot harder for him right now."

"I came back here, didn't I?"

Alex reclaimed the distance. "I saw the look of desperation on your face when you got out of the car. I saw how you were with him. You don't love him. I doubt you even like him very much."

She cleared her throat, brushing the tears from her face. "He's a good man."

Alex sighed and turned away, starting to pace. "I may be new to this whole werewolf thing, but I think there's more to wanting to stay with a man than him being good. There's got to be some love there, Saskia."

"I love him," she repeated.

He turned. "Not as much as you love me, though."

"I—" Saskia floundered, unable to say anything constructive because Alex was right. She did love him more than Zeke. She loved him above her own life.

Walking toward her, Alex slipped his hands onto her hips, pulling their bodies together. "Cut open my chest, Saskia," he said softly, "it's your name etched into my heart."

<hr>

Alex felt Saskia tremble against him. Closing his eyes, he breathed in her scent, memorizing it since this was probably the last time he would get to see her. He'd tried to make her see that now he was one of her kind, they could be together.

But Saskia wouldn't listen. She'd made a promise to Ezekiel and he couldn't hold that against her. She was a better person than him because he would have thrown it all away to be with her.

He guessed he was just hoping she would do that—that he would be important enough to her that she would damn the consequences and just be with him.

Alex realized his error now though.

"It's too late," Saskia whimpered. He looked at her, hating the look of desperation she was trying to hide from him.

"It's never too late," he said in reply, catching a tear as it slid down her cheek. The tiny droplet wobbled on his fingertip for a moment before sliding away. He couldn't help but think that was what his relationship with Saskia had been like.

Fleeting.

Beautiful and perfect, but still fleeting.

Damn it, he couldn't let her go again. "Come away with me," he said again—already knowing the answer but not caring. He'd ask her a million times if on the millionth time she said yes to his request.

"I can't."

Leaning his forehead against hers, he dragged in a deep breath and let it out. "I know. I just had to ask."

Being this close to her made her scent stronger. She smelled amazing to him; the mixture of her shampoo and perfume sure to linger in his memories forever.

"Can I ask you for one thing before I leave?"

Saskia nodded infinitesimally.

"One kiss."

She pulled away slowly. "I can't." The way the words came out made her sound as if she was immense pain.

Alex's grip tightened around her waist. "I won't take no for an answer," he replied, his mouth slanting over hers before she could protest. Saskia's lips were soft against his mouth, the taste of them sweet like fresh strawberries dipped in cream. She melted beneath him, her body falling into the line of his.

His lips trailed down her throat, nipped gently at her skin. Saskia moaned, stifling the sound by closing her lips around it. Alex's wolf was almost purring like a cat. He had wanted this ever since he'd first laid eyes on Saskia.

Right there with you, buddy.

Mate, his wolf echoed.

Alex tried to ignore the call, knowing how futile it was, but his wolf wouldn't let the thing go.

Mate, he repeated.

She belongs to someone else.

That seemed to shut him up for a moment. Alex's mind cleared and he focused on every second he had with the amazing woman in his arms. His mouth was in the hollow of her throat, Saskia's head tilting up to give him the access he so desperately needed.

His new instincts said this was a vulnerable position for her, that she trusted him to be there. Alex groaned and licked his way up the column of her exposed throat. Saskia's fingers dug into his shoulders, her heart beating so loudly Alex couldn't even hear his own pulse roaring in his ears.

He claimed her mouth once more, squeezing his eyes shut tight as the burn of tears told him he'd pussied out in front of her. His one last kiss was coming to an end. His lungs were beginning to scream for fresh oxygen, but he couldn't bring himself to draw away from the soft sweetness of Saskia's mouth.

Reluctantly, he pulled away from her, relaxing his grip around her back.

He was panting, but proud to see that she was, too. Saskia's fingers came to her mouth, pressing gently against her lips. She hadn't moved away from him yet, and he took advantage of the closeness by pressing a light kiss to each of her eyelids.

As he pulled back, she tilted her chin up, forcing their lips to meet once more. "Make love to me," she whispered against his mouth.

Fuck yeah; he was on board with that, but...

"What about Ezekiel?"

Her blue eyes were swimming with tears. "Don't be responsible now," she replied, kissing him again. "Make love to me and let me deal with the fallout."

Saskia let out a little yelp of surprise when Alex drew his arm around the back of her legs, scooping her up and holding her close to his chest. She relaxed into him, her head dropping to rest under his chin.

This was where she belonged, he thought as he walked down the hallway, having no idea which way to go.

"Next door on the left," she murmured without raising her head. Her fingers were clutching at his shirt, holding him to her as if he would change his mind. Well, there was no way that was going to happen.

Alex strode into the room, hooking his foot around the door and pushing it closed. The whole room was painted deep red and gold. The drapes hugging the sides of the window were lush and heavy, matching the bedspread on the bed in the center of one wall.

The scent of vanilla sugar cookies lingered in the air. Alex suspected the candles dotted around the room were used often...probably used by Zeke when he was seducing Saskia. Pushing that thought from his mind, he focused on the woman in his arms. He was finally going to make love to her, and he wanted it to last. He wanted her to remember him when he was gone.

Gently placing her on her feet, Saskia was trembling ever so slightly as she looked up at him.

Even though it killed him to say it, he murmured, "You can change your mind, you know."

"I haven't changed my mind. I'm nervous and excited about being with you. I've thought about this, dreamed about this so many times in the past year. I just never thought you'd be here. I never thought I'd get this chance."

"Baby, I'm going to worship you."

Leaning in, he kissed her slowly; he savored the flavor of her lips, the feel of her warm skin beneath his fingertips. Saskia's back arched, pushing her breasts into his chest. Biting back a groan, he pulled away, feeling his wolf jostling for position with him.

Saskia's fingers traced the side of his face, her usually dark blue eyes aqua. *Mine.*

"Mine," he echoed, his words coming out in a rumbling growl, heavy with possessiveness. Saskia's hands slid down his chest, her eyes following them.

Biting her lip, she looked up. "I'd like to you see naked." There wasn't a demand in her voice. If anything, she almost seemed to be embarrassed to be saying so, but Alex wouldn't deny her anything. How could he?

Dropping his hands from her back, he began pulling the bottom of his shirt up, away from his body. Saskia's hand landed on his and she shook her head.

"I want to do it, if I can?"

"Baby, you don't have to ask permission," he replied, his voice hoarse and thick with desire. Truth be told, he liked that she wanted to take control of the undressing. It would give her the chance to stop if she wanted to. But he hoped like hell that she wouldn't.

With strong, sure fingers, Saskia pulled the shirt from his body. Her breath left her mouth on a shudder, her eyes fixated on his chest—on the scars from his previous life. Licking her lips, her wolf's aqua eyes met his.

One finger traced the outer rim of one of the bullet wounds. "I hate that you were harmed." Lowering her mouth to his chest, her tongue darted out, lapping at his skin, making him draw in a hissed breath. She moved to one of the others close by before he could say anything. He'd opened his mouth to reply, but a groan was all he managed to get out.

One hand wound around the back of her neck, holding her mouth to his chest. He didn't want her to stop. It was almost as if the long-sealed wounds were finally healing.

Saskia's hands found the top of his jeans, her fingers rubbing the top of the fabric while all the time her mouth didn't leave his chest. She'd moved down to his nipple, rasping her tongue against his flesh until he had trouble focusing.

His hips jerked forward when her hand dropped, grazing past his erection pressing greedily against the fly of his pants.

Saskia seemed to purr a little. Looking up, she blinked the aqua from her eyes and smiled sheepishly. "Sorry. My wolf is pushing through."

Tipping her head back with his finger, he said against her mouth, "Don't apologize for that. My wolf is fighting pretty hard right now, too."

She touched his face with a look of amazement in her eyes. "You have such control."

Had he? He didn't think so...at least not where Saskia was concerned. Covering her hands with his, he fused their mouths together again. Saskia's hand fell from his chest to his stomach before brushing against the waistband of his jeans once more.

She pulled at the button until it slipped free. As the zipper slid down, Alex's hips flexed forward again—his body reaching out for her touch. Saskia slid her fingers under the jeans and the waistband of his boxers, guiding them down his legs. Her eyes were on his face the entire time until they finally dropped. Alex watched her lick her lips hungrily, the scent of her arousal kissing his skin.

Seeing her looking at him like that was such a fucking turn-on. Alex kicked the jeans from his ankles, standing long and proud before the woman he loved. Saskia started to drop to her knees, and as much as Alex would have loved to have her mouth on his cock, he didn't want to sully their one and only time together. She deserved to be worshiped, and she shouldn't be on her knees when that happened.

Taking her by the upper arms, he stopped her, shaking his head. With questioning eyes, Saskia asked, "Why?"

"You deserve better than that."

TWENTY-SIX

Saskia allowed herself to be pulled back onto her feet, her heart aching with how perfect a gentleman Alex was being. Her eyes darted down to his waist, a sense of longing gripping her body.

"Hey," Alex said, drawing her attention away. "Let me make love to you properly." She nodded. He took a step toward her. "Now it's your turn," he instructed, but instead of him reaching for her clothes, he seemed to take a step back and wait.

Saskia felt the blush creeping up her cheeks; he wanted her to undress for him. The thought both turned her on and frightened her, but this was the only chance she had with Alex and she wanted him to remember it.

Her hands shook as she reached for the buttons of her blouse. Starting from the top, she slowly undid each one, watching Alex's eyes grow more and more heavy. When the last button was free, she shrugged the fabric off her shoulders and boldly met Alex's eyes.

When he didn't move, she reached behind her and unhooked her lace bra. Pulling it forward, it fell from her breasts—her nipples already puckered and over-sensitive. Alex growled, but remained where he was. It must have been sheer willpower that kept him there, and Saskia appreciated just how strong of a male he was.

She tugged at the button on her jeans, hastily pulling the zipper down. Alex's bright orange eyes dropped, and she knew he would be seeing the matching panties that went with her bra. With her fingers at her hips, she slid the jeans and her panties off together.

Saskia fought the urge to cover herself. Nudity wasn't the issue. It was because it was Alex, and she wanted him to like what he saw.

"You are so incredibly beautiful," he croaked, finally approaching her. He kissed her chastely. "Thank you."

"For what?"

"Wanting me as much as I want you."

Saskia blushed, not having the words to tell him she'd always wanted him—ever since she found him in that alleyway. Cupping the back of her neck, Alex pressed his body against hers, running his hands through her hair. She felt every ridge, every hardness, of his body and never wanted to be without it.

He kissed her with the passion he had in his eyes, claiming her mouth, leaving her dazed when he finally pulled away. Alex moved her toward the edge of the bed, the backs of her knees hitting the mattress. He lowered her down, crawling up her body as she went.

Her skin suddenly felt too tight for her body with Alex stretched out alongside her. She watched his fingers run over her body, starting at her neck, drifting down to her collarbones, her beasts, her stomach. Annoyingly, he missed the part she really wanted him at, skipping over the juncture between her thighs in favor of her legs.

"You have amazing legs," he murmured. "They deserve to be revered just as much as the rest of you."

His hand lifted one of her legs a little off the bed, his thumb pressing gently behind her knee. A jolt of desire shot through her, making Alex laugh gently.

"Turn over for me, baby, and I'll show you just what else I can do."

Saskia did as Alex asked and turned over onto her belly. She felt the mattress shift beneath her as he repositioned himself. Gentle pressure met one foot, Alex's fingers pressing into the ball with equal amounts of strength and softness.

A soft moan slipped from her throat as his hand swept her instep. It felt as if her entire body was on fire, all her nerve endings shooting off at the same time. Alex moved onto the other foot, giving it the same treatment. Saskia was panting heavily when he moved onto her calves. He massaged them with the same tenderness as he had her feet, sliding his thumb up and down the muscle.

"Does that feel good?" he asked.

Saskia managed a sound between a groan and the word "yes" before melting into another puddle on the bed. Alex chuckled, his expert fingers trailing up the backs of her thighs. With each sweep, his thumb trailed higher and higher, getting oh so close to her weeping heart.

She wiggled her hips, trying to guide him closer, but frustratingly his hands swept away. He trailed kisses up over each buttock, his hands following with a soft massage. She'd never experienced that before, but found she enjoyed the way her blood seemed to boil with the attention. Perhaps it was just because it was Alex doing the touching though.

"Be patient," he chastised gently. "All in good time."

Saskia groaned into the mattress, hating how much she was enjoying this attention. She would never be getting this kind of dedicated attention after Alex left her life again. *Stop it. He's here now. I should just enjoy it.*

And that was exactly what she did. Alex asked her to turn over again. He spread out alongside her again, his fingers dragging gently between her hip bones, just missing the mound of soft curls between her thighs. Electricity sparked with each soft caress, making it harder and harder for Saskia to lay still. She wanted his hands on other parts of her body and she wished it could last forever.

Sensing where her thoughts were going, Alex slowly got off the bed. His erection was starting to hurt, but damn it, he was going to take his time with her. Saskia sat up suddenly.

"Is something wrong?"

He shook his head, knowing his voice would be gravel when he finally did speak. "No, baby. Nothing is wrong." He reached for her hand and tugged her from the bed so she was standing in front of him. He tucked a few strands of hair behind her ear, cupping her neck. "Close your eyes," he murmured, staring at her, marveling at her beauty.

Saskia shut her eyes and let out a small breath. Alex leaned down and placed a small kiss on one eyelid, breathing in her delicate scent. She sighed and he kissed the other eyelid. From there, he expanded his territory, dropping light kisses along both temples, the corners of her eyes, her cheekbones. When he reached her jaw, she tilted her head to the side to give him access.

Alex spent some time concentrating on the area behind her ears, kissing her, licking her until her whole body was shivering with anticipation. When he cruised down her neck, he used his teeth to gently nip her skin. Her skin was blistering hot beneath his mouth. Swiping his tongue along the vein, he just sat back and enjoyed the way her body reacted to him.

"Alex. Please," she whimpered, her body writhing beneath his mouth.

"Shhh," he murmured.

"Please," she begged, her hands running through his hair and pulling his head up. She held his eyes. "Please."

Although Alex could have spent the next year exploring her body, he realized that her desperation was partly from desire, and partly from anxiety. Her mate was supposed to be getting home soon, and Alex had to be gone before then.

The fact that he was doing this with Saskia in their bed didn't sit particularly well with him, but he reasoned that he wouldn't get another chance. He kissed her deeply, pushing his tongue into her mouth, drawing even more moaning from her throat. Fuck, he loved the sounds she made for him. When he was worshipping her body, the noises she made for him had driven him on, had forced him to enjoy every damn minute of her body.

Sliding a hand between their bodies, he trailed his fingers down her stomach, through the hair of her mons and down between her thighs. Alex bit the inside of his cheek when he felt how wet she was. Yeah, all that groundwork he'd laid had certainly paid off. He worked his finger between her folds, rubbing her clitoris with a slight pressure. Saskia's body tightened up against his, her mouth next to his ear making small little whimpers.

If she kept that up, he didn't know how much longer he could last. His cock was weeping at the tip, begging to be inside her. Saskia's hand grasped the base of his erection, her fist squeezing gently. Alex's spine bowed without warning, exposing his throat to her.

What Saskia did next shocked the hell out of him. Her teeth were suddenly on his throat—not biting down, but just there. He could feel the pressure of them on his skin. He could sense his wolf mirroring his human form. With his head thrown back, he exposed his throat to Saskia's wolf, wanting to be dominated by her for a moment.

With her mouth against his ear, she said in a growled voice, "Take me."

Alex lost control of his body and thoughts for a moment. One second they were standing beside the bed, the next he had Saskia pinned to the mattress, his cock hovering at her entrance.

Winding her arms around his neck, she pulled his mouth to hers and flexed her hips up, driving the length of him inside her. Warm, slick heat greeted him and Alex could have sworn he'd just died and gone to heaven.

He was panting heavily, unwilling to move because if he did, it would all be over. All the build-up, all the desire would be gone just because he hadn't been able to keep a lid on his orgasm.

He didn't get to think about it for too long though because Saskia's hips swiveled without warning. Desire—hot and sweet—shot through his body. Saskia began chanting his name, her body undulating beneath his. He was powerless to stop her, torn between wanting to come right there and then and pulling out of her so he could have a little T.O to collect his thoughts.

"Saskia," he managed to say, his hips surging forward without his brain's permission. His body knew exactly what it wanted.

"Alex," she echoed, running her hands through his hair. She squeezed her eyes shut for a moment, and Alex was sure he was hurting her. He forced himself to stop only to have Saskia's eyes fly open.

"Don't stop, don't stop, don't stop," she begged. "I'm so close."

He couldn't deny her even if he tried. He began rocking into her body again, feeling his body tighten with the orgasm he'd tried to dam up and keep at bay. He was utterly powerless to stop it though because as soon as she started to pant his name, it was all over.

"I'm coming," he said.

"Me, too," Saskia replied with a groan, her mouth open. Saskia's inner muscles began to contract around his cock, drawing his orgasm out.

"Fuck!" he yelled, his voice hoarse. His cock kicked inside her, jerking over and over again until he was completely spent. Everything else went fuzzy at that point, and when he came to, he was collapsed on top of Saskia.

"I'm so sorry, baby," he said, scrambling up so he wasn't crushing her. She pulled him back down, smiling.

"Don't go yet. I like feeling your weight on top of me."

Alex relaxed back, but rolled a little to the side. With his cock still inside her, he rested his head on her chest. Her free hand ran along the length of his arm, playing with the dark hairs that were scattered there.

She was quiet for so long that he had a suddenly horrendous thought. What if she regretted having sex with him? What if she'd changed her mind, but she didn't say anything? Lifting his head, he looked at her face and instantly relaxed.

She was asleep, a smile tugging at the corners of her mouth. He guessed the doubts were all his own.

TWENTY-SEVEN

Casey woke the next morning, her and Saxon's last words echoing in her mind.

Are you happy?

As happy as I can be.

Lying in his sister's bed, she replayed the entire conversation. She'd had no idea that his parents had done that. She had no idea what she would have done had the situation been reversed. She didn't know whether she could do it. Give up her dreams just because of someone else's actions, someone else's bad decisions?

Then she laughed.

What was she talking about? That was exactly what was happening with her. Her father was dictating what her future was going to be like. Her brothers were doing the same thing. Hell, even her mother had jumped on the Casey-needs-a-mate bandwagon.

At least she still had options. Her father hadn't picked out a mate for her yet, so she still had some time to change his mind.

Yeah, that's been working out great so far.

"Argh!" she huffed, looking up at the ceiling. "I had to be born female, didn't I?" Closing her eyes, she listened to the sounds of the city waking up around her. Buses were rumbling by, car horns were blaring. It was a novelty for her since she was used to waking up to bird song and her brothers' snoring.

Her chest expanded with a large intake of breath, which she held until she could hear her heart pounding loudly in her ears. When her lungs began to burn, Casey released it. She could hear Saxon moving around in the room beside her, and her whole body flushed.

Did he sleep in the nude, or was he a pajama-wearing kind of guy? She hadn't found any when she'd been snooping, but then again, she hadn't gone through his bedside drawers. She continued the fantasy, putting off getting up. If she got up, she'd have to get dressed. If she got dressed, she'd have to leave the apartment. If she had to leave the apartment, she had to leave Saxon behind and her wolf didn't like that so much.

She was doing well until the urge to pee took over.

"Stupid bladder," she grumbled, throwing the blankets from her body and sitting up. Unlike Saxon's room, there was no bathroom attached to Saskia's room. Stumbling to the door, Casey cracked it open a little and did a quick survey of the open-plan living room and kitchen.

Tugging down the hem of the t-shirt she was wearing , she huffed. It barely covered her ass, but at least she still had her panties on, and if Saxon happened to get an eyeful, so be it. He shouldn't be looking anyway, but she was secretly hoping he would.

Opening the door wide, Casey scampered out, her eyes on the bathroom door on the other side of the kitchen. She was so focused on her prize that she hadn't heard Saxon's door open. He walked straight into her path, but there was no way of stopping her momentum. Casey ran into the male, practically bouncing off him. She braced herself for the pain of impact, but when a strong arm wound around her waist and the scent of Saxon filled her nostrils, she just about melted from a combination of relief and contentment.

"Careful," he said, gently righting her. His eyes traveled down her body, going lower and lower until she knew they got stuck on the hem of her shirt. Allowing herself a moment to enjoy the lust in his eyes, she wiggled free of his grip.

"I've gotta pee," she announced, sauntering off in the direction of the bathroom, knowing his gaze was now attached to her ass. With the door shut behind her, Casey relieved herself and washed her hands.

When she finally glanced up at the mirror, she jumped back. Frantically, she began patting her hair down, trying to smooth the little offshoots that were covering the majority of her head. She looked like she'd just stuck her finger in an electrical socket for funsies.

When her red hair had been somewhat tamed, she opened up the bathroom door. Saxon was by the sink, laying a spoon down on the side. In his hand, he had a cup of coffee.

Casey put on her best indignant face. "You could have told me my hair looked like it had been spanked by a Troll doll." Crossing her arms, she waited for his reply, which was a smile and a sip from his mug.

"I have to say I really wasn't paying too much attention to your hair."

Casey flushed and dropped her eyes. Bastard! "Whatever. I need to get dressed." She walked past him, holding her head high, her chin jutting forward. She sank back against the bedroom door when it was closed behind her, letting out a deep breath. Stripping off her shirt, she stepped back into her jeans, slipped on a bra and pulled the tee back on. Sitting on the edge of the bed, she put her feet into her shoes and laced them up.

Stepping back out into the main living space, she felt less ruffled by Saxon's presence. Sitting down at the kitchen bench, she watched him cook breakfast.

"Over easy," she announced cheerfully.

He looked at her over his shoulder, a dark brow arched. "I beg your pardon?"

"My eggs. I like them over easy."

He turned around, crossing his arms over his chest, spatula still in hand. "Who says I'm making you breakfast?"

Casey snorted. "What kind of host would you be if you didn't?"

She watched the way his eyes narrowed in annoyance before he turned back around. "How many do you want?" he asked tightly.

"How many are you having?" She enjoyed the way his shoulders tightened.

"Half a dozen," he replied. There was a smirk in his voice that she didn't appreciate very much.

"Sounds good to me."

Saxon growled, but started cracking eggs into the giant skillet on the burner. Casey watched him work, falling into a blissful Saxon's-ass-in-tight-jeans-stupor till he asked, "Are you leaving after breakfast?"

She blinked. "Huh?"

He turned to look at her, repeating his question. "Gee, don't you ever listen?" he added.

"Not when there are more interesting things to hold my interest, no," she retorted, eyes darting south. The muscle in Saxon's jaw began jumping and he muttered something under his breath as he turned back to the eggs. After a few seconds of terse silence, he snapped, "Well?"

"Well, what?" Casey replied happily.

He growled. "Are you being obtuse on purpose?"

"I don't know. I'm not sure I even know the meaning of that word."

Slamming the spatula down hard onto the benchtop, Saxon whirled around —nostrils flaring, steam practically coming out of his ears. "You know what?" he spat out. "I don't get you."

"What's to get?" she asked with a shrug, her tone the polar opposite of Saxon's. "I'm awesome. End of story."

"Last night we had a serious conversation, the first serious conversation we've had. Why are you being obnoxious again?"

"Obnoxious?" she shouted, standing up. "I might be annoying. I might even be *obtuse*—whatever that means—but I am *not* obnoxious, Saxon McMillan." She started toward the front door, snarling over her shoulder, "Forget about breakfast."

Pulling open the door, she slammed it shut and started toward the lift. Riding down, the car shook and shuddered, which had Casey looking desperately at the buttons, praying that the lights kept descending. After what felt like a lifetime, the doors began to open, but they were taking too damn long. Jamming her body in between them, she braced her back against one door and used her feet to leverage the doors open faster. They resisted for a moment until she heard something snap.

Stepping out into the lobby, she got the hairy-eyeball from an elderly woman. Casey brushed it off, smiling sweetly at the human and pushing out of the building. Looking left and right, she realized she didn't have a ride to the pack house now; she didn't even have any cash for a taxi. Shoving her hands into her pockets, she started walking in the direction Saxon had driven to the pack house.

She had a photographic memory when it came to things like that. All she had to do was be taken to a place once and she remembered the way. Yet another reason why she should be allowed to become an enforcer.

As she walked, she maintained constant vigilance over her surroundings. Enforcer 101 states you should always be aware of what buildings and people are around you.

Check.

Apartment blocks soared above her head, while a lot of shopfronts showed off their wares at eye level. There were a lot of alleyways and private parking areas behind some buildings, which Casey paid particular attention to. She didn't want anyone to come sneaking up on her.

She glanced up as the door of a cafe up ahead opened. A stunning woman dressed in vintage Chanel had the arm of a slick-looking businessman. They were chatting to one another. Casey figured it was some stockbroker having breakfast with his wife before work.

She stepped out of their way as they passed, but then something strange happened. The woman's head turned, her gold eyes boring into Casey. Casey's wolf stood up, her top lip pulling away from her teeth.

Wolf.

Casey dropped her eyes quickly, only peeking up when the woman passed. She didn't know whether she was a Helheim wolf, but if she was, what was she doing with a human male?

Her interest piqued, Casey followed behind the pair, keeping her distance.

TWENTY-EIGHT

"You are such an asshole," Saxon muttered to himself, not for the first time. He shovelled another forkful of eggs into his mouth and chewed. He wasn't hungry anymore. He only ate because he'd cooked a dozen eggs and wasn't in the habit of wasting food.

Casey had stomped out of the apartment fifteen minutes ago, and he had no idea whether she was actually coming back, or when. Placing his fork down, he sat back in his chair and stretched his arms over his head.

He thought that last night he'd finally gotten past the bratty attitude Casey seemed to have in spades. The conversation they'd had had really meant something to him. He hadn't shared that stuff with anyone before—not even Saskia.

Getting up, he scraped all of his breakfast into the trash, rinsed his plate and put it in the dishwasher. The damn female was making him lose his appetite, too.

The harsh shrill of the doorbell brought him out of his thoughts. With quick steps, he pressed the buzzer on the intercom.

"Yeah?"

"It's me. Let me up."

Saxon hit the buzzer and let Casey into the building. She'd obviously only left to walk off her anger, which was a good idea. They had both needed the space after he had lost his temper with her.

He opened up the apartment door before she could knock. Casey marched in like she owned the damn place, making his wolf sit up and pay attention. Grinding his teeth, Saxon shoved the door closed and turned his eyes to the red-head who was slowly turning his world upside down.

Crossing his arms over his chest, he said, "I thought you were leaving."

She groaned in frustration. "I don't have time for this. You need to take me to Rhett, like, now."

Saxon arched a brow at her. "What's the rush?"

"I *knew* you'd be a jackass about this," she huffed. "I just need to get there, get Alex then get the hell of here since we're both so damn unwelcome." Crossing her arms, she came to a stop in front of him. "So, are you going to take me, or what?"

She was sexy when she was pissed. Saxon groaned internally, wanting to kick his own ass for getting so side-tracked. Dragging a hand down his face, he said, "Let me get my keys."

ONE OF CASEY'S LEGS BOUNCED UP AND DOWN IN THE FOOTWELL AS Saxon drove them both out to the pack house. He couldn't help but glance at her from the corner of his eye every few seconds, trying to assess her mood.

The expression on her face was tight—pinched—like she was sucking on a lemon. Her eyes were fixed on the road ahead of them, her fingers rapping against the knee of her other leg.

Saxon hated the silence. Although he'd only known Casey for a short time, he had become used to her inane commentary and general childishness, which made absolutely no sense at all. He preferred more mature women, but his wolf had eyes only for her.

He cleared his throat hoping to catch her attention. When that didn't work, he took his hand off the gearshift and touched her bouncing leg. She startled then twisted around to face him; it was almost as if she'd forgotten he was in the car with her.

"You seem a little distracted," he said.

Casey held his gaze for a moment before turning away.

There was an unbearably long silence.

"Why did you say those things to me before?" Casey said the words to the passenger window, but they were meant for him.

Saxon shifted uncomfortably in his seat. "I'm sorry I said that to you, Casey. I was just—"

"Out of line?" she snapped back hotly, cutting him off. "Being a gigantic asshole?"

He glanced at her quickly before fixing his eyes back on the road. "Both those things, I guess."

"I already knew you were an asshole," Casey retorted, "but I can't figure out what I'd done wrong to make you say those things to me."

Her voice had softened, tugging at Saxon's heart. He let out a deep breath. "I guess I was just upset that the girl I was talking to last night wasn't there anymore," he replied, knowing how stupid it sounded. She was still the same person. "I just thought..."

She turned her whole body toward him. "You thought what?"

Well, he might as well tell her the damned truth. "What I told you last night...I've never told anyone those things before." There, he'd said it. He peered at her to see what she would say, but there was a strange expression on her face. It almost looked as if she was pleased and grateful and surprised all wrapped up in one.

"Not even Saskia?" she eventually asked.

He shook his head. "No, not even Saskia. I couldn't tell her what being admitted into the Helheim pack had cost me. It didn't matter anyway. Saskia was all that mattered and I would have taken any deal they'd offered if it meant Saskia would have a safe place to live, and a chance to be mated to an honorable male."

"You really love her, don't you?" Casey whispered. Saxon nodded. She then said, "After I went to bed, I thought about whether any of my brothers would do the same thing for me—you know, abandon their lives as enforcers just so I could have the opportunity to live a proper life away from scandal."

"And what did you come up with?"

Casey picked at some non-existent lint on her pants. "Only Oliver would do that for me."

"Is he your big brother?"

"One of them." Casey shifted her body to look out the windshield again. "He's the second eldest, after Hunter."

"How many brothers do you have?"

"Four."

"Can you tell me about them?" he asked, not wanting her to stop talking. He had intentionally missed the turn-off for the pack house so she could stay with him a little longer.

"Hunter is my eldest brother. He's the pack's beta. Hunter can be a little stuck-up, but I love him all the same. Oliver has always looked out for me, especially when Hunter was picking on me when we were growing up. Dylan is next and we've been confused for twins before. My youngest brother is Riley. He wanted to be like Hunter so bad that he used to be his shadow when he was younger."

Saxon noticed that Casey's face lit up when she was talking about her brothers, which in turn made him smile. "What about your parents?"

"My dad might be alpha, but he's a real teddy bear deep down. He and my mother have been mated for nearly one hundred and twenty years, but..."

Saxon glanced over. "Casey?"

She shook herself a little. "But nothing. They're still together and happy."

Saxon could tell she wasn't giving him the whole truth, but he let it go. It was getting to a point now where he couldn't hide the fact that they'd been driving for over an hour and hadn't reached their destination yet. He finally pulled off at their turn-off and drove the rest of the way in silence. Casey had told him a lot about her family, which seemed only fair after he had told her so much about his.

When he pulled into the circular drive, Casey seemed a little tense. Could she be feeling as sick in the stomach as he was about her leaving? He cut the engine, and they both sat there for a moment.

"Casey, I—"

"Don't say it, Saxon," she replied without looking at him. She heaved a deep sigh and opened up the door. "Thanks for driving me out here. Have a great life."

TWENTY-NINE

ALEX COULD SMELL SASKIA, BUT HE COULD ALSO SMELL EZEKIEL IN THE sheets they were lying in. The erection he'd been sporting for another round with Saskia suddenly felt so damn wrong, although it was too late for that when he really thought about it.

They had already done what they shouldn't have, and in Saskia and Zeke's bed, too. Saskia sighed gently in her sleep and pushed her ass up against Alex's hips. He was spooning her from behind, marveling at the way her body fit so perfectly into his.

Glancing up, he found the clock on the bedside table glowing patiently. Fuck. He had to go. Their lovemaking had taken longer than he thought it would. Two hours had already passed, and Saskia's mate would be home soon.

"Saskia," he whispered, his fingers stroking the sinfully-soft skin on her belly. She sighed again, but didn't wake up. He tried again. "Saskia, wake up."

Nothing.

He hadn't wanted to resort to what he was about to do since she was so uptight about it already. "Ezekiel will be home soon," he said, pressing a kiss behind her ear.

Saskia jerked up and away from the cage of his arms, the sheet dragging away from her body. Alex's erection suddenly got another injection of blood at the sight of her gloriously naked breasts.

"Oh my god," she breathed, glancing between the door to the bedroom and him. "Oh my god," she repeated, more frantically. Her eyes finally fell down to his waist, taking in the tented sheet hiding his arousal. She blushed and looked away.

"Oh...my," she said once more, except the urgency was gone this time. She looked back at him with heavy-lidded eyes and smiled.

He felt like beating on his chest like a fucking caveman for that look from her, but Alex stopped her from reaching for him. "Your mate will be home soon."

Saskia's eyes widened, her nostrils flared. "Oh!" she jumped from the bed, collecting up her clothes, and throwing Alex's at him. She got dressed quickly then whirled around at him.

"You have to get out of the bed. I need to change the sheets and get these ones in the wash as soon as possible."

Alex stepped into his pants and pulled the shirt over his head. "Baby, calm down. There's still some time."

"No! There is *no* time. Alex, if he smells you on the sheets, he'll know." She was getting frantic now, her blue eyes darting around the room. Alex was still seated on the edge of the bed, watching her unravel.

He shook his head. Here was the regret that she'd given in and made love to him. He should have known it couldn't have lasted. He stood up and started stripping the bed slowly.

"Alex, no, you have to go," Saskia said, still standing on her side of the room. He turned around to look at her. She looked so...afraid. Not wanting to fight, not wanting to ruin what they'd done with each other anymore than it had already been ruined, Alex gave in and turned to leave.

Saskia following him to the door, her anxiety filling his nose with an acrid sting he never wanted to smell on her again. He reached for the handle and stopped. This was it. This was the last time he would see her. He was sure of it this time.

He turned and took her into his arms. She was stiff at first until a sigh shuddered from her mouth and she melted into him. His arms tightened around her back, holding her against him. Burying his nose behind her ear, he inhaled her scent, putting it in a box in the stores of his brain to drag out again when he missed her like crazy.

"I don't want you to go," Saskia sobbed. "I'm sorry I'm pushing you out, but if—"

"Shh," Alex interrupted. "It's okay," he cooed. "I get it. I would only cause you more problems. I don't want that. I want you to have a happy life, Saskia. That's all I ever wanted for you."

She clutched at him a little harder, her sobs getting louder. "I'll miss you," she managed, her words slightly muffled.

He swallowed past the golf ball-sized lump in his throat. "I'm going to miss you, too."

"I only just got you back."

Pulling away from her, he tipped her head up, their eyes meeting. Damn it, he wouldn't cry like some pussy. Ah, fuck, the tears were coming anyway. He pressed his lips to hers, letting them say the goodbye he could never voice.

Resting his forehead against hers, he let out a deep breath. "I love you," he murmured. "I'll love you forever and then for an eternity after that."

The tears leaked from Saskia's eyes as she scrunched them up tightly. "I love you, too."

Alex's heart stuttered in his chest before resuming the *thump-thump-thump* routine. Saskia said she loved him. He already knew that she did, but to hear it from her beautiful lips, was enough to make his chest swell with pride.

With great reluctance, Alex stepped away from her, opened up the door and walked away from the woman he loved, because it was the right thing to do. He started down the road, heading back toward town where he could get a drink. Fuck, he felt like he needed to soak in whiskey to make himself feel better.

After a good three quarters of an hour mentally kicking his ass for leaving Saskia with Ezekiel and their happy life together, Alex found a place that was enough of a dive to suit his foul mood. He slumped down at the bar, ordering a whiskey with the least words possible. He had no desire to talk to anyone more than he had to. No. He just wanted to sit there and lick his damn wounds by himself.

———

Saskia felt numb. Alex hadn't turned back to look at her, which only cemented the fact that he was finally letting her go. Closing the door softly, she laid her forehead against the cool wood and wept for the loss. Her heart was breaking all over again, shattering into a thousand tiny pieces. Losing him once had broken her. Losing him twice obliterated her. She didn't know how long she stayed there for, but the urgency with which she pushed Alex from her apartment suddenly caught her attention again.

Zeke would be home soon, and she had so much to do. Pulling herself together, Saskia wiped the tears from her eyes and straightened her spine. She didn't regret making love to Alex. She was just worried that Zeke would find out, but at least she had the chance to erase every piece of physical evidence that he had even been there.

Walking into the bedroom, she looked at the bed and instantly felt the heat suffuse her body, starting between her thighs and moving up her torso and into her chest.

The way Alex had touched her brought a blush to her cheeks. She had never been caressed like that before. It was almost as if he thought she was the most precious thing in the world to him, and he was determined to be gentle. An involuntary moan escaped her lips, remembering the way his fingers had massaged and applied the slightest and most delicious pressure to different parts of her body. It was more than she had expected of him, and it was perfect.

Snapping out of her sex-haze, Saskia began pulling the quilt cover from the quilt, the sheets from the mattress. Everything had to be washed. All signs of Alex ever having been there had to be removed. Bundling up the linens, she carried them to the laundry, and began shoving them into the machine.

Once the cycle started, she wandered out into the living room and inhaled. Alex's scent was still lingering in the air. Hastily, she ran into the bedroom and picked up one of the scented candles and brought it back into the living room. She lit it quickly then pulled the vacuum from the hall closet to erase the final traces of Alex's visit.

When she was done, she had vacuumed the entire house, paying particular attention to the bedroom. She couldn't afford to have Zeke even suspect that the other male had been there.

Satisfied, Saskia remade the bed, plumping up the pillows and making sure it was just as it had been when her mate had left. She was running through all the places Alex had been when the phone on her bedside table rang.

"Hello?"

"Hello, beautiful," Zeke said. "I'm leaving the office now."

"Okay," Saskia replied steadily. "I'll see you soon."

"Before you go, I thought we could go out for dinner to celebrate," he said. "What do you think?" She could hear him get into his car as he spoke, the engine coming to life.

Celebrate? What could she possibly have to celebrate? She had just let the love of her life slip from her fingers for the second time. "What's the occasion?" she asked, making sure to keep her voice light.

"Honesty, beautiful. I feel like this is a new start for us." The directional signal ticked softly in the background. "I want to mark the occasion."

She bit her lip and looked down at the bed, seeing a flash of her and Alex in her head. "Okay."

"Great. Traffic is light so I should be home in about ten minutes. I'll get changed and we can go out straight away. Wear something nice. I'm going to take you to *Valentino's*."

Saskia swallowed hard, hoping her voice would still be steady. "I can't wait." She hung up and let out a shaky breath. Ten minutes. She had ten minutes to hop in the shower and wash Alex off her skin. The thought made her sad because once that was gone, she would have only her memories to remember him by.

Undressing quickly, she wandered into the bathroom and shut the door behind her. The shower took a long time to heat up, and she waited impatiently, knowing that Ezekiel would be home soon—knowing she barely had time for a shower let alone washing her hair, too. She would just have to leave it.

When the temperature was right, Saskia stepped under the spray, avoiding getting her hair wet. It would take forever for her to dry if it did. Lathering up the soap, she washed her body, remembering the way Alex had touched each part.

When she couldn't smell him on her anymore, she stepped out of the cubicle and started towelling off. She heard the door between the garage and the house close, and her heart started to pound. Nervous energy battered her body. Would Ezekiel notice? Would he question why the house was so clean, or why the sheets had been changed after only a few days?

There was only one way to find out.

With one final deep breath, Saskia secured the towel around her body and opened the bathroom door.

THIRTY

Brax was jolted awake as the Hummer's giant tires rolled over the rutted road, throwing dirt and gravel up in its wake, the engine roaring with the extra torque. Brax looked over at Ulf, seeing the huge grin plastered onto his face.

They'd been driving through the night to get up into Niflheim territory, heading farther and farther north toward the alpha's house. Mathias had phoned just as they'd left Avon and the Jotenheim wolves behind, informing them that Malcolm, the Niflheim alpha, had arranged for them to meet with two of their Bitten wolves.

Happy fucking days.

"You hungry?" Ulf asked, glancing in Brax's direction.

"I could eat," he replied, squinting at the newly rising sun. "Did you sleep?" he added, studying the five o'clock shadow on Ulf's jaw.

"I pulled over for a couple of hours just before we crossed the border."

"You should have woken me up. I could have driven," Brax muttered, rubbing the sleep from his eyes with the back of his hand.

"I tried. You pulled your Beretta on me."

He had? "Fuck, man. Sorry."

"It's fine," Ulf replied, a steady smile pulling up his lips. "So, I slept for a couple of hours then kept on driving."

Brax stretched out his slowly cramping back. "Well, at least we made good time. Malcolm isn't expecting us until mid-afternoon."

At midday, Ulf brought the Hummer to a stop outside a house which was essentially three or four boxes stacked on, or around one central box. They were up in an area called Holiday Hills where thick stands of pines surrounded the property, giving it the shelter and protection many alphas craved.

Getting out of the car, Brax looked up at the modern building, admiring the honey-colored cedar cladding and the glass wall on one side. That stuff was probably bulletproof and had more security features than a prison.

Ulf led the way up the stone driveway, his expression serious. Rapping on the door, Brax stood at Ulf's right shoulder and assumed a similar expression on his face. A few moments later, a young male opened the door.

"Yes?" he asked. Brax scrutinized his face. He had hair so dark it had licks of blue in it. His eyes stirred with his wolf, shifting from ice-blue to gold for just a second. On his neck, a tattoo of a snowflake could be seen skirting the edges of his shirt collar.

"I'm Ulf, and this is Brax. We're here from the Asgard pack to see Malcolm. He's expecting us."

The male looked over Ulf then Brax before giving them a tight nod. "You're early," he said, leading them down a hall.

"We had a good run on the roads," Ulf replied.

"You must have driven through the night," the young male added.

"You must be right," Brax piped up, earning himself a glare from Ulf. Right. *Don't* piss off other wolves in their territory. Brax shrugged and looked ahead again.

They stopped at a room where the Niflheim wolf knocked then opened the door, ushering Ulf and Brax inside. A dark-haired man was sitting in a wing-back chair in front of a fire. In his hands, he held an iPad, his finger swiping over the screen. When Brax looked over, he discovered he was playing Angry Birds, and Brax liked him already.

The male who'd escorted them in cleared his throat. "Malcolm, these are the Asgard wolves you were expecting."

The guy stood up, balancing his iPad on the arm of his armchair. His eyes skimmed over both of them, evaluating their wolves. "You must be Ulf," he said.

"Yes, Malcolm," Ulf replied, his gaze fixed on Malcolm's chin. Brax was looking at the carpet under his boots, but he could feel Malcolm's eyes fixed on him.

"And who is this?"

"Another one of our enforcers, Braxton," Ulf answered for him. Brax grimaced at the use of his full name and looked up for just a moment.

"It's an honor to meet you, Alpha."

Malcolm threw his head back and laughed. "Cut the bullshit, Braxton. I get enough ass-kissing from my own wolves." He looked over at his wolf by the door. "Thanks, Neva. Get us a couple of beers will you?"

Brax gave Ulf a sideways glance and grinned. Damn, he liked this male.

"Take a load off," Malcolm said, sitting back down in his chair and turning off his iPad. There was only one other available seat, which Ulf took. Brax stood behind him, flanking his right.

"Now, what's this about exactly? Mathias said you wanted to speak to some of my Bitten wolves?"

"We'd like to, if that's possible," Ulf replied, sitting forward in his seat, resting his elbows on his knees. "Mathias sent us here to interview some of the newly Bitten wolves so we know what we'll be up against, as we think whoever is biting these humans will be moving east soon."

"What..." Malcom started, but glanced at the door where there was a knock. "Excuse me. Come in," Malcolm called.

It was Neva with the beers. He handed them out to everyone, starting with his alpha, then excused himself from the room. Brax put the bottle to his lips and sucked back a gulp. It wasn't Lag, but it would do. Brax glanced down and noticed that Ulf hadn't sipped from his bottle yet, just had it resting on the arm of the chair.

Malcolm took a drink and placed the sweating bottle onto a small table near his chair. Pulling a phone from his pocket, he slid his finger over the screen.

"What's your number? I'll send you the name and number of one of the wolves you can speak to." Ulf began reciting his cell number to Malcolm, who punched it into his phonebook. "His experience was relatively normal and safe, so he'd be more likely to speak to you about the experience. He also knows you'll be stopping in to see him today."

"How many Bitten wolves do you have?" Brax asked.

Malcolm glanced up from the screen. "We had three. One we had to put down because his wolf dragged him too far when he went through the Change. The other wolf we still have is a little...damaged from going through his first shift."

"All right, got the info," Ulf replied, checking his own phone. To Brax, he said, "Are you ready to go?"

Brax drained the rest of his beer and placed the empty on the desk in the corner. "Yep."

Brax and Ulf hopped back into the Hummer, entering the address Malcolm had given them into the GPS. They were heading to a place around fifty miles away. Ulf put the Hummer into first and started down the road, the cage of metal vibrating along the unsealed road as its wheels hit the ruts and runnels grooved into the surface.

Once they were on the highway again, Ulf sank back into his seat and cruised through the traffic. Brax noticed that most of the cars simply got out of his way, and he didn't really blame them. The car was nearly five thousand pounds of driving steel and guaranteed death if someone got in the way.

Ulf flipped his directional signal on and pulled off the highway twenty minutes later, following the directions the GPS gave him. Another half an hour of semi-sealed roads and more fir trees than Brax thought even possible, they pulled up onto the gravel shoulder in the middle of fucking nowhere.

"Let me do the talking," Ulf said as he opened his door. Brax nodded and followed Ulf up the mud and gravel driveway concealed by the low-lying fir branches bordering the road. The house that appeared in front of them was small and redefined the word 'dilapidated' all on its own. The only thing that didn't fit with the rest of the facade was that the drive had been cleared recently—salt and grit sprinkling the surface and crunching under their boots as they hiked up to the front door.

Ulf lifted his fist and hammered on the thing when they got there, waiting just a few seconds before repeating the process. His beta looked at Brax over his shoulder, a brow raised in question. Brax shrugged.

"He could be out?" Brax suggested, peering through one of the windows beside the door.

Ulf grunted. "He knew we were coming."

There didn't appear to be any movement that Brax could see from the crack in the gingham drapes. "So what do you want to do?" he asked, his breath fogging up the glass as he spoke.

Brax got his answer half a second later. Ulf brought his boot down onto the door, sending sharp splinters of wood flying in every direction, snapping the locking mechanism with a sharp crunch.

Brax cocked an eyebrow at him. "Overkill much?" he said, squatting down onto his haunches and pulling the doormat up. He felt around with his fingers until they clutched at a key. Brax showed it to Ulf with a smile. "All you had to do was find the key."

The big guy shrugged. "Whatever. My way was faster."

Ulf cautiously entered the house. Brax followed, figuring there was no need to keep up the nice-and-quiet routine when they'd announced themselves so well.

Stepping over the entrance rug, Brax's gaze drifted up to the mezzanine level of the hunting-style lodge. An old couch rested like a downed animal in front of the stone hearth, a musty blanket draped over the back. Opposite that was a dated kitchen with olive-green appliances and a chipped Formica bench top. There was a doorway on either side. While Ulf took the left, Brax went right, pushing open the narrow wood door. It was the bathroom, decorated in the same olive-green as the kitchen. Brax looked around, opening drawers and the vanity above the sink. The place had been cleared out.

Ducking back out into the main part of the house, Brax saw Ulf emerge from what must have been the bedroom.

"He's gone. The drawers and closet are empty."

"Same in the bathroom."

Ulf cursed and pulled out his phone.

"Who are you calling?" Brax asked, crossing the distance between them, running his fingers over the blanket on top of the couch.

"Malcolm. Maybe he'll know where he might be."

Ulf put the phone to his ear, speaking softly to the alpha on the other end. While they were talking, Brax had a closer look around the place and noticed that there weren't any photos hanging on the walls or on the mantle.

Moving to the kitchen, he opened up the cupboards and checked out the situation in there. There was a solitary pot with a lid, one plate, one bowl, one cup, one fork, knife and spoon. Brax looked up, frowning as Ulf said his goodbyes.

"What's the story?" he asked.

Ulf shook his head. "Malcolm said he'd spoken to the guy this morning, who'd told him he wasn't planning on going anywhere today since he knew we were coming."

Brax leaned back against the counter and crossed his arms over his chest. "So what now?"

"Malcolm suggested we go to the other Bitten wolf's place to check that out. He's going to text me the address."

Ulf's phone beeped right on cue. "According to Malcolm, this other guy's place is about thirty clicks east of here."

Pushing himself upright, Brax straightened his tee and moved toward the door. "Let's get this done then."

ALEX WAS DAMNED NEAR DROWNING IN LIQUOR AT THE BAR WHEN HE WAS finally thrown out after being unable to pay his tab. The little issue of money had started to become a big issue.

Running a hand through his hair, he decided he should get back to the pack house. After hitching for as long and far as he could, he legged the last five miles, arriving to a full house.

As he stood in the entrance hall stomping the snow from his boots, he heard the clinking of silverware on China plates coming from the dining room. He wasn't interested in playing happy families, though, not with his foul mood, so he proceeded to the stairs that would lead to the room he was shown when he'd first arrived.

"You smell like you bathed in whiskey," Vaile said from the doorway. Damn, the bastard was quiet. "You need to eat."

"Not hungry," Alex replied, putting his hand on the banister.

"You can lose your wolf to hunger."

"I don't care."

He growled. "Don't make me order your ass around, motherfucker."

Alex glared at him, still not used to Vaile speaking to him like that. "Fuck you," he snarled back, his fuse shorting out.

Vaile's eyes flashed blue. "Get your ass in here, right now."

Alex felt the power in his words, and he suddenly had no choice in the damned matter. Stifling a groan, he followed the guy into the dining room where a large group of wolves and humans were eating dinner together.

"Sit," Vaile commanded, pointing at a free chair. Alex glanced at the people on either side of him. One was Sabel. Beside him was a female wolf with blonde hair and black eyes. On the other side of the empty chair was Larissa. She smiled at him warmly, watching him walk around to take his place.

"It's good to see you, boss," she whispered once eating had resumed.

"It's good to see you, too, Grey."

"Turkey?" she asked, gesturing to the spread set out in front of him. There were three huge turkeys along with a dozen plates of vegetables. Alex's stomach growled loudly at the sight of it all.

"Sure."

Larissa leaned over to grab him some slices of turkey from the serving dish, but Vaile stopped her with a hand on her arm.

"Serve your damn self, D'Angelo," he muttered, taking the plate from Larissa's hand and practically throwing it back in Alex's face.

Alex did just that—loading up his plate with turkey with all the trimmings. As he ate, he looked around the table. Rhett was at the head—of course—but to his right was a stunning, dark-haired female with violet eyes without a plate in front of her. She turned those eyes on him.

"I wouldn't make eye contact with her," Vaile said under his breath. "Rhett doesn't like it, and it's only because of his good graces that you're staying in the house tonight and not in the cage in the basement."

Alex turned to look at Vaile. "Who is she?"

"Indi, Rhett's mate."

"Why isn't she eating?"

"She already did," Sabel replied. Alex looked at him quizzically.

"Am I missing something?" he snapped.

"Yeah, a whole damned lot. Indi is—"

"Sabel," Rhett said quietly, drawing everyone's attention to him. The alpha shook his head at the other wolf, who simply shrugged and went back to his food.

"Eat," Rhett commanded. "You'll need your strength for the return trip tomorrow."

THIRTY-ONE

Ezekiel shut the door to the garage behind him and let out a deep sigh. He was glad to be home. His client—the less-than-legitimate businessman whose name had thankfully been supressed from the media—was out on bail under strict orders not to leave the city. Ezekiel had left his associates to handle the rest of the fallout, desperate to get home to his mate.

"Saskia?" he called when she didn't come to greet him at the door. He put his briefcase down. "Saskia, darling? Are you here?"

Figuring she was getting ready for their dinner together, he walked down the hallway, noticing how clean the house was. She must have done it after he'd left so he could come home to a tidy home. He was so lucky to have her.

Pushing open the bedroom door, he saw that she had changed the sheets on the bed, too. Maybe it was a cathartic thing for her to do—to clean the house—almost like wiping the slate clean. The shower was running in the ensuite, Saskia's gentle humming barely audible over the drum of water.

A pile of her dirty clothes was just by the door, looking out of place in such a spotless home. Unbuttoning the first few buttons on his shirt, Zeke bent down to scoop up the dirty laundry to put in the hamper.

He paused, a sudden haze of red slipping over his vision. His wolf had pushed forward forcefully in his mind for a moment. As he righted himself, his nostrils flared and a possessive growl escaped his throat.

What was that smell?

Sticking his nose into his mate's dirty clothes, he drew in the scent and snarled. That male—Alex—was all over them. Ezekiel took in the spotlessly clean room, the changed bed sheets, but refused to let the traitorous idea stick, not until he could ask Saskia himself.

The water was suddenly shut off. Zeke spun around to face the door, waiting for his mate to open it up. Before the door was all the way open, he pounded closer to her, putting them nose to nose.

"Zeke?" Saskia gasped, clutching at the top of her towel. "What are you doing?"

She tried to step away, but he took her arm and held on tight. Saskia winced at the strength in his fingers, her eyes widening, her heart rate increasing.

"Zeke? What's wrong? You're scaring me," she said in a small voice. Her eyes darted down to her clothes still bundled under his arm. "W-why do you have my things?"

"Why do they smell of Alex?" he asked in reply, his voice twisting with his wolf's growing rage.

Her blue eyes were back on his face, but not looking him directly in the eye. "They were the same clothes I was wearing when I found him and Casey," she replied unsteadily.

Zeke didn't know whether that was true or not, his wolf's hackles rising even further. He had to trust his mate, and he had to mark her as his own in order to push the murderous thoughts about killing Alex from his mind.

Dropping Saskia's clothes, he pulled her to him, forcefully pushing his mouth against hers. She tasted like she always did, she felt like she always did, but his wolf wasn't happy. His mouth broke from hers. Roughly, he tilted her head back until her throat was exposed. She gasped and whimpered, but even her surprise wasn't enough to stop him. His lips trailed down her jaw to her throat, his teeth opening over her delicate skin and biting down. Ezekiel was aware he was being too rough with her, but he was driven by a baser instinct to mark his territory again.

Saskia's gasp was accompanied by the taste of her blood.

"You're hurting me, Zeke," she whispered, her head still tilted up. "Please."

Zeke's jaw clamped down harder, causing his mate to jerk away in pain. Blood was dribbling down her throat, the indentations from his teeth clear. She wiped at the wound, her eyes wide when she looked at her hand.

She had taken a few steps away from him. Zeke snarled low in his throat and tackled her again; his wolf raged on the inside. He wasn't satisfied. He needed more.

Taking large clumps of her hair in his hands, he wrenched her head back. She cried out in pain, but Zeke was too far gone. He forced her mouth to his, but she managed to turn her head away despite the hold he had on her hair. Zeke's nose ended up behind her ear, buried in her hair. There was no mistaking it this time. Alex was all he could smell.

Rearing back from Saskia, he forced her to look at him. Tears were rapidly tracking down her cheeks.

"Why can I smell Alex on you?" he snarled.

Saskia winced and tried to pull away. He yanked her back hard. Zeke heard her cries, but ignored them.

"Why. Can. I. Smell. Alex. On. You?" he demanded again. "He's all over you." He released her to pick up her panties. They were wet, the combined scents of Alex and her overwhelmingly strong. "Did you fuck him?" he asked, throwing her soiled panties into her face.

Saskia caught them, her head bowed as she looked at the sheer fabric in her hands. "Please, let me explain," she whispered. "I can explain."

"Explain what?!" he roared. "How my mate *fucked* another male?" He ripped the quilt from the bed, pulling the pillows, throws and sheets off with it. "Did you fuck him here in our mated bed, too?" he spat, picturing the two of them tangled up together.

She looked up, tears running freely down her cheeks. "I can explain."

Zeke blinked, letting the rage wash over him. He couldn't fucking look at her. He turned to leave, and had made it to the hallway, when Saskia tugged on the back of his shirt.

"Zeke!" she cried. "Please give me a minute to explain."

Without thinking, he raised his hand to her, slapping her hard across the cheek. Saskia's head spun around, her hand over the place where his palm had just been. Zeke was breathing heavily, his chest pumping up and down at a frenetic pace. He wanted to tear Alex apart for what he had done, and a small piece of him wanted Saskia to suffer, too.

That was all it took—the want—and his wolf took over. He dropped to his knees, tearing at his shirt.

"Ezekiel," Saskia whimpered. Zeke looked up at her and snarled. She began backing up a few steps, looking hastily at the bedroom door. When his wolf began punching through his body with snapping bones and torn ligaments, she disappeared. The door slammed shut and Zeke let his wolf have him.

———

Saskia's cheek stung so much her eyes were still tearing up. When his palm had connected, she could have sworn she heard bone crack, too. With her cool palm against the injured cheek, she just knew that it was fractured at worst and going to bruise at best.

On the other side of the door, she could hear Zeke going through the Change. The whole time she'd been talking to him, his eyes had been his wolf's. She'd always liked his wolf because he was a gentle soul who would do anything to protect her. But now she knew better. Now she knew that his wolf could be dangerous, and she also knew that she would never be able to get the image of his silver-eyed wolf from her mind.

The bedroom door suddenly rattled violently on its hinges. Saskia jumped back, her legs hitting the edge of the bed. A snarl curled under the door, hitting her senses on more than one level, her heart beginning to pound too hard in her chest.

Ezekiel hit the door again, an ear-splitting creak shooting through the room.

Saskia dragged herself into the middle of the bed, her arms locked around her knees. Zeke was going to break into the room and tear her to pieces. She knew it, and god help her if she didn't deserve it.

Her eyes bounced around the room, looking for something she could use as a weapon should Zeke manage to knock the door down completely. The idea of hurting him any more than she already had made her feel sick, but she couldn't just lie down; she would defend herself the best she could.

Her gaze fell on the nightstand beside the bed. The door shuddered again, the sound of Zeke's claws scratching at the wood getting louder, more urgent. Saskia glanced between the door and the phone on the nightstand. She could call Saxon, but the chances that he'd be able to force Zeke to shift back were slim to none.

No, there was only one person now who could help her. With shaking hands, she picked up the phone and dialed the pack house. Rhett picked up on the second ring.

"Saskia?" he asked when he answered.

She squeezed her eyes shut, tears of relief leaking out. "Rhett, I—"

Her words were drowned out when Ezekiel's wolf charged at the door again, a split forming in the wood.

"Saskia? What the hell was that noise?"

Zeke snarled loudly through the door before striking it once more.

"Saskia? Talk to me. Tell me what's happening."

"It's Zeke," she whispered. "He's shifted and is trying to break down the bedroom door." She didn't want to explain why this was happening. She was too ashamed of herself for giving in and making love to Alex, even if it was only to say goodbye.

"Are you hurt?" Rhett asked, his voice edged with sharpness. Her skin prickled with his power.

"I'm fine, but please hurry." Zeke struck the door again, causing Saskia to whimper. "Please," she begged.

"I will. Saskia, get into the bathroom. If there's another door in his way, it'll give us the time to get to you."

Zeke slammed his giant body into the barrier between them again, a large chunk of wood punching out from the impact.

"Please hurry. He's almost through the door."

"I will. Get in the bathroom. Lock the door and sit tight. We'll be there as soon as possible."

Saskia hung up the phone, quickly found some clothes to change into and shut herself inside the bathroom. She flipped the lock shut, pointless as it was. Shaking, she closed the lid on the toilet and sat down. Her whole body was trembling, goosebumps breaking out on her skin. Waiting to be rescued from her enraged mate wasn't quite how she pictured she'd be spending her Saturday.

As she waited, she could hear Ezekiel's claws going to work on the wood, his teeth tearing through the door to get to her. And when she closed her eyes, all she could see were his silver eyes so full of rage.

THIRTY-TWO

"It just doesn't make any sense," Ulf said, his hands cranking down hard on the steering wheel. "Why would both Niflheim Bitten wolves just up and leave without telling their alpha?"

Brax shrugged into his seat. "Maybe they didn't realize they had to?"

"They'd been with the pack for near-on six months. That would have been plenty of time to learn the rules."

"Maybe they're rebels?" Brax suggested, earning himself a glare from Ulf. "What? I'm just spit-balling here."

His beta muttered under his breath, but kept his eyes fixed on the road ahead.

"Ulf? Did you notice anything about the places of the last wolves?"

"Apart from them being empty, no."

"While you were on the phone to Malcolm, I had a poke around in the kitchen and the living room. There weren't any personal photos hanging on the walls or on shelves or anything."

"Maybe they aren't the sentimental types? They probably didn't have any memories to bring with them if they'd been bitten in another city."

Brax looked out the passenger window, his mind churning. "Maybe, but in the kitchen, there were only the bare essentials and in the second place, the fridge had been cleared out and turned off. Why would someone do that if they were only going away for a little while? It was almost as if they weren't planning on coming back at all."

Ulf grunted—his version of assent. "Let's just wait and see what things are like with the Midgard wolves. If they're missing, too, I'd say your theory might have some legs to stand on."

"THE PACK HOUSE SHOULDN'T BE TOO FAR AWAY," ULF SAID AS HE MADE A sharp left onto a quiet country lane. They had been driving for a couple of days. As he looked out the window at the apparently infinite number of trees closing in around the car, he came to the realization that alphas were all creatures of habit; none of them made their homes in city centers. They all seemed to need trees, trees and more trees...plus a shitload of land for their wolves to run in.

Tall, thick oaks lined the road, framing it as the Hummer tore up it. Brax let his head fall back against the headrest, his brain rattling around in his skull with each jolted movement. Eventually, the car pulled to a stop and Brax got his first look at the Midgard alpha's house.

The giant red-brick house stood proudly in the middle of the woods, claiming its position. Out the front, three small children were all bundled up against the chill in the air. They were playing under the watchful eye of a female. Her head jerked up when she saw the car, her eyes narrowing before calling the kids back to her and hustling them into the house.

"Berke is expecting us, right?" Brax asked. Ulf pulled the handbrake up and peered through the windshield.

"Yeah. Mathias called him this morning to confirm we could come around today." Ulf slid from the car, slamming the thing door behind him. Brax followed because, really, what other choice did he have? He dragged in a lungful of cold air and stretched out his back noisily.

Ulf was already at the door, knocking. Brax had just ascended the short flight of stairs onto the porch when the door opened. The guy on the other side stepped out onto the porch, his dark, shoulder-length hair swinging with his easy gait.

He smiled at them both, revealing his straight, white teeth. "You must be Ulf," he said, holding out his hand. Ulf took it, the men pumping their hands up and down a few times. "I'm Glendon, the beta of the Midgard pack."

"It's nice to meet you," Ulf replied. "This is Brax," he added, gesturing with his chin to where Brax was standing. Glendon offered his hand to Brax, also.

"Come on in. Berke is just finishing up a meeting with some of our pack members. Would you like some sweet tea while you wait?"

"No, thank you," Ulf replied, his eyes doing a sweep of the entrance hall.

"I'll take you up on the offer," Brax said cheerfully. Glendon nodded and excused himself.

A moment later, a line of five or six males walked past the living room, disappearing from view. Brax and Ulf looked at each other then turned their attention to the male now standing in the doorway. He looked too young to be the alpha of a pack, but then again Rhett was also considered too young.

Nice one, you asshole. You almost made it a whole day without thinking about the past.

Brax lowered his eyes when Berke walked into the room, Glendon on his heels carrying a tray of glasses and a pitcher of sweet tea. The alpha settled into the armchair opposite Brax while Glendon played home-maker, serving everyone with a smile.

"Mathias told me you wanted to talk to some of my Bitten wolves," Berke began, taking a sip of tea.

"Yes, Alpha," Ulf said. "We'd like to speak with them to find out details of who bit them and maybe get a description."

Berke nodded. "Yes, of course." Pulling out his phone, he asked Ulf for his number. "I'll send you their business cards and you can contact them directly. If they ask whether I'm aware of you being here, tell them to call me. I'm sure it won't be an issue, but if they do make a fuss, I'll make sure they cooperate."

"Would they be unlikely to cooperate otherwise?" Ulf asked mildly.

"They can still be a little skittish around strangers, especially strange wolves."

"Did they make it through the Change unscathed?"

Berke shrugged. "More or less. It's a traumatic experience—being bitten and shifting for the first time—and there are bound to be some long-lasting side-effects."

Ulf's phone beeped.

"How long do you think you'll be in our territory?"

Ulf and Brax shared a look before Ulf answered. "If we can talk to them right away, I would say no more than two to three hours."

Berke smiled. "Perfect. Call me if you have any issues with my wolves."

"Thank you, Berke. I will," Ulf replied, his eyes lowered in deference once more. Brax stood up, placing his empty glass on the tray and following Ulf from the room.

Back in the car, Ulf punched the address into the GPS without bothering to check the details of the text message again. Starting up the engine, he drove them in silence to the first of the two addresses they'd been given. The house they pulled up at was just as they'd expected it to be—empty. They went through the place after a little B&E and found the same scenario as before; the house was barely lived in.

"Let's hope we have better luck with the other address," Brax said, hoisting himself up into the Hummer and buckling himself in. It was only a short drive to the next place, and Brax stepped onto the sidewalk of the middle-of-the-range suburb and stared at the house. Maybe this place would be different.

"We might be in luck," Brax said, thinking aloud.

Ulf grunted. "Don't get ahead of yourself. The guy has to answer the door first."

Ulf knocked and Brax could hear footsteps approaching. The door opened quickly, a petite blonde standing on the other side of the jamb.

"Yes?" she asked, brushing some of her long hair behind her ear.

"We're here looking for Samuel," Ulf said, taking a step back, probably to appear less intimidating.

Brax inhaled her scent, his brain logging that she was human and probably didn't know about werewolves and other things that went bump in the night.

"You're looking for Sam? Why?" the human shot back suspiciously.

"We're a couple of his buddies," Brax broke in, dropping one of his dimple-encrusted million-dollar smiles. When she spoke again, her words were directed at Brax rather than Ulf.

"Sam left this morning on a business trip."

"Do you know where he went?"

She frowned. "East. He said he was heading east."

"What kind of business is he in, sugar?" Brax asked, gently shoving Ulf out of her line of sight. His beta stiffened at his touch, but moved.

She laughed nervously. "Do you know what? I really don't know. He never really speaks about it. We only met each other a month ago."

"But you live together already?" Ulf retorted, disgust clear in his voice.

Fuck. Brax gave Ulf a sideways glance and pressed on. "What my *buddy* meant to say was you must be a special woman to keep Samuel content at home."

The female's chest inflated a little at the compliment. "Sam's a great guy."

Brax dazzled her with another smile. "I'm sure you being a great woman helps things along."

The female blushed that time.

"So, do you think you could give us his cell number? We haven't seen him in a few years and actually had to look him up the old-fashioned way."

The woman's eyes darted to Ulf quickly then back to Brax. Pushing open the screen door, she stepped back. "Let me just get my phone. I have a terrible memory for numbers."

Ulf let Brax lead the way inside, stepping to one side in the small hallway, waiting for the girlfriend to return. She came back with a pen and grabbed Brax's hand. She etched Samuel's number onto his palm.

"You can reach him here," she said. Brax smiled and dipped his head toward her ear.

"Thanks, sweetheart," he murmured before looking at Ulf. "Let's go and catch up with old Sammy-boy."

THIRTY-THREE

Alex was climbing the stairs up to his room when the sound of a ringing phone drifted up from the office caught his attention. Peering over the banister, Alex could see the door had been left ajar, a small sliver of light slicing out into the hallway. He watched as Rhett appeared from the dining room and strode toward the office. He disappeared inside, but left the door open.

"Saskia?" Rhett asked when he answered. "Saskia? What the hell was that noise?"

He crept back down the stairs, staying out of sight.

Rhett's fist came down hard onto the blotter. "Saskia? Talk to me. Tell me what's happening... Are you hurt?"

Alex could suddenly taste his pulse. Saskia was in trouble? He glanced up and down the hallway, wondering whether he'd be able to take one of the cars. He had to go to her.

"I will. Saskia, get into the bathroom. If there's another door in his way, it'll give us the time to get to you."

Another door in his way? Alex didn't have to ask to know what was going on. Somehow Ezekiel had found out about them. Rhett repeated his instructions to Saskia, tacking on, "Lock the door and sit tight. We'll be there as soon as possible."

Damn straight they were going to be there as soon as possible. If Zeke had harmed one hair on her head, Alex was going to tear the male apart with his bare hands.

"What the fuck are you doing lurking out here?" Rhett demanded. Alex spun around, surprised. The alpha crossed his arms over his chest. "Were you listening in to my conversation?"

"I was just passing when I heard you talking to Saskia." Alex licked his lips and kept his head bowed. "Is she all right?"

"No, she's not, but her welfare doesn't concern you."

The fuck it didn't. Of course, Alex didn't say that exactly. "If she's in trouble, I want to be there for her." He lifted his gaze slightly higher on the male, his scrutiny fixed on his nose rather than his chin.

"You will, but not now."

"But—"

"Look," Rhett interrupted. "I know you're new to this whole wolf pack thing, but let me give you some advice: if an alpha wolf tells you to do something, you do it. If you really want to help Saskia, shut the fuck up and let me do my job."

Alex remained silent, his wolf cowering from the power coming off Rhett's body.

"Vaile, Sabel, I need you with me," Rhett called into the kitchen before grabbing a pair of keys off a hook on the wall and marching toward the front door. Vaile and Sabel filed out of the kitchen, their expressions grim.

Turning around, Rhett said, "On second thoughts, Vaile, stay here. Sabel, come with me."

Helplessly, Alex followed Rhett and Sabel out of the door and down the front steps, watching their SUV tear out of the driveway. Lacing his fingers together on top of his skull, he tipped his head back and looked up at the first few stars that had come out for the evening.

He wanted to punch something so badly. He could feel his wolf pacing, growing agitated. He was demanding that he follow them, but Alex did his best to ignore the demands.

"I've never seen you like this," a soft voice said behind him. Alex spun around, the sound of gravel crunching under his feet. Larissa was bundled up in a coat, breathing into her hands and rubbing them together. "It's cold, huh?" she added with a smile.

"Grey, I—" He couldn't think of anything to say. His wolf was baying inside his head; the cacophony of sound was getting on his nerves. He turned around to look down the driveway again, wishing he'd been in that SUV too.

Alex startled when Larissa touched his arm. "They'll be back soon. Come inside where it's warm," she insisted.

"I don't think I can," he replied honestly. "I feel like I want to tear things apart."

"Larissa? Come back in the house." Alex glanced over to see Vaile standing on the porch.

"They don't trust you yet," Larissa murmured.

"I don't blame them."

"Don't be too hard on yourself. From what I've heard, you've actually got better control of your wolf than many other newly bitten wolves."

Once Larissa was back in the house with Vaile, Alex turned and walked back in, too. He didn't know what to do though. He felt as if there was a maelstrom of energy battering around in his body, under his skin, that if he didn't expend it somehow, there was going to a massive explosion of furious energy.

"D'Angelo, follow me," Vaile said, turning down the hall. He disappeared through a door and Alex picked up the pace. He stepped inside, coming face to face with a room containing a full-sized boxing ring and fighting equipment.

"Catch," Vaile said, throwing a pair of focus mitts at him. Alex looked at the curved pads in his hands and shook his head.

"Wolfe, I don't—"

Vaile brought his fists together and raised his guard. "Come on. Don't be a pussy. This will make you feel better."

Alex slid the pads on just in time for Vaile to throw his first punch with bare knuckles. "Aren't you going to put gloves on?" Alex asked as another jab came at him.

Vaile smiled, his top lip curling away from his teeth, but said nothing more. Vaile threw different combinations at Alex, the skin over his knuckles splitting and weeping blood. Alex wanted to stop, but the bastard just kept throwing punches. If he didn't keep the mitts up, he would have got one to the mouth.

They kept it up until Vaile was breathing heavily and sweat was trickling down his forehead and making the front of his shirt stick to his chest.

"Swap," Vaile demanded. Alex obeyed because he simply couldn't fight the order. Being a wolf was fucking hard. Alex eyed Vaile's busted knuckles, watching in fascination when he saw the wounds beginning to close up on their own.

Vaile did that half snarl, half grin thing again. "The perks of being a werewolf." He put the focus mitts on and held them so the curved edge was facing down. "Upper cuts."

Alex bunched his hands into fists and squared up to Vaile. As soon as his fists made contact with the padded mitts, he could feel his tightly wound body begin to relax. The boxing training he'd had as a kid came flooding back, his hips starting to swivel with each punch, delivering more and more power. Each strike became harder and quicker—all his anger and aggression being forced out of his body through his fists.

He punched until Vaile stood back with the mitts held up, fresh sweat marking his brow. "Feel better?" he asked, pulled the mitts free.

Sweat soaked Alex's face and shirt. Did he feel better? "Yeah."

Vaile nodded. "Listen to your wolf. He wants to destroy something? Let him do it in a controlled way. You have to learn to manage his baser urges otherwise he'll take over." Alex nodded. "Good. Get a shower. They should be back soon."

Vaile's words shocked Alex. The impromptu boxing session had made him forget all about Saskia, but he guessed that had been the point. Following Vaile out of the room, Alex made his way upstairs and into the bedroom he was using. After showering quickly, he came out to find a fresh pair of sweats and a new shirt folded up on the end of the bed. He had just pulled the shirt over his head when he heard the front door open.

SASKIA HAD HER BACK TO THE TUB, HER EYES FIXED ON THE DOOR, WHEN she heard a gentle knocking.

"Saskia? It's Sabel. Open up."

Sabel's here! She stood up on numb legs. Flipping the lock, she opened up the door, sagging with relief to see the wolf that had been dubbed the Butcher.

His serious blue eyes took her in. "Are you okay?"

She nodded. "Where is he?" she asked in a whisper.

"Rhett has him in the living room, forcing him to shift back. Pack a bag with enough clothes for a couple of days. I'll meet you out in the hallway in a minute."

Saskia followed Sabel from the bathroom and stopped when she saw the state of the bedroom door. The wood had been completely shredded, slivers of the door both inside and outside the room. On the hallway wall, there were huge, deep gouges taken out of the drywall.

She shuddered.

That could have easily been her body torn to pieces.

"Saskia?" Sabel called, pulling her attention away. "Clothes. Now."

"Right," she replied, pulling out the same carry-on suitcase she'd used a few days before and putting it on the bed. She had the strangest case of déjà vu as she moved from her tallboy to the bed, filling the bag with clothes. After a few minutes, the carry-on was filled and Sabel was taking it from her hands.

"Come on."

Sabel led the way down the hallway, the sound of Rhett's voice drifting toward them.

"Zeke, shift back now," he commanded, and Saskia could feel her own wolf surface, being drawn to the power in her alpha's voice. As she entered the living room, she gasped and took a step back, bumping into the wall.

Rhett was standing in front of Zeke, his back to them, while the huge chocolate-brown, silver-eyed wolf fixed its gaze on Saskia.

"Zeke, look at me," Rhett demanded, forcing her mate's eyes back to him. "Shift back now, or I will force you to do it."

Zeke whined and sat back on his haunches, lowering his head in submission.

"Saskia, follow Sabel to the car. I'll be there in a minute," Rhett instructed without taking his eyes off Zeke.

"Come on, Saskia," Sabel said, taking her gently by the arm. That earned him a snarl from Ezekiel, but Sabel simply bared his teeth and growled back.

Sabel opened the SUV's door for her, ushering her inside with her suitcase and shutting it behind her. She watched him walk around the hood and get in the passenger side.

"What's going to happen to him?" she asked softly. Ezekiel had been hurt enough by her.

"Don't worry about that now. Once we get back to the pack house, we'll discuss everything that needs to be discussed."

Saskia nodded, knowing she wouldn't be getting any other information from the Butcher and sank back into the leather seat. She had just dozed off when a door opened, jolting her upright.

"Rhett, what happened?" she asked. Her alpha glanced over his shoulder, his mismatched stare full of pity. Without answering her, he started the car, shifted it into gear and backed out of the driveway.

SASKIA MUST HAVE DRIFTED OFF AGAIN BECAUSE ONE MINUTE SHE WAS watching the trees smear past, and the next she was in front of the pack house. Sabel opened her door, took her suitcase and helped her from the backseat—her legs were still a little shaky now that the adrenalin had worn off.

She followed her alpha into the house, her eyes searching for Alex as she was ushered into the office. Rhett took up his position behind his desk while Sabel folded his arms across his chest and stood to Rhett's left.

"Sorry," Vaile murmured when he walked in. His shirt was stuck to his body, sweat still beading on his brow. He took up his position on Rhett's right, his eyes narrowing on Saskia's face with a slight frown.

She put her hand to her cheek gingerly, dropping her eyes. The bruising had obviously started coming out. "Where's Alex?" she asked softly.

"Taking a shower. He should be here in a minute," Vaile replied, like he knew she was going to ask to have him in there with her.

There was a soft knock, and Alex's scent wafted in through the door. Saskia stood up in an instant, throwing herself into his arms. Alex grunted in surprise, his strong arms wrapping around her. Tears sprung to her eyes and the sobs she'd been holding back finally took over.

Scooping her up into his arms, Alex walked her back over to the couch, but instead of placing her down beside him, he sat down and cradled her in his lap. She looked up and his eyes darted to her cheek.

The burnished orange eyes of his wolf surged forward, calling to her wolf, too.

"Did he hit you?" Alex asked, his voice taking on a sharp edge.

"I'm okay," she whispered. "I'm okay."

"Saskia, what happened?" Rhett asked, drawing her attention away. She turned to her alpha and blushed. She'd completely forgotten they were in the room.

"I...I..." How was she supposed to explain this to them? They were all happily mated males who would die for their female. They wouldn't understand.

"Saskia, I won't judge you. Just tell me what happened."

"Zeke...Zeke came home from work. I was in the shower and when I came out, he was enraged." Saskia slipped from Alex's lap and sat beside him, making sure to put some space between them. Alex possessively took her hand in his, squeezing her fingers until she had to tell him to ease up.

"He struck you?" Rhett asked.

Saskia nodded, unable to look at Alex. There was no doubt there was a murderous glare there.

"Why would he do that? From everything I've seen he seems like a very placid wolf."

She let out a deep breath. She had to tell Rhett about what had happened, but the idea of saying it in front of everyone embarrassed her. She had shamed herself, shamed Zeke and shamed their mating.

"Is it okay if I tell just you?" she asked softly. Rhett's eyes softened before glancing at Vaile and Sabel.

"Give us a minute," he said before fixing his eyes on Alex. "That means you, too," he added.

"No. I stay," Alex replied.

"That wasn't an invitation," Vaile growled in response. "Get your ass out here now. Saskia will still be here when you're allowed back in."

Alex looked at her desperately, but she nodded at him, whispering, "I'll tell you later, okay?" Saskia touched his face when his eyes flared with his wolf as they fixed on her bruised cheek. "Okay?"

"Fine," he spat. "But I'll be just on the other side of that door," he replied, jabbing his finger at the office door to his right. He didn't move to get up until she nodded, and even then he left reluctantly.

When they were alone, Rhett rounded the desk, dragging another chair toward the couch until they were sitting opposite each other.

"He hurt you," Rhett said, reaching out to touch her cheek. She recoiled a little at the sting. "Sorry," he murmured. "Saskia, you'll have to tell me what happened if you want me to help you."

"I thought you were speaking to Zeke while we were waiting in the car."

Rhett shook his head. "He wouldn't say anything else other than you'd explain everything, answer all the questions that needed to be answered."

Saskia nodded, knowing she had no choice but to tell him everything that had transpired between her and her mate. Tears began to well at the thought of admitting her transgression with Alex. She hadn't thought her giving in would have led to all this.

"Zeke and I have been having some problems," she started, playing with the hem of her t-shirt.

"He did mention something about that when he called to report Alex and Casey."

"I'm not sure how much you know about it, but before Alex was bitten, he and I dated very briefly, but I broke it off because I knew it was wrong to want to be with a human. Saxon was insisting that I get mated, so I chose Ezekiel since he was a male from our old pack, and my brother thought it would help to mend the bad blood between them and our family.

"Even though I was doing the right thing by the pack, my heart still belonged to Alex. The last few weeks I've been depressed because it was coming up on the one year anniversary of when I walked away from him. Zeke was beginning to notice, but I couldn't tell him that I loved someone else. It would break him."

"He does love you, Saskia," Rhett replied.

She nodded. "I was so confused about my feelings, and Zeke was pushing me to try and talk, but in a gentle way—nothing forceful. Anyway, I went to stay with Saxon one night and the next morning I went for a run, and that was when I found Alex and Casey. I knew that nothing could happen between us since I was mated, but when he came around to say goodbye, I couldn't stand the thought of him leaving without knowing how much I loved him, how much I still love him and will always love him."

"You slept together?" Rhett asked.

Ashamed, Saskia dropped her eyes. "We did. After he was gone, I cleaned the house and stripped the sheets from the bed, putting fresh ones on, but when I stepped into the shower, I forgot about the clothes I'd been wearing. They would have still smelled of Alex. Zeke came home and smelled him on me."

"And he struck you?"

She nodded again, remembering the sharp crack and the searing pain exploding along the length of her cheekbone. "What's going to happen?" she asked on the barest whisper. "To him?"

Rhett sat back in his chair and looked her over. "Is this the first time he's hit you?"

"Yes."

"And he hasn't been violent toward you before?"

"Never," she replied emphatically.

"I'll tell you, Saskia, I don't enjoy seeing a woman getting knocked about, but breaking the mate bond is serious. It will ruin your reputation, and Zeke's, too."

"I know."

"Do you love him?" he asked.

"Zeke?" she asked. Rhett nodded. "I... No, I don't. I never have."

"Why did you agree to mate with him then?"

"I couldn't have Alex. I had to do what was right for the pack, and for my brother, too."

Rhett grunted. "I'm going to need to think about this, all right? He will be punished, but I don't know how. For now, I want you to go and stay with your brother for a few days."

"What about Alex?" she asked, wiping the tears from her undamaged cheek.

"He's leaving tomorrow morning with Casey as planned."

"He's not going to be punished?"

"I don't see why. You were two consenting adults even if you made a really poor decision. Don't worry too much about it, Saskia. I'll let Alex take you home, say your goodbyes tonight and we'll deal with the fallout tomorrow."

"Okay." Saskia uncurled herself from the couch and stood up, Rhett shadowing her.

"I'm sorry this happened to you, Saskia," Rhett murmured. "No woman should have to see that side of their mate."

Saskia nodded solemnly. "Thank you."

THIRTY-FOUR

Alex's jaw was beginning to hurt from grinding his teeth together. Pacing back and forth outside the office, he glanced at the door every few seconds even if it was pointless. His desire to have Saskia in his arms again, to check her over and make sure she was okay, was an overwhelming need inside.

Mate. Hurt. Mate. His wolf was pacing impatiently in his head, Alex's legs mimicking his wolf's frenetic pace.

Just a few more minutes, he replied.

"Take it easy, D'Angelo," Vaile said. Alex glanced over at the guy. He was leaning up against the wall with his arms crossed over his chest. "She's safe."

"That bastard hurt her," Alex growled, letting his wolf push out.

"And he'll be punished for that, but *not* by you."

Alex's wolf snarled at Vaile, showing his displeasure at not being able to dish out the punishment.

Mate, his wolf repeated.

Not ours. Ezekiel's.

Want.

Alex was about to mentally kick his own ass for having the thought that Saskia could be his when the office door opened, and Saskia stepped out with Rhett following closely behind her.

"Saskia?" he croaked. He could see her eyes were still red, still sore from crying. "I'm—"

He couldn't finish his words as Saskia slammed into his body. Her delicate arms wound around his waist, her cheek resting against his chest. Alex wrapped his arms around her, holding her close. His wolf purred his approval.

Safe.

"Alex," Rhett said, "take my car and drive her back to Saxon's apartment."

He nodded. "What's going to happen to Ezekiel?"

"That doesn't concern you," the alpha replied. "Take her home. Say goodbye then come back here. You and Casey will both be leaving tomorrow morning as planned."

"I don't want—" Alex began to say, but clamped his lips shut when a growl broke free from Rhett's throat.

"Take her home. Now."

Alex looked down at Saskia. "Come on, baby, let's get you home to your brother."

Saskia nodded and straightened, looking back at Rhett. After she thanked him for coming to rescue her, they left the pack house hand in hand. Once outside, Alex opened up the passenger door, waiting until she was all the way in until he shut the thing. Circling the hood, he opened up his door and got in. Alex started the car, slowly accelerating down the driveway and out onto the road.

Saskia reached across and took his hand, squeezing it gently. Alex returned the gesture before bringing her hand to his mouth and brushing his lips against her knuckles.

"How are you feeling?" he finally asked, hating that he hadn't been the one to rescue her.

"I'm okay."

"What about your cheek? It's bruised as hell."

Saskia's free hand touched her damaged cheek, wincing as she did. Alex's grip around the steering wheel tightened until something cracked. Sucking in a deep breath and releasing it, he loosened his hold and tried to relax. Destroying the alpha's car was *not* a good idea.

"I'll kill him for hurting you like that," he spat, eyes fixed on the road. He didn't want her to see his rage. Seeing it in the eyes of her mate would have been enough.

"Alex? Look at me," she commanded, her voice soft. He blinked rapidly a few times until he felt his wolf retreat, and then looked at her. "Rhett will punish him for what he has done."

"I want to be the one to do it," he replied, his jaw tense. Fuck, he was going to have one helluva headache later.

"Why?" she asked.

He looked at her sharply. "*Why?* Because...because you're my..."

"Your what?" Her voice was still soft, still calm. "I'm not your mate. We don't even belong to the same pack, Alex."

"Don't say that, baby. I would claim you as my own in a heartbeat if it were possible."

"You wouldn't do that." Saskia sighed and pulled her hand away, twining her fingers together in her lap. Alex had the horrible thought that she was trying to say good bye to him now. Well, fuck that.

"This isn't goodbye, Saskia," he practically growled.

"Yes, Alex, it is." When she turned her head to look at him, tears sat unshed in her eyes. "If Ezekiel chooses to break the mate bond with me, I'll be ruined. No male would ever choose to be with me."

"*I'll* choose to be with you," he said desperately, reaching over and gripping her hands. "I'll choose you until the very day I die."

She gave him a watery smile. "I know, but you're leaving tomorrow to go to a pack over four hundred miles away."

"Come with me, then," he said, the words spilling out of his mouth without any real thought. "Come with me and we can start over."

"Alex— "

"Just hear me out," he said, talking over her. "You can come with me and Casey. You'll get a new life, away from the pack and Ezekiel. Away from—"

"My brother?" she interrupted. "Because if that's what you're asking me..."

Was that what he was asking? "I love you," he blurted out. "I love you, and I would never ask you to do that."

"Good, because I love you, too, and I would never ask you to give up your family for me."

"So, you're going to stay, but are you going to stay with him?"

She gave him a sideways glance. "If by him, you mean Ezekiel, then I don't know."

"What's not to know?" he snapped back, suddenly angry with the thought of letting the other male touch his woman again.

Saskia sighed, exhausted by the conversation. "Breaking a mate bond isn't like getting a divorce. I can't just decide that I don't want to be mated to him anymore. Pack magic bound us. Blood binds us still."

That revelation left Alex cold. "So, you're joined together forever?"

She shrugged. "Kind of, I guess."

"This can't be the first time this has happened," he muttered more to himself than to Saskia.

She shrugged. "Wolves mate for life."

The thought of Saskia being stuck with Zeke for the rest of her life made Alex's gut twist. "If there is a way, would you take it? Would you break the mate bond?"

Alex knew he was torturing himself with the questions. She had told him she wouldn't already, but he had to make her see that she wouldn't be tainted. He would take her. He was a Bitten wolf. As far as their society was concerned, he was already the dirt they walked on.

She sucked in a deep breath again. "If I did, I would be irrevocably ruined."

"So you'd stay with Zeke just to keep up the pretence of being happy, even though you're desperately unhappy?" he demanded.

Saskia's denim-blue eyes shot to his face. "I'm not desperately unhappy."

"Really? So all the running away from your mate meant you were ecstatic with your whole life? Fuck, Saskia! Why can't you take the out I'm giving you?"

Alex's voice had risen and Saskia's expression had become more and more shocked.

When he was finished, she sat there in the passenger seat, twisting her hands together, her eyes fixed on something far away. "If you love me as much as you say, you wouldn't have to ask that question. You would know why I can't give everything up. I made my decision, Alex. I choose Zeke."

Her mate's name left her tongue on a whimper, and Alex could tell she was lying. He narrowed his eyes on her face, scrutinizing the tight lines branching out from her eyes, the tenseness of her jaw. She was pushing him away on purpose.

But Alex let it go. He didn't want his last few hours with Saskia to be tainted with such heartache. He followed the city traffic through downtown Buxton until they reached Saxon's apartment. Taking the last spot out the front, Alex put the car into park and let grief wash over him.

Saskia popped open the car door, looking over at Alex when he touched her face softly. "Can I come up?"

She looked between him and the building. "I don't think that's such a great idea," she replied softly.

Alex took back his hand, anger filling him. Pushing it away, he took one final look at the woman he would love forever. Tears sat in her eyes, and he would have done anything to erase them for her, to make sure she never had any reason to cry ever again.

But he didn't have that power.

He didn't even have that right.

"Thank you for driving me home," she whispered; her voice was so incredibly soft and gentle—haunting.

"Is this goodbye?"

"Yes," she breathed. "I'm afraid it is."

Fuck, this wasn't getting any easier. "Stay there. I'll come around to your side." Without waiting for an answer, he popped open the door and stepped out into the street. When he made it around to the other side, Saskia was trembling. Alex helped her from the car, taking her hand and pulling her into the line of his body.

She whimpered and melted against him, wrapping her arms around his waist. With one hand on her back, Alex's other hand found the back of her head, pressing her to him. He didn't want to forget the way she felt, or smelled, or sounded, or looked. He wanted to memorize every instant of this heartbreaking goodbye.

His tears fell into her hair. Roughly, he scrubbed the others from his face. When Saskia started to pull away, he pulled her in closer for half a second before finally giving in and letting her step away.

With arms wrapped around her middle, Saskia looked up at him, the misery in her eyes unbearable. Alex looked down at his boots, but it was Saskia's warm palm on his cheek that drew his head up once more.

Placing his hand over hers, Alex closed his eyes and hoped she was changing her mind.

"I love you."

That was all she said to him before running up the stairs and into the apartment building, catching the door as someone left. He watched her silhouette disappear from view.

Saskia chest was hurting so badly. There was a burning in her throat, and a sting in her eyes that wouldn't go away either. As she raced up the stairs to her brother's apartment, all she could hear were Alex's words to her.

Really? So all the running away from your mate meant you were happy? Fuck, Saskia! Why can't you take the out I'm giving you?

His words had shocked her, but the truth of them wounded her more. Yes, she was unhappy, but she wouldn't let him ruin his life too by being associated with her. She just couldn't do it.

While she'd been pressed to his hard body, she'd felt loved and protected and worthy. She'd felt his tears, smelled his sorrow, wanting so badly to reach up and tell him she was sorry and yes, she would go with him. It was only her honor that had stopped her.

By the time she reached the third floor, the few tears had become a torrent, running down her cheeks, blurring her vision. Fumbling with her keys, she opened up the apartment door and shut it behind her before breaking down completely, slumping against the wall.

Was she doing the right thing? Of course she was. There could be no future with Alex. He was being shipped off to Casey's pack in the morning. It was a mercy to finish it when she did. She knew all of these things, but her wolf was fighting her decision. She knew her mate—her one true mate—had come and gone from her life.

For the second time.

Dragging her knees to her chest and wrapping her arms around them, she bowed her head and let the tears come. She wept for Zeke and Alex and Saxon. But mostly she wept for herself.

"Saskia?" Saxon asked. Saskia lifted her head slowly, her neck stiff and her face puffy from crying. She blinked up at her brother, watching as his confusion turned to concern. Getting down onto his haunches, he pushed some of the hair away from her face, exposing her swollen and bruised cheek.

"What the hell happened to you?" he snarled, gripping her chin and tilting her head in different angles. His eyes had slipped to his wolf's, a low steady growl building in his chest. "Who did this to you?" he demanded. Saskia could feel the power of his wolf emanating from his body, something she hadn't felt in such a very long time.

"Zeke hit me," she whispered. Saxon was stock-still except for his nostrils. They were flaring wildly, dragging fresh air into his lungs. The growling became louder, forcing Saskia to lower her eyes.

"Why?" he demanded, his voice more wolf than man.

She drew in a cleansing breath and released it before telling her brother the whole story. Everything. Even the part where she and Alex made love. When she was done, Saxon was pacing in front of her, agitated like a caged...well, wolf. Each time she mentioned Zeke's name, he clamped his teeth together, growling around a curse.

When he eventually calmed down a little, he asked, "What did Rhett have to say?"

"He'd have to think about a suitable punishment."

Oh, boy. She really shouldn't have said that. Saxon was back to raging beast in a heartbeat. "A suitable punishment?" he snarled. "Death would be fitting."

"Saxon, please just listen," Saskia pleaded. "We've both done something wrong here. I betrayed my mate, and he lashed out at me."

As soon as the last words had left her tongue, she knew she'd made a mistake. Saxon marched toward her, getting up close into her personal space. In her mind, she could see her wolf's ears flatten against her skull, her lips peeling back from her teeth.

"Don't make excuses for him. He struck you, and that's not okay. No worthy male would strike a female. Ever."

Saskia nodded because that was all she could do and watched him resume his pacing. "All right, so this is what's going to happen: you're going to move back in here with me and I'll go around and get the rest of your clothes and anything else you want from the house over the next few days."

"I don't think you should go around there," she managed to say, quickly adding, "If Zeke is there, you'll get into a fight."

"I can take him," he shot back, cracking his knuckles like he was picturing the fight already. There was no doubt her brother would win. He was a strong fighter, and he would be fighting for her. "For your sake, I'll go when we know he's at work."

Yes, that sounded like a much better plan. Getting up slowly, Saskia stretched out her legs. "I'm going to take a shower then go to bed," she announced softly, moving toward her bedroom.

"Wait," her brother called. "Where's Casey?"

"I'm not sure. Isn't she staying here tonight?"

He scrubbed a hand through his hair. "Yeah. The last I saw her, though, was when I dropped her at the pack house this morning. She wasn't there?"

Saskia shook her head. "No, I didn't see her." She noticed how worry was pinching his expression, making him look older. "I probably just didn't see her while I was there. I had other things on my mind."

His jaw muscles popped. "Get some sleep, Saskia. We'll talk about this in the morning."

She nodded and slipped into her old room. Taking off her jeans and pulling on an oversized tee, Saskia curled up under the blankets and tried to forget about the look of utter desolation on Alex's face as she turned to leave him behind forever.

THIRTY-FIVE

Casey became aware of her surroundings very quickly—a sharp, vivid rush of awareness that left her floundering for a moment until she reminded herself that if her eyes were open, and she was still drawing breath into her lungs, she was still alive...for now.

She may have been awake, but lucidity wasn't with her yet. She was lying on her side, her face mashed up against something rough. Her head felt too heavy, too slow to function properly. Taking in a deep breath, she let it out, willing some of the fuzziness to go with it. Casey kept up with the breathing routine until her eyes and brain were once again linked together and working in harmony.

What had happened to her?

The last thing she could really remember was leaving the pack house after telling the Helheim alpha everything that she'd seen in town.

"And what is it that you saw?" Rhett had asked.

"A female werewolf with a human guy. She bit him." This statement had made Vaile chuckle. She glared at him. "She bit him then drove off."

"And the guy she bit? What happened to him?" Rhett asked calmly.

"She took him with her. Duh."

Rhett turned to Vaile. "Did she just say 'duh'?"

"I think so, yes," the Helheim beta replied with a smirk.

Argh, they were so infuriating. "Look, I memorized the licence plate. All we have to do is look it up and we'll find her." She looked at Vaile. "You're a cop. It should be easy enough."

Rhett sat forward in his seat, lacing his fingers together on top of the blotter. "Casey, you must be mistaken about what you thought you saw."

She'd stormed from the house, refusing their offers to take her back into town. She'd been so angry. It was just like being back home where she was pushed out and dismissed by her father and brothers.

The details of what happened next were unclear, but she pushed through the mental haze and the events slammed against her like a wrecking ball against a building wall.

She remembered that a car had stopped, had pulled up right beside her on the empty road. She couldn't see past the dark tint on the windows, but the next thing she knew, she was hitting the gravel, her body losing complete control. Touching her cheek, her fingertips came back flaked with dried blood.

"I see the little snoop is awake," a female purred sweetly. Casey's eyes swiveled around. The woman who had spoken was standing in the doorway. Casey's instincts kicked in. She tried to sit up but found her wrists and ankles bound.

The woman took a few more steps into the room, crouching down elegantly in her vintage Chanel. Her perfume was cloying, making Casey's nose wrinkle.

"What's your name, female?" the woman asked.

"What's yours?" she snapped back, grunting as she tried to break through the bonds.

"I don't think you are in any position to make demands," the woman replied in a sugared drawl. "Answer me."

Casey's wolf wasn't afraid of this woman. They were probably equally ranked when it came to dominance, which wasn't a bad place to be in. "Crystal," she spat.

Vintage Chanel tutted. "Don't lie to me, or I'll be forced to put you to sleep again. You wouldn't like that, would you?"

Fuck. Casey couldn't afford to have any more drugs pushed into her system. She needed to remain as alert as possible. "Casey," she replied, hating that she'd had to submit.

"Where are you from, Casey?"

"I'm a Helheim wolf," she lied.

Vintage Chanel laughed. "No, you're not." She leaned closer and inhaled. "You don't smell like a Helheim wolf."

"Alfheim pack," she muttered in reply.

"What are you doing here?"

"Helping out a friend."

The woman *harrumphed* then stood up.

"What are you going to do with me?" Casey asked frantically, watching as the woman turned around to leave. She glanced over her shoulder, her golden eyes glowing.

"I don't know yet."

EZEKIEL'S SKIN WAS STILL TWITCHING FROM BEING FORCED TO CHANGE back so quickly. Rhett had just left his house, taking Saskia with him. When Sabel had ushered her out the door, Zeke saw the huge red welt on the side of her face, the outline of his fingers clearly visible on her soft skin.

He hadn't meant to lash out and strike her, but his wolf was in pain. He'd lost himself completely and by the looks of things in their house, his wolf had raged, destroying almost everything.

Being forced to shift back had been a humiliation for both him and his wolf, but there was no way he could have resisted the command from Rhett. Forcing himself onto his feet, Zeke wandered into their bedroom and rummaged around for some clothes to put on as well as some shoes to avoid getting his feet cut up on the shards of glass scattered around the floor.

As he walked past the door, he eyed the huge hole gouged into the wood by his claws and shuddered. His wolf would have hurt Saskia if she hadn't shut herself in their bedroom. At the time, that was what he'd wanted, too, but now that common sense and his humanity had returned, the thought of harming a single hair on her head made him feel sick.

Fully dressed, Zeke set about picking up the pieces of furniture he'd knocked over and sweeping up the other pieces that hadn't survived his rampage. He just couldn't believe Saskia would do that to him—bring another male into their mated bed and betray him and his love.

Although, if he was truly being honest with himself, he had seen it coming; he just didn't realize it would be so spectacular. He knew she was unhappy even when she'd told him everything about who Alex was and what he meant to her. She'd said she'd chosen him, Zeke, but he *knew* she wasn't happy. It really was only a matter of time.

When the house was relatively straightened up, he pulled a spare blanket and pillow from the linen closet, dragging his sorry ass over to the couch. There was no way he could sleep in their bed tonight, not after finding out what he had. Slumping down onto the cushions, he ignored the huge tear in the fabric, ignored the foam spilling out from it, and pulled the blanket over himself, praying he could forget about the whole night.

A HEAVY POUNDING ON THE DOOR WOKE HIM. SITTING UP, HE STARED AT the front door for half a second as the hammering continued. Blinking, he realized it was morning. His legs protested as he stood up from the couch. Stretching his arms over his head, he padded to the door and opened it.

Standing on the small front porch were Vaile and Sabel—both looking as serious as a heart attack.

"You have ten minutes to get dressed and come with us," Vaile said, his voice hard. Zeke's gaze bounced from his beta to the captain of the guard then back again. They were here to take him to see Rhett. Ezekiel nodded mechanically. After dressing in a pair of black slacks and a collared shirt, he returned to find Vaile and Sabel exactly where he'd left them.

Following them out to their car, he got in the back, made suddenly nervous by the silent routine they were both holding up. He let out a resigned sigh and sank deeper into the car's leather.

What was the worst that could happen? What he'd done was not generally treated as a crime punishable by death. He could be forced to break the mate bond, but Saskia would be the one to suffer the most from that. Maybe Rhett was going to make him apologize to Saskia and that would be it? Could a slap on the wrist and a stern talking to really be too much to ask for?

Probably.

Ezekiel must have been deep in thought because when he looked up, Vaile was just pulling into the pack house drive. The new pack house had been built after the other had burned down the previous year. It was around the same size as the original one, just more modern inside with better security and a better equipped gym for the enforcers who lived on site to use. As soon as the car rolled to a stop, Sabel was out of the car, pulling open the passenger door. Sabel followed at Zeke's back as he moved toward the pack house while Vaile walked ahead of him.

The house still smelled of breakfast—sausage and bacon still hinted at on the air. Zeke was led down the hall to the office. Rhett was behind his desk, his expression tight. As Zeke turned around, he saw Saskia and her brother sitting on the couch. His mate glanced at him quickly, offering him a weak smile before dropping her eyes to the tightly twisted fingers in her lap. Her unease unsettled both him and his wolf.

"Take a seat, Ezekiel," Rhett said, leaning back further into his chair. Zeke took the only remaining spot—a dining room chair placed strategically in the center of the room—and tried to ignore the tension all around him.

Rhett cleared his throat. "I'm sure you know why you're here," he began, pausing for a moment. Zeke's gaze drifted up to his alpha's face for a moment before dropping again. "Do you deny striking your mate last night?"

"No," he croaked. There was no point lying about it. Both Rhett and Sabel had seen the mark on Saskia's face when they'd rescued her from his wolf. They had both been witness to the destruction he had left in his wake.

Rhett leaned forward in his chair, forcing both Vaile and Sabel to subtly shift their stance. "Striking your mate is a serious offence in this pack, an offence which deserves punishment."

"I understand," Zeke said, hoping to be and sound as repentant as possible.

"The extent of that punishment also relies heavily on the will of the effected party—in this case, Saskia." Rhett tilted his head in the direction of Zeke's mate. "I've thought long and hard about this, and have thought up two possible options."

Zeke heard Saskia shifting uneasily behind him. His shoulders tightened instinctively, his mind reeling. Would he be whipped? Forced to break the mate bond? Killed?

"I cannot break the blooded mate bond between you two. However, I can make your mating null and void if that is what Saskia wants."

Silence filled the room before Saskia asked, "But we'll still sense one another, right? We'll still share some sensations?"

Rhett nodded. "That's right. I cannot reverse the magic that binds you together, but in the eyes of pack law, I can make it so you are no longer connected."

"What's the alternative?" Saskia asked quietly.

"Expulsion from the pack," Rhett replied steadily, his eyes on her face.

Both options were just as bad as each other. Breaking the mating would ruin them both. Expulsion from the pack would mean he would have to start all over again. He'd already left his old pack behind, but maybe he could return there.

"Like I said before, the decision, ultimately, comes down to Saskia. She can choose to sever your connection, or she could choose to send you away. In either case, you will no longer be mated, but whether you remain as a Helheim wolf is a different story."

Saskia cleared her throat delicately. "Can I have a moment to think about this?" she asked. Zeke took a deep breath in, already knowing what her choice would be. She never wanted to be mated to him, and when she eventually mated with that other male, she wouldn't want Ezekiel hanging around.

"Of course," Rhett replied. Zeke stood up and followed Rhett, Vaile and Sabel out the door. When Zeke glanced over his shoulder at Saskia, she was gripping her brother's hand, silently begging him to stay.

Ezekiel sat in the living room in a daze as Rhett, Vaile and Sabel milled between their mates and children. Larissa came down from the second floor with a little girl in each arm. Vaile glanced up when he heard her, rushing to take one of the kids from her.

He kissed her gently on the cheek, before kissing each one of his daughters. "You should have called me," he murmured.

"I can handle them both," Larissa replied.

Vaile grunted. "For now."

Ezekiel tuned out at that point. He didn't need to see the happy family scene. He would never have that with Saskia. Ever.

Just then the office door opened. Everyone's gaze swung around to find Saxon standing in the doorway.

"She's ready," he said. Vaile gave his squirming daughter back to Larissa and followed them back into the study.

Saskia was pacing in front of the couch as they filed in, her eyes focused on the ground.

"Have you reached your decision," Rhett asked, taking a seat behind the desk.

Saskia stopped and faced her alpha. "I have."

"And what have you decided to do?"

She took in a shallow breath and raised her eyes. "Expulsion," she replied in a small voice. "Expulsion."

Rhett nodded. "If that's your decision." Clearing his throat, he said, "As Alpha of the Helheim pack, I hereby break your mating. You are to split your estate equally—"

"She can have it all," Ezekiel interrupted.

"What?"

"Saskia can have it all—the house, the car, everything."

"Zeke—" Saskia said, finally looking at him.

"I'll pack my bags as soon as we're done here and leave."

"But where will you go?" she asked. "What will you do?"

"Does it matter? This is what you wanted. Our association is over, and I'll be gone from your life."

He wanted her to tell him no. He wanted her to beg him to stay. But she didn't. She just fell onto the couch beside her brother, her eyes lowered.

THIRTY-SIX

Saskia kept her eyes down as Ezekiel said his goodbyes to Rhett and the others, leaving the room and her life. Her fingers, wrapped tightly around Saxon's, were squeezed gently, lending her the support she needed. She didn't know whether to be relieved or sad or guilty or any other feeling about what had just happened. She'd got what she wanted—to not be mated to Zeke anymore. But at what cost?

Ezekiel was tainted by her, and Saskia's reputation was ruined. Resigned to her fate, she sighed and finally lifted her eyes to find Rhett watching her carefully.

"You did the right thing," he said softly. Saskia dropped her gaze to his chin and she nodded.

"I just feel..." She struggled for the words. She didn't know how she felt, and trying to justify her reasons for not wanting to be mated to Zeke anymore just made her sound like a petulant little girl.

"Don't feel as if you owe him anything," Rhett replied. "He hit you. I won't stand for that in our pack. Females are too precious to be treated that way."

Saskia nodded, feeling a blush creep up her cheeks. She wasn't defending Zeke and what he did, but she did feel as if she was partly responsible for how he'd reacted. She'd cheated on her mate and, granted she'd never expected Ezekiel to find out, she couldn't help but feel like his punishment should also be hers somehow.

"Saxon, how about you take her home and let her get some rest?"

Saxon squeezed Saskia's hand gently and motioned for them to stand up. After thanking Rhett, she followed her brother out to the car. The ride home was a blur. All Saskia could think about was how easily Ezekiel had given up. He'd said she could have everything—that he would be leaving straight away.

Those feelings of confusion bombarded her once more. She was glad their mating was effectively broken, but she couldn't help but feel guilty for being happy. She'd ruined his life. She'd selfishly wanted to have one solid memory with Alex before he disappeared again, but she'd never considered the cost.

"Hey, are you all right?" Saxon asked, breaking through her thoughts. Looking around, she saw they were already at the apartment. Squeezing the bridge of her nose, she tried to clear her head. She had to stop thinking about it. It was done. Zeke was moving on and so would she.

"Yeah. I'm good." She followed Saxon up the stairs. Once they were inside the apartment, Saskia shut the door and leaned back against it.

This was real.

This was all real.

"Are you hungry?"

Saskia focused on Saxon, focused on the faint lines on his face as he stared at her with concern. She smiled. "I'm fine. I just have to get used to the idea that I'm no longer mated."

He nodded. "Do you want something to eat?" he asked gently.

"No, I think I'm just going to go have a long hot soak in the tub."

Saxon started rummaging through the fridge. "Damn it," he muttered.

"What?" she asked, turning back.

"I need to go to the store to get some supplies. Will you be all right on you own?"

The look of pity and concern on his face didn't sit well with her. She didn't need to be wrapped up in cotton wool just because she'd sent her mate away and willingly ruined her standing.

"Saskia?" Saxon asked, taking a step toward her.

A bubble of hysterical laughter suddenly burst out of her mouth, startling them both.

He frowned. "What's so funny?"

The laughter died on her lips. "All this time, you've been trying to protect me from getting a bad reputation, but I've managed to get one all on my own." She looked down at her feet. God, what a sobering thought. She'd ruined her life, and Ezekiel's. She jerked when Saxon's arms wound around her, holding her shaking body to his chest.

With his lips to her ear, he murmured, "You did the right thing. I shouldn't have pushed you the way I did. Zeke struck you, though, and that is unforgiveable."

Tears stung her eyes, burning the back of her throat. "I cheated on him."

"That's doesn't mean what he did was right. He struck his mate."

"And *I* cheated on him," she repeated. "I chose to do that. He didn't choose to strike me. He was under the influence of his wolf."

Saxon pulled back, his eyes hard. "That doesn't make it right."

No matter how many times she heard it, she couldn't help but feel guilty. Ruining her life was one thing, but to ruin someone else's, too?

Stepping from her brother's embrace, she kept her eyes on her feet and said, "I'm going to take that bath."

Saxon tilted her head up and studied her in silence for a moment. "I won't be long at the store."

"Don't rush," she replied, trying on a smile, but finding it didn't quite fit yet. "I'll probably still be in the tub when you get back."

Saxon continued to study her, trying to figure out whether she was telling him how she really felt or what she thought he needed to hear. Before he could ask, she turned toward the bathroom. Pressing the plug into the hole, she started to run the hot water, barely hearing the jangle of keys being picked up and pocketed before the front door closed quietly after Saxon.

She sighed, undressing slowly. What would she do now? Would she live in her and Zeke's house, or would she sell it and move back in with Saxon? She didn't like the idea of living alone. She'd become too accustomed to having someone else around. Maybe she could get a roommate? Maybe even a human? She also supposed she could start dating humans since she would never get an offer to mate again.

But that's not true. Alex said he'd have you, a little voice whispered.

She shook her head. Saskia couldn't think that way. Alex didn't know what he was asking for.

The bath was almost ready, the level having crept up to near the lip while she'd been daydreaming about a future that couldn't possibly be. Shutting off the water, she lowered herself into the bath and let the hot water cocoon her body. With a bath pillow propped up behind her head, Saskia let her mind go slack. The quiet didn't last too long, though. There was a sudden insistent knocking on the front door of the apartment. Saxon must have forgotten to pick up his apartment keys when he picked up his car keys.

Hauling herself from the bath, she wrapped a towel around herself and headed toward the door.

"I'm coming," she groused when the knocking became more frantic. "Geez, Saxon," she said, flipping the lock and pulling open the door. "Didn't you... Alex?"

She wasn't prepared to see him again. Mentally and emotionally, she'd said her goodbyes. "What are you doing here? I thought you'd already left."

"Is it true?" he fired back in response. Saskia stepped back from the door and let him in. The neighbors didn't need to hear all the details.

"Alex," she began, shutting the door. She didn't want him to torture himself like this. She turned to face him.

His warm palm slid against her cheek. "Tell me. Is it true? Did Rhett break the mate bond? Are you free of him?"

"Yes," she whispered, watching all the light come back into Alex's eyes.

Pressing his forehead against hers, he whispered, "Thank god. Thank god you're free of him."

She wrapped her fingers around his. "I'm free of him," she repeated, "but at what cost?"

He pulled away, his brows drawn down. "What are you talking about?"

"I'm ruined, Alex."

"Don't say that."

"It's true," she replied, hugging the towel to her chest. His eyes slid down, his eyelids lowering as he realized she was naked under all the terry cloth. A blush crept up her cheeks when she smelled his arousal.

She had to put some distance between them before they both did something stupid. Saskia backed away from him, but Alex followed, stalking her.

"I'd mate with you, Saskia. You know this. I've told you this already."

"I know, but I can't let you do that."

"Why?" he spat back. "Because you're *tainted?*"

She didn't like the way he'd said that—like she was dirty and spoiled. Lifting her chin, she defiantly stared at the wolf she loved.

"You love me," he stated.

"It doesn't change anything."

"Of course it does. I love you. We belong together. Wait, let me finish," he said when she opened her mouth to argue. "My wolf has not shut up since we found out about Rhett's decision. I want you. I don't care what people think. I never have." He approached her in two long strides. "I. Want. You. I don't know how many more times or ways you want me to say it, but they'll always be true. I want you."

Tears scalded her eyes, but she couldn't bring herself to turn him away. This was her chance at happiness. Alex was staring at her intently, his wolf pushing forward. What could she say to him? How could she apologize for acting the way she had?

There was only one thing to say.

Loosening the towel from around her body, she let the fabric fall to the floor between them. "Mark me as yours then, Alex. Claim me as your mate, and I'll go wherever you want me to go. As long as I'm with you, I'll be happy."

Desire.

Need.

Lust.

All these things coursed through Alex as he watched the towel drop from Saskia's body. She was accepting him. She wanted him, and damn it he would follow through on his promises. He would protect her with his life.

He had no idea what he had to do now, but remembering Vaile's words to listen to his wolf's instincts, he loosened his grip on the animal inside his body and let the bastard come to the forefront of his mind.

Bite, his wolf urged. He took a step toward Saskia. Her eyes were fixed on his face as he moved, watching him. Without having to ask, Saskia tilted her head back, exposing her throat to him. Alex's mouth opened over her carotid, his tongue darting out to taste her skin. She moaned, her hands coming to rest on his shoulders, her fingers digging into his skin.

Bite.

Alex could feel his teeth getting longer, starting to become his wolf's. He grazed them along the delicate, paper-thin skin on Saskia's neck, feeling her shudder but not pull away. The scent of her filled his nostrils, imprinting on his brain.

One of Saskia's hands on the back of his head drew him in closer, urging him to do what his wolf was already demanding. His jaws opened on her throat, his teeth pressing into her skin, breaking it open. Warm, sweet blood flooded his mouth, his lips sealing over her neck, his throat working down one solid mouthful of her blood.

Saskia pushed him off her gently. Alex licked his lips, rolling her flavor around on the back of his tongue. Blood ran slowly from the shallow bite, pooling in the depression of her collarbones. He leaned forward to lap it up when she stopped him with a hand on his chest.

Her eyes flashed aqua. "My turn," she whispered, her voice a few octaves lower than normal. Tipping his head back, Saskia brought her mouth to his throat.

A sharp sting.

A groan of pleasure.

Alex drew her closer, letting her take all she wanted from him. When she pulled away, a trickle of blood hung delicately from the side of her mouth.

"To seal this, repeat these words after me, okay?" she whispered, her eyes still bright blue. He nodded.

"I take this wolf to be my mate," Saskia said. "No other shall come between us." She leaned toward his still weeping throat. "With blood we bind ourselves," she added, placing her lips to him and taking him into her body. Alex's head was swimming with sensation. His whole body felt like it was wound far too tightly. Still, he repeated back to Saskia the words she had said.

With a smile, she guided his head back to her throat, and he took another deep pull from her vein. He stumbled back when a tingle went through his body. The air seemed to crackle between them, charging the very blood in his veins.

"What's happening?" he asked as Saskia lapped at his neck again while her hands worked his shirt up over his head.

"Pack magic. We're bound now." She stepped back and stared at him. "Make love to me."

THIRTY-SEVEN

Saxon walked the aisles of the local grocery store, filling his cart with some of Saskia's favorite things—Chubby Hubby ice cream and peanut butter M&Ms. He was hoping they would go toward cheering her up after the day she'd had. As he browsed the shelves looking for the right brand of marshmallows, he smiled a little to himself; it was great to have his sister back again even under these circumstances. When he was sure he had everything he needed, Saxon went to the checkout, perfunctorily handing over his credit card. His groceries bagged and paid for, he left the store and started walking back toward the apartment.

Juggling the bags around, he found the keys in his pocket and opened the front door of the building. He rode the elevator up alone and wandered slowly down the hallway. As he got closer to the apartment, a lingering scent on the air became stronger. It took him a few moments to realize who it belonged to.

He opened up his apartment door, his gaze finding Saskia's bedroom door closed. There was a husky laugh followed by a groan. Trying his best to block the sounds of Saskia and Alex's lovemaking, he switched on the small radio on the countertop in the kitchen and turned up the volume. He'd just opened the fridge to put away the groceries when the intercom buzzed.

"Yeah?" he asked into the speaker.

"Saxon? It's Vaile. Rhett needs to see you."

Saxon frowned at the metal box on the wall. Rhett wanted to see him? Hadn't they said all that had to be said before? And why hadn't he just called and told him to come back to the pack house?

A dark voice whispered, *They know it was you.*

"I'll be right down," he replied, releasing the button. He put the ice cream away, left a note for Saskia and left the apartment. When he made it downstairs, Vaile was leaning up against a car, waiting for him.

"Get in," Vaile said. Saxon wanted to ask what was going on, but kept his trap shut. It seemed no more than a few minutes before they were pulling up at the pack house. Vaile got out of the car, waiting for Saxon to do the same. Saxon heaved a sigh and got out. Starting toward the house, he felt his beta move like a shadow behind him. Before he could reach out to knock on the door, it was pulled open from the inside. Sabel stood there, glaring at him as he stepped into the entrance hall. Keeping his head low, Saxon walked in the direction of the open office.

Rhett was already there, his expression unreadable.

"Take a seat," he said in a flat voice. Saxon's heart rate picked up slightly, but he did as he was bid and sat down. Behind him, Vaile and Sabel filed in and closed the door behind them.

As Saxon waited, he started to sweat. No doubt every single one of them could smell his anxiety. He sat there for a good five minutes, and nobody said a word. When he finally had the guts to look up, Rhett was watching him with predatory eyes.

They all know, that same voice said again. *And they'll punish you for it.*

"Saxon, I asked Vaile to bring you down here because we have a little... problem." Rhett spoke slowly, purposefully.

He seemed to be waiting for Saxon to reply, so he managed to spit out the word, "Okay."

"As you know, Alex was bitten..."

Oh, fuck. Saxon's hearing took a little holiday at that point, a whole load of white noise filling his eardrums. He watched Rhett's mouth make the words he could only assume were: *You bit him. Biting wolves is a punishable offence. You will be sentenced to die in front of the entire pack, including your beloved sister.*

"I did it for her," he croaked, cutting off Rhett. His alpha's stare intensified, making Saxon's skin crawl.

"I beg your pardon?" he replied coolly.

Saxon cleared his throat, his dry tongue rasping along the roof of his mouth. "I bit him," he admitted.

"We know that. Vaile picked up your scent on Alex the first time we saw him. What we want to know is why. You said you did it for her? You mean to say you did it for Saskia?"

Saxon nodded. Sucking in a breath, he tried to put into words all the guilt he'd been feeling, all the regrets he'd had ever since seeing how unhappy Saskia had been.

"I forced Saskia to get mated to someone she didn't love. She did her duty, but I couldn't stand to see her so unhappy. I found Alex out hunting one day. He shot at me, but I dodged the shot. He fought me, but he also wanted to die. I could see it in his eyes—like everything he had lived for was now gone. I made the decision to bite him then because Saskia deserved to be happy."

"Even though it meant signing your own death warrant?"

Saxon shrugged. "I just wanted Saskia to have a chance at happiness."

"She was mated to another male," Rhett said, disappointment in his eyes.

"I know," he whispered. "I bit him on some stupid impulse. I knew then that it wouldn't change anything. I knew I would be punished for what I did," he added, looking up and meeting Sabel's then Vaile's and finally Rhett's gaze. He stared at them boldly, knowing there was no going back now. He was already dead. "And I would do it all over again if Saskia could be as happy as she is now."

"She's just condemned herself to a mateless existence. What makes you think she's so happy?" Rhett demanded, his lip curling up in one corner.

"Alex is with Saskia right now, and I think they've mated. If Saskia is happy, then I've done my duty as a brother. I'll happily go to my death."

Rhett sat back in his chair, biting on his thumbnail as his eyes churned with his wolf. Saxon could feel the waves of power washing against him, trying to break him down. "You've mentioned being willing to die a lot. Why?"

Saxon started. "Death is the punishment for creating a Bitten wolf."

Rhett glanced at Sabel on his left for a moment. "Maybe in the time of my uncle's rule, but I'm not so sure we should be following the same path. Our pack's bloodline is still pure, but for how long?" He sighed. "I've seen firsthand what it's like to be shunned in your own pack. Bitten wolves are still wolves."

"So, what are you saying?" he asked in a small voice.

"I'm going to get Alex down here and he's going to decide."

The phone rang then.

"Rhett," he said into the receiver. "Acario, how are you? No, she hasn't left yet...I'm sorry, I don't know where she is right now...Of course I'll get her to call you when she gets in...Fine...Thanks."

Rhett hung up and said to Vaile, "Where's Casey?"

Saxon looked up. "Is she still not home?" he asked.

Rhett glanced in his direction but he didn't say anything. Saxon's gut twisted. "Something's happened to her."

He didn't know how he knew, but he just did.

"Why do you say that?" Sabel asked, his tone edged with a snarl.

Saxon moistened his lips. "Something spooked her before—I don't know what. She didn't tell me. All I know is she was desperate to come and speak to you about it."

Rhett frowned. "She was convinced she'd seen a female wolf who didn't belong to our pack in town. She thought it was the same wolf who was biting the humans across the other side of the country."

"Not all the humans," Sabel muttered, not bothering to hide his glare.

Saxon shrugged him off, unwilling to pick a fight with the Butcher. "What did you tell her?" he asked softly, keeping his voice low and his eyes even lower.

"That she was mistaken about what she thought she'd seen. If there was a rogue wolf in our territory, I would have known about it."

"What if she was right?" Vaile asked. "What if she saw what she thought she had?"

Rhett turned to his beta. "What are you saying?"

"I'm saying we've lost the location of an alpha's daughter—a female we should have been guarding with our lives, a female we ignored."

Rhett sank into the back of his chair, his hands steepled in front of his chin. "Suggestions?" he barked angrily. His power was leaking from him, getting stronger and stronger, more unbearable with each lungful of air Saxon breathed in.

"Pray we find her in one piece," Vaile replied, already moving toward the door.

* * *

Casey's eyelids fluttered open, her brain slowly registering the pins and needles in her arms and legs. Beneath her, the ground was ice-cold, smelling of dirt, blood and fear. Silently and quickly, she took stock of any injuries she might have, slowly stretching out and testing different parts of her body. Everything moved as it should have, and there was no pain except for the numbness that came along with the loss of feeling in her legs.

It was dark wherever she was, dark and cold and filled with pain. Casey's nostrils flared, trying to pinpoint just how alone she was, but it didn't help; the cloying scent of death was too strong. Moaning and screaming surrounded her, but it was a wet sound followed by a crunch breaking through the inky blackness that made Casey's pulse spike.

She forced her breathing to slow. She needed a clear head, and wouldn't allow fear to cloud it. She searched the darkness, seeking out a pinprick of light like a moth. She squinted, thinking she saw something there in the shadows and drew back when there was a pained moan. Casey pushed herself into a squatting position, but jumped up when a cold hand clutched her bare foot. Kicking the hand away, Casey edged backwards until her spine collided with regularly spaced metal bars and she realized she was in a cage.

"H-h-help..." The ghostly words were cut off with another moan.

Shaking and scared, Casey pressed her back into the bars and closed her eyes. This wasn't happening. This was all a bad dream.

"P-pleasssse..." the person repeated.

Casey tried to block out the pleading voice, tried to focus on something else. She turned around, wrapping her fingers around the bars and pressing her face against them. A warning snarl trickled through the darkness in front of her. Her wolf snarled loudly in her head, forcing Casey to move away just as the bars rattled and the fetid stench of snarling werewolf breath invaded her senses. Slowly, her eyes began adjusting to the darkness. She could see the outline of a large wolf on the other side of the bars, its breath puffing out in front of its mouth. A rumbling growl vibrated through its chest.

Whoever they were, they were too far gone to their wolf to be of any help. Casey yelped when the hand landed on her foot again. Her back slammed into another set of steel bars.

"H-h-help..."

Casey dropped into a crouch, the outline of a woman breaking through the darkness. She was on her hands and knees, and judging by the strain in her voice, she was going through the Change as well.

What the hell is going on?

"Who are you?" Casey asked, reaching for the female to feel her forehead. She was past the fever stage, maybe only a day in.

She whimpered at her touch. "E-Emily," she replied, her words as broken as her body was going to be in about thirty-six hours.

"What is this place? Where are we?"

Casey felt Emily shake her head. "Dying," she replied after a minute.

"No, you're not dying," Casey replied, taking her hand and holding it. Emily sighed gently.

"W-what's happ—"

"Shh," Casey whispered. "You've been bitten. You're going through the Change."

"I d-don't understand."

"A wolf bit you, right?"

"N-no. Wo-woman did."

A woman had bitten her? "What did she look like?"

Emily swallowed loudly, shivering under Casey's hand. "Black h-hair. Gold eyes."

It was the same woman. It was the same goddamn woman! Casey's mind started to work, the gears churning. Rhett hadn't believed her. Nobody knew she was missing. Nobody knew where she was, which meant she had only herself to rely on.

"Emily, where are you from?" Casey asked again, hoping to get a coherent answer from the female.

The woman shivered. "Buxton."

Were they even still in Buxton? There was every possibility that she was thousands of miles from the Helheim pack or her brothers and father.

"Is it just the woman here?" she asked, frantic now. The male to her left snarled at the mention of the raven-haired female. He obviously was holding a grudge.

Emily shook her head, crying out as her spine bowed, drawing her stomach closer to the ground. "A man," she panted. "A man comes with her," she moaned then screamed when a fresh wave of agony washed against her.

Gripping the woman's shoulders, Casey got her face nice and close, forcing Emily to focus on her. "When? How often?"

Just then the harsh grind of metal on metal shuddered through the room. A square of light forced its way into the confined space, throwing light on Casey's surroundings. She forced herself to look, to blink her night vision away. She saw Emily in front of her, her blonde hair damp with sweat and hanging down in her face. All the color had drained from her face, leaving her pale and gaunt.

Casey's eyes swiveled around, taking in the cage she and Emily were sharing. To her left were two males. One was furry and snarling. The other was dead, his body twisted and deformed, unable to fully Change back as his heart had given out mid-shift. The snapping wolf bared his fangs at Casey before turning around to his dead jail mate, his jaws closing around one of the deceased man's legs. That same wet sound drifted up and Casey's stomach revolted, bile burning up her throat.

She looked away, wishing she could cut the sound effects. She focused on the right side of her this time. There was another cage with at least half a dozen men in various stages of the Change.

"Go and see who's made it," a woman's voice said from the opened door. Casey flopped back to the ground, playing dead as footsteps tromped down the stairs. They punctuated the darkness with all the subtly of a jackhammer. The wolf to Casey's left snarled as the male approached.

Casey remained still, praying that Emily's whimpering didn't draw his attention.

"Number six didn't make it," the man called, the sound of shoes scuffing on concrete telling Casey he was moving in front of their cell now. With her back to him, she had no idea whether he'd figured out she was awake yet.

He tapped the bars loudly. Casey watched as Emily's glazed eyes rose to his face. "The bitch isn't going to make it," the man said, spitting on the floor. Emily whimpered.

Casey listened as he continued onto the next cage, calling out a report as he went.

Number nine: dead

Number ten: dead.

Number fifteen: dying.

Number twenty-three: Changed and shifted back.

His footsteps moved back toward her cage, stopping there. His breathing was slow and steady, and Casey could feel his eyes burning in her back.

"What about our clever little pup?" the woman called.

There was a thick silence, thick enough to suffocate Casey, to still all the air in her lungs. She could hear her heart pounding a frantic tattoo in her chest and she prayed he couldn't hear it.

"Still asleep," he replied. Something hit her in the back then, bouncing off her spine. When the man spoke again, his voice was low. "Get out while you can."

THIRTY-EIGHT

ALEX MOVED OFF SASKIA'S BODY WHEN HER PHONE BEGAN TO VIBRATE ON the bedside table. His mate's—his *mate's*—hand shot out to pick the thing up, swiping the screen and putting it to her ear.

"Hello?" Her voice sounded well-used, making Alex proud he'd made her scream his name on multiple occasions over the last hour or two. "He's here. Hold on a second." Saskia passed him the phone, a puzzled expression on her face.

"Who is it?"

"Rhett. He wants to talk to you."

Alex took the phone and held it to his ear. "Hello?" he answered cautiously.

"Alex, I need you down here."

Oh fuck, he thought. *Rhett was getting ready to kick him out.* "All right. I'll be there within the hour."

"Good." Rhett hung up.

"What did he want?" Saskia asked, a fearful look in her eyes as Alex handed her back her phone.

"He just said he needed to see me," he replied, scrubbing anxiously at his incoming beard.

Saskia stilled his hand by taking it gently in hers. "Don't worry, Alex. We're mated now. If we have to leave, then we leave, but we do it together."

Alex stared at her, marveling at how in the hell he'd gotten so damn lucky. Pulling her into his arms, he placed a kiss to her forehead, murmuring, "I love you." Those three words didn't even come close to explaining the depth and breadth of his feelings for her, but they were a start.

An hour later, Saskia pulled to a stop in front of the pack house. Alex stared up at the big house. Saskia took his hand in hers and squeezed gently. "Everything is going to be fine," she whispered, bringing his knuckles to her mouth and brushing them against her lips.

"How do you know?" he asked, not just asking in some rhetorical way; he genuinely wanted to know.

"I just know," she replied, smiling a little. "You came back to me when the odds were against you. You fought for me, and I've finally accepted that I've always been fighting for us. So, I'm not letting you get away. If we've got each other, we're going to be just fine."

Alex found he could hardly argue with that logic. Opening up the car door, he stepped out onto the frozen ground, watching his breath hover in front of his mouth for a moment before disappearing completely. Saskia's body warmed one side of him. He looked down at his mate, leaning down to plant a chaste kiss on her lips.

He chuckled. "I'll never get sick of being able to do that."

Saskia rolled her eyes and said, "Come on."

Despair at the upcoming confrontation made the knot in Alex's stomach tighten painfully, but he made his feet move one in front of the other until they'd taken him to the front door. Saskia pulled away from his side to knock, but Alex only let her go for a moment. Tucking his mate into his side once more, he took comfort in the fact that she was there, and as long as he was touching her, there was no way he could mistake it as a dream.

The door was opened by a young, blonde female. Saskia smiled at the other woman. "Hi, Ivy. Rhett wanted to see us," she said cheerfully.

Ivy's eyes scanned Alex for a moment, her nostrils flaring before she nodded and opened up the screen door.

"This is Alex, by the way," Saskia added, tilting her head in his direction.

After the close scrutiny, Alex didn't expect the female to introduce herself properly, but she did, thrusting her hand out to him. "I'm Ivy, Sabel's mate," she said by way of introduction.

Alex took her hand and shook. "Alex D'Angelo."

"Just go on through. All the boys are in there right now," Ivy replied, shutting the door behind them. Saskia led him down the hall to the alpha's office, knocking quietly before pushing into the room.

Alex's eyes bounced around, landing on each wolf individually for just a moment. When they got to Saxon, though, he paused. What was Saskia's brother doing here?

"What's going on?" he demanded, forgetting what he was now, forgetting he wasn't talking to his subordinates down at the station. Vaile's growl sent his wolf back, his ears and head lowered.

"Sit down, Alex," Rhett said. He waited until Alex had sat down beside

Saxon on the couch before continuing. "I asked you here because we know who bit you."

Alex just stared. That was the last thing he thought they'd bring up. In fact, he didn't give a damn that he'd been bitten at all. It had been the best thing that had ever happened to him.

"Who was it? The same person who's been biting the others?"

Rhett shook his head, his eyes fixed on Saxon. "Saskia's brother did."

"Saxon?" he asked incredulously, turning to look at the guy.

"Yes," Saxon croaked. "I'm sorry, but yeah, I bit you."

Alex barked a laugh, startling Saxon. Clapping him on the back, he said, "Don't be fucking sorry. I should be thanking you for what you did."

"Thanking me?" Saxon all but sputtered. "Why would you want to do that?"

Alex glanced at Saskia, whose expression was just as horrified as her brother's had been. He took his mate's hand and brushed his lips against it. "You brought me back to her."

"Why did you do it?" Saskia asked in an incredibly small voice.

Saxon's dark blue eyes fixed on his sister. Orange danced in his irises for the barest moment. That flash of color resonated with Alex; whenever he closed his eyes, he saw the bright orange gaze of the wolf who had bitten him.

"I did it for you, Saskia. I could see how unhappy you were. All I ever wanted was for you to be happy."

Saskia began to cry softly beside Alex, making his chest tighten a little. He didn't like to see her upset.

Rhett cleared his throat loudly, drawing everyone's attention. There was a small smile on his lips as he said, "Right, now that's out of the way—Alex, the reason you're here is to decide on the punishment."

He frowned. "Punishment?"

"For creating a Bitten wolf in this pack, the punishment is death," Sabel replied, his tone cold, his eyes arctic. It seemed as if he didn't give a fuck either way.

"That was the law under my uncle's rule. Being on the receiving end of a lot of shit handed down by antiquated rules and out-dated regulations, I don't see the point of them anymore. I've decided that the Bitten wolf can decide on a fitting punishment for the one who committed the crime," Rhett replied in a deliberate way, choosing his words carefully.

Alex looked back at Saxon. The guy just stared at him with sad eyes. "I get to choose how to hurt you?" he asked, making sure he'd heard Rhett correctly.

"Death is no less than I deserve," Saxon replied softly.

Fuck. No.

Alex wasn't going to kill Saxon. He gave him a new life with Saskia. "I don't want you killed."

Saxon's whole body sagged, relief washing over his features.

"All right, so death is off the cards," Rhett interrupted. "But you must choose a suitable punishment."

"Whipping is always a good one," Sabel said with a predatory grin. Rhett glanced at his captain of the guard over one shoulder.

"Whipping is an option," the alpha conceded with a grimace.

"What else?" Alex croaked. He didn't want to hurt Saxon—not after what he did for him and Saskia.

"Banishment from the pack is another fitting option."

Alex glanced over at Saxon. Could he banish him? He wouldn't be physically hurting him, but the emotional pain he'd cause him by leaving his sister and pack behind would be great.

But what other choice was there?

"Banishment then, but I want him to return to the Asgard pack with Casey. Do you think her father will let him go?" Alex glanced around the room. "Where is that little hellcat anyway?"

He had to admit that he missed her. He saw her as somewhat of a little sister.

Rhett shifted in his chair slightly, signaling his unease. Alex looked between the three males sitting and standing in front of him, not understanding. "Where is she?" he asked again, a tight knot forming in his gut.

CASEY POCKETED THE KEY SHE HAD BEEN SLIPPED. THE MAN HAD LEFT A few minutes before, shutting the door behind him and plunging the room into utter darkness. It took her eyes a little less time to adjust that time around, the outline of Emily coming into view first.

The woman was still curled up in a ball, her whole body shaking violently. Casey crouched down beside her, resting her hand lightly on her shoulder. Despite the feather-light touch, Emily recoiled with a hiss.

"Sorry," Casey whispered, "but we have to get out of here."

"H-how?" she asked on a whimper.

"Don't worry about that. I need you to stand up, okay? Believe me, you can do it. The pain is all in your head. Come on," she coaxed, "stand up, Emily, and I'll help you get out of here."

The woman eventually made it to her feet with Casey's help. Once she was vertical, Casey wrapped a solid arm around her waist, holding Emily against her.

Gently leading the other woman, Casey led them to the front of the cage. Her free hand slipped through the bars, her fingers searching for the keyhole. When she found it, Casey slid the key into the lock and twisted it as smoothly as she could. The mechanism clicked and the door eased outwards.

Casey let go of the breath she'd been holding and, with Emily tucked up against her side, she stepped out into the small space. A growl from the cage on her right made her turn. The wolf who'd been snacking on his cellmate snarled at her, his eyes drifting from her to the door of his cell.

"I don't think so," she replied snidely, backing further away. Casey looked up at the stairs, wondering when to make the move. There was only one chance at this and she couldn't fuck it up. Placing her foot on the last tread, she applied a little pressure and hoped like hell there wasn't a squeak in the wood.

"Hey," a guy called quietly from one of the other cages. "Let us out of here, too."

Casey glanced back at the male who was standing at the door of his cell. Her gaze dropped to the two men propped up against the cell walls. They were still breathing, their chests rising and falling shallowly. Her first instinct was to leave them all behind, but if she did, she couldn't live with herself. Casey wasn't so sure they would make the trip back, but she had to try. She had to give them a chance at life.

Emily moaned as Casey placed her down on the bottom step before she moved toward the door of the third cell. Letting her wolf push forward just a little, she assessed the men carefully. The one at the door had survived the Change; his mind was intact and he was in complete control of his wolf. The other two were still —a lot like Emily was suffering.

She bit her lip, thinking over her options. Would this man leave her as soon as they were free of the house, or would he stay? She was taking a risk, but she wouldn't knowingly leave them there to the fate of the raven-haired woman. Casey slid the key into the keyhole and unlocked the door. Stepping back, she watched the man come toward her.

Offering her his hand, he said, "I'm Mark."

"Casey," she replied, ignoring his hand. "Can you handle the other two?"

Mark looked over his shoulder. "Yeah, I think I can manage."

Casey turned back to Emily, her heavy panting drawing Casey's brows down in concern.

She didn't have much time.

Gently, Casey bent down and picked up Emily, cradling her gently against her side. Emily trembled when Mark's voice cut through the near silence.

"What's the plan?" he asked.

Casey whispered over her shoulder, "Get out of here in one piece."

The guy snorted. "And then what?"

Emily shivered and Casey's arm tightened around her. "Then I get these people the help they need." Without waiting, Casey turned back around and looked up into the dark maw of the stairs. She had no idea how many people were up there; she had no idea what was waiting on the other side of the door. All she knew was that she had to get Emily and the others out of there.

"Come on, Emily," she whispered, leading the woman up the stairs. Behind her, Mark moved with quiet confidence. She wondered who he had been before he'd been bitten.

Once she reached the top, Casey pressed her ear to the door, listening for any movement or voices, but she heard nothing. Letting out a breath, she lifted her hand and placed it on the handle, pressing down firmly but cautiously.

The door clicked open, the sound too loud in the darkness, and Casey froze. She waited for a long minute until she was sure nobody was going to come and investigate before fully pushing open the door and peering into the darkened room. Her eyes scanned the shadows. She was confident the house was empty.

Over her shoulder, she said to Mark, "Looks like they've left. It's now or never."

"Let's go then. But where will we go?"

"Leave that to me," she replied, tightening her grip on Emily and stepping from the basement.

"Which way?" Mark asked with a grunt. The weight of the other two semi-conscious men was taking its toll on him.

Casey's nostrils flared, taking in the scent of crisp air and freshly fallen snow. "This way."

"Is that fresh air I smell?" Mark asked, his voice strained.

Casey nodded. "Just through there," she replied, lifting her chin in the direction of an open doorway.

"Thank Christ for that. I couldn't handle the smell of blood for a second longer."

Casey couldn't have agreed more. She could still smell the tang of the stuff in her nostrils. She shifted Emily, a small whimper escaping the woman's lips with the movement. Apologizing softly, Casey urged her forward again.

Through the doorway, they stepped from carpet to tile. Casey's eyes swept the area, seeing the countertops, recognizing it as the kitchen. And the back door was their salvation. With her gaze fixed on her prize, Casey led the group out of the house, taking the first steps to freedom out into the snow.

Casey scanned the area, trying to figure out which way to go. Glancing up at the sky, she got her bearings and began trudging through the three-foot high drifts.

"A girl scout, huh?" Mark asked from her right shoulder.

Casey grunted. "Grow up with four brothers and you learn enough."

With a single-minded determination, Casey led the band of survivors away from the house, her senses alert. After what seemed like hours of nothing but snow, and agonized moans from the three surviving humans, Casey lifted her head and took in the sight she'd been hoping to find again. The Helheim pack house loomed in front of her, the house lights shining warmly through the darkness and snow.

"Where are we?" Mark asked.

"Somewhere safe."

THIRTY-NINE

Saskia couldn't breathe. It was if all the air had just been sucked out of her lungs. She looked at her brother, feeling as if she both knew him inside and out, yet didn't know him at all. She didn't know how he could have bitten Alex. He'd known the consequences. He'd known the risks. Yet he had done it still.

For her.

Fresh tears pricked her eyes, a burning at the back of her throat threatening to tear down her carefully constructed facade. Clearing her throat, she drew Saxon's gaze.

"Thank you." Her voice came out on the barest whisper.

"For what?" he replied, reaching out to touch her hand resting on the couch cushion between them.

"For always being there. For always looking out for me. You knew exactly how I felt and you wanted to make it better for me."

"I just wanted to make you happy, Sass. Couldn't you see that?"

Saskia couldn't stop the tears this time. Wiping them away, she said in a broken voice, "I could always see that."

Saxon looked between her and Alex. "Please tell me my sacrifice hasn't been in vain. Please tell me you and Alex have completed the mate bond."

She looked over her shoulder at Alex and felt her heart flutter. He was her mate, and she was utterly in love with him. When she felt eyes on her, Saskia looked up to see Rhett watching them both carefully.

"We are mated," she replied, addressing both her brother and her alpha.

"Will you remain in Buxton?" Rhett asked.

Saskia glanced at Alex, asking him silently what they were going to do.

When he shrugged, Saskia said, "We hadn't really thought that far ahead, actually."

"You should stay," Saxon said softly. Taking her hand, he added, "You should stay here and be happy."

Saskia's face flushed. "I don't even know whether Rhett will let us stay. Alex was supposed to be sent away."

"Your mating changes things," Rhett interrupted. "Saskia, you are one of our wolves, but Alex doesn't have a pack yet, not officially. If you would like to stay, we would be happy to have you—both of you."

Saskia's heart suddenly felt lighter. She was getting everything she had ever dreamed off, and just as suddenly as she was happy, she was utterly devastated. She was getting everything she'd ever wanted, but the person she loved the most was getting nothing at all.

"Hey," Alex said, tilting her chin up to look into her eyes. "Whatever you're thinking, stop it. You deserve to be happy."

"He's right, Saskia," Saxon said. "We all make choices. Sometimes they're good and sometimes they're bad, but they're our choices and we have to own them either way. I knew what I was doing and I have no regrets, not when I can see how happy you are right now."

Saskia threw herself into Saxon's arms, not knowing when she might see him again. She couldn't imagine Rhett would let him stay any longer than necessary now that the decision had been made. She pulled away when there was a knock on the office door. Turning, she watched Sabel pull it open and frown.

Casey stepped into the room, her face scratched up, her clothing bloody. All the color had leeched from her cheeks and she was shaking.

Both Saxon and Alex stood up. Saxon took a step closer, but seemed to stop himself. Alex eventually went to her, gripping her by both arms and peering at her. "What the hell happened?" he growled. He led her into the office, trying to press her down into the seat he'd just been occupying. But Casey resisted, edging back toward the door.

"Tell me what happened to you," Alex demanded, his wolf pushing forward, and for the first time, Saskia felt his power.

Casey's gaze darted to the door. "I have to show you something first." Without waiting, Casey left the room, leaving the men to follow. She led them out the front door and the group stopped abruptly. Saskia skirted around the mass of bodies and gasped. Three men and one woman sat huddled on the front porch. They were bedraggled, their clothing ripped, their slack faces covered in dirt and blood.

"Casey, who are these people?" Rhett growled.

"They've all been bitten," she murmured. Turning to Rhett, she said, "I was abducted and drugged when I left the pack house after I came to speak to you about the female wolf I saw downtown. When I woke up, I was in a cage with Emily."

Saskia looked down at the only woman in the group and her heart went out to her. Her hair was caked with blood, her cheeks were hollow and there were dark circles under her eyes. From the tremor passing through her body, it seemed Emily couldn't even find peace in sleep.

Casey weaved slightly then caught herself on the side of the house. "Mark," she said, nodding weakly at one of the men, "survived the Change. He was in the cage beside me, although I have no idea how long he'd been there either. He helped me rescue everyone we could." Casey rubbed at a blood patch on her face with a shaking hand.

Saskia studied her and saw she was going into shock. The adrenaline that had helped her through the escape was wearing off. "There were more people imprisoned with me, but I could only help..." Casey fell silent as more color drained from her face.

Saskia's gaze trailed over to Saxon. His hands were curled into tight fists, and like before, it was like he was holding himself back from going to Casey.

Casey sucked in a deep breath through her mouth. "They'll be going through the Change in less than twenty-four hours. They need a safe place to do that." She paused, shutting her eyes tightly. "I didn't know where else to take them," she whispered.

"Casey," Rhett replied, taking a step toward her, "you did the right thing."

Casey exhaled slowly right before she passed out. Saxon sprang into action, lunging forward and catching her before she could fall. Scooping her into his arms, he cradled her tightly against his chest. Saskia studied the fierce expression on her brother's face, seeing something she never thought she'd ever see.

"Saxon, get her to bed," Rhett commanded. "Vaile and Sabel, help me get these people into the house." Rhett slung one of the men over his shoulder and went inside. Casey's head jerked up suddenly as Saxon started to follow his alpha. She blinked slowly, looking around as if she didn't recognize where she was for a moment before struggling feebly in Saxon's arms. He put her down gently. She moved toward the porch steps and tripped, but caught herself on the railing.

"We have to go back," she muttered, looking around with glazed eyes. "We have to go back and stop them."

"Casey—" Saxon started, gripping her arm as she tried to take her first step away. She pulled away and stumbled, falling to one knee.

"Casey," Saxon repeated, this time his voice was softer, more compassionate. He helped her to her feet and cupped her face in his hands. "Casey, please. You've been hurt. Let me take care of you."

Casey shook her head. "No. We need to go back now." Her voice grew fainter with every word. Saskia thought she might pass out again.

Rhett stepped back out onto the porch. "What's going on out here?"

Saxon said, "Casey wants to return to the house, but I don't think that's such a good idea."

"Saxon's right, Casey. You're injured and probably going into shock. Stay here and recover."

Casey looked around desperately, and Saskia could tell she was trying to fight Rhett's order. "But—"

"No buts, Casey. Your father has trusted me with your care. I've already lost you once. If he finds out you're injured further, the pact that survives between our two packs will be broken, and I cannot have that. Rest. I'll send out a group now to check things out, but I want you to rest."

Reluctantly, Casey allowed Saxon to take her back into the house. Vaile approached Emily and gently picked her up, and followed Saxon inside. Saskia stayed with Emily until she was sure the woman was warm enough and comfortable. She stood up to leave when she overheard a conversation out in the hallway.

"Vaile, Sabel, I want you to go and speak with Casey. We need to find this building she was being held in. Find out whether she can tell you which way to go," Rhett said.

"I want to go with them," Saxon said. A heavy silence fell and, for the first time, Saskia was fearful for her brother. Making demands of their alpha now was not the best idea.

"Why?" Rhett asked.

"If I am to join the Asgard pack, Casey is my responsibility, too."

There was another long stretch of nothing. "Fine," Rhett said. "Go with them."

Saskia pulled open the door, seeing Vaile and Sabel already heading toward the room near the end of the hall. As Saxon passed her, she caught his arm.

"Saxon," she murmured. "Don't do this. I can't lose you."

"I'll be fine, Sass. Just do me a favor?" he asked.

"Anything."

"Look after Casey until I get back."

What more could she do but do as her brother asked? "Of course."

Saxon squeezed her arms gently then started after Vaile and Sabel. Following Saxon into Casey's room, Saskia found Vaile sitting uncomfortably on the edge of the bed. Sabel had his back pressed against the opposite wall, arms crossed tightly over his chest.

"If I had to guess, it was probably a five or six mile walk. We found a road, but stayed off it in case they came looking for us."

"Which direction did you walk to get back here?"

"South-east."

"That's old Dragos lands," Sabel said from his side of the room.

Vaile glanced over at him. "Yeah."

"What are we waiting for then?" Saxon asked, pacing anxiously between the two males.

"Take it easy, Saxon. We'll leave in a minute." Vaile's words should have calmed her brother, but they had no effect. "There's no point rushing into this," he added, turning his attention back to Casey. "If I show you a map, would you be able to trace your way back?"

"Yes, of course," she replied.

Sabel disappeared from the room, reappearing with a folded up wad of paper in his large hands. Opening it up, he brought it over to Casey and laid it flat in front of her. Casey's tired eyes studied the map for a long moment before her finger landed on a feature on the map.

"That mountain there is where the cabin is. It's surrounded by forest."

Vaile and Sabel both cursed at the same time.

"What is it?" Saxon asked.

"We've been here before. This was where Eaton was held when Marcus took her. Whoever this female is, she knows about the location of the cabin."

"You think she's a Dragos wolf who escaped the raids last year?" Sabel asked, his voice coming out as a snarl.

Vaile grunted. "Maybe. It doesn't matter. We'll go there tonight and check it out. Maybe we'll find out more."

FORTY

"WE LEAVE IN TEN MINUTES," VAILE SNAPPED, STALKING FROM THE room, Sabel following closely behind him. Saxon felt Saskia hovering at his back. She was worried about him. He could sense that, but he had to ignore her anxiety. Focusing on Casey, he sat on the edge of her bed and tucked a strand of hair behind her ear. He hated how small and fragile she looked, lying there so still.

He began to reach for her hand, but stopped himself at the last moment. "Are you hungry?"

Casey shook her head. "Just tired," she murmured, her eyelids already fluttering shut. Blood was matted in her red hair, turning it a shade darker.

Saskia laid her hand on his shoulder. "You should go. I'll watch over her."

Saxon grasped her fingers and squeezed gently. "I'll kill whoever did this to her," he vowed, his voice dropping a few octaves.

"You really care about her, don't you?" she replied. Saxon glanced quickly at Casey then back at his sister.

"Yeah, I do," he said, admitting it to himself for the first time. "I want to protect her."

She nodded. "You will. But first you have to take care of those wounds. I'll go get her something to eat. She should be able to heal more quickly then."

Saskia left the room. Saxon turned around to look down at Casey. The scrapes and cuts around her face and neck were slowly healing, but he went to find some supplies to clean up the wounds in any case. Casey couldn't die from an infection, but he felt a whole lot better knowing he'd done everything he could to help her heal as soon as possible.

He'd just thrown the last wad of saline-soaked gauze into the bin when Saskia returned. She was holding a plate piled with four rare roast beef sandwiches. Casey's eyes fluttered open as she smelled the meat. Perching himself on the side of the mattress, Saxon accepted the plate Saskia handed him and picked up one of the triangles.

"Try and eat something," he murmured gently to Casey, lifting his hand to her mouth. Casey's lips parted over the sandwich he offered her, his wolf prowling closer, enjoying that he was the one to feed her. He shoved the feelings away for a moment and concentrated on the delicate-looking female lying helpless in front of him. Casey's teeth bit through the bread and meat, her lips closing over them, her jaw working.

As she ate, Casey's green eyes remained on his face, scrutinizing him without saying a damn thing. Saxon looked away, unable to bear the mistrust in her eyes. The last time he'd spoken to her was still a very vivid memory for him.

Have a great life, she'd said like he was someone she would forget about as soon as her back was turned. *Have a great life*, I-don't-give-a-fuck-about-what-you-do-from-now-on.

"I'm sorry," he said softly, the words spilling out of his mouth. Why did he have to go and say that?

Casey swallowed. "Are you going with them?" she asked, the color already seeping back into her cheeks.

Saxon gave her a stiff nod, glancing over his shoulder when the sound of people walking quickly down the hallway drew his attention. Had it already been ten minutes?

"I have to go," he said, pressing the plate into her hand and standing up. Her green eyes didn't leave his face for a second. Turning his back on her, he stalked from the room, running into Sabel because his eyes were fixed on the floor.

"Watch it," the other male snarled, his wolf's chartreuse green eyes flashing in his irises.

"Sorry," he muttered, keeping his eyes low. Sabel was not a wolf you wanted to get on the wrong side of. Saxon trailed a few feet behind the Butcher, keeping his other senses sharp.

At the bottom of the steps, they stopped in front of Rhett, whose expression was hard. Vaile stepped out of the living room, joining them.

Meeting each of their eyes, Rhett said, "Check the cabin out. Avoid engaging with them. Just follow them. See what you can learn. We need to know why they're doing this." Rhett looked to his beta. "Vaile, pick up their scents if you're able. If they've left the area, we need to be able to identify them in the future."

Vaile nodded, palming his gun and checking the hardware. "You ready?" he asked, the question directed at Saxon and Sabel.

Saxon nodded, following the other two men from the house. The cold hit him like he was walking straight into a wall of ice, wrapping around his body, threatening to squeeze the last ounce of heat from his body. Looking down, he realized why. He was wearing only a thin cotton tee and jeans.

Wading through the snow, they all piled into an SUV, Vaile behind the wheel, his presence alone filling the rest of the car. Adding Sabel to the mix didn't make the car ride any more comfortable.

They'd been cruising along the highway for a long while before finally pulling off onto a dirt road. Vaile stopped the car on the hard shoulder, killing the engine and turning around in his seat to stare at him.

"I don't want any fucking heroics out there, you hear me?"

Saxon dropped his eyes and nodded.

"Follow my lead or I will have you killed rather than just banished." The guy got out of the car, and when Saxon looked up, Sabel was smiling at him.

"I hope you do fuck up tonight."

All right. So Vaile and Sabel obviously didn't agree with Rhett's idea of letting Alex choose the punishment.

"Did you hear me, fucker?" Sabel snarled.

Saxon nodded again, a jerking movement that gave away his fear—not that the stench of it leaking from his body wasn't enough of an indication. Sabel snarled again and opened his door. Saxon watched them through the windshield and shivered slightly.

In unison, the males looked over at the car, Vaile's eyebrows popping up in question. Saxon let out a shaky breath and tugged on the handle of the door. Cold air swirled in, diluting the scent of his fear.

"We walk from here," Vaile announced, taking off into the underbrush. Sabel gave Saxon that same sadistic smile and followed their beta into the trees. Saxon had to do this for Casey, so he shoved his fear aside and followed the other men.

After about a mile, the trees began to thin out and Saxon could see a cabin sitting in a clearing. The closer they got, though, the more he could see just how dilapidated it was. Shingles hung from the roof, the guttering running off the rails at the edges. All the window panes were intact, but they were boarded up from the inside.

Vaile's low whistle redirected his attention. Gesturing with his hands in a series of simple commands, he told Saxon to go around the back while he and Sabel took the front and side.

Saxon nodded to show he'd understood and emerged from the cover of the trees, keeping his body low to the ground. The surge of adrenalin that shot through his blood made him a little dizzy for a moment. This is what he missed. He was born to be an enforcer. Positioning himself underneath one of the windows, he looked around, noticing the edge of a rear porch.

Saxon approached the back of the building slowly. Testing the strength of the wood with one foot, he stepped onto the porch, gaze swinging around, searching. The door ahead of him was ajar. Nudging it with his foot, he pushed it open. Falling back to the side of the door, he waited to see if someone came to investigate. Two heartbeats later, he peered around the corner. The place looked empty.

Movement at the far end caught his attention. His body reacted on instinct, his muscles contracting, preparing for a fight. He only relaxed when he saw Vaile stalk through what was the living room of the cabin. Saxon stepped through the back door and into a small kitchen with flagstone floors and surprisingly modern appliances considering the state of disrepair on the outside. But maybe that was the point—make it look like a piece of shit so nobody would try to break in.

Vaile gestured with his hand for Saxon to get behind him. He did as he was directed, taking up position behind the broad expanse of his beta's back. Vaile's ribcage rose and fell with his breath, his shirt straining over his highly-defined muscles. His beta had drawn his weapon, flipping off the safety and moving down a short hallway.

At each door, Vaile opened it and stepped into the room, his gun raised, tracking across the space. After no more than a few seconds, Vaile backed out of the room, forcing Saxon to retreat also. Once the two small bedrooms and bathroom were cleared, Vaile stalked down the hall and into the kitchen.

He moved to a doorway that Saxon hadn't seen when he'd first walked in. Pulling the door open, Vaile surveyed the darkened stairs, his nostrils flaring. Saxon smelled it too.

Death.

Blood.

Pain.

Moving down the steps with fluid grace, Vaile led the way, his weapon still raised. Saxon idly wondered where Sabel was as they were swallowed up by the darkness.

Some movement at his back.

The trickle of a familiar scent hitting his nostrils.

Sabel had finally joined the party.

There was a snarl in warning and Saxon froze. A wet tearing followed the non-verbal *fuck-off*, the sound making Saxon's stomach turn violently. The smell of fresh blood wafted out of the darkness, the thick *squelch, squelch, squelch* of jaws going to work on raw meat giving him a quick mental image.

Sabel shoved him forward, a lot more gently than Saxon would have expected. He felt the power of both of his pack mates pressing against him, giving him a sense of safety. He continued down the stairs, unconsciously holding his breath.

When they reached the bottom of the stairs, Saxon blinked just to make sure he was actually seeing what he thought he was seeing.

"Fuck," Sabel muttered. Vaile grunted in agreement, slowly approaching the only unopened cage in the room.

A wolf prowled its confined length, its bloody jaws dripping with sticky strands of scarlet-stained saliva. On the floor behind him was a half-devoured body. If Saxon had to guess, he'd have said the other guy had died during the Change and become a meal for the bigger, meaner wolf sharing his cage.

Unlucky bastard.

A twinge of guilt flickered somewhere inside him. Alex could have ended up as either one of those guys. The two extremes. He could've simply died, or lost himself to his wolf. He had been so incredibly lucky Casey's pack had taken him in and brought him through the Change.

"What do you want to do with him?" Sabel asked, a predatory gleam in his eye. He'd moved up close to the bars, getting his face right into the wolf's, staring him in the eyes. The growl that vibrated from the animal's body made Saxon's blood run cold.

"Put him down," Vaile replied.

Sabel smiled, baring his teeth. "With pleasure." He withdrew a hunting knife from inside his boot.

Vaile pulled another gun from a holster around his shoulders and shoved it under Sabel's nose. "Humanely."

Sabel glanced between the two weapons and the wolf that still had his muzzle pressed between the cage's bars. Muttering under his breath, Sabel slid the blade back into his boot and took the gun from Vaile.

After checking the chamber for a round, he cocked the gun, aiming straight between the wolf's eyes. "Sweet dreams."

The crack of gunfire made Saxon jump, but it wasn't just that. It was the unabashed look of enjoyment on Sabel's face; he was a killer through and through.

Blood poured from the wound, spilling out onto the floor. The smell unsettled Saxon's wolf, making it hard for him to rein him back in. He forced himself to look at the rest of the room, at the other cages. Moving away from Sabel, Saxon looked into the next cage over. He growled when Casey's scent registered. It was all over the thing along with her fear. The other female scent was still human, but it must have belonged to the woman Casey had brought back with her. He couldn't smell any other people in there, so he assumed it was just a cage for the females.

The next cage had two bodies in it. Vaile was crouched over one of them, rolling the body over and looking at the ID.

"This guy was from Buxton, and I'll bet my canines so is the other guy."

Saxon had no doubt about that. If Casey had been right and this was the same person, they'd been biting people all across the country. He just couldn't figure out why.

"Can you get any other scents?" Sabel asked, coming to stand in the doorway, his fingers hooking into the overhead bar, suspending his arms above his head.

Vaile shuffled around the enclosure, his nostrils flaring. Saxon didn't know of any wolf with a better sense of smell than Vaile. He knew no other pack had someone with such advanced olfaction.

"All I can smell is the other men who shared this space and a fuckload of fear and pain." He walked out of the cage and moved toward the stairs. His head swept from side to side, pausing every now and again to take a second hit of an odor.

"I think I got the guy Casey said came down to check on them. His scent is unfamiliar, but there's another element here I can't figure out. I'd need to get an untainted sample to determine exactly what it is."

Vaile started up the stairs, leaving Saxon and Sabel to follow. Just as they reached the doorway, Vaile directed them to stop with a raised fist in the air. He turned around, speaking to them in hushed tones. "I just heard a car engine cut out, out the front. Keep low and stay hidden."

Saxon did as he was asked, bending at his knees and ducking down behind the small benchtop jutting out from the wall. Sabel, bent at the waist, ventured into the living room along with Vaile. The Helheim beta stood behind the door while Sabel took up position behind the armchair near the stone fireplace.

Feet pounding up the porch stairs vibrated through the room, followed by the handle of the door twisting. The door opened with a squeak. There was a sudden shuffling of feet on the floorboards.

"Sabel, get the woman," Vaile growled, urgency in his voice. Saxon stood up, glancing between Vaile, who had a man pinned to the wall with his gun to his temple, and Sabel's back disappearing out the door. The roar of a car engine drowned out Sabel's cursing—gravel and snow spitting out from under the tires of the car.

When Sabel returned, his anger was like another person standing in the room.

"She got away," he growled, stalking toward Vaile and the strange wolf. Vaile spun the male around, leaning in close, his nostrils flaring as they took in his scent.

"Who's the woman?" Vaile demanded.

The male's dark hair was long in front, flopping over his forehead. When he came closer, Saxon could see yellow flashing violently behind his blue eyes. The male grinned, showing all his teeth. "I'll never tell you," he replied.

Vaile cocked his weapon, an empty expression on his face. "Who's the woman?" he repeated.

The male's eyes darted to the gun for a fleeting second, licking his lips. "I don't know."

"Fuck you," Sabel growled. "Tell us who she is," he demanded.

"Did she bite you?" Vaile asked, pressing the muzzle into his temple. The guy started to laugh, the sound bordering on hysterical.

"You guys are so fucking dead," he boasted. "You're so ignorant to what's coming."

Vaile and Sabel glanced at each other. Sabel shrugged and Vaile pulled the trigger, releasing the guy and stepping back as his body slumped to the floor.

Sabel kicked the guy with the toe of his boot. "We could have got more information out of him."

"It didn't matter. He wasn't the male I smelled downstairs, but that guy and this piece of shit were bitten by the same person. And if I'm right, and I am, that person was the female hauling ass out of here. But that's not the best bit."

"Come on, don't leave me hanging," Sabel drawled back, resting his shoulder up against the wall.

"The base scent was Marcus'."

FORTY-ONE

"Casey, it's so good to hear your voice," Oliver said on the other end of the phone. Casey couldn't help the tear that slid down her cheek in response. She'd missed her big brother, too. She'd missed all her brothers. Hell, she'd even missed her stubborn-ass father, who thought she was nothing more than a walking womb ready to birth the next generation.

"When are you coming home?" Oliver asked.

Casey breathed in deeply, finally able to complete the action without wincing. It turned out all she'd needed was food and rest to fully recover from her ordeal. She winced as the memories of her imprisonment marched to the forefront of her mind. Being in that basement with all those people had been one of the most difficult things she'd ever experienced. She didn't understand why they'd been left to suffer as they had. It was cruel and pointless and—

"Case?" Oliver prompted.

"This morning," she replied. Saxon was coming with her, along with Mark. The Bitten wolf had said there was nothing left in Buxton for him. Unfortunately, the other two men Casey and Mark had escaped with hadn't made it, but Emily—against all the odds—had survived.

"Is Rhett loaning you a car?"

"He doesn't need to. Saxon—the wolf I told you about—is coming with me and he has a car."

"Remind me again why he's joining our pack," Oliver asked suspiciously.

Casey fidgeted on the bed. "Because Dad told me to bring him back."

He grunted. "What's his story anyway?"

She let out a sigh. While Casey had been forced to rest, Alex had caught her up on what had happened while she was missing. The biggest bombshell was that Saxon was the one who had bitten Alex. That little bit of information had completely blindsided her, but when she really thought about it, she completely understood his motivations.

"He bit Alex. Rhett told Alex to choose the punishment—either expulsion, whipping or death."

"And he chose to expel him," Oliver murmured. She knew exactly what he was thinking. He was thinking Alex was being weak, that he should have made Saxon pay the ultimate price for biting him.

"He did it to make his sister happy," she explained. "She was mated to someone she didn't love. She was horribly unhappy, and Saxon couldn't bear to see her like that."

Oliver snorted.

"I'd like to think you'd do the same for me," Casey snapped back venomously.

Oliver sighed. "*If*, and that's a big if, you ever found a male you wanted, and he also happened to be human, I'd probably offer to do that for you, too."

Casey's heart swelled at the thought. She was grinning from ear to ear when she said, "I've got your back, too, in case you ever find a nice female you'd like to settle down with."

Oliver laughed, the familiar sound booming through the phone. "Yeah, right. Like that's ever going to happen, Case. I'm a career bachelor."

"I don't know," she replied in a sing-song voice. "One of these days you might just meet a woman who sweeps you off your feet."

He snorted, making Casey's grin grow even larger. "Not going to happen, sis."

"Whatever. It'll happen and when it does, I'll remind you of this conversation."

She could hear voices in the background when Oliver said, "Casey, Dad wants to talk to you. I'll see you when you get home."

"All right. Talk to you then."

There were muffled murmurings and a loud, sharp knock before Casey heard her father's voice on the other end of the line.

"Casey, how are you?"

"I'm good, Dad. How are you? Did you miss me?"

He grunted, which was as good as "yes" and she smiled. "I hear you're coming home today."

"Sure am. I can't wait."

"How are your injuries? Have you fully recovered?"

Casey rolled her eyes. He knew full-well that she had. He'd been the one to ask Rhett to keep her there until her strength had fully returned. "You know I have, Dad."

He made that same grunting noise again. "I'll see you tomorrow then."

"Bye, Dad," she replied, waiting for the line to go dead.

"Casey?" he asked softly after a long minute.

"Yeah?"

"I'm sorry I doubted you."

The words she wanted to say choked in the back of her throat. Instead, she nodded then laughed when she realized he couldn't see her. "Thanks, Dad."

"Drive safe. Love you."

Casey hit the end call button and stared down at the phone. Inside, she felt like she would burst. She felt free, vindicated after the constant accusations that she was seeing things or blowing things out of proportion. Maybe her father would take her request to be an enforcer more seriously now. Surely she'd proven herself with her ninja enforcer skills.

There was a knock on the bedroom door, bringing her out of thoughts of a possible future. Alex poked his head around the door and smiled. He looked so different from when she'd first met him. His whole body had relaxed, and his features were softer somehow. He smiled more easily now, and all of that was possible because he'd gotten Saskia back.

"How are you doing, kid?" he asked, stepping inside and nudging the door closed with his foot.

"I'm good," she replied with a smile.

"That's good to hear. Are you ready to leave?"

Casey nodded. "Yeah. I can't wait to see my brothers again."

He grinned. "Come on then. Stand up so I can give you a proper hug."

Slipping her legs off the bed, she got up and walked into Alex's open arms. Wrapping her arms around his waist, she leaned her cheek up against his chest and breathed him in.

"I'm going to miss you, kid," he murmured, his lips pressing to her forehead.

Casey felt all warm and a little flustered by his words. "I thought I annoyed you," she shot back, still smiling into his chest.

His laugh rumbled through his chest, running directly into her body. "You're the biggest pain in my ass, but I'll still miss you. You looked out for me when your brothers and father wanted me gone. You...saved my life. For that, I will always be grateful."

Casey was shocked by the strength of emotion that surged through her. Her throat felt tight, burning slightly. The tears weren't stinging her eyes yet, but if she swallowed down, she was sure they wouldn't be too far behind. She tried to shrug him off. "It was nothing."

"No, Case. It was everything." He took her by the arms and pulled her back so they were looking into each other's eyes. Casey felt vulnerable standing there, facing up to his honesty and gratitude. "You brought me back to Saskia." He smiled. "You and I? We're going to be best friends from now on. Hell, I might even name my first daughter after you," he announced.

"Is Saskia pregnant?"

He laughed and dragged her back against his chest. "No. I was just saying that when she has our first girl, we'll name her after you."

Casey didn't stop the tears that time. They leaked out over her lashes, falling down her cheeks and chin, leaving splotches of darker patches on Alex's grey shirt. She'd never thought she'd have a kid named after her.

"Come on now, Casey. Don't cry. I'm sure Rhett and your father will allow visits and stuff."

She nodded stiffly. Of course they would. She just hated goodbyes. She cleared her throat a little more loudly than she'd intended, stepping back and swatting away those emotionally traitorous tears.

"Where's Saskia?" she asked.

"Downstairs with Ivy and Larissa." Adoration lit up his entire face at the mere mention of his mate's name. Casey hated to admit it, but she wanted to have that feeling, too. She wanted a man to just beam when he thought about her, like she was their entire world—their sun and their moon.

She gently pushed Alex from her room. "Go on and get back to your mate. I'll be down to say goodbye in a minute, okay?"

He nodded and left. Casey sat on the edge of the bed, slipping her feet into her shoes before leaving the room. At the bottom of the stairs, she was stopped by Rhett.

"Casey, I'm glad to see you've recovered quite well."

Casey stared at his chin, but nodded. "I'm feeling just peachy."

"Good," he said, smiling. "I spoke to your father this morning and explained everything that has happened in more detail. I've also called the other alphas and told them to be on their guard. I don't think we've seen the last of this female."

Casey nodded then doubled over as an inexplicably sharp pain stabbed at her gut. She cried out and clutched at her stomach. Rhett squeezed her shoulder gently and she could feel the power flowing through him and into her.

"Are you okay?" he murmured, not raising his voice to draw any unwanted attention to them.

"No," she gasped, trying to breathe through her nose, to control the pain. "I feel like I'm being stabbed."

Rhett's expression grew serious. "Can you move?" he asked, still touching her.

"I don't know," she whispered, still feeling as if a rusty knife was being plunged into her flesh. Experimentally, she straightened then groaned.

"Let's get you into the office," Rhett said earnestly, already leading her away.

Casey leaned heavily on the alpha. Shuffling her feet along the ground in an effort to keep the non-existent wound from throbbing, she let out a relieved breath as the veil of pain lift from her almost as quickly as it had come. Standing up straight, she probed her stomach, lifting her shirt up and expecting to find some physical sign of what she'd experienced.

There was nothing there.

She looked up at Rhett.

"What was that?" he asked.

"I...I don't know. It's never happened before."

He was suddenly grim-faced. "You need to get home, Casey, and you need to get home now."

Confused, she said, "I don't understand."

Gripping her shoulders, Rhett put his face close to hers. "Trust me on this: leave now. Don't stop driving until you get there."

Casey's heart started to pound erratically. "You're scaring me."

Rhett let her go and stepped back a few steps, but the intensity of his mismatched gaze burned. "Leave now."

FORTY-TWO

"So, I was thinking, what do you think of ten?" Alex said, wrapping a handful of newspaper sheets around a vase. He and Saskia were both in the kitchen, packing up her and Ezekiel's house. They were placing it on the market, and Alex was glad for that. Although the place would always hold a special place in his heart because it was where he and Saskia had finally stopped with the bullshit, he understood why Saskia had wanted to sell it.

Too many memories.

Too many *bad* memories.

Saskia was on clean-out duty, her head shooting out from inside the fridge at Alex's question. "Ten what?" she asked suspiciously.

Alex grinned, sauntering over to his woman. Wrapping an arm around her waist, he pulled her in close to his body, dropping a soft kiss to the side of her neck. "Kids, of course," he replied softly, licking her earlobe. Saskia's body lost all its rigidity then, sort of just puddling against his body.

"Kids?" she breathed.

Oh, fuck. Was it too soon? "I mean, if you want to...oh, fuck. Saskia, what I meant to say was—"

Alex's words were cut off by the warmth of Saskia's lips. He groaned into her mouth, holding her tightly against his body. She moaned, too, but pulled away.

"No," she replied with a smile.

"No, what?" he asked, suddenly panicking. No to what? Kids? He sure as shit hoped not. He wanted to have at least three. He was Italian, after all, and big families were what they were good at.

Saskia gently cupped him between his legs, dragging a ragged gasp from his throat. "No to this." She kissed him chastely and laughed. "We wasted three hours in bed this morning and we have to have this whole place packed up by this afternoon."

Oh, thank fuck for that. He grinned at her lazily. "I wouldn't call those three hours wasted, baby," he drawled in reply, brushing his mouth against hers once more before releasing his hold. His fingers already ached to have her back.

Forcing himself to move back to the bench, he picked up a few more sheets of newspaper and stuffed them into the belly of the vase. "So, ten?" he asked again.

Saskia laughed. "Maybe not ten."

"All right, six then."

Saskia leaned her arm against the door of the open fridge and sighed. "How about we split it down the middle with three?"

"Deal," he agreed, smiling broadly. "When can we start?"

Saskia rolled her eyes at him. "We've been mated for all of a week and you want to start a family already?"

"I lost you for a year, Saskia. I have to make up time here," he replied, only half seriously. He could wait. From what he'd been told, werewolves were quite long-lived. He just loved Saskia so damn much he thought his heart would burst right out of his chest.

"Once we move into our new house and get settled then we can start to think about it, okay?"

He nodded happily. They were due to move in about a month. For the moment, they were staying in Saxon's apartment while the sale of the house went through. Alex couldn't believe how happy he was. Only a few weeks ago, his whole world had seemed dull and lifeless. Now his sun was back in his life, shining on him, warming him from the outside in.

"What are you thinking about?" Saskia asked, ducking under his arm and laying her cheek against his chest. Alex leaned forward and dragged the scent of her hair into his nostrils. Damn, he loved this woman.

"Just how much I love you," he said, pressing a kiss to her hair.

"I love you, too, Alex. Don't ever leave me again, okay?"

"Promise." His voice cracked over the word, but he'd be damned if he didn't mean it.

EPILOGUE

"WHAT'S THAT?" CASEY ASKED, PEERING THROUGH THE SNOW-BLANKETED windshield. They'd been driving for about four hours already, Rhett's words of warning still echoing in her head. Ever since she'd left the Helheim pack house, she'd been trying to come up with possible reasons for the sudden and short-lived episode. Werewolves couldn't get cancer, so that was out. An ulcer? She had been under a lot of stress over the previous days. But a possible ulcer didn't explain Rhett's warning.

Saxon slowed the car. "It looks like a tree has fallen over the road," he replied, putting the car in park and reaching over the back of his seat to wake up Mark.

"What?" the other male grumbled loudly, wiping the drool from his chin.

"Get up. I need your help with something."

Casey met Saxon's eyes as he turned back to her.

"Stay here where it's warm."

No. Something isn't right. Something told her they couldn't be delayed, not even for a few minutes. "But I can help—"

"Casey, stop being a pain in the ass and stay here. We won't be long."

Casey fumed as she watched Saxon slam the door and walk a few feet in front of the car. Mark was already there, looking over the huge trunk, his hands on his hips. Saxon jogged up and joined him. They spoke a few words before splitting up. Saxon went to the large base while Mark moved toward the top where the branches lay out on the road.

They seemed to count before Saxon pushed and Mark pulled. After ten or so seconds, Saxon made a cutting motion with his hand across his neck. Mark let go of the branches, but stooped down to pick up something. Saxon had his hands down on the trunk, his head bowed as he studied something.

That was when Casey noticed Mark walking toward Saxon with a gun pointed at him.

She screamed, her voice deafening in the small interior of the car. She'd screamed, but Saxon hadn't heard her. His hand swatted at his neck for a moment before he lifted his head and saw Mark with the gun pointed at him.

Saxon stepped out from behind the trunk, but his movements were jerky, sloppy even. He must have shot him with a tranquilizer dart. Casey watched in horror as Saxon fell to the ground, his hands clenching into fists weakly. Mark turned his attention to Casey, a malicious smile turning up his mouth.

Casey's heart began pounding hard against her ribs, her heartrate accelerating to an unmaintainable speed. *Was this what the pain was about?* she thought desperately. Mouth dry, a small strangled sound escaped her lips as she realized Mark was coming for her next. Fumbling with the seatbelt across her body, she wrenched the door open and bolted into the woods.

The powder beneath her feet hushed her steps, but her frantic breathing was too loud. Looking around, she tried to find something to give her enough cover. The thought of leaving Saxon out there made her feel sick, but if she stayed safe, there was a chance she could save him, too.

Just ahead there was a fallen log, snow dusting the top. Casey dived under the thing, into a small gap only she would be able to fit in. Her whole body shivered and shook, the combination of cold and adrenalin and shock all taking their toll.

Forcing her breathing to calm, she took a few deep breaths and focused on listening for Mark's stalking footsteps. The only hope she would have would be his inexperience. He didn't know how to use his nose properly yet. Casey squeezed her eyes shut. How could she have been so stupid? She'd led him straight to the Helheim pack house. She'd endangered everyone.

"Stupid, stupid, stupid!" she whispered.

Approaching footsteps made her heart bounce into her throat, and she held her breath. A pair of well-worn work boots appeared just in front of her hiding spot, shuffling slightly.

Mark's breathing was steady and even, the complete opposite to Casey's.

"Did you find her?" a woman asked. Her hushed steps could just barely be heard.

"No," Mark replied.

"Kade, the task was easy enough. How could you let our little snoop get away?"

Kade? His name was *Kade?*

"She won't be getting anywhere anytime soon. She's still two hundred miles from home and it's another two hundred and some change back to the Helheim wolves. She's on foot."

"That may be," the woman said, her voice arctic, "but she is imperative. The other male is dispensable, but she is not."

"Sorry, babe. We'll come back in the morning, okay?" The woman didn't say anything, but then she moaned. Casey peeked out a little to see Mark-AKA-Kade kissing the golden-eyed woman. "I've missed you," he murmured. "Spending three days with that pack was hell. I thought the enforcers would figure it out and kill me."

"They wouldn't have figured it out. You were the victim in their eyes." The woman's eyes scanned the forest for a long moment before she turned back to Kade. "You have to find her in the morning, Kade. I won't have my plans ruined by some idiotic mistake you made."

"I promise I'll be back at first light to look for her," he replied. Casey ducked back in, listening to their retreating footsteps. The sound of the car starting echoed through the cold, empty forest.

She wiggled out from her hiding spot, following their steps back to the road. Approaching the tree slowly, she could see where Saxon had fallen, following the drag marks in the snow to where the car had been sitting. They'd taken him, and she had no idea where.

Backtracking, she looked at the end of the tree trunk, recognizing the teeth of a saw that had gone to work on the thing. They'd sabotaged them. The woman's words echoed in her head for a moment.

She is imperative.

Casey shivered and it had nothing to do with the cold. It had to do with fear.

Plain and simple.

FROM THE AUTHOR

If you enjoyed reading this book, please consider leaving a review.

ALSO BY LAUREN DAWES

The Half Blood Series

(Available on Kindle Unlimited)

Half Blood

Half Truths

Half Life

Half Cast

Half Bound

Half Blood Bundle (Books 1-3)

Half Blood Novellas

Hunter

The Dark Trilogy

Dark Deceit

Dark Desire

Dark Devotion

Dark Trilogy Bundle: The Complete Series

Blood Bound Series

Shadowed Lover (2020)

Shadowed Pain (2021)

Shadowed Past (2022)

Shadowed Lust (2023)

Shadowed Secrets (2024)

ABOUT THE AUTHOR

Lauren Dawes is a USA Today Bestselling Author. She writes dark urban fantasy and paranormal romance and is the author of the Half Blood series, the Dark Trilogy and the Blood Bound Series. She likes her vampires dangerous, her shifters vicious and her Norse gods ruthless.

When she's not writing, she's reading, hanging with her young daughter or designing book covers. She currently lives in Canberra, Australia.

Visit her at: www.authorlaurendawes.com
Or sign up to her newsletter